BLOOD ROSE

Margie Orford is an award-winning journalist, photographer, film director and author. She was born in London, grew up in Namibia, and attended university in Cape Town. While there, she was detained for student activism under the newly declared State of Emergency, and ended up writing her final exams in a maximum security prison. Since then, she has moved back to Namibia, studied in New York on a Fulbright scholarship, and eventually settled in Cape Town, where she now lives with her husband and three daughters.

Visit her website at **www.margieorford.com**

THE CLARE HART SERIES

LIKE CLOCKWORK
BLOOD ROSE
DADDY'S GIRL

Margie
Orford

BLOOD ROSE

CORVUS

First published in South Africa in 2007
by Oshun Books.

First published in Great Britain in 2010 by Atlantic Books Ltd.

This paperback edition first published in Great Britain in 2011
by Corvus, an imprint of Atlantic Books Ltd.

1 3 5 7 9 10 8 6 4 2

A CIP catalogue record for this book is available from
the British Library.

ISBN: 978 1 84354 945 1 (Paperback)
ISBN: 978 0 85789 428 1 (Ebook)

Printed in Great Britain.

Corvus
An imprint of Atlantic Books Ltd
Ormond House
26-27 Boswell Street
London WC1N 3JZ

www.corvus-books.co.uk

For my parents Jock and Rosie

Walvis Bay
22.95°S, 14.50°E

Here is a place of disaffection
T. S. Eliot, 'Burnt Norton'

scorpio rising ...

No moon. The desert wind knifes down the gully, rattling the dry grass. Stars hang heavy above the dunes. To the east, the sky is clear. In the west, the retreating fog hovers over the sea. The vehicle crests the dune, its lights malignant twin moons. Car doors open, spilling a peal of laughter, music, the tang of tobacco.

Later, the heft of a pistol in your hand. Perfect. Circled forefinger and thumb slide down to trace the blind eye. A fingertip dipped inside the barrel fans desire, warms your cold body. Pace back one step, two. He watches, the target. Hands bound. Breath held. Eyes riveted. Filled with the hope that you mean something else. Not this. Not you.

Your finger curled around the trigger anticipates the weight needed to fire. Uncurls, extends the ecstasy. Your eyes on the metal marker, an erect nipple on the barrel. Breathe out. Your breath mists the desert air. Breathe in. Breathe out as you beckon. Release. The force of it explodes through your arm, chest, head, groin and erases everything.

Turn and reach for a cigarette. The match flares into the night, filling again with calls and stars. The cigarette glows; the nicotine stills the choppy sea that is your blood. You yearn for what is coming.

Oh. His final breath tongues up your back. You turn to look. Wonder lingers in the unblinking eyes, almonds above the high cheekbones. The crumpled whorl of the ear is innocent of the blood marking the forehead. The open eyes glaze. You go home to sleep, tail lights red in the dark.

Scorpio's tail is poised over the numinous star at its base.

Winking in the centre of the constellation, the star-eye mocks the dead face. The blood soaking into the sand summons the first wave of tiny scavengers. Insects, flies, bacteria marshal themselves for the onslaught.

one

The sound sliced open Clare Hart's Monday morning, dragging her out of a catacomb of sleep. She sat up, heart pounding, and pushed a tousle of hair from her face. It was her cellphone writhing on the bedside table. She reached for it, knocking over a glass of water. She shook the droplets off the phone and onto the sleeping cat. Fritz hissed and dug her claws into her mistress's bare thigh. Clare caught the tiny bead of blood on her nail before it trickled onto the sheet.

'Witch!' she hissed. The cat strutted out of the room, flicking her tail in regal affront.

'Dr Hart?' the phone crackled.

Clare pulled the duvet around her naked body. 'Who is this?' The reception was always bad in her bedroom.

'Captain Riedwaan Faizal. South African Police Service.'

Clare sat up, zero-to-panic alert. 'Where are you?' The other side of her bed was empty.

'I'm downstairs. Buzz me in.'

'You bastard!' Clare could not hide the relief in her tone.

'Tell that to my mother.'

'Where's my tea?'

'Come on, Clare. It's freezing out here and the security guard is getting suspicious.'

'You know the deal, Riedwaan. You get sex and a bed for the night; I get tea as I wake up.'

'I'm trying to break your habit. I've got you a cappuccino and hot croissant instead.'

Clare wrapped her gown around her body. 'Fair enough.

Hang on.' She pushed the red button on the intercom, listening for the thud of Riedwaan's shoulder against the glass door. He came upstairs, bringing with him a blast of cold dawn air and two steaming coffees.

'Giovanni's. My favourite.' Clare took the coffees from him and led the way to the kitchen.

Riedwaan followed her down the passage. 'Maybe you should give me some keys. I could have brought you this in bed.' He tipped the croissants onto a plate and opened the microwave.

Clare opened the plastic coffee lid. 'Maybe.'

She snatched the *Cape Times* he had clamped under his arm and went back to bed. Clare had allowed her defences to be breached once, long ago. The consequences had been devastating. It would take more than breakfast in bed for her to lower her defences a second time.

But Riedwaan pinged the microwave optimistically a second time and put his coffee and the croissants onto a tray.

In the bedroom, Clare had propped herself up against the pillows. The soft fabric of her wrap fell open as she leaned over to get a croissant.

'I love this about you.'

'What?' asked Clare, her mouth full.

'That you wake up ravenous.' Riedwaan reached forward, cupping her breast on an upturned hand. The air seemed thin, as if there was only just enough oxygen, which he would have to use judiciously. He moved his hand down her body, onto her hip. Clare put her cup on the table and slid down the bed. She pulled him towards her, practised hands undoing buttons, seeking the satin warmth of the skin on his belly, his back.

'I'm glad you came back,' she whispered.

Riedwaan smiled down at her. 'I'll be back any time for a welcome like this.'

When he reached for his coffee again, it was cold …

'It's time to get up,' said Clare.

'Stay a bit.' Riedwaan tightened his arms around her. 'You're going away.'

'I've got things to do.' Clare slipped from his grasp and went to the adjoining bathroom.

Riedwaan listened to her hum as she splashed and opened and closed cupboards. 'Do you hum when I'm not here?' he asked.

The humming stopped. 'None of your business.'

He rolled over and looked out at the grey sea heaving itself against the rocks. He had meant to tell Clare last night about his wife's decision to return to South Africa.

When she came out of the bathroom, she was wearing a tracksuit. 'You coming?' She bent down to put on her running shoes.

'You must be joking.'

Clare reached under the duvet, her hands cold on Riedwaan's chest. 'I'm not. You need to do more exercise than occasionally getting it off with me.' She turned towards him at the door, sunlight catching her face and the trace of a smile.

'Clare, I wanted to—'

'What?' She raised an eyebrow.

But Riedwaan could not spoil the happiness he had coaxed from her. 'Your eggs, fried or scrambled?'

'Hardboiled would be apt, don't you think?' Then she was off, two steps at a time.

'Feed Fritz,' she yelled up the stairs. 'Then she won't attack you.' The door slammed and she was gone.

two

One thousand six hundred kilometres north, as the crow flies, Herman Shipanga lay waiting, the cold biting through his thin mattress. The houses hunkered together for protection from the wind that moaned across the exposed dunes of the Namib Desert, only breaking into its hyena-laugh when it slunk between the houses. The wind probed cracks in the bricks, places where doors and windows had shrunk from their frames; it sought out and found tender limbs uncovered in sleep.

At last it came: the siren's wail, tearing through Walvis Bay. Shipanga threw back the covers, his damaged hip protesting. He stepped over the huddle of children asleep on the floor, filled a bowl with water and went outside to wash. As he threw out the icy water, the siren wailed again. The fishmeal factory looming over the pinioned houses belched yellow smoke. Shipanga gagged at the stench.

His wife was up, stirring porridge on the two-plate. 'You should be used to it by now. The smell of money,' she said by way of a greeting as she handed him a bowl. He shovelled down the porridge without appetite.

He pulled his jacket on over his blue overalls. The children stirred, puppies burrowing back into the warmth of each other's bodies. He bent down to stroke the smooth forehead of his youngest before leaving.

Outside, he broke into a steady trot, footsteps echoing down the empty streets. The viscous fog parted for him. A dustbin, a chained bike, a woman walking her dog materialised just in time for him to avoid colliding with them. He took a short cut through the alley running between the sandy yards. It spewed him out at the back of the school. Walvis Bay Combined School was perched on the edge of the town. Here, the shifting red sand shored against the perimeter fence as if looking for a way in. Shipanga slipped through a gap in the fence and fetched a rake from his caretaker's shed.

He made his way to the youngest children's playground and closed the tall wooden gate behind him. The jungle gym reared up in the mist. The swings hung mute beneath their frames. Vacant, except for the last one.

The child's knees were drawn close to his chest. He was leaning, with adolescent nonchalance, against the chain looped around the yellow swing.

'What are you doing?' Shipanga called.

The boy did not answer. These swaggering older boys always taunted Shipanga, mimicking with pen marks on their own pocked cheeks the ritual scars on his face. The triple verticals were the last trace of the home Shipanga had left to seek his fortune in this sunless port.

A cat's paw of wind buffeted the swing, but still the boy remained silent. Anger welled hot and painful in Shipanga's chest. He grabbed the chain, turning the boy to face him.

The startled insects paused only for a moment before returning to their busy feasting. Where the forehead should have been, a third eye leered.

Shipanga's rage gave way to horror. He backed away, his eyes riveted by the swing's cargo. When he reached the gate, he turned and ran towards a pair of lights raking over the parking lot.

'Mr Erasmus,' he gasped, his chest raw with exertion and shock.

'What?' The headmaster was unlocking the boot of his car. He did not bother to look up.

'Someone's there.' Shipanga put his calloused hand on the man's arm. 'On the swings.'

'Speak to Darlene Ruyters. She'll deal with it.' Erasmus took his briefcase out of the boot.

'It's a child, sir.' Shipanga blocked the man's path, anger returning. 'Another boy.'

'The same as the others?' asked Erasmus, looking at the caretaker now.

Shipanga nodded. Erasmus walked towards the enclosed play area, opening the gate to reveal the figure twisting on the bright-yellow swing.

'Who brought him here?' Sweat beaded Erasmus's forehead.

'I don't know.'

'The first one in town,' Erasmus said, flicking open his cellphone. Calling an ambulance sustained the illusion of hope. 'Go and wait for the police, Herman. I'll watch him. And don't let anybody through the gates.'

Shipanga walked towards the gate, the corpse's staring eyes prickling his back with dread. The leaden sky was silvering the truck approaching the gate. George Meyer, always first, rolled down his window. 'What is it?' asked Meyer.

'An accident,' Shipanga explained. 'In the playground. We're waiting to see what the police say, Mr Meyer.'

'Thank you,' said Meyer. He shot a sidelong glance at the small red-haired boy sitting next to him. Oscar was craning his neck forward to see what was wrong. Mrs Ruyters was Oscar's teacher. Her car was there. That part was right. Herman Shipanga stopping them at the gate wasn't, even though his familiar smile was a comforting white flash in his face.

A shiny new Mercedes Benz skidded to a halt behind them. Herman Shipanga stepped forward as a man hurled himself from the driver's seat and planted his hand on the caretaker's chest.

Shipanga cracked his knuckles and stood his ground. Twenty years on fishing trawlers gave him the edge over a manicured man who spent his days in a heated office.

'Why is this car blocking my path?' demanded the man.

'No school today, Mr Goagab,' Shipanga said. 'You must wait here, please. There was an accident at the—'

'I must speak to Mr Erasmus.' Goagab pulled out his phone. Before he could dial, Erasmus appeared, attracted by the noise.

'Explain this, Erasmus,' Goagab shouted. 'Why can't I drop off my sons? I demand an explanation.'

'I'm sorry, Mr Goagab, but you'll have to wait. Everyone will have to wait. The police are on their way. They'll decide.'

Erasmus was relieved to see a blue light glowing in the distant mist. A pair of cars pulled up. Two men got out of a white 4x4. Elias Karamata was dark, shaven-headed and compact, just the hint of a beer belly pushing at his crisp khaki shirt. Kevin van Wyk was lithe and precise. In the right light, he could pass for a movie star.

'Who's in command?' asked Erasmus, looking from one to the other.

A woman heaved herself out of the other car, a clapped-out bakkie. 'I am,' she said. 'Captain Tamar Damases.'

Erasmus suppressed a sigh and took her hand. It was smooth to the touch. 'Thank you for being so quick. You know Mr Goagab?' he asked.

'I do. Good morning, Calvin.'

'What about my meeting? I've got to get to the mayor,' bellowed Goagab.

Tamar Damases's jaw set hard under her soft skin. 'You'll wait here. Either in your car or outside. You choose.'

'I'll report you to Mayor D'Almeida, Captain Damases,' said Goagab.

'Would you?' she said. 'I'm sure that he'll appreciate the time to tell the media that we've a third dead child to bury within the same number of weeks.'

Goagab looked apoplectic, but when Karamata folded his muscular arms and stepped forward, he retreated, his sons scrabbling after him into his car.

'Now,' said Captain Damases, turning to Erasmus, 'where's the body?'

The headmaster opened the gate to the kindergarten play-ground. The high wooden paling shielded only three sides of the area. The fourth side was an open stretch of sand that sloped down to the barbed-wire perimeter fence. A red jungle gym, blue roundabout, a wall painted with rabbits and squirrels in aprons and hats. The yellow swings. A gust of wind twisted the body. The chain creaked, dismembering the silence.

'Oh.' Tamar Damases's voice was soft with pain.

'Strange fruit,' murmured Van Wyk. Tamar looked at him, surprised. She would not have marked him as a jazz man.

'Shall I send the scene-of-crime officers here when they come, Captain Damases?' asked Erasmus.

'You've been watching too much American TV,' said Tamar with the ghost of a smile. 'This is Walvis Bay. Scene-of-crime officer? That's me. Police photographer? That's me. Forensics? That's me. Ballistics? That's me, too.'

Erasmus stared at her blankly and she softened her tone: 'Would you call the mortuary and see which pathologist is on postmortem duty? It should be Dr Kotze. Get her to send a van round.'

'I'll leave you to it then.' Erasmus hurried off, relieved to have a task.

'Get some crime-scene tape, would you, Sergeant van Wyk?'

Authority crackled in Tamar Damases's voice. 'Cordon off the area. I want to limit access to the crime scene. Both the previous investigations were compromised because everyone was everywhere.'

'Pity you weren't here to take charge, Captain.' Van Wyk didn't bother to hide the sarcasm in his tone. 'Must be difficult to do a good job' – he ran his eyes over her full belly – 'the state you're in.'

Tamar watched him go, relieved to be alone with the body. The wind was picking up now from the south, chilly and mean. She zipped her jacket up to her chin and turned to examine the dead boy. Looking at him on the swing, his back to her, he could be just another child carrying on some game for that moment too long. If he could climb out of the swing, if they could stand back to back, she and the boy, as growing children love to do, they would have been evenly matched.

When she moved towards the swing, marking her path, the boy's eyes seemed to follow her progress like one of those trick portraits, beckoning her towards him. Tamar obeyed, her feet as small as a child's, picking through the stony litter, recording each detail on her camera. The sand at the base of the swing was slightly disturbed, punctuated by a series of neat, tapered holes. She inserted an index finger into one. It was about two inches deep.

The swing that cradled the body faced due north. It was the only one at an angle. It was also the highest off the ground, the most difficult to reach. If Tamar had to hazard a guess, she would say it had been chosen for the view, but the sullen fog had its back hunched low and she could see nothing of the desert. She turned her attention and her camera to record the macabre display before walking down to the edge of the playground.

There were several gaps in the fence. She bent down, her

camera steadied by her elbows on her knees. Tamar was comfortable squatting like this. She had learned to do this alongside her grandmother; the old lady explaining to the sharp-eyed child how to read the hidden signs that told if an animal had moved through an area, if a person had stopped to think or eat, or if a woman had been there to do her secret business. Hurrying. Ambling. Hunting. Hiding. There were signs for all actions if you knew how to look.

The jungle gym was livid against the fingers of grey mist. The fog flattened everything, bleaching detail from the landscape. Tamar straightened up, waiting for the fog to thin and for an anaemic sun to cast its short-lived shadows. When it did so, she could just make out the marks. They were so faint as to be almost absent: blades of grass broken and angled in the same direction, an impression on the salt-encrusted sand as faint as a palm print on glass. She increased the contrast reading on her camera and snapped pictures until the sun withdrew. She unclipped the loop of yellow tape from her belt, fingering the service pistol nestled below her rounded belly en route. She stepped backwards into her own footsteps and taped off the area, finishing as her phone rang.

'Helena,' she answered. There was no need to check the caller identity.

'What is it?' asked Helena Kotze. 'Another weekend stabbing?' Working in a port had hardened the young doctor's heart and sharpened her eye.

'I almost wish it was,' said Tamar. 'It's another dead boy.'

'Same as the others?'

'Looks like it,' said Tamar, her voice catching. 'A boy again. Young. Maybe fourteen. This time in a swing at the school in 11th Street. Looks like a bullet that's punctured the forehead. Ligatures on both wrists. Wrapped in a dirty sheet.'

'Was he killed there?' asked Helena.

'No. No blood to speak of. Nothing on the ground. Smells as if he's been dead a couple of days, too.'

'I'm in the middle of surgery. I can't come for another hour or so. Can you do the preliminaries?'

'I'm about to,' said Tamar. 'Your guys are here. I'll speak to you later.'

Tamar looked up at the two mortuary technicians skulking at the gate. The two Willems, she liked to call them. 'How are you, boys?' she greeted them.

'Cool. You?' mumbled the taller Willem. His skin was raw from a rushed shave.

'I'm okay,' said Tamar. She shook out two evidence bags.

'Who's that?' asked the other Willem.

'Don't know yet,' said Tamar. 'We'll only get an ID later.'

The two Willems stuck their hands in their pockets, hunching their shoulders like a pair of bedraggled crows. 'Why so sad?' asked Tamar.

They shrugged. The taller Willem lit a cigarette. Tamar knew their disconsolateness wasn't for the dead boy. The pair moonlighted for Human & Pitt, the most enterprising of the flourishing undertaking franchises in Walvis Bay. The funeral director paid them one hundred upfront for the first call to a fresh body, provided it brought in business. A three-day-dead body that nobody had reported missing was not worth getting into a suit for first thing on a Monday morning.

They watched listlessly as Tamar walked back to the boy and steadied the swing between the uprights and her knee. The stench of decay haloed the body. Another day and it would have been unbearable. Tamar took a deep breath and bagged the hands bound with nylon rope. The boy's shoes were covered with fine sand. She bagged those too. She looked at the wound

13

in the middle of his forehead. It was seething with larvae. Two, maybe three, days in the life cycle of the blowfly, Tamar guessed.

Trusses held his arms locked around his knees, but the shroud had loosened. There was a large area of bloodied flesh where the boy's oversized shirt gaped. Tamar probed the writhing mass of feeding larvae, her nausea dissipating as she worked. She checked the boy's pockets. She did not trust the pair at the gate. If there was anything of worth on the body, it would be gone by the time the corpse got to a hospital gurney.

One trouser pocket held nothing but a black pebble. Tamar held it in her hand. She could see why the boy would have picked it up. It was symmetrical, smooth. There was some change in the other pocket and a greasy till slip for twenty-four Namibian dollars. This she dropped into a separate bag. In the other pocket was a pencil stub. There was an initial, looked like a K, inked into one ridge of the pencil. Could be his initials; could be something he picked out of a rubbish bin.

Tamar stood up and signalled to the two men. Like acolytes, they stepped forward with the stretcher, placed the frail body on it and covered it with a sheet. Tamar opened the wooden gate and walked with them as they carried their small burden to the van where Karamata and Van Wyk were keeping the curious at bay. The two Willems put the stretcher down to open the doors.

'The same thing?' asked Karamata.

'Looks like it to me,' said Tamar. 'Have a look. See what you think.'

Karamata knelt down beside the dead boy and pulled the sheet back. He pushed the grimy shroud aside and traced the boy's decaying cheek.

'You know the boy?' asked Tamar, prompted by the burly man's tenderness.

'He played soccer with my sons.' There was a sheen in Karamata's dark eyes when he stood up. 'Be careful with him,' he said as the two technicians picked the body up. The taller Willem sneered, but his swagger stopped at the hips and he picked up the boy without jolting him.

'His name?' Tamar asked.

'Everyone called him Kaiser,' Karamata replied.

Tamar nodded. The pencil with the K was his then.

The bang of the mortuary van's doors seemed to release the crowd of onlookers. They pulled out cellphones to tell those who had been unlucky enough to miss the excitement what had happened: that there was another body; another boy was dead, another of those street children who wheedled money at every traffic light these days.

'His surname?' asked Tamar.

'Apollis,' said Van Wyk. 'He has a sister. Sylvia. A whore, like he was. That'll be why he's in the van.'

'You knew him too?' asked Tamar.

Van Wyk spat out the match he had been using to clean his teeth. 'It's a small town, Captain.'

Captain Tamar Damases watched the vehicle bump down the road. Twice before this had happened and she had been unable to do a thing. Boys caught, killed, displayed, buried.

The violent secrets encrypted on their bodies turned Tamar's mind to Dr Clare Hart.

three

Riedwaan Faizal pushed back the covers and went to the window, wrapping a towel around his waist. After a couple of minutes, Clare appeared in the distance, taking the curve of the Sea Point Boulevard in her stride. At this distance, in the thin September sunlight, she was a stranger to him, despite his intimate knowledge of her, gleaned in secret and hoarded. He watched her until she had disappeared, then he pushed his hands back through his hair. It had caused him a lot of trouble at high school, the way it grew straight up. He was always being sent to the headmaster to prove that he hadn't gelled it. That was long ago now. Two decades, give or take a year or so. Now it showed careless streaks of grey in places.

Riedwaan wandered through Clare's flat, picking up her things, putting them down, running a finger along the alphabetically arranged spines of her books. Mainly hardbacks. Above the television were a couple of shelves of Clare's documentaries, VHS copies of her broadcast investigative pieces, and an award for a film she'd done on human trafficking in the Congo. Putting the world to rights, that's what her investigative work was about, her beliefs giving her the courage to go where there were no nets to catch her if she fell. It fitted with her profiling work, her conviction that she could find the source of evil and eliminate it. Riedwaan was less sure about that.

He rifled through the heap of classical and acoustic CDs. 'How much Moby can one person listen to?' he asked Fritz. The cat flattened her ears and hissed in reply.

In Clare's bathroom, he opened one of the small pots of cream and held it to his nose. The jar carried the scent of her: tender, secret. Riedwaan put it down. He had done this so often in the homes of strangers. It had become second nature to look through the everyday artefacts of a woman's life after her broken body had been found, searching for reasons why that woman stepped out for that minute and never returned to finish half-used jars of expensive cream or to serve the meal cooking in the oven.

Clare was tired – he knew it – wrung out by the last case they had worked on together, profiling a killer whose refinements of cruelty had turned the stomachs of men who considered themselves inured to depravity. She needed to visit her reclusive twin, Constance. She needed to be alone, away. But Riedwaan didn't want her to leave him. He liked to live with the woman he slept with. The patterns of a long marriage like his, even if it was broken, ran deep.

He looked at himself in the mirror. He could get away without shaving. He showered and dressed, repressing the anxiety riffing down his spine. He fed Fritz. Clare would be back in half an hour. He went to watch for her. The sitting room was sparse, the way she liked it. The wooden floor a pale expanse that merged with the waves hurling themselves against the boulevard. He sat down on her sofa and picked up the pile of books she had been busy with before he had arrived the previous evening. There was a book on desert plants, the pollen of a forgotten cutting staining the index. A history of the Richtersveld, the harsh area around the Orange River. A novel about an early and murderous journey into that desert: Coetzee's **Dusklands**. She had made notes in her guide to southern African seabirds. He snapped it shut, amused at the thought of Clare with binoculars around her neck, bird list in her hand.

In the kitchen, Fritz glared as Riedwaan waited for the kettle to boil. He took his coffee through to the spare room. Clare's suitcase was open on the bed, half-packed. Clothes lay in methodical order, waiting to be placed in the suitcase. He picked up a dress, ran the silky black material through his hands and held it to his face. She must have worn it recently, because his touch released the feral tang of her sweat that lay just beneath the perfume she always wore. Jealousy surged through him. Who had she gone out with in that dress? Who had made her sweat?

He put it down and picked up a bra and a matching pair of panties – expensive, silky, low on the hip. Who were these for? Riedwaan could hear her mocking voice: for me is what she'd say. She was right, but her self-containment made him feel adolescent. He folded the dress again. He folded the bra and put it back. Her panties he slipped into his pocket. A memento for while she was away.

In the kitchen, Riedwaan put tomatoes on to grill and eggs to boil. He watched the last city lights go off. Cape Town in the light of the morning looked to him like a stripper past her prime. The lines were good, the breasts firm, but it was silicone and make-up that gave the nights their charge.

The front door opened. Riedwaan's hand curled around the filleting knife on the sink. 'Clare,' he called.

'You missed the best part of the day.'

Riedwaan looked at the knife in his hand in surprise. He passed a drying cloth over it and reached for a ripe melon.

Clare came in dripping, cheeks scarlet.

'I'm not going to kiss you.' She evaded him. 'I'm sweaty and disgusting.'

'Just how I like you.' Riedwaan sliced the spanspek. He didn't think much of fruit, but Clare loved it.

She picked up a slice and bit into it. 'Perfect.' She opened the window and put the skin on the sill for the birds waiting there. 'Come and talk to me in the shower.' She stripped, dropping her sweaty clothes into the washing machine.

'In a minute,' said Riedwaan, watching her disappear naked down the passage.

Clare stood under the shower. She loved the jet of water hot on her face, washing the sweat away. It took with it, though, the imprint of Riedwaan's warm skin on hers. She was going to miss him, being away for a month. She massaged shampoo into her blonde hair, working it down to the ends that hung below her waist. Damn. She had meant to have it trimmed before she left.

'You distract me with your clothes off.' Clare had not heard Riedwaan come into the bathroom. 'Especially when you look guilty like that. You thinking dirty thoughts?'

'I'm not telling.' Clare reached for the soap and scrubbed her shoulders.

'I can do that for you.' Riedwaan watched her deft hands lathering her body.

'You've seen all this before.'

'I'm not going to see it for weeks,' he pleaded.

Clare rinsed her hair. It coiled over her shoulder like a snake, the water making it almost as dark as Riedwaan's. She switched off the tap and stepped out of the shower.

'I didn't know you were interested in birds.' Riedwaan did not take his eyes off her. Dripping wet, she was as easy with herself naked as she was clothed.

'Well, I am. My father taught us. He would slam on the brakes in the middle of the highway, do a U-turn and hurtle back to identify some tiny ball of brown feathers. I decided that if I was going to die, at least I should know what I was dying for.'

'Why didn't you tell me?' Riedwaan asked.

Clare caught the look on his face and laughed. 'You never asked.' She put on cream, smoothing out her arched brows. She reached for her red kimono and tied the cord tight, emphasising the curve of her hips.

'I'll come find you in Namaqualand. You can show a city boy what there is to like about all those flowers and birds.'

The thought of him at her sister's farm bobbed bright as a lure, hiding the hook that lay beneath.

'I'd love that.' The need in her voice caught them both by surprise.

Riedwaan opened the door, letting in a blast of cold air. He reached for the words to tell her that things were more complicated than this morning routine. That Shazia was coming back. His wife. Instead, he pulled Clare towards him.

'Not now,' she said. 'It's freezing with the door open and I want my breakfast.' She kissed him on the mouth and slipped out of his arms. 'I'm going to get dressed.'

four

On the desolate southwest coast of Africa, Mara Thomson turned between the houses to take the short cut to school. A year ago, she had arrived as a volunteer teacher in Namibia with hope and two suitcases. The summer heat had buckled her knees as she stepped off the plane in the capital, Windhoek. The light had seared her eyes, but her heart had soared and she had walked across the blazing tarmac as if she was coming home. She had expected acacia trees etched against an orange sky. Instead, she was assigned to Walvis Bay. She cried herself to sleep for a week; then she'd decided to make a life for herself amongst the grime and the fog. A life that she was going to miss, now that she was leaving.

Mara jumped off her bike and wheeled it up the narrow alley, wondering why the dogs were barking. Elias Karamata was standing guard at a breech in the fence that was looped with chevronned tape. Black and yellow, nature's danger signal.

'Morning, Mara,' Elias Karamata greeted the girl. Skinny and brown, in her hoodie and jeans, she looked like one of the boys she coached rather than a volunteer teacher.

'What's wrong, then?' asked Mara, the clipped vowels marking her as foreign. English.

'Kaiser Apollis,' said Karamata, a gentle hand covering her arm. 'He was found dead in the playground.' He felt Mara tremble. At nineteen, she was still a wide-eyed child herself. 'Go around the other way.'

Mara walked around to the main entrance of the school, glad that she had her bike to lean on. Her legs were shaking.

'Where are you going, Miss Thomson?'

Mara had not seen Sergeant van Wyk until he had peeled himself off the wall and blocked her path.

'I volunteer here,' she said.

'I'm sure you do. ID.'

Mara handed it to him, even though he knew full well who she was.

Van Wyk looked her passport over. 'Only two weeks left on your visa.'

'Since when did you do immigration?' she shot back.

'The dead boy.' Van Wyk's eyes were cold. 'He's wearing one of your soccer shirts.' Mara paled. 'Interesting coincidence.'

'I know what you did to him. To Kaiser,' said Mara. 'I reported you.'

'Oh, I know you did.' Van Wyk was dismissive. 'Didn't get you or your little friend very far either, did it?'

Mara made for the entrance. That's when Van Wyk moved, trapping her body against the frame of the door. His breath was hot with intimate menace. 'I hear that you've been picking boys up in the clubs.' His fist, hard and hidden from view, came to rest on the soft mound between her legs. 'A step up from a rubbish dump, but sailors are a dangerous game, don't you think?'

'Why won't you leave me alone?' whispered Mara.

Van Wyk's thin lips twisted into a smile. 'It was you who started—'

'Sergeant,' Karamata interrupted. He was standing at the wall, his arms crossed. 'The staff are waiting to be interviewed.'

Van Wyk dropped his hand, and Mara pushed past him, tears in her eyes.

'I was just checking on Miss Thomson's movements,' Van Wyk said to Karamata as they walked back to the playground.

Tamar was sealing the last evidence bag, noting the time and date on each one. Karamata handed her the list of people who had been at school before they had arrived. 'Who've you got here, Elias?' she asked.

'Calvin Goagab, of course, and his sons,' said Karamata.

'Really made my day, seeing him so early in the morning.' Tamar grimaced. 'Who else?'

'Erasmus, the headmaster. Herman Shipanga you met, the caretaker who found the body. Darlene Ruyters, the Grade 1 teacher. She was in at six-thirty, but says she saw nothing. The only other person here was George Meyer. He drops his stepson Oscar early. Darlene Ruyters is his teacher and she keeps an eye on him until school starts.'

'Oscar's mother?' asked Tamar. 'Wasn't she killed in that car accident six months ago?'

'That's her,' said Karamata. He held the door open for Tamar. The school staff fell silent as she stepped into the stuffy staffroom. The preliminaries were soon over: statements, times for interviews, arrangements to close the school, the staff dismissed for the day.

Tamar drove back to the station, glad that she could lock her office door behind her. She let her head drop into her hands, allowing the first tears to splash onto the desk. It didn't help to dam them all. When she decided it was enough, she made tea while she waited for her photographs to download. She wrapped her hands around the hot mug and stared at the images of the dead child on her screen. Again, she thought of Clare Hart.

She found Riedwaan Faizal's number and dialled. 'Captain Faizal? Tamar Damases here, Walvis Bay police.'

'Tamar, it's been a while,' said Riedwaan. 'You've got a body if you're calling me.'

'A dead boy in a school playground. Looks like the third

in a series,' said Tamar. 'I'm going to need your profiler friend Dr Hart.'

'We'll need to pass it via the official channels,' said Riedwaan. 'But if you can get it past Supe Phiri I'll persuade Clare.'

'You're on first-name terms now?'

'You could put it like that,' said Riedwaan, with a smile.

Clare closed her suitcase and went into the kitchen. Jeans and a white T-shirt. No make-up yet, her damp hair in a twist on top of her head. Riedwaan was leaning against the counter, the paper spread out in front of him. Her stomach grumbled as she kissed him.

'I'm hungry,' she said.

'You look nice.' Riedwaan drew her against him.

Clare dampened down the lick of desire that flared between his hands. She would lose the rhythm of her day if she let her body distract her.

'We'll be late,' she said, prising herself loose. She sat down and helped herself to breakfast. 'Who were you talking to?'

'Phiri.'

'So where's the body?'

Riedwaan felt in his pocket for cigarettes.

'Don't smoke. It's too early,' said Clare.

Riedwaan shrugged and started stacking the dishwasher. She watched the muscles on his back flex under his shirt as she finished eating.

'Very domestic,' she said. 'Maybe I should just stay here with you. Play housey-housey.' She handed him her empty plate and slipped her arms around him.

Riedwaan laughed. 'Ja, right.'

'The other call?' She had him, trapped between her and the dishwasher. 'When I was in the shower?'

'Captain Tamar Damases. From Namibia,' said Riedwaan. Clare didn't miss a thing. Why did he always forget that about her? 'She came to your lectures last year on serial killers.'

Clare's right eyebrow shot up.

'Pretty. Soft voice. Tiny waist,' said Riedwaan.

'No wonder you remember her,' said Clare. 'Just your type.'

'*Was* my type. You're my type now. Skin, bone and attitude.'

'So there *is* a body.'

'It's Monday morning,' said Riedwaan. 'There's always a body.'

five

'Hello?' Clare's phone was ringing as she opened her front door, laden with shopping bags.

'Dr Hart? Please hold for Superintendent Phiri.'

'Okay, I'm holding.' She put down her bags, wondering if she had heard wrong.

'Dr Hart?' She hadn't. The clipped formality could belong to only one man. 'This is Phiri here. How are you?'

'I'm well.' Clare buried her surprise in pleasantries. 'How nice to hear from you. How are you?'

'Very busy, but well.' Phiri took his cue from her. 'I hope I haven't got you at a bad time?'

'Not at all.' Clare could no longer ignore the growing knot of anxiety. 'Has something happened to Riedwaan?' she asked.

Phiri laughed. The low, melodious sound didn't fit with Clare's picture of him: precise moustache, stiff and exact in his uniform. 'He's fine,' Phiri said. 'Looks as if someone's been looking after him.'

Clare blushed. She was glad there was no one except Fritz to see.

'I have a situation that needs … lateral thinking. And tact – something I couldn't get from Faizal for love or money. He suggested that I speak to you.'

Clare was taken aback. Phiri had always been reluctant to use her services as a profiler. He had a policeman's distrust of civilians and a man's scepticism about giving a woman authority.

'How can I help you?'

'I'd like to discuss it with you in person. In an hour. My office at twelve.'

Clare put down the receiver, took her shopping to the kitchen and packed it away.

Two weeks ago, Riedwaan had stayed the whole night with her, slipping into domesticity as if it were a second skin. It was not so easy for Clare. Doubling her shopping seemed easier than talking about boundaries and space and her secret pleasure at being held in the morning, but Phiri's call warranted a few questions.

Riedwaan picked up on the fourth ring.

'I'm meant to be going on holiday,' said Clare. 'Do you want to tell me what's going on?'

'I'm coming to the meeting, too. I'll meet you outside the nut house.'

At five to twelve, Riedwaan pulled up outside the newly built Psychological Crimes Unit. It had been dubbed the nut house before the first brick was laid, and the name had stuck, much to Phiri's chagrin.

Clare wrinkled her nose. 'You smell horrible.'

Riedwaan ground his cigarette under his heel. 'That's a nice way to greet someone who just got you a job,' he said, reaching his hand under her thick hair. Clare arched her neck. 'Are your hackles always raised?' he asked.

'Only when I'm suspicious,' Clare laughed. 'Explain. Phiri's my new best friend?'

'Let's just say he sees you as a way out of a tricky political corner.' Riedwaan followed her up the marble stairs of the unit.

'Since when was I the answer to someone's political problems? Or you for that matter?'

'Captain Tamar Damases,' said Riedwaan.

'Who called this morning?'

'That's the one.'

'I don't trust you, Riedwaan. There's something going on that you're not telling me.'

'She called. Out of the blue. She was looking for you, not me.' Riedwaan knocked on Phiri's door before Clare could interrogate him further.

The senior superintendent gave the impression of a man in uniform, despite his civilian clothes. Phiri was lean to the point of thinness. He moved with the agility of the champion athlete he had been as a young man, desperate to escape the legacy of grinding poverty that illegitimacy had bequeathed him.

'Thank you for coming, Dr Hart, Faizal. Can I offer you some coffee?'

Clare declined. Phiri's coffee was notoriously strong and he only ever served it as he drank it – with three sugars and powdered milk.

'You'll have some, Faizal.' It was not a question. It had taken Riedwaan twenty years with the police to learn which battles were worth fighting. This was not one of them and he accepted the cup without demur.

Phiri opened the Manila folder in front of him. 'I have an unusual request to make, Dr Hart,' he said, steepling his fingers over the single page of spidery notes, the careful handwriting of a man who had started school at twelve.

'You know about the policing cross-border cooperation agreement signed between the South African government and some of our neighbours?'

'Yes,' said Clare. 'It was signed in April as I remember.'

'Correct,' said Phiri. 'Extremely tricky negotiations, as you can imagine. Very often what South Africa offers regionally is seen as interference, domination even, rather than cooperation.' Phiri looked pained at the thought.

'The agreement focuses on terrorism and weapons of mass destruction and car hijacking syndicates, doesn't it?' asked Clare.

'That and the upsurge of armed gangs. We know that increasing numbers of soldiers from our … how shall I put it … less affluent neighbours are moonlighting as hired guns in South Africa for cash-in-transit heists and armed bank robberies. So the South African Police Service is providing expert assistance to our neighbours' developing police forces.'

Clare looked from Phiri to Riedwaan. Riedwaan had just ventured his first sip of coffee and had a stricken look on his face. He was not going to be of any help.

'That's not my field of expertise at all,' she said. 'I specialise in head cases: psychological crimes, sexual murders in particular.'

'I know,' said Phiri, impatient at having his presentation speeded up. 'That's why I've called on you. One of the subclauses – 6.6 of the agreement if you want to read it – deals with unusual violent crimes. The current terminology for predatory sex crimes, serial rape or murder and unusual crimes against children.'

'It excludes the more usual murders or assaults of children,' Riedwaan added, 'committed by their very own loving parents, teachers, relatives and—'

Phiri cleared his throat. 'Thank you, Faizal. It was the best that could be produced in a short period. At least we've something to work with.'

'I do apologise, sir,' said Riedwaan with just sufficient sincerity to pacify his boss. 'As I was saying, Dr Hart,' said Phiri, turning back to Clare, 'section 6.6 deals with unusual violent crimes. As you know, few of our neighbours have either the manpower or the scientific expertise to investigate crimes such as these. We've had our first request for assistance of this nature.

I'm very keen that we're successful with this particular case. It'll go some way in showing that the agreement's worth something and that we can provide a service beyond our borders.'

'So what happened where?' asked Clare. 'And why me?'

'We've had a request from the Namibian police, from Captain Tamar Damases of their Sexual Violence and Murder Unit. Faizal said she was keen that we ask you.'

'Ask me what exactly?' asked Clare.

'That you go up to assist with an investigation. She thinks they need a profiler.' Phiri picked up his rose-speckled cup and sipped and put it back on its saucer. The clatter was loud in the silence. He was the only policeman Clare knew who drank from a cup and saucer. His mother had given the set to him when he had been made a senior superintendent. She did not think it fitting that her only son should drink from the chipped assortment of mugs the rest of the force used.

'I'm flattered that you asked me,' Clare said into the silence that stretched between them. 'But surely it'd be easier if someone employed by the police went up. Captain Faizal, for example.' She looked at Riedwaan. He pretended to drink his coffee and avoided her gaze.

'Dr Hart, the protocol is new, the bureaucracy not quite in place and the Namibians are territorial. What Captain Faizal suggested was that you go and work with the investigation. We send him up next week when we have all the formalities sorted out.'

'Where would I be based?' asked Clare.

'Walvis Bay,' Faizal interrupted Phiri's answer. There was a note of apology in his voice. As there should be. Clare had spent two godforsaken months there working on a documentary. The hot desert wind had whipped red sand off the dunes and ruined her camera.

'Faizal tells me that you know the place,' said Phiri.

Clare wondered what else Riedwaan had told the superintendent. 'I know it a bit,' she said.

'Will you consider it?'

Clare shifted in her seat, repressing an uninvited flash of memory: stars hanging low as lamps in the sky, the desert's nocturnal creatures calling, and her yielding to a man who had taken measure of her loneliness and her desire. She had given herself to him for a week, then flown home, edited her film and ignored his phone calls until they stopped.

'Tell me more about the case,' she said.

'A dead child. Bizarre killing. The body displayed in a school-yard. Bullet to the head, but ritual marks and other peculiarities on the corpse. Reminiscent of at least one other. Maybe more. Interested?'

Clare was intrigued and Phiri could see it. He knew how to play her and she wondered how much of that was thanks to Riedwaan. 'I am,' she confessed, despite her misgivings at being the subject of discussion. 'But I need some more detail.'

'Faizal has all the notes. He'll brief you,' said Phiri with a tone of finality. 'There are the crime-scene photographs. No autopsy yet. They're holding that up until you get there. A few preliminary interviews. She's smart, this Damases. Organised.' He picked up Riedwaan's abandoned cup and put it on the tray on the counter behind him. He closed the file in front of him and stood up. The meeting was over.

Clare stood too. 'Thank you, Superintendent Phiri.'

'I watched you work the last time, Dr Hart. You were very … effective. Let me know what you decide and what you need. You'll be working under Faizal.' He straightened the immaculately arrayed files on his desk. 'Not a position I'd have chosen. But not everyone has the same taste I suppose.'

No secrets in the force, thought Clare. Everyone knew that Phiri, at fifty, still lived with his mother and that she made his lunch every day.

So, no reason that they wouldn't know that Riedwaan had been staying with her, although the breach in her hard-won privacy – secrecy, her sisters call it – rankled.

She followed Riedwaan to what he called his office. More a corner of chaos that his colleagues avoided like a domestic incident on a Saturday night.

'You've got some explaining to do, Riedwaan,' she said, closing the door. 'I don't for one minute imagine that Phiri thought this little scheme up by himself.'

'It's nearly lunch time. I need something to eat before we discuss this.' Riedwaan picked up a file with Tamar Damases's notes. 'You going to feed me?'

six

'What has Captain Damases got so far?' asked Clare, carrying a tray of fresh bread, carpaccio and a salad onto her balcony.

'Three dead boys. All in and around Walvis Bay. This boy, they found this morning.' Riedwaan turned over the top page of the faxed docket. 'And two others: Nicanor Jones and Fritz Woestyn. All found about a week apart.'

Clare stroked her cat, winding in and out between her ankles. 'And?'

'Same age, same cause of death. Vulnerable kids, easy targets. No one to report them missing. All the weird stuff with the binding, the risky display on the swing. It just said serial to her. She thought, rightly I imagine, that if she gets someone up there now there's a better chance of cracking it before another body washes up.'

'Sounds like a textbook case,' said Clare. She rolled a piece of paper-thin fillet between her fingers and ate it. 'What's the new boy's name?'

'Waiting for a positive ID, but they have him as Kaiser Apollis. Looks fourteen, could be sixteen. Been living on the street like the other two victims. Aids orphan, apparently. There's a sister around somewhere, but no interview yet. That's scheduled for the day after tomorrow. With you,' said Riedwaan. 'Here, have a look at Captain Damases's photographs.'

He pushed away their plates and spread out the pictures on the table. His phone rang. Not his usual ring tone, but one a little girl had recorded before she left for Canada with her mother. The child's voice, sweet and plaintive, called him:

'Daddy, Daddy, it's me.'

'Yasmin?' asked Clare.

'Yup.' Riedwaan looked at his watch. 'My biweekly father-hood ration.' He stood up, phone already to his ear. 'Hello, baby girl. How's Canada?' Clare heard him say as he closed the door so that he could speak privately to the seven-year-old daughter he had not seen for almost a year.

Clare turned her attention to the images in front of her. They were eerie; the body huddled like any child escaping on the finite flight of a swing. The image nudged a buried memory. The tug of that weightless second at the top of the arc before the free fall of return; the solemn face of Clare's twin sister, watching her swing up higher, higher, higher. Away from her. Until Constance could stand it no longer and caught the swing, tumbling Clare out, dissolving Clare's rage with tears. Their father had removed the swing after that. To keep Clare safe, is how he had explained it. Clare and her older sister Julia had seethed, knowing that the real reason was to keep Constance calm. Clare felt for the forgotten scar on her elbow. The smooth ridge of skin was still there.

'You look like you've seen a ghost.' Clare had not heard Riedwaan return. He put his hand on her arm, drawing her back into the present.

'This tyre swing. We had one when we were children. I loved it. It made me feel free.' She turned to face him. 'How are things with Yasmin?'

'Fine,' said Riedwaan. 'She's fine.'

'Shazia?'

A shadow crossed Riedwaan's face at the mention of his estranged wife. He shrugged and did not meet Clare's gaze. 'The same.' He picked up the crime-scene pictures. 'What do you think of this?'

'So spiteful to kill a child on a swing,' said Clare, leaving the painful subject of Riedwaan's broken family.

'It looks like he was killed elsewhere; no blood in situ.' Riedwaan's attention was focused back on the soluble problem in front of him. 'He was dead a good couple of days before he was dumped at the school. Maybe kept out beyond the fog belt, in the heat. The body was starting to smell bad,' said Riedwaan, scanning through the faxed notes.

'Why in a playground?' mused Clare.

'That's the thing with nuts. It makes no sense unless you get inside their heads. Why put him on show a couple of days after he's dead? What were they doing together all that time?'

'The other two, were they also found near schools?'

'No. Tamar has linked them because they were all head-shot wounds, same calibre gun. Intermediate range and similar victim profile. Ligatures or remnants of ligatures. And the timing, too – looks to her like there's a pattern. A killing, then a cooling-off period.'

'You think you have me stitched up then?' Clare asked. The image of the dead boy had sapped the tentative spring sun of warmth, but she could not be sure that he was the source of her unease. She packed away the photographs and ushered Riedwaan to the front door.

'Come on, Clare. You're not going to say no. I'll be there next week, when Phiri gets the paperwork done.' Riedwaan, as usual, was reluctant to leave.

'I must phone Constance first,' said Clare, distracted. On the far side of the bay was a ribbon of white beach and beyond that the mountains, softened by distance. Clare imagined the road she would have taken up to Namaqualand, to see her twin. She felt the old tug deep within her. 'Tell her I'm not coming.'

'You and your twin,' Riedwaan sighed. 'I watch you, but don't ask me how your minds work.'

'It's one mind,' said Clare, 'divided in two.'

She closed the front door behind him and walked through her apartment, picking up clothes, CDs and books that Riedwaan had discarded. Before she realised what she was doing, she had bundled his things into a bag. She dropped it at the front door, feeling lighter. The thought of a working journey felt good, right; this holiday idea, going to stay in the middle of nowhere with Constance, had not. Two birds with one stone, you could say. Clare took a deep breath, releasing the tension in her neck, and went to phone her twin.

As she dialled she pictured Constance as if she were with her. The hip-length curtain of dark hair; the shoulder blades and angular hips jutting against the seamless white she always wore over her scarred body. Clare let the phone ring three times. She put it down. Redialled. Another three rings. She hated these subterfuges, this pandering to a neurosis so deep it had worked into the marrow of her sister's existence. And her own, she thought, irritation and hopeless love welling up together.

'Constance,' said Clare, envisaging her twin in the dim farmhouse of their childhood.

'Are you all right?' Her twin's voice had the same soughing as wind in pine trees. You had to lean in to her to hear her. Which meant that when she spoke, which was rarely, everyone stopped, leaned in close, listened.

'I'm fine,' said Clare.

'You aren't coming.' Constance laughed, a silvery peal. 'I've been waiting for you to call.'

'I'm sorry, Constance. Something came up. A work thing. I have to go.'

'The dead boys.' Constance said it simply, a statement of fact.

'How did you know?' Clare's skin crawled.

'Television. We pick up the Namibian broadcasts here sometimes. I saw a snippet about a boy on a swing in a school in a desert. I thought, she'll go to him, instead of coming here to me.' The mocking, musical laugh again. 'I thought, he's waiting there for Clare.'

seven

Early the next morning, Riedwaan picked up the picture on Clare's hall table. The mom-dad-me-and-my-dog drawing, a gift to her from her little niece. He was overwhelmed with longing for his own child. Yasmin. His daughter. The undoing of his heart and his career. When she had been kidnapped, the husk of his desiccated marriage had blown apart, and he had signed the emigration papers that allowed Shazia to take Yasmin to Canada. Yasmin used to draw him pictures like the one before him now, but the drawings she sent from her new country were less exuberant. She had told him proudly that she could colour inside the lines now. Shazia would like that: getting Yasmin to stay within the lines. Riedwaan unlocked Clare's front door. That's what he liked about Clare, her disregard for limits.

It was cold on the street, and his breath misted and hung on the dawn air as he hefted Clare's suitcase into his old Mazda. The boot was temperamental and had been since a drunk in a Porsche had rear-ended him. As he slammed the boot, he felt cold metal against his carotid artery, warm breath on the back of his neck. Fury whipped him around, his fingers gripping the wrist, twisting hard. It felt wrong. Plump. Soft.

'Still fast, Captain.' A giggle, not a grunt. 'That Bo-Kaap skollie in you.'

'Rita.' Riedwaan dropped her wrist, angry, out of breath. 'You'll get shot doing that.'

She laughed again. 'You trained me, Captain. But I'm younger and faster, so watch your back. Is Clare upstairs?'

'She's there. Go up, it's open.'

Sergeant Rita Mkhize sauntered to the front gate. Riedwaan knew, without rancour, that she would out-captain him soon. That was how things worked now.

'I'm here, Clare,' Rita called through the intercom. 'Sorry to be late.'

Clare met her halfway down the stairs. 'Here are the keys. Fritz's food is where it always is. The vet's number is on the fridge. I made a bed for you in the spare room.' She gave Rita the keys and a thick envelope. 'Those are the things that Fritz likes. I thought it might be useful. Don't tell Riedwaan about it.'

'It's our secret, but you'll owe me big time,' said Rita, keeping a straight face. She handed Clare a much thinner folder.

'I've put together everything that Captain Damases sent for you.'

'Brilliant, Rita,' said Clare, flicking through the file. 'Use my car if you want to.'

'I'll walk,' said Rita, picking up the cat and following Clare to the gate. 'The station's three blocks. It'll be a pleasure not being shot at coming to work. I've had enough of this taxi war.'

'Thanks for taking care of Fritz for me,' said Clare. 'She's not as fierce as she looks.'

'Don't believe her. Look at this.' Riedwaan showed Rita a scabbed scratch on the back of his hand.

'He teased her,' said Clare.

'I'm sure he did,' said Rita, stroking the cat purring in her arms. 'Don't let him tease you.'

'Get in,' said Riedwaan. Aeroplanes always made him irritable. Clare let her hair swing forward to hide her smile as she slammed the door shut. 'It's international, so you need some time.'

Clare put her hand on Riedwaan's knee, moving it up his thigh. 'I'm going to miss you,' she said, her breath warm in his ear.

'Hey, let me drive,' he said, smiling. 'You'll make me have an accident if you do that.'

Riedwaan drove along the elevated highway that cordoned off the city from the harbour. The lanes were already clogged, and overloaded taxis weaved between the cars as they raced into the city. Clare checked her face in the mottled mirror dangling from the sun visor.

'Have you got a comb in here?' she asked, opening the cubbyhole.

Riedwaan stretched across to close it. 'Leave that,' he said, swerving to avoid two schoolboys dashing across the highway.

A torch, a bar of mint chocolate, bills, letters, a map and a comb spilled onto the floor.

'Are you planning to live in your car while I'm away?' Clare asked. She bent down to pick up the scattered papers. 'When last did you do any admin? Rates. Water. Electricity. Telkom. Insurance.' She smoothed out the papers on her lap. She bent down to retrieve the last one, swearing as she bumped her head on the dashboard. A scrap of lilac paper fell out from between the stapled sheets. The childish script caught her eye, and she read, almost without thinking:

> *Hey Dad this is Yasmin. Can't wait 2CU2. Mom got me new shoos. It is cold here when it is hot where you live. They look nice on my feet and we put paint on our nails. Red color.*
> *CU soon. I ♥ u daddy.*
> *Ps the tooth faree fairy gave me six dollars.*

Clare looked at Riedwaan. His profile had set. A muscle on the underside of his jaw jumped. She smoothed the piece of white paper that had held Yasmin's handmade card and stared down at the unfamiliar handwriting. This time she read deliberately:

Riedwaan

It looks like we will both come. I'm not sure if this is the best thing for me (or for you), but I think we have to try to work out how to move on. We arrive on the 13th. Friday. I'm not sure if it will be lucky or unlucky. Your mother has all the details. I hope this works. I'm tired of waiting. I need a decision

Shazia

Clare folded the letter and put it back into the cubbyhole. The comb lay forgotten on her lap. She opened the window, the air cooling her hot face.

'You weren't meant to read those,' said Riedwaan.

'You didn't tell me she was coming.'

'I did tell you Yasmin might come.' Riedwaan knew he was clutching at straws.

Clare turned to him, anger flaring from the spark of hurt. 'I'm glad that you'll see your daughter,' she said, teeth clenched, voice low. 'But you didn't tell me they were both coming.'

'I only knew for sure a few days ago.'

A truck hurtled past on the inside lane, hooting. Riedwaan swerved again.

'A few days?' said Clare. 'And you didn't think to tell me?'

'I thought you'd be angry.'

'I am angry.'

Riedwaan took the off-ramp to the airport. 'Shazia and I have a child together. We've been married for twelve years. I have to talk to her to sort things out.'

'I know.' Clare looked out of the window, dashing the tears from her eyes with the back of her hand. 'But you should've told me.'

'You'd still have been upset,' said Riedwaan.

'I'd have been able to make a choice then.'

'Let me explain.'

'No! You had your chance. Just drop me and go.'

There was a steel edge to Clare's voice. The armour she used to protect herself from feeling too much moved along familiar grooves to protect the vulnerability she had risked with Riedwaan. His separation was too recent and his ties to his family were too strong. It was her fault for letting him insinuate himself into her life, her heart. She was as angry with herself for letting it happen as she was with him for doing it.

Riedwaan ignored her and parked the Mazda. 'Talk to me, Clare.' He switched off the ignition and turned to face her.

'About what?'

'About all of this.'

'Why didn't you think of that before, genius?' Clare opened the door.

Riedwaan got out too, waving away the porter. 'I can explain.'

'You've had weeks to explain,' said Clare. 'Yesterday, when Yasmin called. Perfect opportunity to explain. Not telling me is worse than lying to me.'

'It's complicated.' Riedwaan put his hands on her arms.

'It was complicated,' said Clare, shrugging him off. 'Now it's simple.'

'It's hard to talk to you about this, Clare,' said Riedwaan. 'It's hard for me to tell you anything. I don't know what you think. What you feel. What you want.'

The blinds came down over the hurt in Clare's eyes. 'There's a bag of your things at the front door,' she said. 'Fetch it from Rita.'

'Clare, I'm so sorry.'

'It'll be simpler professionally.'

'I'll call you,' said Riedwaan.

'About the case. This subject is closed.' Clare touched his cheek, back in control, fingers cool, more dismissive than a slammed door. She strode towards the international departures terminal and into the embrace of the automatic doors.

'Fuck it,' Riedwaan said and went back to his car.

He threaded through the cars offloading passengers at domestic departures and joined the sluggish flow of traffic making its way into town.

'Fuck it,' he said again as the traffic gridlocked on the Eastern Boulevard.

eight

Clare handed over her ticket and passport, submitting to the pat-down when the security machine beeped.

'Your bra,' smiled the woman who searched her. 'The under-wire always sets this thing off. But what can you do? We all need a bit of lift.'

'Don't we just,' said Clare.

The morning mist was still wreathed across the Cape Flats, stranding Table Mountain and the leafy suburbs that clung to its base, but as the plane headed north, trees, fields, roads, towns, then villages, fell away and the land became drier, stripped of any vegetation except the hardiest plants. Clare opened the file that Rita Mkhize had put together. Precise notes in convent-school cursive. A plastic sleeve for expenses and petty-cash slips. A list of contact numbers. Empty file dividers for the post-mortem report, forensic analysis, ballistics report, and Clare's profile. Anticipation tingled up her spine.

Tamar Damases had e-mailed an aerial photograph of Walvis Bay. It showed a marshy river delta south of the port. Extending northwards was a slender sand peninsula that protected the lagoon and the harbour. At the tip of this encircling arm was Pelican Point, around which the calmed Atlantic tides swirled into the bay. The little town squatted behind the harbour. It was a bleak place, pushed closer to oblivion by the collapsing fishing industry. The town had ceased to grow as planned, so the school where the body had been found was right on the edge of the town, a bulwark against the red dunes that marched northwards until the dry Kuiseb River halted them.

A lonely place to live and an even lonelier place to die.

Clare looked at the photographs Tamar had taken of the dead boy. Kaiser Apollis might have been fourteen, but he was so undernourished that it was hard to view him as anything but the child he had been. The thin arms were clasped around the angled knees, the arms and legs shielding the stilled heart. Slender ankles disappeared into too-large takkies. Even in the grainy low-res prints, Clare could make out Nike's expensive swoosh. The forehead rested on the knees, and the back of his skull was missing. The autopsy was scheduled for the next day. Then the pathologist's knife would peel open any secrets hidden in the body of this dead child.

Clare closed the file and rested her forehead against the window as the plane started its descent. To the west, the surf-white beach corralled the red dunes. Beyond it stretched the restless Atlantic. The sun, angled low, revealed the Namib Desert's wind-sculpted dunes, dotted with tiny impoverished settlements. Every now and then, Clare glimpsed a flash of a corrugated-iron roof or the flurry of a flock of goats browsing on the acacias growing along the subterranean Kuiseb River bank – evidence of sparse human habitation. Walvis Bay, blanketed in fog, was invisible.

Clare let her thoughts drift back to Riedwaan. Her anger had burnt itself out, but it had left cold ash in its wake instead of calm. She missed him with an acuteness that hurt. Who would have thought?

'Thirty days.' The bulky customs official dropped Clare's immigration form into an untidy box at her feet. An unexpected smile dimpled her round cheeks as she handed back the stamped passport. 'Captain Damases told us to expect you.'

Tamar was waiting at the arrivals terminal when Clare exited. Her heart-shaped face was as beautiful as Clare remembered, but the tiny waist was hidden by a pregnancy that seemed ominously close to term.

Tamar's green eyes lit up with recognition. 'Let me help you.' She reached for Clare's suitcase.

'You're not carrying anything,' Clare protested. 'You look as if I should drive you straight to hospital.'

'It's just because I'm so short that I look huge,' laughed Tamar. 'I'm glad you could come.'

Tamar led Clare to a white Isuzu double cab. An officer was leaning against it, smoking. His black shirt stretched tight across a muscular chest. His hair was cropped close, giving his handsome face a hard look.

'Sergeant Kevin van Wyk,' said Tamar, 'this is Dr Clare Hart.'

'Welcome.' The man shook Clare's hand but made no move to help her load her suitcase.

As they exited the airport, Van Wyk turned the radio up just loud enough to make conversation an effort. Clare took Tamar Damases's cue and watched the desert slip past in silence, wondering how much had changed since her previous visit.

Two years ago, the factories perched like hungry cormorants around the harbour had gorged on bulging catches. Clare had filmed vessel after vessel offloading their silver harvests. Namibia's suited elite, circling like sharks, had allocated ever-bigger quotas to themselves, buying farms and BMWs hand over profligate fist, ignoring the scientists and their warnings. Now the fish had all but vanished and an eerie lassitude pervaded the town. The bounty that had followed the retreat of the South African army, itself leaving a gaping hole in the town's coffers, was gone.

Walvis Bay still wasn't much to look at. The town huddled around the harbour, ready to suck what it could from passing ships. The Walvis Bay police station faced a black coal-heap that waited to be loaded onto increasingly intermittent trains from the uranium mines deep in the desert. The gaunt cranes were sinister against the leaden sky. A seagull startled when Clare slammed her car door, its cry harsh on the raw air.

'Not as nice a view as you have in Cape Town, Dr Hart,' said Van Wyk, his gaze a lazy trawl across her body as she walked ahead of him. The fine hairs on Clare's neck rose.

The station was a low, featureless building with grenade mesh on all the windows. Someone must have thought that swimming-pool blue would make it more cheerful, but the coal dust had settled on every available surface. Two outlandishly pink pots marked the entrance, but all that flowered in them were cigarette butts. A few lipstick-stained, most not.

A stocky man was putting out a cigarette as they walked up the steps.

'Sergeant Elias Karamata, this is Dr Hart,' said Tamar. 'Elias is also working with us on the case.'

'Welcome to Namibia, Doctor.'

'Please call me Clare,' she said. Karamata looked like a prize-fighter – bull neck, broad shoulders – but his handshake was gentle, his smile warm. 'It's good to be back.'

'You've been here before?' asked Karamata, pleased.

'A couple of years ago,' said Clare, filling in a visitor's form. 'I made a documentary about the fishing industry.'

'All that corruption business is cleared up now.'

'Elias would be better off working for the Walvis Bay Tourism Board,' Tamar interjected. 'He spends his spare time trying to persuade me that it's heaven on earth.'

'People cry twice in Walvis Bay, Captain,' said Karamata, shaking his head. 'Once when they get here, once when they leave. You'll grow to love it too.'

Clare followed Tamar down the dim passage. Right at the

47

end, a tattered sign saying 'Sexual Violence & Murder' was sticky-taped to the door.

'Welcome to S 'n' M.' Tamar gave the door a practised kick and it swung open, revealing a surprisingly spacious office. There were four new desks, each with a plastic-covered computer.

'This is where Van Wyk and Elias work,' Tamar said. 'You can use that computer by the window.'

'It looks brand new,' said Clare.

'It is,' said Tamar. 'I got Elias after the marine-poaching unit was closed down, because there's nothing left to poach. Van Wyk was transferred from the vice squad.'

'Why was he moved?'

'Gender-based violence is the government's flavour of the month, so in theory it was a promotion.'

'Someone should let him know,' said Clare.

Tamar led the way to her own office. It was private and painted a sunny yellow. One corner of the room was covered with children's pictures. There were toys and two red beanbags next to the blue sofa, and a low table was covered with paper and crayons.

'The kiddies' safe corner,' she explained. Her soft mouth hard as she picked up a drawing and handed it to Clare. It was of a child's idealised house – red door, cat on the window sill, yellow sun smiling in the corner, smoke curling from the chimney. The family stood on green grass. A little girl, her head haloed with ribbons, with panda eyes. A mummy with bruises to match. A suited daddy with bunched fists, his groin scored out with black crayon. Someone had written 'Joy' at the bottom of the page.

'Her name,' said Tamar. 'I went to her funeral last week. Her stepfather beat her to death. Said she was cheeky.'

'How old was she?' asked Clare.

'Six.' Tamar's voice wavered.

On the wall were framed photographs of a laughing boy of eleven and a dimpled little girl dressed in Barbie pink.

'She's pretty,' said Clare. 'Your kids?'

'My sister's. She passed away, so they live with me now.'

'I'm sorry,' said Clare.

'They're sweet kids.' Tamar patted her belly. 'This one'll be born into an instant family. You've got no children?'

'Not for me,' said Clare. 'I'm an aunt though. My older sister has two girls.'

Tamar put on the kettle. 'Some tea?'

'Please. Rooibos?' asked Clare.

'The only thing for lady detectives,' Tamar said with a grin, handing her a cup. 'Here's a schedule.' She pulled out a sheet of paper with a list of names and dates. 'The city manager wants to meet you.'

'That's fine,' said Clare, 'but why does he want to see me?'

'You're a novelty and this murder has been a shock. Usually the only murders we get are the odd prostitute floating in the harbour or a drunken sailor stabbed in a shebeen.'

'Or little girls like Joy,' murmured Clare.

'Or little girls like Joy, yes.' Tamar's cup clattered in its saucer. 'My decision to bring in outside help hasn't been unanimously welcomed,' she said. 'Serial killers don't quite fit in with Walvis Bay's new vision of itself as a tourist Mecca.'

'Is this a bit of a political minefield for you?'

'That,' said Tamar, 'is an understatement. Important people have been jumpy since the fishing collapsed. They've pinned all their hopes on tourism, and dead boys don't attract many tourists.'

'I'm going to need a bit of specialised sightseeing.' Clare turned her attention back to the schedule.

'Elias will be taking you tomorrow,' said Tamar. 'He was born and bred here, one of the few, so he knows this place like the back of his hand. He even speaks the language the Topnaars speak.'

'Topnaars?' Clare frowned. 'Are they those desert people?' She vaguely remembered them from her previous stay.

'That's right. They live in the Kuiseb River and know the desert really well. You probably saw their huts when you came in to land this morning.'

'I did,' said Clare. 'White goats all over the dunes. Looked like snow for a second.'

'That's them,' said Tamar. She put her teacup aside. 'I need to eat something before our meeting with the big boys; otherwise I'll unravel.'

nine

'The Venus Bakery. This is the best place to eat,' said Tamar, parking under a palm tree on the other side of town. A group of boys uncurled themselves from its base.

'I'll watch your car,' said the tallest boy.

The bakery was on a corner, the walls painted a festive blue. Succulent cakes and pies were on display behind the glass counters of the self-service area, behind which were several tables, most full with a satisfied-looking lunch crowd.

'Why aren't you at school, Lazarus?'

'Sorry, Miss.' The boy looked down at his shoes, his shoulders bowed in well-practised contrition until Tamar walked past him. Then he moved his hustle over to the next car, pushing a smaller boy out of the way when he saw that they were tourists. He was wearing a grubby white shirt with a silver fish emblazoned on it.

'Pesca-Marina Fishing's still going?' Clare recalled the fishing company from her documentary.

'It is. One of the few. The company sponsors anything and everything. They're trying to clear their name of fishing this coast to death. Calvin Goagab, the city manager, who you'll meet later, has shares in it. They only do specialised fishing now, export added-value products.'

'What does that mean?' asked Clare, following Tamar to a table in the corner.

'It means packaged fish to the rest of us,' said Tamar with a smile. She ordered rolls and coffee, which arrived promptly.

'This is good,' said Clare. She hadn't realised how hungry

she was. 'What's the meeting about then, if there's nothing to report yet?'

'The mayor established a community policing forum to deal with family violence. After this body was found in the playground, Calvin Goagab called me in to see how we were going to tackle it. I told him then that I'd approached your new cross-border unit for help and that you were coming. He said he wanted to meet you.'

'Sounds fair enough,' said Clare.

'Goagab is a difficult man and he seems to have taken it as a personal insult that the dead boy made him late. It's best just to let him say what he has to say. He's not thrilled that our arrangement with the police was a fait accompli.'

Clare and Tamar walked the two blocks to the municipal building.

'Somebody had delusions of grandeur,' said Clare when she caught sight of the concrete bunker that reared up in an extravagant wilderness of lawn. The building dwarfed the few citizens scurrying up its steps, disputed bills clutched in fists.

'Army money,' said Tamar. 'South Africa's two fingers to the desert.'

Once inside, it took Clare a few seconds to adjust to the dim light of the cavernous entrance hall. Tamar pushed open the carved double doors to the executive wing, where their footsteps were absorbed by the pile of a garish carpet.

'Hello, Anna,' Tamar greeted an exquisite young woman who looked out of place behind the vast desk. 'We're here to see Mr Goagab.'

'Do you have an appointment, Miss Damases?' the girl asked, glossing her full lips.

'It's Captain Damases, my dear. And it was you who arranged the meeting.' There was enough irony in Tamar's voice to penetrate even Anna's self-absorption. The girl scrolled a crimson fingernail down the desk diary, before uncrossing her legs and leading Clare and Tamar down the passage.

'Damases and the doctor from Cape Town,' she said, flinging open the door to the mayor's conference room. Cigar smoke undulated on the overheated air. Gilt chairs with spindly legs and red cushions were arranged around a shimmering table. The velvet swagged across the windows was held in place with thick gold tassels, which would have been more at home in a bordello. The effect was both ludicrous and oddly sinister.

'Ladies, you're welcome.' The man closest to them stood up, his charcoal suit tailored within an inch of its life. 'I'm Calvin Goagab. CEO of cleansing. You are Dr Hart?'

'I am.' Clare held his gaze. 'It's good to meet you.'

'This is His Worship, the Mayor, Mr D'Almeida.' Clare thought Goagab was going to bow, or make her curtsey, but he managed to restrain himself.

'Call me Fidel,' said the mayor. 'Calvin likes all this protocol, but I'm a simple man. Sit down, Tamar. In your condition, you must not strain yourself. Sit. Sit, Dr Hart. Anna, bring the ladies tea.' The secretary closed the door a notch below a slam.

'You're a runner, no?' D'Almeida was a compact man of about fifty, with iron-grey hair that set off his olive skin. He took Clare's measure appreciatively.

'I do run,' she said.

'Well, you must run by our lagoon then. You can watch the flamingos.' He turned to Tamar. 'She's staying in the cottage? I hope you'll be comfortable.'

Anna brought in a tray and set it down. She slopped tea into four cups before flouncing from the room. The mayor turned to Calvin Goagab. 'You wanted to have this meeting, Calvin. Please go ahead with what you wanted to say.'

Tamar, Clare and D'Almeida all turned to Goagab expectantly. 'I just wanted to welcome Dr Hart.' Goagab put his fingers together. They were slender, manicured. His sleeve slipped back to reveal an ornate Rolex watch. 'And to make sure that she understands that she is working for Captain Damases and the Namibian Police at all times.'

'Calvin is sensitive about South African imperialism,' D'Almeida explained. 'Trying to make up for the time he spent in closer-than-intended proximity to the South African army. Independence rather took him by surprise.'

Goagab flushed. He did not like to be reminded of his two menial years shunting trains in the desert for the army.

'I understand,' said Clare. 'I'll be doing preliminary work here while Captain Riedwaan Faizal's paperwork is sorted out. He'll be joining me when that's done. Then you'll have a direct police counterpart here. My own expertise is more specialised.'

'A profiler, yes.' Goagab stared up at the ceiling. 'I'm sure that it is a difficult skill to bring across cultures. I'm sure you'll find that this ... unpleasantness will have the usual explanation. We've many foreigners who come to our port who have' – again he ferreted for a word – 'needs. Unusual needs. We had a case before Captain Damases was posted here. A girl was found dead, but she'd been seen frequenting nightclubs where such services are for sale. I'd be careful of jumping to conclusions.'

'I'm not that way inclined, Mr Goagab.'

Tamar concentrated on her tea. Goagab started to speak again: 'Of course, I didn't mean—'

'Thank you, Calvin.' D'Almeida silenced him. 'I'm sure that Dr Hart will bear that in mind during her investigation.' D'Almeida stood up and Clare took the cue and rose to her feet. The mayor walked the two women to the door. 'I'm sorry we have so little time,' he said. 'But we've a land claim to deal with. Some of the rag-and-bone people from the Kuiseb.'

'The Topnaars?' asked Clare.

'Ah, I see you know something about this place.' D'Almeida's grip on her arm was just short of painful. 'Yes, them: pastoral nomads following an ancient way of life if you're a romantic foreigner; poverty-stricken squatters who drink their pension money away and litter the desert, if you're from Walvis Bay. The one man who knows everything about where their so-called ancestral lands are won't speak'.

'Spyt?' asked Tamar.

D'Almeida nodded. 'The problem pre-dates us, unfortunately. The South African military has more than just the war to answer for. This is some confused claim about sacred sites. Apparently the ghosts of the dead must walk the land because of what went on here in the past.'

'Walvis Bay is a busy place for ghosts at the moment,' said Clare.

'These murders, yes.' D'Almeida waved a dismissive hand. 'People in the town are getting anxious. The rumours are getting increasingly exotic, as you can imagine. We must deal with them, of course.'

'With tourism, image is everything,' Goagab added. 'And we depend on it now that the fish are gone.'

'That, and of course the fact that we've a series of unpleasant crimes on our hands, Calvin. Not just a PR problem. I trust you won't forget that.' D'Almeida made sure that he had the last word. 'Please, Dr Hart, let us know what you need to make your investigation work.' He inclined his head towards her. 'And I do hope to see you running.'

ten

'I'll get Elias and Van Wyk,' said Tamar when she and Clare got back to the station. 'Then we can get started on our display.'

Tamar, Clare and Karamata made their way to the special ops room. Evidently, Van Wyk had more important matters to attend to, declining Tamar's invitation to join them without even looking up from his computer screen.

There was a roll of maps and a neat stack of autopsy photographs on the trestle table in the middle of the room. Stacked alongside were three murder dockets, sheets of coloured paper, scissors, Blu-tack, drawing pins and marker pens.

'We'll work backwards,' said Tamar. 'Let's start with Kaiser Apollis.' She wrote his name large in red.

'Monday's Child …' Clare pinned up the photographs of the boy drifting on the swing.

'Was fair of face,' Tamar finished. 'We'll have to wait for the autopsy before we can finish him.'

'There's a police file for him,' said Clare, checking through her documents.

'He was caught trespassing a month or so ago,' said Karamata.

'He was beaten?' Clare asked, glancing through the scrawled report.

'He worked the docks when he had to,' said Karamata. 'Van Wyk handled the case. The volunteer teacher, Mara Thomson, accused Van Wyk of beating Kaiser but it could just as easily have been the Russians on the old Soviet ships.'

'What are they doing here?' asked Clare.

'They've been rusting here since perestroika,' said Karamata.

'They don't dock because they don't want to pay harbour fees. They can't go home, because the state that owned them disintegrated with Gorbachev.'

'They like rough stuff,' Tamar continued. 'And they pay, but you've got to be desperate to go out there. The bar girls have stopped going after they beat up one of them for fun and threw her into the water. Some guy working on the *Alhantra* pulled her out.'

'Alive?' Clare asked.

'Just. Gretchen was lucky to survive. She worked at Der Blaue Engel, the most expensive of the sailors' bars. The "Gentleman's Club" is a new one in Walvis Bay. God knows where the money's coming from, but the local politicians and businessmen lap it up.'

'Gretchen von Trotha,' Karamata picked up the story. 'Unfortunate surname. Von Trotha was the German general who gave the extermination order for the Hereros a hundred years ago. My great-grandfather survived, so it's just luck that I'm here today.'

'Did she lay a charge?' asked Clare.

'Not likely in her line of work,' said Tamar. 'And she wouldn't know any better. She's been selling her body since she was thirteen. Van Wyk told me she's working the clubs again.'

'Van Wyk keeps tabs on things,' Clare noted, picking up the second slim file. 'Nicanor Jones.' She checked the date that he was found. 'A Wednesday's Child. Full of woe,' she said, shuffling through the photographs. An eyeless face leered up at her, a small neat hole blown clean through the skull, filigreed flesh peeling back from the snowy bone underneath.

'Looks like something got to his hands.' Clare pointed to a close-up of his hands. The palms were scored with callouses, freshly healed. The second finger of the left hand ended in a nailless stump.

'A trophy collection.' Tamar pulled the autopsy report out of the folder. 'That was post-mortem. The gunshot was ante-mortem.' She shook her head. 'Only a pathologist would define life as being pre-death.'

'If death's your main business then it is, I suppose,' smiled Clare. 'Where was he found?'

'Right near the dump. It's on the edge of the Kuiseb River. It's on the aerial map there.' Tamar showed her. The dry river with its fringe of hardy plants held back the dune marching north. The Kuiseb curved along an ancient faultline until it dissipated into the salt flats on the cusp of the lagoon.

'How did you find him?' asked Clare.

'An anonymous tip-off,' said Tamar. 'Two Wednesdays ago. The call came through to the switchboard operator and she told Elias. He went out and looked until he found the body.'

'Do you know who called?' Clare asked.

'The operator said it was a foreign woman,' Karamata told her. 'But Namibians speak more versions of English than I can count.'

'And a boy's voice could be mistaken for a woman's,' Clare suggested. 'Who else but another homeless kid would have seen him out there? I can't imagine these kids want any police attention themselves.'

'No, they don't,' said Tamar. 'But they're very frightened. Those who can have moved back to whatever families they have.'

'Nicanor Jones had no family, by the looks of it,' said Clare, reading his file. 'Who's the last boy?'

'Fritz Woestyn. He was found three weeks ago, last Saturday.' Tamar handed her a sheaf of photographs.

'Saturday's Child,' said Clare, 'works hard for his living.'

'Woestyn, his name. It means desert,' said Tamar. 'And that's where he was found by some municipal workers doing a pipeline inspection.'

'On a Saturday?' asked Clare, disbelieving.

'Water's more precious than gold here. The foreman identified him. He'd seen him scavenging.'

'Peculiar that there was anything to find,' said Karamata. 'A hyena, even jackals make quick work of anything dead.' Fritz Woestyn stared up at Clare from the autopsy photograph. She looked over the small evidence boxes. Each contained the remnants of the boys' lives – shoes, some bloodied clothes, a note found in a pocket – making the displays look like small, morbid shrines.

'Easy targets, street children; many different reasons to do them in and no one around to report them missing.' Clare paced up and down in front of the boxes. 'You don't think it could be some kind of unofficial clean-up operation? Out at the dump where there are plenty of homeless kids scavenging. The school, too' – she checked Tamar's notes – 'where it looks like this Mara Thomson was running some soccer thing for homeless kids. That might make sense of the killer's desire to display them: that the bodies are a kind of threat. That's what happened to street kids in Rio.'

'It crossed my mind,' admitted Tamar. 'But with those Rio killings, you always had two or three together, kids sleeping in doorways in a city of ten million. You're not going to get away with that in a town of forty thousand people.'

'Have you done a search for a similar pattern in other ports?' asked Clare.

'I did. Nothing came up on any of the databases I have access to,' said Tamar. 'Rita Mkhize did a search in South Africa too. Nothing.'

'Nasty, brutish and very short, these lives,' said Clare. 'Unless the killer's left town, there'll be another body before too long.'

'I have to get home,' said Tamar, stretching her arms up to loosen her shoulder muscles. 'Let me drop you off at your cottage.'

Clare picked up her bag and the three files. 'I'll go over these again tonight.'

Tamar drove alongside the deserted harbour. It was fenced off from the road by twenty feet of razor wire. The barbs were festooned with grimy plastic bags: Africa's national flower.

Tamar stopped outside a secluded series of stone cottages, all of them closed up. Shadows were deep beneath the palm trees and narrow service alleys. 'Lagoon-Side Cottages' said a sign hanging from the bleached whale-ribs that arched up over the entrance.

'The view is great on the few days when the fog lifts,' said Tamar.

'You don't like this weather?' Clare asked, taking her suitcase out of the car.

'I hate it,' said Tamar. 'I grew up in the sun, so this cold worms its way into my bones.'

'How did you get posted here?' asked Clare.

'It was my choice.' Tamar fished in her bag for keys. 'My sister needed help before she died, and there's plenty of scope for promotion in the police force.'

'Your husband?'

Tamar ran her hand over her swollen belly. 'There's only me for this little one.' Her tone invited no further questions.

'I'd like to see where Kaiser Apollis was found before the autopsy tomorrow morning,' said Clare, switching tack effortlessly.

'You have to see everything yourself?'

'Photographs flatten things. I've looked at your pictures, but there's something about being where the body was found.'

Tamar opened the door of the cottage. 'I hope you aren't superstitious. It's number 13; that's how the police got it cheap. No one ever wants to rent it.'

'Did you think I might be?' asked Clare.

'From your lectures,' said Tamar. She unlocked the French doors onto a small stoep. The sea air was welcome in the stuffy room.

Clare was glad to put her suitcase down. It had been a long day. 'I usually get accused of being too scientific,' she said.

'There was one thing you said that stayed with me.'

'What was that?'

'You said that when you go to a crime scene you like to sit there a while alone or with the body. That sometimes a feeling of what happened washed over you like a warm breeze. That spooked me.' Tamar was quiet for a second. 'You weren't talking about the feeling of the victim. You were talking about the killer. What you feel is what the killer leaves behind. His heart, that's what you find. When I saw that body in the school playground it raised the hairs on the back of my neck. I had that feeling, Clare. The one you described.'

'I wouldn't put that down in the case file, if I were you,' Clare laughed.

'I won't.' Tamar looked tired, older than her thirty-two years. 'Stranger killings are the hardest to solve,' she said.

'Hard to be a stranger in a town this size,' said Clare. 'Hard to keep a secret, I'd imagine.'

'You'd be surprised how many secrets there are.' Tamar opened the fridge. 'I put some wine in for you. And some milk and bread.'

'Very thoughtful,' said Clare, walking outside with her.

'I'll see you at 7.00 a.m., then?'

Clare nodded and watched Tamar ease her bulk into the

front seat of the vehicle. Within moments, the mist had swallowed her car. She was heading due east. Clare guessed that she lived in Narraville, a windswept township that had uplifted itself into a suburb. There had been a few nice gardens there, if she remembered correctly. Roses flowered in some of them, despite the desert.

eleven

Out of habit, Clare locked the front door to the cottage. It didn't take long to put away her tracksuit, T-shirts and jeans. She hung up her black dress and put a framed photograph next to the bed. Three little girls next to a childhood swimming pool laughed up at her. Two identical in frilled white swimming costumes: Clare and Constance. The third stood in the middle: Julia, older, breasts budding in her yellow bikini top, her arms around her twin sisters. Clare always carried the photo with her.

She opened the sliding doors and stepped onto the sheltered stoep. The lawn sloped away towards the boulevard that circled a tempting five kilometres around the lagoon. Clare reckoned she still had another hour of light. She was tired, her limbs sluggish, but the nausea from the small plane lingered. She needed a run.

It was a release dropping the weight of the day with her clothes and replacing them with her tracksuit.

The lagoon stretched towards the horizon, burnished a deep copper by the setting sun. A swathe of flamingos took off in a startled flurry of pink. They whirled out to sea before banking to fly inland, stragglers trailing like the tails of a kite. A boy of about seven hurtled past Clare on his bicycle, his hair set aflame by the setting sun. He waved shyly before turning in to the yard of a dilapidated double-storey house.

The wind was picking up, carrying the ice of the Benguela current with it. The last kite-boarders were peeling off their wetsuits and packing up their equipment. Clare was glad of her hood. The thick grey fabric cocooned her, the rhythmic thud of her feet on the ground as familiar now as her own heartbeat. For the first time since she had opened that Pandora's box in Riedwaan's car, her mood lifted. She ran faster, pushing the thought of him from her mind, burying it beneath the task that lay ahead of her.

Some problems are better buried. The boy on the swing, for instance; he would have been less trouble if he had been buried. To the killer, at any rate. Clare wondered what lesson had been intended.

She reached the end of the paved boulevard, but she wasn't ready to go back to the empty cottage yet. She kept on, running past the arc of streetlights and towards the salt marshes. Beyond them, if she remembered correctly, lay the Kuiseb Delta, an area of treacherous tributaries and restless sand blowing off the dunes. She repressed an atavistic fear of the dark and pressed on into the wind, losing herself in the comforting rhythm of her loping stride. A truck materialised without warning, forcing her off the road.

'Hey!' she yelled after it, fright making her furious. She stopped, leaning forward, trying to get her heart to slow down. The vehicle accelerated into the thickening fog, flashing its hazard lights in apology. It was time to go back.

Clare turned towards town, the wind at her back now, the chatter of the sea birds feeding in the shallow water to her left. She rounded a dune, planted with a copse of dusty tamarisks. The trees cut out the sound of the lagoon, but here the wind carried the faint, percussive echo of unfamiliar footsteps. The sound of it goosefleshed Clare's arms and made her stomach feel hollow. She picked up her pace, certain now that she could also hear the sound of breath rasping in lungs unused to running.

Just before she broke free of the trees, a wiry arm snaked around her, yanking her backwards. The other arm twisted into her hoodie, snapping her neck back. Clare kicked hard backwards. There was a sharp gasp of pain as her foot reached a shin, but the arms around her body did not lessen their hold. Her hood had pulled tight across her throat. She could smell him, the feral tang of adrenaline and wood smoke on his skin. Clare pulled forward, but that made it more difficult to breathe, so she leaned her weight in to her attacker, using the momentary slackness in his arms to twist loose. They both fell onto the damp sand, Clare beneath him. She calculated the distance to the lights beyond the trees. Three hundred metres. The takeaway restaurant she had passed earlier would still be open. She needed fifteen seconds, twenty at the most. She looked at her attacker, trying to see if he had a weapon. There was no glint of steel in the dim light. No knife out. No gun. Clare took a deep breath and fought again to slow her heart rate.

'I'm sorry, Miss.' The voice was light, almost girlish. Not what Clare had expected. So was his body, lighter than hers, now that she thought about it. 'But I need to talk to you,' the voice said.

Clare's heart was still hammering against her ribs. She took a breath, trying to slow it down. He wouldn't be the first man to attack a woman and say he just wanted to talk. But it gave her a gap. 'Let me sit up,' she said, the steadiness of her voice hiding her panic.

The figure of a young boy came into focus. 'Don't run away,' he pleaded.

'I won't,' said Clare, although the unwashed smell of him turned her stomach. She moved slowly so as not to startle him. Still no knife that she could see. She realised now that she was sitting up that she was taller than him.

'I saw you outside the bakery today.' Clare's heart was returning to normal. 'Lazarus. That's your name.'

The boy nodded, pleased that she had remembered.

Clare stood up cautiously. The boy rose with her. He came up to her shoulder. 'What do you want?' she asked. 'I've got nothing on me.'

'I'm scared,' said the boy.

'You're scared,' said Clare.

'Nobody helps us. Sometimes we die,' said Lazarus, 'but then it's just a drunk person who didn't mean to kill us dead.'

'Is that what happened with Kaiser?' Clare asked gently.

A car pulled in to the lot outside the takeaway, the shards of light from its beams raking through the trees, the glare catching the boy's face. He looked very vulnerable, very young.

'Kaiser, he went to stay with his sister.' The boy blurted the words out. 'He thought he'd be safe with her.'

'That's the last you saw of him?'

The boy nodded. 'Friday morning. He went to town.'

'What happened to him?' asked Clare.

The boy shifted his weight. 'I don't know. No one saw him. He never came back.'

'Lazarus, I'm going to start walking now,' said Clare, moving slowly so as not to alarm him. 'Do you want something to eat?'

'You go home, Miss,' Lazarus said, glancing nervously in the direction of the car. 'I'll be in trouble if someone sees me with you. We go to jail if we bother the tourists.' He looked down at his scuffed shoes. 'Mr Goagab said so.'

'Okay,' said Clare. She checked instinctively for her keys and her phone. They were both still in her pocket. Clare looked Lazarus in the eye. 'Was there anything specific you wanted to tell me?'

His gaze slid away. He shook his head.

'Okay,' said Clare again. 'But you find me if you hear anything. Just don't knock me down again.'

'There are people who won't like you if you help us. Be careful, Miss.'

'Who won't like it?' asked Clare. She looked at Lazarus, but it was too dark to read his expression.

'I don't know,' he shrugged. 'There are so many people who think we're just trouble.'

'Is that what happened with Kaiser?' Clare asked a second time. Another car turned in to the parking lot. Clare put her hand up to shield her eyes. When she turned to Lazarus for an explanation, he had blended into the darkness cascading in from the desert. Like a ghost. The thought made her shiver.

She was glad she had left the lights on in her room; the yellow light made it seem like a haven amidst the unlit cottages. She let herself in, locking the door behind her before taking a shower.

When she was dry and dressed, she poured herself a glass of wine and made toast. Then she fanned the dockets around her on the bed and set to work. Monday's Child: Kaiser Apollis. Nicanor Jones: Wednesday's Child. Fritz Woestyn: Saturday's Child. She was becoming accustomed to the unfamiliar names, but she had to reach behind the violence of their deaths to conjure an image of what they had been alive. She picked up a news clipping about the homeless soccer team. The key to the dead was in the living. To find their killer, Clare would have to resuscitate, if only for a moment, the laughing boys they had been, taking a shot at the goal posts at the end of a dusty soccer pitch.

twelve

It took Clare three cups of coffee to get going the following morning. Tamar arrived early to take her to the school. The streets were still empty, and wide – wide enough for an ox-wagon to turn. A hundred years ago, they would have been the only form of transport into the waterless interior. The dusty streets would have been the only way inland for the ingredients of civilisation – tea, coffee, sugar, alcohol, and later guns – and the route out for colonial spoils – copper, uranium, gold and diamonds. The only reason anyone would live here, Clare thought, is to take a cut of whatever passes through.

It was five past seven when Tamar stopped before the school's locked gate. The caretaker eyed them warily, but waved when he recognised Tamar.

'Herman Shipanga,' Tamar said to Clare. 'He found the body.'

'When will the school re-open?' Clare asked.

'Maybe Thursday; otherwise next week. The headmaster Erasmus took it badly. I was surprised. He was such a tough guy when he was in the army.'

'South African?'

'Ja, he took Namibian citizenship and stayed on after they pulled out in '94.'

'Did many people do that?'

'A few. Some said they loved this place. For others it was a good way of avoiding Bishop Tutu and his Truth and Reconciliation Commission. Us up north of the Orange River, we decided to just brush our little atrocities under the carpet.'

Tamar parked beneath a wind-ravaged palm tree. 'Come this

way. A path runs behind the school. This is how the boy got in.'

'You think he was alive then?'

'No, sorry. I'm sure not,' said Tamar. 'I meant the body, which Helena Kotze will confirm during the autopsy later.'

Clare picked her way down the path. It was strewn with chip packets and empty bottles. In places, used condoms had been snagged by the barbed-wire fences.

'Prostitutes bring their clients here?' she asked.

'They do, but we don't do anything unless there's a complaint,' said Tamar. 'I've checked with the regulars. Nobody saw anything.'

'You think that's the truth?'

'That I can't say.' Tamar stopped when the playground came into sight.

The houses had their backs to the alley. In the yards, dogs barked, chained to wires staked into the ground. Damp clothes hung on sagging lines. In the yard opposite the flapping strip of crime-scene tape, a faded-looking woman hung up her last item of washing and hitched the empty basket to her hip. A pudgy toddler tried to push his scooter through the sand.

'Hello,' greeted Clare, stopping at the fence.

'What you want?' The woman's tone was belligerent.

'These dogs always bark like this?' Clare asked.

'Only for strangers.' The woman fished out a cigarette from her pocket.

'Did you hear anything on Sunday night, Monday morning very early?'

'She asked me already.' The woman jerked her cigarette towards Tamar. 'I was watching TV.' She blew a smoke ring. 'Then I was asleep.'

'It's important, anything unusual,' said Clare. 'A boy was murdered.'

'Ja, the third one. You tell the police to do their job, so that our kids are safe instead of bothering innocent people.' With that, the woman turned and went indoors, yelling at her child to follow her.

'Who uses this alley?' Clare asked Tamar.

'People taking a short cut to the school,' answered Tamar. 'The rag-and-bone men used to come through here with their donkey carts.'

'Not any more?'

'Not as much,' said Tamar. 'Most of the recycling is done at the municipal site. The Topnaar carts were banned from coming into town. Hygiene reasons apparently, according to our CEO of cleansing. But they still come from time to time.'

'My friend Goagab?' asked Clare.

'The very one.'

The playground stood at the top of a gentle incline. A new wooden fence sequestered the youngest children's area. It had been decorated with a garish mural, the laughing Disney characters mocking in the childless silence.

'That's the swing?' Clare pointed to the last tyre hanging from the yellow frame.

Tamar nodded. 'And this is the gap in the fence where he got in.'

They walked together through the desolate playground. The bright-yellow paint had flaked off the links of the chain from which the seat was suspended. Clare sat down on the inverted tyre. The smell of the rubber, the metal sharp against the back of her legs, tipped her down a tunnel of memory again. It took her breath away, the immediacy of it. Herself a solemn six-year-old, swinging in the hot school playground, bare legs pushing time behind her, brown arms bending into the future. Willing herself older so that she could get away. Watched by Constance, her twin, whose face mirrored hers except in what it concealed, watching her, willing her to stay. Constance, a thought fox sniffing out Clare's most secret desires to be the only one, whole in and of herself.

Clare stopped, aware that Tamar was looking at her. She steadied the swing and hopped off.

'It's got the best view,' said Tamar. 'That swing.'

'You tried it?' asked Clare, looking out at the expanse of sand circled by the dark arm of the Kuiseb River to the south.

'I wanted to get a sense of him. Of his death. To see if there was anything left of the violence of it.'

'And was there?'

Tamar blushed and shook her head. 'There were some indentations in the sand, though,' she remembered. 'Like someone had poked it with a thin stick. Maybe a cane.'

Clare nodded and went over to the classroom block. A single window overlooked the playground. She peered into the dim classroom. The rows of miniature red desks and cheery yellow chairs were empty. A pile of marking lay abandoned on the teacher's desk. The writing on the board caught her eye: Mrs Ruyters, Grade 1, Monday's date.

'Ruyters,' said Clare. 'That rings a bell.'

'She's on your list for interviewing. She was here early, before Herman Shipanga arrived,' said Tamar, looking at her watch. 'Shall we get going? I need to get some coffee and pastries on the way. I can't do pregnancy on an empty stomach. Post-mortems neither.'

The Venus Bakery was bustling with early-morning trade when Tamar pulled up on the opposite side of the road. At the stop street ahead, a familiar figure peered into the windows of cars caught by the traffic light.

'That's the boy I met last night,' said Clare, feeling the bruise on the side of her arm. 'I'll need to talk to him again.'

'Lazarus,' said Tamar. 'Lazarus Beukes. He's sharp. Been living on the streets most of his life. He'll spin you whatever story he thinks you want to hear.'

'You wouldn't believe him?' asked Clare.

'Put it this way,' said Tamar, 'Lazarus rarely lets the truth interfere with a good story.'

To the left of the bakery entrance, a wiry girl, her hair a wild black halo, chained her bike to a blue column. Lazarus approached her, trying to sell her a tatty-looking newspaper, his bony shoulders sharp against his worn jersey.

'That's Mara Thomson. The English volunteer.' Tamar pointed to the girl as she entered the store.

'They look so alike,' said Clare as they crossed the road. 'Funny to think they grew up six thousand miles apart.'

'Two rolls with cheese, please,' Mara was saying when they entered the bakery.

The woman behind the counter pulled two buttered rolls out of a tray, slapped the cheese onto them and wrapped them in plastic. She pushed them across the counter to Mara. 'You shouldn't talk to these street boys.' Disdain curled her thin upper lip. 'Six Nam dollars.'

'They're good kids,' said Mara, 'living a bad life.'

'It's easy for you foreigners to feel sorry for them, but we have to live with them. Aids orphans are just trouble.' The woman counted out Mara's change. 'Look at that one who got himself killed. And the other two they found in the desert. What do they think that'll do for our tourism?'

'I'm sure they'd have avoided being shot,' Tamar interjected tartly, 'if they'd known what their murders would do to your business.'

'Hello, Captain,' said Mara, her relief at being rescued palpable.

'Morning, Mara. This is Dr Hart,' said Tamar. 'She's here from Cape Town, working with me.'

'Yeah, well, I'm glad somebody's bothered,' said Mara, shaking Clare's hand. 'Nice to meet you.'

'And you,' said Clare. 'You knew Kaiser? And the other boys, I understand?'

'Kaiser plays ... played in the soccer team I coach. So did Fritz and Nicanor, on and off,' said Mara, moving towards the door, out of earshot of the sour-faced shop assistant. 'Fritz Woestyn's death, that was part of the odds they play with anyway,' she went on. 'There've been murders before this. Nicanor Jones's death made them scared. This last one ...' Mara's voice trailed off.

'I'll need to talk to you,' said Clare. 'About the boys.'

'All right,' said Mara. 'I rent a room in that double-storey on the lagoon. George Meyer's house, if you need to ask for directions.'

'I've seen it,' said Clare. 'A little redhead on a bike went in there.'

'That's Oscar,' said Mara. 'I'll be back after soccer practice this afternoon.' She nodded goodbye and walked outside. Clare watched her give a roll to Lazarus.

'No meat?' he asked, pulling off the wrapping and dropping it to the floor.

'How about a thank you?' said Mara, picking up the discarded wrapping.

'Thanks,' he said, throwing the cheese roll into the bin as Mara turned the corner.

'Her visa's almost expired.' Clare had not heard Tamar come outside. 'She's got to go home, whether she wants to or not.'

73

'And does she?' asked Clare.

'I don't think so,' said Tamar. 'She's fallen for a beautiful young Spaniard called Juan Carlos. I doubt she can think straight at the moment.'

thirteen

The Walvis Bay private hospital was a drab building. The mortuary, housed in a weather-beaten prefab round the back, was the grim heart of the establishment. A young woman in hospital greens opened the door when Tamar knocked.

'Welcome.' She stood aside for Clare and Tamar. The lemony scent of her hair held the institutional smell of disinfectant and instant coffee at bay.

'You must be Dr Hart.' The hand she offered Clare was broad and capable, the square nails cut short.

'Call me Clare. I feel like a fraud around proper doctors. You're Dr Kotze?'

'Helena, please,' the woman said. She turned to Tamar, looking her over. 'How are you?'

'Fine. Here's some breakfast for you.' Tamar gave Helena a pastry.

'Thanks. It's good to meet you, Dr Hart. I've read some of your work.'

'And your old professor, Piet Mouton, was singing your praises.' Clare returned the compliment.

'I'm just sorry I wasn't here to do those other two boys,' Helena said. 'A medical intern did the autopsies on Fritz Woestyn and Nicanor Jones. They're about as much use as a politician's election promises. Those boys were buried and the intern went back to Cuba, so a lot rests on this post-mortem.'

Helena gave Clare and Tamar gloves and gowns, ushering them into a cubicle off the entrance hall. Clare pulled the shapeless green gown over her clothes and tucked her long hair into the disposable hairnet. Helena opened a door, releasing the smell of the morgue. The ammonia was biting, but it was no match for the cloying stench of decay. Thick plastic curtains thwacked against metal when Helena Kotze wheeled in the metal trolley.

Kaiser Apollis's scrawny body was curled under the white shroud Clare had seen in the photographs. Helena pulled back the cover to reveal the child's head and face. The back of his head was missing and there was a small, neat hole in his forehead, the caked blood erasing the delicacy of his features. The three women circled him.

'A single gunshot wound to the forehead,' Helena said, more for her tape recorder than for Clare and Tamar. 'Probably a pistol. Nasty exit wound at the back, so no bullet for ballistics. Cause of death, I'd say. Put the call through to Piet Mouton, won't you Clare? The red button switches it to speakerphone.' She pointed to a machine near the window.

Clare busied herself, relieved to have something to do. She was also glad to have Mouton orchestrating this, even if it was remote. His experienced eyes missed nothing.

'Dr Hart,' bellowed Mouton, right on cue. 'You girls ready?'

'We're here, Piet. Me, Dr Helena Kotze and Captain Tamar Damases of Nampol.'

'Where's that useless bastard Faizal? He leave you in the lurch in the desert?'

Clare kept her voice light. 'Looks like it.'

'Tell him from me that absence makes the maiden wander. Doc Kotze, what you got there?'

'You've got the photos?' Helena asked.

'Yes, of course I have the photos. They jammed my e-mail all morning. Photos help me bugger-all. Forensics is science in court. On the slab, it's intuition and luck. Put me in your head and let me see through your eyes.'

Helena took a deep breath. 'Body of a child. Male. Looks twelve. Sixteen next week, according to his ID book. Weight: forty-two kilos. IDed as Kaiser Apollis. Bullet to the head. Close range. Body placed in a rubber swing. Blue and white nylon ligatures around both wrists. My guess is washing line.' Helena moved closer to the still form on the gurney and looked at the rope that had held the child's wrists together. 'A clean cut. Looks like—'

'Cut with what?' interjected Mouton.

'Looks like it was a pair of pliers,' Clare finished for Helena. 'Something rough.'

'Body folded into a foetal position,' Helena continued. 'Arms wrapped around the legs when discovered. Wrapped in an old piece of cloth. All held together with riempie. Riempie also used to attach the child to the swing where he was found.'

Helena untied the leather strips holding the shroud loosely in position. Kaiser Apollis looked as though he could have been asleep. His limbs had flopped wide, palms up. She pulled the shroud from underneath him and spread it out. There were no bloodstains. His life had seeped away before he had been swaddled in the cloth.

Helena continued: 'The top joint of the ring finger is missing.' Tamar brought her camera up close to the mutilated digit.

'The only finger with a dual nerve supply,' Mouton noted. 'Double the nerves; double the pain. No wonder it's the wedding finger.'

'An unlikely bridegroom.' Clare picked up the boy's hand and spread out the fingers. 'Some bleeding. If it was done post-mortem then not too long after he died.'

'Dr Kotze,' said Mouton, his disembodied voice startling them. 'What's your time of death?'

'The body was cold when it was found,' said Helena. 'But I'd say at least thirty-six, maybe forty-eight hours before we got to it. There was only a little stiffness left. Weekends are generally our murder nights anyway. So Friday.'

'Any other wounds? From the photographs it looked like his chest was a mess.'

'Yes,' said Helena. 'Considerable post-mortem cutting. Surface wounds on the chest and abdomen. Not much oozing. Done quite some time post-mortem. We'll wash it off and have a closer look.'

Helena and Tamar laid the slender boy out on the trolley, his hip bones twin peaks under the bloodstained white shirt. 'The Desert Rats' was emblazoned across the front of the grubby shirt.

'Mara Thomson's soccer team,' said Tamar.

Helena removed his clothes. He had no underwear on under his jeans. His feet were too small for the shiny new Nikes.

'Expensive shoes for a homeless child,' Clare commented. She bagged and tagged the clothes and shoes.

'Fake,' Helena explained. 'Chinese Nikes. Thirty Namibian dollars. That's what? About four US dollars. Try China Waltons in the middle of town. That's where everyone gets them.'

Helena looked away from the still face, androgynous in death, and put her hand on a dirty knee. 'Old scars on the knees and elbows. Uncircumcised. No tattoos. A leather necklace with a beaded pouch at the end.'

'It's for protection.' Tamar reached forward. She untied it and dropped it with the clothes. 'He'd have worn it since he was a baby. Whoever gave him that loved him.'

'Didn't do him any good in the end,' said Helena. 'Will you help me turn him, Clare?'

Clare nodded reluctantly. The naked boy was insubstantial. When they laid him on his stomach, his heels flopped outwards, leaving the feet pigeon-toed. Helena leaned forward, oblivious. She pressed a forefinger against the naked buttocks. 'The discolouration on the back of the legs is quite marked. Buttocks, back, thighs, calves. The blood looks like it's pooled.'

'What's that telling you?' barked Mouton.

'That he lay on his back for some time before he was trussed up for his trip to town.' Helena ran her finger over the boy's matted hair. His drying blood had trapped fine sand. She held a glass strip beneath the locks and tapped a bit of sand onto it, holding it up to the light. It glinted. 'See that? It's mica. Fool's gold. You don't get that at the coast. At the coast the sand's darker, purple even.' Helena put the glass aside.

Clare's eyes traced down the lattice of scars on his back. 'Kaiser Apollis took a few beatings in his life. I'd like to hear what Van Wyk says about his weekend stay in the cells.'

Helena turned on the tap, and warm water spurted out of the garden hose she had rigged up. She and Clare turned Kaiser onto his back. The water ran pink, clearing the boy's face of the crust of blood. Bone and skin filigreed over the hole the bullet had punched into his forehead.

'The killer was close when he fired. Look at this.' Helena pointed to the boy's forehead. Fanned out around the entrance wound was an intricate stippling. 'It's called tattooing. You see this if the victim is shot at close range. Between ten centimetres and two metres. Further away than that you don't see it.'

'What's it from?' Clare asked.

'The propellant and gas that travels with the bullet as it leaves the muzzle embeds itself into the tissue, like a tattoo,' Helena explained. She moved the hose down, rinsing blood from the boy's neck and chest. She turned the water down and washed the wound on his chest. Marks were deliberately scored into the flesh with a few deft, deep strokes.

79

'It looks like a 3,' said Helena.

'There had better not be a number 4. There was a cutting like this on Nicanor Jones too,' said Tamar. 'He had a 2 on his chest.'

'Did Fritz Woestyn have a 1?' Clare asked.

'Nothing. The finger joint was missing. Head shot the same, same type of gun, but not this mutilation,' said Tamar.

'How was this done?' Clare turned back to Kaiser Apollis.

'Non-serrated knife, I'd say,' guessed Helena. 'Very sharp. A fisherman's knife, something sturdy like that. Look here.' She pointed to the chest. 'It's nicked the ribs in places. But there isn't much blood here, so definitely done some time post-mortem.'

Helena washed the rest of the frail body, hands gentling the healed lash wounds on his back and buttocks. She examined his feet, pulling apart the toes. The tender flesh between them was still pink, the last vestige of a truncated childhood. There was sand and salt crusted around his toes, as if he had dug them into sand and then let a wave run over them.

'It looks like he walked in sand before he put his shoes on,' she said, taking a scrape of the soil. 'I could see if this sand is the same as the sand in his hair.'

'You studying soil to go with your gunshots?' Tamar asked.

'My boyfriend's a geologist. He thinks the best way of getting me to give him a blow job is to tell me in graphic detail about all the soil types of the Namib.'

'Does it work?' asked Clare.

'Put it this way, it keeps him quiet.'

'Have you thought about giving him something to eat?' asked Tamar.

'Gross,' said Helena, shocked. 'I hate cooking.'

'Ladies, I have work to do. Call me when you're done, Dr Kotze.' Mouton cut the connection, leaving a disapproving silence in the cold room.

'Oops!' Helena gave Clare and Tamar a grin. 'I'm going to start with the cutting now. It's a bit gory. Organs, brain and splatter. I'll do you lung slices too. If he vomited before he died, we might be able to see what his last meal was. If you two want to get on, I'll finish up here.'

'We've got an interview with Kaiser's sister anyway,' Tamar said. 'Clare, Lazarus told you that Kaiser had been going to her a lot lately. Maybe she can tell us why.'

fourteen

The crisp air outside the mortuary was a relief. Kaiser Apollis's secrets would be scalpeled from him. The nestled organs separated. Liver, heart, lungs laid out in stainless-steel dishes to be weighed and tested. Clare doubted that this bloody grubbing would reveal much. The truth of his death lay in the dark maze of someone else's mind. This was her labyrinth; she an Ariadne armed with nothing but the slender thread of instinct.

A firm foot on the accelerator had taken Clare and Tamar past the warehouses and low-cost houses that sprawled north of the town. The wind lashed the washing, Mondrian blocks of blue, green, yellow and red, pegged to the fence defending the last row of cramped houses. The dunes seemed to sidle closer with each gust. A thin girl was sweeping the apron of cement at her front door. She had the same heart-shaped face and delicate build as the dead boy Kaiser. On her high cheekbone was a bruise, butterfly-winged around the almond-shaped eye. Tied to her back was a baby, perhaps a day or two older than the bruise.

'Captain Damases,' the girl whispered as soon as they were in earshot.

'Hello, Sylvia,' said Tamar. 'This is Dr Hart.' Tamar unlatched the gate and they stepped into the neat yard. A scrawny dog yapped. Sylvia raised a threatening hand. The dog cowered and was silent. She looked back at the two women, dazed. Tamar put a gentle hand on the girl's arm. 'Shall we go inside?'

'Sorry.' Sylvia jumped. The house was empty, but the air was laden with a fug of sleep, cheap coffee and sadness. A snowy television spluttered into the gloom. It was hard to move among the over-sized furniture. Sylvia switched off the TV and the radio, and silence crackled into the chilly little house.

'How are you?' Tamar touched the girl's swollen cheek.

Sylvia dropped her eyes. Two fat tears appeared, rolled down her cheeks and splashed onto her milk-swollen breasts. That was it.

'The baby?' The swaddled infant mewled. Sylvia retied the blanket and he puckered his rosebud mouth and went back to sleep. 'What's his name?' asked Tamar.

'Wilhelm. For his father.' Then a surge of defiance glowed in Sylvia's eyes. 'I call him Kaiser.'

'For your brother?' asked Tamar.

'For my brother.' Sylvia looked down, the unblemished side of her face illuminated by the morning light. She would be beautiful without the bruises.

'The boys at the dump say that Kaiser didn't always stay with them?' Tamar inflected the sentence into a question.

Sylvia's face had the look of a secretive child who refuses to tell tales. Her eyes flicked at the kitchen table. Tucked beneath the overhang of Formica was a thin blue mattress rolled tightly around a grey dog-blanket.

'Your brother slept here sometimes?'

'When my boyfriend worked night shift. He didn't like Kaiser to be here ...' Her voice trailed off. Clare wondered how long the infant's plump cheek would stay unmarked.

'Did you know your brother's friends?'

'We were always alone,' Sylvia said. 'Then Wilhelm took me to live here.'

'When was that?' Clare asked.

'Two years ago.' There was shame in the girl's voice. 'I had nothing to eat.'

'How old were you then?'

Sylvia shrugged. 'Maybe thirteen. I'm not sure.'

Clare supposed that at thirteen a regular fist from a man you knew was better than a knife in the guts from a man you didn't.

'And Kaiser? Where did he go?' asked Clare.

'He was with me sometimes. Sometimes on the street. I gave him money when I had some.'

'When last did you see him, Sylvia?' Tamar asked.

The girl slumped. She looked for an uncanny instant like the crone she would be at thirty. If she lived that long. 'My baby's father changed his shift,' she said. 'Kaiser had to go for good.'

'Try to remember when,' Clare pressed. Patience would get them what they wanted.

'Last week he stopped working night shift. When I came back from the hospital with the baby he told me that Kaiser had to go.'

Her hand touched the bruise on her face. That explained the timing: the bruise was younger than the baby, but only by twenty-four hours.

Sylvia took a deep breath. 'I left him a note.' She raised her head, the brief spark in her eyes snuffed. 'I never saw him again.' Her voice was so quiet that Clare could hear the tiny panting breaths of the baby sleeping on its back.

'And Wilhelm?' asked Tamar. 'Where was he on Friday night?'

'No,' Sylvia said, 'he was with me all night.'

'Do you mind if we look round?' Clare asked.

Sylvia shook her head. She sat down and opened her blouse. The baby's mouth parted, clean and pink. A fat little hand kneaded her soft flesh. Sylvia cupped her hand over the child's fragile head. Tamar put on the kettle to make tea, asking Sylvia about the birth, the breastfeeding. The soothing talk of mothers.

Tuning out Tamar's gentle murmur, Clare unwound the worn

bedroll. The faded Superman pyjamas brought her up short with the realisation of how recently the dead boy had been a child. She slipped her fingers inside the frayed blue cuffs. His skinny wrists and ankles would have protruded from them as he grew into his malnourished and delayed adolescence. She picked up the top and held it to her nose, breathing in the lingering, wood-smoky smell of him.

Someone had stood close enough to the boy to breathe in the same essence, to feel his warm, frightened breath on their hands. They had stood that close and then discharged a bullet into the unlined forehead. Tears prickled hot in Clare's eyes.

'What else was his?' she asked Sylvia.

The girl pointed to the window sill: a jagged scrap of mirror, a yellow comb, a jar of Vaseline. A blue bowl stood on the drying rack. The boy would have filled it, perhaps catching a glimpse of his small, peaked face before plunging his hands into the cold water to rub the accumulation of the night's sleep from his eyes. Outside, he would have heard mothers calling their children for breakfast, as Clare could hear now. Inside, the house was quiet, just the click of the baby's throat as it suckled, oblivious of the harsh life that awaited it.

Clare opened the Vaseline jar. Kaiser would have opened it one last time to dip his finger in for a final gob of pale jelly. He might have rubbed the grease into his cheeks. The cupboards would have been empty as they were now, and the child's belly would clench around the water he drank for breakfast. Kaiser's cheeks would have glowed brown in the morning light, creeping over the desert as he stepped into the cold. At least with his cheeks shining, his teachers wouldn't get angry with him for looking hungry.

Clare looked into the shard of mirror. It fragmented her face. She could see her mouth or eyes, a cheek or the chin. Her picture of the dead boy was the same, fragmented. A shattered face. A flayed chest. A delicately turned foot in a white Nike, a full bottom lip. A discarded child she had never met and into whose begging hands she probably wouldn't have dropped fifty cents.

Clare imagined the last afternoon the boy had come home, turning left at the bent fig tree that grew outside the shebeen where his sister's boyfriend drank before he beat her on Fridays. When he saw his sister's note, the boy might have wished that he could not read, but he would have read the lines on his sister's face anyway. The message was clear in black and blue. He would have just turned around and gone back to town. He'd have scoured the dustbins outside the fast-food restaurants.

The voice would have startled him and he'd have looked up to find the driver of a car asking him if he was hungry. Did he nod? Or was he too proud? His eyes would have flared wide at the proffered banknote.

'Get me a Coke. Something for yourself,' the driver would have said. 'Get in.' As the fog thickened, the boy had done just that. Nobody would have seen the car glide into the mist.

'Shall we go and watch the sea?' the driver might have asked. Or the desert. Or the lagoon.

The boy would have nodded. Why not?

At the edge of the lagoon, the tide would be rising, water rushing in over the exposed mud and around the pink legs of the stilted flamingos, necks down, looking for food. The birds would have raised their heads in unison at the sudden retort of a car door slamming. The car would've traced the curve of the lagoon towards the fog-blanketed salt flats, the boy watching the fingers on the steering wheel.

'You got a family?'

Perhaps the boy had thought about the wooden cross that marked his mother's resting place, or of his sister's battered face, before shaking his head.

'You busy now?'

The boy shook his head again.

'Would you like a drive?'

The boy had obviously thought that he would. They knew that much. Clare wondered if he had known it was going to be his last. If he had sought out what was coming, even welcomed it …

'Clare, we should go.' Tamar's voice drew Clare back into the small, stuffy house. Tamar was holding the baby, and Sylvia held a Mickey Mouse rucksack in her hands.

'He left his school bag. Take it,' she said. 'Maybe it'll help you.'

Clare looked back at the house as they reached the end of the street. Sylvia was standing at the gate where they had left her, the wind wrapping her skirt around her thin legs. Clare opened the bag. There was a pencil case, a dog-eared *Harry Potter* in Afrikaans, and a diary. She rippled through the pages: homework assignments at the beginning of the year with longer and longer gaps between them. One hundred Namibian dollars fell out. Clare put her finger in the place where it had been secreted. August. A month earlier when all three boys were still alive.

'A lot of money not to spend.' Clare tucked it back into the book as Tamar turned into the station parking lot.

'I'm going to take a walk,' said Clare. 'I need some fresh air.'

She headed towards the water, the wide sweep of it a relief after the confined space of the mortuary and Sylvia's cramped house. The sun, gilding the drab buildings along the shore, was as warm as a hand on her skin. She missed having Riedwaan as a sounding board for the ideas whirling in her head. All she had to do was swallow some pride and phone him to discuss the case.

She swallowed and dialled, but his cellphone went straight to voicemail. She called his office. It rang for some time and went through to the switchboard.

'Special Investigations Unit. Can I help you?'

'Clare Hart here. Put me through to Captain Faizal.'

'He's not in. He took a personal day.'

Clare knew the reservist. She was a bosomy law student with a uniform fetish.

'A personal day,' she said. 'That must be a first in the SAPS. You've been reading too many magazines.'

'Something about his wife and daughter, I'd call it personal.'

That silenced Clare.

'You want to leave a message, Dr Hart?'

'No.'

'I'll tell him you called then?'

Gabriella. That was her name, Clare remembered.

'Don't bother, Gabriella.'

Clare's stomach growled, reminding her that it had been a long morning and she needed lunch. On her way back to the police station, she stopped at the bakery and ordered rolls and coffee to take away.

'Twelve-fifty,' said the cashier, the same thin-lipped woman who had given Mara the third degree that morning. 'You're the expert from South Africa.'

'I'm from Cape Town.' Clare searched through the unfamiliar notes in her purse.

'A waste of money. One dies, and they spend how many thousands of our tax money to bring you here.' A vein pulsed in the woman's temple. 'Where are you staying?'

Clare was so taken aback that she answered: 'On the lagoon.'

'I knew it. In a town with no money and no work.'

Clare picked up her lunch and went outside, shaken by the woman's venom. She stepped off the pavement, right in front of a big Ford truck.

The driver slammed on his brakes and she jumped back. Her heart skipped a beat when she recognised him: Ragnar Johansson. She hadn't calculated on his still being in Walvis Bay.

'Hey, Clare.' Ice-blue eyes in a weathered face. Ragnar Johansson put out a vein-roped hand to restrain the Labrador whining next to him. 'I was wondering if you'd call.'

'It didn't take you long to find me.' Clare pushed her hair out of her eyes, playing for time.

'Not in a town as small as this,' said Ragnar.

'I wasn't sure if you'd want to.'

'Well, I found you,' he smiled. 'I'll tell you later if it's what I wanted.'

'How've you been?'

'Good.'

'Iceland?' she hazarded.

'Didn't work out. Cape Town?'

'It's been fine.'

'You alone?'

Clare looked away and nodded.

'You want a lift?'

'No, thank you.'

He put out his hand and touched her cheek. 'It'd be good to catch up.'

'It would.' It seemed churlish to step away from his forgotten touch.

'Dinner?'

'Okay.'

'I'll pick you up at eight-thirty tonight.'

'I'm staying at the Lagoon-Side Cottages.'

'I know.'

The light changed and Ragnar drove off. He and his wet dog huddled together on the front seat. Both grinning. Clare's face felt hot where he had touched it. She rubbed her cheek, then licked her finger. It tasted salty. Like blood.

fifteen

Tamar Damases had arranged a vehicle for Clare's interview with Shipanga. Clare signed for it, picked up the keys, and within five minutes was guiding the 4x4 along the wide avenue that led to Kuisebmond, the township where the caretaker lived. The quiet streets of the town gave way to a warren of lanes, and she slowed to avoid the darting children and mangy, slinking dogs. The cracked pavements were crowded with stalls selling single cigarettes and plastic bags holding an onion and two potatoes. Women squatted by low fires, tending fragrant vetkoek and frying pig trotters. Men with glazed eyes and the concentrated precision of the permanently drunk watched Clare drive past the dark shebeens, before turning back to the pool tables.

The address Tamar had given Clare didn't mean much in the thicket of houses. She hazarded a guess and turned down a newly laid road that took her away from the larger houses and into a maze of narrow paths. Tin shacks and tarpaulins had been replaced with brick boxes. Green, red, pink, yellow, brown: brightly coloured, poorly built. The Smartie houses. A flock of chubby-legged urchins ran alongside the car. Clare parked. An entourage of children clustered around their minder, a girl of nine or ten, staring at Clare getting out of the enormous car.

'Where does Herman Shipanga live?' Clare asked the girl.

The fat baby on the girl's hip gave a terrified wail and buried its face into her neck.

'Come,' the girl beamed. Clare followed her through backyards where washing snapped and forlorn patches of mielies somehow grew.

'There.' The girl pointed at a yellow house. The little boys backed up against her skinny legs. A few plugged their thumbs into their mouths and watched, solemn-eyed, as Clare knocked on the door. She could hear the radio blaring inside. It sounded like a church service, but the language was unfamiliar.

The door cracked open a few inches. A man, wiry and short-er than Clare, looked out from the gloom. His hair was sprin-kled with grey; cheekbones high and wide; dark eyes, kind.

'Herman Shipanga?'

The man nodded, wary. The air that escaped was stale, laden with the smell of too many bodies in too small a place.

Clare held out her temporary police ID. Shipanga opened the door wider and took it. 'I'm Clare Hart. I'm investigating the death of Kaiser Apollis.' The man's eyes flickered with fear, anger, sadness; Clare couldn't say which. 'I wanted to ask you about him. About how you found him.'

Shipanga did not respond. Clare repeated the question in Afrikaans. Her train of urchins scuffled closer.

'One minute.' Shipanga answered in English. He closed the door, and the radio stopped. Then he opened the door again and set down two Coke crates in front of the house. 'Sit, *asseblief.*'

Clare obeyed.

'*Voetsek*!' Shipanga raised his hand at the children and they scattered like gulls to settle at a safer distance.

'English?' Clare asked.

Shipanga looked down and spread out his hands.

She switched back to Afrikaans: 'You found the boy?'

Shipanga nodded. He ran his hands over his eyes, as if trying to erase the image.

'I read your statement,' said Clare. 'But I wanted to hear from you what you saw on Monday, from beginning to end.'

Shipanga did not take his eyes off her face. The beginning? His fingers sought the ridged scars on his cheekbones. Precise incisions that had been filled with ash so that he would be forever marked as someone who belonged. But that had been forty years ago. The close-knit structures of family and clan up north had fractured and then broken apart. The force of that implosion had landed him here on this tract of bleak sand. It had kept him in the heaving bowels of a factory ship until it had crushed him beneath falling crates of filleted fish. Then it had spat him out again to find woman's work, sweeping and cleaning toilets, dragging his injured leg behind him until he had come face to face with the dead child in the swing. The end? Hard to say. Shipanga looked down at his shoes.

'We used to find them like that,' he said at last. 'Outside the villages.'

Clare waited, watching as Shipanga gathered memories, sought words in a language that did not belong to either of them.

Shipanga looked at Clare, frustration clear in his eyes. The words were inadequate for what he wanted to tell her, the shock of a buried past colliding with the present. 'I found him,' he said. 'The bullets to the head. Like the executions when the army was here, in the north …' His voice trailed off.

The absence of war, thought Clare, did not result in the presence of peace. The elemental force of it, the trauma, shaped a man in unnatural ways, much as the wind along this Skeleton Coast bent the alien trees.

'You found him,' prompted Clare. 'Tell me how you found him.'

Shipanga straightened the seam in his trousers. Someone had ironed them with care. 'I ate early. I left after the first siren. Before six. I went straight to the school. Got my rake to clean.'

'Which way did you go in?'

93

'I went in the back. I take a short cut down the path between the houses.'

'Don't the dogs go crazy?' asked Clare.

'I always go there,' said Shipanga. 'They're used to me.'

'Did you see anybody?'

Shipanga shook his head. 'My wife was here, my kids. At the school, on the way there, the fog was too thick. I saw nobody. Nobody saw me.' He paused, thought about the implications.

'No one was at school before you?'

'Just Mrs Ruyters. Her car was there. I didn't see her.'

'Did you expect her to be there?' Clare asked.

'She's always first.'

'You always start with the kindergarten playground?'

'Always. Some of the children come early. Mrs Ruyters likes it to be ready for them.' Shipanga picked at his fraying cuff. 'When I saw him there,' he continued, 'I thought it was one of the older children teasing. Then the wind turned him and I saw the flies on his face.'

'Did you touch him?'

'I told Sergeant van Wyk,' said Shipanga, 'I ran for help. The headmaster was there and he called the police. I didn't see the boy again. My job was to stop anyone coming into the school.'

'Who came?'

'There were only a few,' said Shipanga. 'Mr Meyer, of course. He's always early. The little boy, Oscar. He sometimes helps me or he goes to Mrs Ruyters.'

'The other early people?'

'They all went away when they saw the police vans and the ambulance. Only Calvin Goagab caused trouble.' Shipanga's mouth twisted, as if the name was bitter on his tongue. 'He wanted to drop his sons at school.'

'Is he often early?' Clare asked.

'He does what he wants. He's a powerful man. He works for the mayor now. He has a smart house. He forgets that he came from here.' Shipanga gestured to the grimy dilapidation around him. The silent, staring children shrank out of sight again.

'Does anyone else use that back entrance?' Clare changed tack. Tamar had told her about Goagab. She needed more.

Shipanga shrugged. 'Sometimes the children. The ones who come from the other side of town. Mara Thomson sometimes. She comes by bike.'

Clare was about to get up, but Shipanga put his hand on her arm, restraining her.

'It was a warning, the boy. Like a warning from the spirits. This is a bad place. I told you we used to see them left dead to warn us, telling us to keep our heads down, not see things, to leave. That boy was a warning. Like the old ones we had during the war.'

'Who was the warning for?' Clare asked.

Shipanga shook his head. 'There are many ghosts in this desert. The desert sees everything. All our secrets.' He paused, waiting for a distant siren wail to cease. 'It keeps secrets only as long as it feels like it. Then the sand moves and there are all the skeletons. It is a message.'

'And what was the message?'

'That I must go home to my village,' said Shipanga. 'I mustn't die here.' He traced a curved line in the sand: the river on whose verdant banks he had spent his boyhood.

Clare stood up to go. Shipanga looked up at her. 'Did you speak to Miss Mara?'

'Not yet,' said Clare.

'Miss Mara knew that boy well. He was in her team. The other boys, too, the dead ones.'

To the left of the house, a woman turned the corner, laden

with old plastic shopping bags. She stopped when she saw Clare, her brow furrowed with concern. 'Herman?' she said as she approached.

Shipanga stood up. 'This is my wife. Magdalena, this is the police doctor.' Clare took the woman's plump hand. It was as soft and worn as an old glove. Magdalena looked at her husband.

'He can't sleep,' she said to Clare. 'Since he found the dead boy, he keeps us all awake with his nightmares or with walking about. He says the boy was there to call him home.'

'What do you think?' asked Clare.

Magdalena shook her head. 'I was born in the city. I see no ghosts. There are sailors here, truck drivers, and foreigners from everywhere. It's one of them. Whoever did it is gone.' She sat down beside her husband. 'Gone, Herman.'

Shipanga leant against the sturdy body of his wife, the strength drained from him. 'You'll excuse us.' Magdalena pulled him to his feet, limp as a rag doll. Clare watched the little house swallow them. The radio crackled back to life.

The children drifted away when she returned to her car. She sat for a minute, wishing she still smoked. The caretaker had given her nothing new, nothing concrete.

The hand tapping on her window snapped her into the present. It was Shipanga again. 'I found this,' he said, reaching for Clare's hand and placing a tangle of gossamer threads in her palm. It was a cast, a compact ball of insect remains; wings, shimmering and transparent, some still attached to fragments of insect bodies.

'What is it?'

'It's from insects, after they've been eaten. You only find these ones in the desert.' Shipanga pointed to a red-streaked pair of wings, longer than the others. 'They come out if it rains.'

'Termites?'

Shipanga nodded.

'Why are you giving me this?' The tangled limbs moved in the breeze, their husky weightlessness horrible in Clare's hand.

Shipanga stepped back from the car window as Clare tipped the little corpses into the cubbyhole. 'After they took the boy away,' he said, 'I went back to the swing. I found it stuck in the tyre where his head had been.'

sixteen

Karamata was finishing his coffee in Tamar's office when Clare got back to the police station. 'Are you ready to see the sights?' he asked. He was scheduled to take Clare to the dump site where Nicanor Jones was found.

'I'm ready. Are you coming, Tamar?' asked Clare.

Tamar shook her head. 'I am still going through all the ship logs to see if there's any pattern with which ships were in and these murders.' She leant back on her yellow couch. She looked so slight, despite her pregnancy.

'Find anything yet?'

'Not much. The Russian ships, of course. The *Alhantra*'s been in all the time. Ragnar Johansson's the skipper. You know him, I think.'

'I do,' said Clare. 'From the last time I was here.' She couldn't read Tamar's expression.

'There've been a couple of others, but there's no consistency,' said Tamar. 'I need to do a few more checks. I'll catch you later.'

Clare picked up her files and followed Karamata to the Land Cruiser. He opened the door for her, before heaving himself into the driver's seat.

Karamata took the road past the lagoon, but soon turned off onto a dusty track. Clare opened Nicanor Jones's file. A class photograph, taken several years earlier, was stuck in the front. A little boy with shiny eyes and a wide mouth smiled up at her, frozen in his last recording of an official moment. In the next picture, his eyes were hollows and the white cheekbones shone through. There was one of his torso. It was bloody, the skin on the bony chest torn away. Clare looked away.

'Not pretty,' said Karamata.

'No,' said Clare.

Karamata turned right, into pure sand. The wheels held and the Land Cruiser topped the dune. Hidden below at the foot of the dune lay a scavenger's paradise.

'That is where I found him.' Karamata pointed to the rusting razor wire looped along the edge of the dump. He pulled out a panoramic shot and held it up. The composition foregrounded the boy's limp body, giving perspective to the vast expanse of the sand.

From their vantage point, Clare could see the road that led back to town, the lagoon and the harbour beyond it. 'On this side of the fence?' she asked.

'Yes. He had been tied to that pole.' Karamata pointed to a sturdy log that held the swags of razor wire in place.

'Whoever dumped him didn't come through the dump then. If he'd gone through that wire, alive or dead, it would've lacerated him. Whoever dumped him must've come across the sand. You didn't see any tracks?'

'I didn't,' said Karamata. 'But the wind had been blowing, so anything would've been covered with sand.'

It was as sparse a crime scene as the schoolyard, according to the docket. 'He wasn't killed here, was he?'

'No,' said Karamata. 'He'd been dead five days when he was found.'

Clare pictured the shrine she and Tamar had made to the child full of woe, Wednesday's Child. That made the time of death Friday, the same as Kaiser Apollis. She looked at the autopsy pictures again. The mutilation was the work of human hands. So where was he? Why keep his body away from scavengers? When was he put here?

Clare looked over the unforgiving sand and rock. It made no sense, the risky display, the complications of transporting a corpse several days dead, the exhibition in a public place. Or was it intended that children see it? A warning of sorts, like Shipanga had said.

'The body must've been in full view of where the waste-pickers sleep,' she observed.

'They say they saw nothing and heard nothing,' said Karamata. 'They certainly said nothing.'

A blue dump truck moved along the black ribbon of tar. It lumbered past a windowless brick building then onto a weighbridge. A man with a clipboard took note of the number plates and weight before waving the truck on.

'George Meyer. The boss.' Karamata cut the engine. 'That's his incinerator.' The chimney, dark against the grey sky, spiralled smoke into the still air. It drifted towards the town.

'So much easier to just burn a body,' Clare said, half to herself.

'You'd think so,' said Karamata, 'but you'd have to get it past George first. He's very German about his record-keeping!'

'His movements have been checked, I suppose?'

'We spoke to him,' said Karamata. 'He was at home all weekend. Him and that funny little boy of his, Oscar.'

The truck stopped in the middle of the dump site. Scrawny supplicants emerged from the heaps of waste and swarmed around the vehicle, heads bowed, hands lifted. The driver jumped out and walked over to the foreman standing to the side, sjambok at the ready. The waste-pickers worked with practised efficiency, filling sacks with discarded affluence.

'The other economy,' Karamata noted. 'At the moment it's the only one that's stable.'

'The fishing is over?'

'Finish and *klaar*. Not even jobs left for pals.'

100

'You didn't put money in fishing?' Clare asked.

'Not me,' he laughed. 'I didn't have the right surname or the right connections. I suppose I should be glad about that now.'

Karamata started the engine, and the vehicle pitched forward down the vertiginous dune. He pulled onto a track that led to the dump and parked outside the entrance to the building.

'Let's say hello to George Meyer,' he said. 'A courtesy.' He pushed open the screen door and Clare followed him down the immaculate passage. The third door was open.

'Mr Meyer?' Karamata ducked slightly as he stepped inside the office. His bulky form dwarfed the furniture.

George Meyer was at his desk. The little redhead Clare had seen cycling along the lagoon was sitting at a small table. The boy's eyes widened in recognition when he saw her.

'Sergeant Karamata. Madam.' George Meyer stood up and smoothed down his hair, nodding at Clare.

'This is Dr Hart,' said Karamata. 'Dr Hart and I want to talk to the boys who live on the dump.'

'Sign in, please.' Meyer pushed a ledger towards Karamata. 'New policy since that body was found here. The boys are afraid. This makes them feel safer.'

'And are they?' asked Clare.

'I doubt it,' said Meyer. 'Whoever's killing them wouldn't start out here on the dump.'

'Why not?' asked Clare.

'Well, everyone here would recognise a stranger, wouldn't they?'

'They would,' said Clare, 'if it was a stranger.' She went over to look at what the child was drawing while Karamata took care of the formalities. Oscar had covered the page with drawings. Flowering people, winged trees, dolphins. The eerie whimsy was so at odds with this rough place.

'Those are beautiful.' Clare smiled at the boy, but the child looked down at his freckled hands, twisting them in his lap. 'What's your name?' She bent down beside him.

'This is Oscar,' Meyer answered for the child. 'He's been mute since his mother died six months ago.'

The pieces clicked into place: Meyer, Virginia Meyer. Clare remembered a book she'd read the last time she was in Walvis Bay. She turned back to the child. 'Your mother studied the Kuiseb plants, didn't she? She worked with the desert people, trying to understand how they use them.'

The boy's eyes lit up, confirming Clare's question.

'She was my wife.' George Meyer looked down as he spoke. 'Before that, she and Oscar lived in the Kuiseb for many years.' He held out his hand, and the child sidled over, but Meyer did not draw the child into the shelter of his arms. The two of them stood, side by side, watching Clare and Karamata get back in the vehicle.

'Unusual colouring Oscar has,' she said as they drove away.

'He takes after his mother,' said Karamata. 'Virginia was like Moses's burning bush with all her red hair. And such a white skin, no good for this country.'

'She wasn't from here?'

'She was American. She came here to work at the desert research centre. Then her visa ran out and she found George somewhere and married him. I think for her it was like collecting a rather dull specimen. A husband was something she needed. Oscar is what she wanted. The two of them were always alone out in the Kuiseb, her trying to preserve things, stop any kind of development. That's where she died, in a car crash.'

'George Meyer's not his father?'

'No. That child has no one now she's gone. No one came from America to claim him, so he stayed here with the stepfather.'

Karamata stopped the car. The rubbish truck they had seen from the dune stood empty, everything of value winnowed from the rotting black mass lying around it. The truck driver waved as he headed back to town. A group of boys had left off scavenging and were watching them. The foreman came towards them, caressing his palm with his whip, a flock of ragged children at his heels. 'You looking for work, Karamata?' asked the thickset man.

'Good afternoon, Mr Vermeulen. This is Dr Hart from South Africa. She is working with us on the murder of the boy here, and the one at the school.'

'*Nee, fok*, Karamata. Foreign experts for a couple of dead street kids.' He glared at Clare, his muscled neck bulging. 'Don't you have enough corpses of your own down south?'

'Nice to meet you, Mr Vermeulen.' Clare extended her hand; Vermeulen wiped his palms on his overalls and held her fingers for a moment.

'These poor little fuckers, their mothers throw them away.' Vermeulen caught the child closest to him, a boy of five or six, by the scruff of the neck.

'Who's your mother, hey?' The boy giggled and Vermeulen tossed him aside. 'He never even knew. He's lived on the streets since he was three. When he gets a bit sicker, then maybe those nuns will come and get him. They'll take him to their place out there.' He gestured eastwards with an arm as thick as a pole. 'So what you want here now?'

'I'm not a social worker,' said Clare. 'But I might be able to help find who's killing these boys.'

'Ag, you can believe what you want, lady,' Vermeulen sighed. 'It's nice of you to try to help. Not many do.'

'Where do these boys sleep?' Clare looked around the site; it was hardly an orphan's haven.

'A few go sleep in town,' said Vermeulen. 'The rest sleep here at the dump. You want to see?'

'Sure,' said Clare.

'Lazarus!' he bellowed. A scrawny boy was pushed to the front of the group.

'We've met, I think,' said Clare. Lazarus gave her a shifty smile.

'Why weren't you at school?' Vermeulen demanded. 'You know how I had to *gatkruip* that headmaster to get him to take you back?'

'School's a waste of time.' Lazarus was careful to stay out of Vermeulen's reach.

'This is our Einstein,' said Vermeulen. 'Knows everything, cocky bugger, which is lucky because the school won't take him back again this time. Take the doctor and show her where you sleep.'

Clare and Karamata followed Lazarus into an enclosure behind the truck. An old tarpaulin served as a roof, and a nest of mattresses was arranged underneath, neat bundles of clothes at the top of each one.

'That was Fritz Woestyn's bed,' said Lazarus. 'And Kaiser's.' Clare looked down at the yellowed sponge mattress. There was a photograph next to the bed.

'That's our soccer team.' Lazarus came and stood next to her. His breath was rank. 'We were in the newspaper for the Homeless World Cup,' he said. 'See, there's Kaiser and there's me. There's Fritz and the other boys. Mara took it. She gave us all a copy. Look, here's mine.' He dived onto the last mattress and pulled out an identical shot.

Clare took it and turned it over. There was an inscription on the back. *From Mara*, it said. *For my boys. Remember to always believe.*

'When was that?' she asked.

'I don't know.' Lazarus shifted from one foot to the other. 'I suppose about four weeks ago. We went away for a weekend and she took it then. It was when she got us our new uniforms. Look, it says "The Desert Rats".' He pointed to the photograph.

It must have been cold when it was taken, because the boys were huddled together. They all wore the same shirt that Kaiser Apollis had been wearing when he was killed.

'Cool shirts,' said Clare.

'Pesca-Marina Fishing sponsored them. Look, it says so here on the back.' He whipped up his sweatshirt and turned around to show Clare the logo, pleased to have a witness to the small joys of his life.

'Can I keep this?' Clare asked.

'Keep Kaiser's picture,' said Lazarus, handing it to her. 'He won't need it. Maybe in Cape Town you can get us some more sponsorship, find us a new coach.'

'What about Mara?' asked Clare, slipping the picture into her pocket.

'She's going back to England.'

'When?' asked Clare.

'I don't know,' said Lazarus. 'But they all do. What's there to stay here for?'

There was no answer to that. 'Is she still coaching you?'

'Ja, we have a practice later. But it's not the same any more.'

'The boys who were killed, you knew them all,' said Clare.

'None of us live long, Miss. They went quick. You try going like him.' Lazarus pointed to the darkest corner of the makeshift tent. There was a small mound of blankets. 'He's afraid to go to the nuns. If the sisters come for you, then you know you're over and out.' Lazarus gave a bleak laugh. 'It's not much of a team any more. Three dead.'

'Who do you think did it?' Clare asked.

'Someone they went with, that's what everyone's saying,' said Lazarus, watching the other boys kicking a makeshift soccer ball on the level patch of gravel that was their pitch.

'You got any names?' asked Clare. 'Anyone in particular?'

Lazarus looked at her briefly, but the focus of his attention had shifted. 'A sailor? Maybe one of the old men who live alone here in town. A lawyer from Windhoek? It happens like that to us boys.'

'Is there anyone …' – but Lazarus was gone, dribbling the ball expertly towards the goal posts – 'regular?' Clare finished the question.

'Too much glue,' said Karamata, watching Lazarus score.

'Or too afraid,' said Clare as Lazarus careened across the field, arms extended in the universal language of football victory. 'I want to ask him some more questions.'

'Another time,' said Karamata, checking his watch. 'We've got to get going now, if you want to get to the next crime scene before dark.'

Clare followed him reluctantly back to the car. She waved at Lazarus. He lifted one hand in salute, watching them drive away.

Karamata drove towards the Kuiseb River, a sinuous line of green that parted the vast ocean of the Namib. A group of oryx made their way in single file, their measured pace only emphasising the stillness. The road they took snaked through stands of dusty tamarisks. Their branches whipped against the windscreen as Karamata picked up speed.

'Topnaars,' he said, pointing at the donkey cart rattling home, feathering golden dust into the sunset. Clare could hear the crack of a whip above trotting hooves, the shouts of the driver urging his tired animals home.

'You know this place well,' she observed.

'Like the back of my hand,' said Karamata. 'I grew up around here.'

Old flood-marks had scoured a wall out of the sand. Debris from upriver was stranded high above the dry bed. The road petered out into a sandy track, pocked and scarred with the previous year's rains. The mud had dried and cracked as it had retreated from the relentless sun.

Karamata cut the engine. 'Fritz Woestyn. This is where he was found.' He pointed towards a bleak stretch of sand. The ridge of an old railway was visible in places where the water had churned and frothed in the riverbed, desperate to reach the sea.

'Who found him?'

'Pipeline maintenance. There was a leak and they came out to check. They found Fritz staring up at the sky with a hole in his head. Van Wyk was on duty. He came out.'

'Saturday's Child. Where exactly?'

'Under that big tree.' Karamata pointed to a spreading acacia.

'Tied up?'

'Curled up in a piece of cloth. His hands had been tied, but the rope had been cut through, like with Kaiser.' Clare knelt down in front of the tree, photograph in hand. She traced the area where his head had lolled sideward. The bark was rough, pitted with age and heat.

'You got the autopsy photographs there?' she asked.

Karamata handed her the gory close-ups. Bare feet, calloused hands. She flicked through until she came to the close-ups of the bullet wounds. The bloom on his forehead was clear, the petals of crusted blood and bone delicate around the dark centre. The back of the child's head was intact.

'No exit wound?' asked Clare. 'So the bullet was still in the brain. I haven't seen anything for ballistics. The autopsy?' Clare knew what the answer would be; Helena Kotze had said that it had been cursory. So cursory that a bullet in the brain went undetected.

'Not detailed,' said Karamata. 'Just enough to give a cause of death. Gunshot wound, easy. He was buried three days after he was found.'

'Why?' Clare tried to hide her frustration.

'The head of cleansing ordered that the city pay for all the paupers' funerals.'

'Calvin Goagab?'

'That's him,' said Karamata.

'Generous.'

'The state morgue is always full these days. Families can't afford to bury their loved ones, and then the cooling systems broke down. The mayor is a practical man, so he went along with Goagab's request to clear the backlog and get everyone buried. It had been ordered before the murder. Fritz Woestyn just happened to benefit from it.'

'Captain Damases went along with it?' asked Clare.

'She was on sick leave,' said Karamata. 'Complications with her pregnancy. The case was with Van Wyk.'

'Burying murder victims,' said Clare, standing up. 'It's a novel way of getting rid of a caseload.'

'I don't know if this stuff seems worthwhile to him,' said Karamata, opening a packet of biltong.

'Murder?'

'Street children. There are so many now. He says it's just Aids orphans; that they're going to die anyway. A lot of people think like that.'

'Do you?'

'I'm a policeman,' said Karamata. 'I don't think about it. I do my job. To me a life is a life. I was like those boys once. Just a piece of rubbish.' His eyes were so dark it was impossible to read any expression in them. 'And now look.'

seventeen

The sun, all day a hot, unseeing eye behind the fog, was sinking towards the sea when Tamar Damases switched off her computer and stood up, arching her back. She couldn't find any pattern in the dates on which the ships had docked in Walvis Bay Harbour and when her three boys – how she was starting to think of them, her three dead boys – disappeared.

Her own baby kicked, one tiny protesting foot bulging the tight drum of her belly. She put her hand there, feeling the foetus glide away from her touch, safe in its dark, secret world. From the parking lot outside came snatches of shouted conversations, arrangements to have a beer, talk about a soccer practice, the night shift arriving. It was time for Tamar to steel herself for her own long night shift.

She straightened her desk and rinsed the teacups, ready for tomorrow. She had never liked the thought of the night peering in at the windows, so she closed the curtains. She picked up her handbag and the groceries she had bought at lunch time. The hard-earned package from the chemist was tucked deep in her jacket pocket. It cost her a substantial chunk of her salary. She felt for it again, like an anxious passenger checking their passport, their ticket, just to make sure.

Tamar locked her office door behind her. Karamata was out in the Namib with Clare. There was no sign of Van Wyk. She went through to the special ops room where a light was burning. There was a scarlet pashmina tossed over the back of Clare's chair. Tamar picked it up and folded it before sitting down.

She considered the boys from Clare's perspective: Monday's Child. Wednesday's Child. And Saturday's. Three ephemeral children who had slipped into the river of life with barely a splash. Who would have sunk without a trace if Tamar had not reached out for their spectral hands. She held out her own hands now, in front of the desk lamp. They cast a startling silhouette across the display. Tamar read Clare's notes. First about place, of the crime scenes virtually devoid of physical evidence. They would be; the bodies had been moved and deliberately displayed.

She thought of the bodies, of the boys they had been, wondering about this killer who managed to pick up his victims without witness, without leaving a ripple of anxiety. In such a small town, why did no one notice someone away for hours and days on end? Unless it was someone who was working shifts. Someone who could be all over the place, no questions asked. On the ships, in the factories, in the bars, a truck driver passing back and forth, ferrying goods. The silhouette of a killer, just the shadow of a man on a blank wall. Malevolent, shifting, shape-shifting, like a Javanese shadow-puppet theatre. Tamar thought of this figure moving unseen through the fog and she shivered. Who? Why? And where? The questions beat an urgent rhythm.

A siren wailed, insistent as a hungry baby. It was time to get on to her next shift.

Tamar found her niece leaning against the wall outside her day-care centre.

'What are you doing out here, Angela?' she asked.

'The other children …' The little girl's eyes glittered with tears.

Tamar put the sobbing child into the back seat of her car and strapped her in, feeling once again for the package of ARVs in her pocket. Her talisman. She drove home fast, relief flooding her when she realised that Tupac, her nephew, only eleven, had already cooked the macaroni.

She held Angela in her arms and coaxed five, then six, then seven, slow, painful spoons of buttered pasta into the child's mouth. The boy hovered on the kitchen steps, staring into the darkness. When Tamar thought it was enough, she took her precious package from her pocket and counted out the pills into a Mickey Mouse saucer that Tupac had put out.

Angela pressed her lips together and closed her eyes, but the tears seeped out anyway. They made her feel so sick, the pills. Tupac knelt down beside her, his thin brown hands cupping her face.

'Please, Angela,' he said. 'You're a dancer. You can do anything.'

Nothing.

'Take them for me.' Desperation edged his voice. 'I'll tell you a story later.'

Angela opened her eyes. 'About Mommy?'

Tupac was quick. He popped a tablet in and held her mouth closed. 'About her and the day you had your first dance class,' said Tupac.

Angela swallowed. Tamar breathed.

'Here. Just three more.'

'Tell me about what she said about me.'

Tupac popped the pills into her mouth, like coins into a slot machine. Tamar was not religious, but she was praying that the expensive drugs would repel the virus that had prowled Angela's blood since her birth, the virus that had wrested the life from her plump, laughing, fecund sister five years ago.

She put the little girl to bed and helped her arrange her princess puppet. The child had given her a doek, so that the shadow looked like her mother leaning over the bed, always just about to kiss her.

Tupac lay down next to his sister.

'They wouldn't play with me today,' Angela told him. 'The other children, they say I'm dirty and that I'll make them sick. Will you get them?'

'I'll get them.' Tupac had defended his baby sister since their mother had died the previous year. 'But first let me tell you a story.'

Tamar closed the door on his once-upon-a-time. It was always the same story: a little girl and a mother who didn't really die, who just went away somewhere for a while, who was coming back.

She went to lie on her bed, too tired to eat or change. It was quiet on the edge of the desert when the children stopped murmuring. From far away came the cry of a jackal; further away the answering call of its mate. Tamar folded her fingers over her belly.

Her child might be fatherless, but it was safe.

eighteen

Ragnar Johansson was hesitating between two blue shirts. Clare Hart, she made him worry which near-identical shade would be best. He chose the darker of the two, walked over to his apartment window and did up the buttons, looking out at the emptied street. The night had settled in, but he could still make out the cranes offloading the trawlers that had berthed that afternoon. The girls would be busy already. It was eight-thirty and cold out, but Ragnar Johansson decided to walk. He liked the fog. It blocked out the flat desert lines of Walvis Bay, let him pretend that he was somewhere else, not immured here at the arse end of the world, no better off than when he arrived. The security gate rattled shut behind him as he strode towards the lagoon.

Clare was easy to find in the deserted holiday complex. Hers was the only cottage spilling light onto the worn grass, as she had not closed her curtains. Ragnar stopped beyond the pool of light to watch her through the open window. She had her back to him and he could see the curve of her waist, the slim hips in faded jeans. She slipped her hands under her hair and twisted her hair up, exposing the nape of her neck. She pinned up the thick coil, then turned and looked out into the blackness. Wary as a gazelle. Ragnar lit a cigarette, ignoring a tug of desire. When he had finished smoking, he went across the dark garden and knocked. She opened the door, standing aside so that he could enter.

'Hello, Clare.'

'How are you?' She closed the door behind him.

'You look beautiful,' said Ragnar.

'You were watching me.'

'How did you guess?' Ragnar kissed her cheek. 'Same perfume.'

'No. 19.' Clare picked up her jacket and they walked along the water's edge, immediately falling into step. They had been easy together, physically. She let him take her arm, glad to put the day behind her.

'What happened to your boat?' she asked.

'Money's tight. Had to sell it.' Ragnar could taste the bitterness of failure on his tongue.

'I didn't know,' said Clare, walking up the steps to the Raft.

The restaurant was built on stilts against which the lagoon's dark water lapped. It was usually frequented by tourists or locals celebrating rare special occasions. Tonight, the candlelit tables were mostly empty.

'You didn't stay in touch, did you?' said Ragnar.

'I never said I would.'

A waitress showed them to a window table, the lights rippling on the lagoon beneath them. The lighthouse at Pelican Point pulsed on the horizon.

'What are you doing now?' Clare asked. 'I can't imagine you without your boat.'

'Lots of kite-boarding, a little consulting for the mayor and his team. I just got a new ship to skipper, the *Alhantra*,' said Ragnar. 'And a licence for orange roughy. Very popular in the US and in Spain. Expensive, so worth fishing. Tonight can be a celebration, if you like. That and seeing you again.'

The waitress brought the wine and bread. Ragnar poured.

'It didn't take you long to track me down,' said Clare.

'A single woman under two hundred and fifty pounds is always news in Walvis Bay.'

'Come on,' she said. 'Who told you? I can't believe that your nearly running me over was a coincidence.'

'Actually, that was,' said Ragnar. 'But Calvin Goagab had told me you were here. I saw him yesterday afternoon. After you'd been there. There's official concern about this incident, about what it'll do to tourism here.'

'What about official concern about finding who hung a child's body in a playground?' Clare bristled.

'Oh, there is, but this is a port.' Ragnar leant towards her. 'Goagab's saying that what they found in that playground was just a quick midnight transaction gone wrong. Whoever did it was back on board ship before the body was discovered.'

'And the others?'

'Unrelated probably,' said Ragnar. 'Captain Damases is inclined to jump to conclusions.'

The waitress arrived with their food, before Clare could respond.

'You did well with that documentary.' Ragnar noted the flare of anger in her eyes and changed the direction of the conversation.

'It worked,' said Clare.

'You made some people uncomfortable.'

'Good,' said Clare. 'I meant to.'

'Some quite influential people, Clare. People lost money. A lot of money. Goagab was one of them.'

'You too?' asked Clare.

'That's not what I lost when you left.' He took her hand, turning it over and running his thumb over the vein pulsing in her wrist.

'Let's not go there, Ragnar,' said Clare, withdrawing her hand to pick up her wine glass. The nights they had spent alone together up the Skeleton Coast … she would had to have been an ice queen to resist him.

Ragnar let it go, and they ate their meals without further conflict. They talked of people Clare had met on her last visit: who'd made money; who hadn't. The bill arrived and Clare reached for her purse.

'Let me get this.' Ragnar put his hand over hers. 'If you owe me I'll be sure of having dinner with you again.'

'I'm finessed then,' Clare smiled.

'Shall we get a brandy?' asked Ragnar as they stepped outside into the cold wind.

'Where were you thinking?' Clare was tired, but she wasn't quite ready to go back to her lonely bed.

'Der Blaue Engel.'

'Where is it?' The name was familiar. Clare tried to place it.

'It's a club down near the harbour.' He saw Clare hesitate. 'Think of it as anthropology.'

Ragnar put his arm around Clare's shoulders and they walked back towards the harbour. Clare remembered where she'd heard the name. From the story about the lap dancer who'd come off worse for wear after a visit to one of the rusting trawlers anchored outside the harbour.

'Gretchen von Trotha,' said Clare, 'doesn't she dance there?'

'How do you know her?' Ragnar asked with obvious surprise.

'I don't,' said Clare. 'Elias Karamata, one of the cops who's working on this case, told me that she'd been beaten and thrown off a Russian ship. The name stuck.'

'Someone fished her out, a South African,' said Ragnar. 'Ironically, he had a Russian name. Gretchen owes her life to that man.'

Clare could feel the dull thump of the bass long before she could hear any music. The club's logo was a naked pole-dancing angel, complete with wings and a halo.

'That must drive the fundamentalists nuts.'

'It does,' said Ragnar. 'Sundays, there are always pickets by the Christian Mission ladies, lying in wait for their husbands, I suppose.'

Inside, the air was thick with smoke. Around the pool table, girls were leaning along their cues to the advantage of their cleavages. A few couples were dancing, and waiting women nursed Coca-Colas at the bar. A group of drunken Russians working their way through a bottle of vodka at the bar looked Clare over then returned to their drink. Only two tables were occupied.

'That's him.' Ragnar pointed to one table where a man sat alone. 'The guy who pulled Gretchen out of the water.' The man's shirt was moulded over his lean belly, long legs stretched out, the steel caps glinting at the end of his dusty suede boots. A cigarette dangled from one tanned hand. He had tilted his chair back and his face was hidden in the shadows.

'Is he trying to play Clint Eastwood?' asked Clare.

'I don't suggest you ask him,' said Ragnar. 'He's not much of a joker.'

Clare recognised some of the occupants at the other table, groaning with champagne bottles, near the stage. D'Almeida had his secretary, the beautiful Anna, on his arm. He raised a glass to Clare. Opposite him sat Goagab, in conspicuous Armani. Two heavy-set men in their forties were with them. One of the men held a delicate girl on his knee, a smile plastered over her discomfiture. The other one ran lazy eyes over Clare, his tongue flicking across his moist, parted lips.

'Politicians?' asked Clare.

'Businessmen. Politicians. One and the same in this part of the world. My new bosses,' said Ragnar. 'They own the *Alhantra*. They're celebrating the licence too.'

'You want to join them?'

'Not now that I have you to myself.' His hand brushed hers. It was disconcerting, the intimate roughness of his skin.

'What will you have?' he smiled.

'A brandy, please.'

The bar was filling up as men drifted in singly and in compact, eager groups. Chinese, Spanish, Senegalese, South African, freshly showered, hair slicked, eyes darting towards the women unpeeling themselves from bar stools, the pool table.

'When's the show?' Ragnar asked the barman pouring their drinks.

'Ten minutes, maybe fifteen.' The barman pushed across a brochure that showed a young woman – maybe twenty-five – coiled around a pole.

Five minutes later, the lights flickered, then stayed off. A pre-recorded drum roll drowned out Clare's objections. The velvet curtains opened, and a nubile blonde stepped into the spectral light, her body voluptuous beneath the transparent layers of blue chiffon, the scar beneath her left eye a slender crescent bleached white by the spotlight. Her eyes, shadowed by dark, arched brows, revealed nothing.

'Der Blaue Engel?' asked Clare.

'That's her. Gretchen von Trotha. Not yet in all her glory. Then she's quite something,' said Ragnar. 'Another?'

'One more,' said Clare. 'Then home?' Her interest was piqued.

'Nicolai,' called Ragnar. The barman filled Clare's glass, his eyes on her face. 'Enjoying the show?' he asked.

'It works for the audience,' she said.

Gretchen moved effortlessly, disdain infusing her movements with an erotic menace. The rowdy groups of men sat transfixed. She peeled off first one garment then another, until she stood naked except for her tattooed wings, a tinsel halo and the wisp of silk between her thighs.

A movement to Clare's right drew her attention to D'Almeida's table. A fat politician was snapping his fingers at the barman. Nicolai bent low for the man's order. He looked up at Gretchen and nodded. A whispered word from Nicolai and she left the safety of the stage. The fat man leant back in his seat and beckoned her into the space between his splayed knees. She stepped closer, nipples glinting in the dim light as he tucked money into the thigh-high boot gripping her soft flesh. Her skin was milky; her limbs were smooth and firm. The shaved pubis lasciviously childlike as she twirled out of his grip and made her way to the lean man sitting alone at the table in the corner.

The man took a note and slipped it into her halo before standing up and sauntering out. Gretchen removed the rolled-up note and looked at it as she walked back to the stage, ignoring the beseeching, empty hands that reached after her.

'I think I've had enough lap dancing for tonight,' said Clare. 'Let's go.'

It was cold out. Clare pulled her collar up and her beanie down as they walked towards the unlit cottages.

'If I didn't know better, you could pass for a boy,' said Ragnar.

'Maybe I should be careful then,' she said, unlocking the door. 'Walvis Bay is not the safest town to be a boy in.'

'You should be careful anyway, Clare.'

'You're the second person to tell me that.' She turned to face him, remembering Lazarus's clumsy attempt. 'Is that a warning or a threat?'

'A warning.' Ragnar's hand was cold on her cheek. He slid a finger down her neck, finding the warm skin under her collar.

'From a friend.'

'I'll keep it in mind.'

Clare stepped away from his caress and into the cottage,

ignoring his wry look as she said a swift goodnight and locked the front door. But as Ragnar's footsteps died away and the stifling silence draped the night again, she did wonder if she'd made the right call.

nineteen

Clare woke the next morning, her limbs leaden and her head aching, but she pushed back the covers and pulled on her running clothes. She washed down two aspirin with a glass of water. The wind had come up in the night, and the unfamiliar sounds meant that her sleep had been fitful.

The bracing air and the morning light cleared her mind and she found her stride, running faster until the paved boulevard petered out into sand. There had been a high tide; straggles of seaweed lay across the path. A flock of startled flamingos took off ahead of her. Clare scanned the path to see what had disturbed them. It was Goagab in a black velvet tracksuit, complete with gold chain, approaching her.

'Dr Hart,' he called. Clare came to a reluctant halt. 'You're up early. I trust Johansson let you get to sleep at a reasonable hour.'

'He did.' To her annoyance, Clare found herself blushing at his innuendo.

'I've got a PR nightmare on my hands with this case.' Goagab turned around and walked alongside her. 'I trust you're making progress.'

'Some,' said Clare. 'The groundwork: talking to people who knew Kaiser Apollis and the other two boys. The autopsy's done, but we'll need to wait for the forensic reports from Cape Town.'

'Any suspects yet?' asked Goagab, stopping beside his silver Mercedes sports car. 'We need an arrest soon to justify the expense of foreign expertise.'

'It's only been a couple of days,' said Clare. 'And the first two victims were buried without proper autopsies, on your orders.

That makes for sparse evidence.'

'I understand,' said Goagab, without missing a beat. 'But there's pressure, I'm sure you can see that. I'd appreciate it if you let me know as soon as possible what shape our killer is taking.' He opened the car door, reached into the cubbyhole and gave her a card. 'If you need anything, here's my private number.'

'What do you imagine I'd need?' Clare turned the white square over in her hand.

'It helps to have as many friends as possible in a strange town,' said Goagab, sliding into his car. He pressed a button, and the window closed. For a second, Clare stared at her own pale reflection, then she slipped the card into her jacket pocket and ran back, but the unexpected meeting had put her off her stride.

By seven-thirty Clare was showered, dressed and breakfasted, her scattered thoughts in order again. She had time to see Mara Thomson before she met Tamar at the police station. She locked up, taking her small bag of rubbish out with her and dropping it into the bin standing in the narrow strip of sand between her cottage and the next one. She froze, ignoring the gulls scrapping over a stolen fish head, riveted by tracks in the sand.

A single set of human footprints stopped at her bedroom window. Clare followed them to the entrance to the service alley, but the night wind had erased any marks except her own. She followed the prints back, stepping carefully so as not to disturb anything. Whoever it had been had stood there for a while. The sand was compressed, as the watcher had scuffed about to keep warm. Or get a better view. She had opened her curtains the night before, hoping that the moon would break through the fog for a while. How long had he stood there? What had he wanted? She searched through the disturbed dreams she had had the previous night to see if one

123

of them had been triggered by the proximity of a stranger. There were bars on the windows, but her bed was close. He could have put his hand through an opening and held it over her face, feeling her breath soft and trusting with sleep on his skin. Her throat closed at the thought of it.

Clare squatted down next to the footprints. Whoever had stood there had been wearing some kind of trainer, but, even in this sheltered spot, the dawn wind had blown a cover of sand over any detail. Clare could not even tell what size they were. There were a few old cigarette butts lying against the fence, but that would have woken her, surely, if he had smoked. She stood up and looked in at her own window, as a stranger had, at her dishevelled bed, at the book on the bedside table, at yesterday's lace underwear abandoned on the floor.

Her breath came in a gasp, misting the glass and bringing to life the crude outline of a heart. He had stood here, breathing open-mouthed against the glass, looking in at her as she had slept, tracing with a lingering fingertip. She breathed out again, harder this time, to see if he had finished his drawing. He had. A sailor's tattoo, it was scored through with a jagged arrow, and blood was pooled below the heart.

twenty

Mara Thomson picked up the photographs propped against her clock. Her team of homeless boys in their brand-new football kit, holding up a silver cup in triumph. The other picture was worn at the edges: Mara and her mum in the park next to the London council estate that she had survived by learning to be invisible. She pressed the photographs between her hands, bookending her journey to the point where she sat now – with Kaiser Apollis's dead body bobbing on the periphery of her thoughts. It drove her to the kitchen in search of tea and company.

Oscar was at the kitchen table alone, uneaten cornflakes congealing in his plastic bowl.

'You're up early.' Mara smiled at him.

A door slammed upstairs and the boy's delicate throat constricted around the food. Oscar looked up. Mara did too, imagining George Meyer stepping from his other lodger's bedroom into the chill passageway upstairs, closing the door on the woman inside: Gretchen, who always paid what she owed, exuding contempt for her landlord, for his lonely dribble of pleasure.

'Go on,' said Mara, breaking the spell, 'eat your breakfast.'

Oscar, conditioned to obedience, picked up the spoon. The mournful wail of a ship's siren came from the harbour.

'The *Alhantra*,' said Mara, putting on the kettle.

Mara had taken Oscar on board once and he had seen Juan Carlos kiss her when they thought he wasn't watching. But the boy was always watching, so he had seen Juan Carlos, Mara's boyfriend, slip into her room in the middle of the night, and away again just before dawn.

George Meyer came into the kitchen, buttoning up his jacket. He greeted Mara and poured coffee, drinking in silence.

'Come, Oscar,' he said, putting down his mug and looking at his watch. Oscar reached out a tentative hand, but George thought he was reaching for his lunch and handed the boy two slices of cling-filmed white bread. The two of them stepped into the trails of fog hanging low over the desolate yard, the washing limp on the line, just as Clare Hart opened the gate.

'Good morning, Dr Hart,' said Meyer. 'Can I help you?'

'I'm here to see Mara Thomson,' said Clare. 'Is she in?'

'In the kitchen,' said Meyer, opening the door to his truck. 'Get in, Oscar. You're coming with me today. You can draw some more plant specimens for me. Your mother would've liked that.'

Oscar climbed in and placed his bag at his feet. He let his forehead rest against the cold glass. It could have been a nod.

The doorbell chimed, interrupting the tangled drift of Mara Thomson's thoughts. She had been half-expecting Dr Hart, but seeing her on the doorstep gave her heart a little jolt.

'Please, come in.' She opened the door for Clare and led her down a dingy passage off the kitchen to her bedroom.

'Sit here,' said Mara, offering Clare the only chair and sitting on the unmade bed. A splash of sunlight framed her face, setting her apart from her anonymous bedroom. The only place that revealed any personality was the crowded table next to her bed.

'Lazarus told me you were at the dump,' said Mara.

Clare nodded, picking up a photograph. 'You?' she asked.

Mara nodded. 'That was taken just before I came to Namibia. Me and my mum.'

You had to have a charitable eye to see the blood that linked them. Where Mara was all tawny shades and wild hair, her mother was pale, her lips as prim and pressed as her blue suit.

But it was there, in both their narrow faces, the wide-set eyes.

'My father was Jamaican,' Mara explained. 'But I never knew him. He was killed in a fight before I was born. So it was just me and my mum. It was hard for her when I left.'

'And for you?' Clare asked.

Mara sighed. 'I expected a village of light and heat and throbbing cicadas. Instead, I got Walvis Bay. Somebody had to,' she said, with a wry smile.

'That bad?' asked Clare.

'Oh, it's been okay. Till all this. I threw myself into my work, answered the kids' questions, read to them and organised a soccer team. My mum clipped out the sports pages from the Sunday papers and taped soccer games and films. *Bend It like Beckham* was a real hit. It all worked,' said Mara. '*I* worked and that was a first.'

There was a framed photograph of Mara with her arms entwined around a dark-haired man. 'Your boyfriend?' asked Clare.

'Juan Carlos.' Mara leant back against the wall. 'You want me to tell you about Kaiser?' she asked. 'The others?'

'Let's start with Kaiser,' Clare suggested.

'What don't you know?' asked Mara.

Clare thought of his body on the mortuary table. No secrets there. She knew how much he weighed; that he still had a couple of milk teeth; that he had been violently sodomised, but that he had healed; that his back was covered in scars; that someone had stood so close to him that their breath had mingled. Someone had looked the bound child in the eye, cocked his gun, pulled a trigger and shot him in the face.

'Tell me what he was like,' said Clare. 'What he did, where he went, who he hung out with, where he slept, what he ate.'

'What he ate?' repeated Mara, fiddling with the frayed hem

127

of her hoodie. 'He ate what he could scavenge. Meat, if he could find it.'

Clare thought of Lazarus throwing away the roll Mara had bought him, her hurt and disappointment clear in the set of her narrow shoulders. 'Who were his friends?' she prompted.

'Lazarus, I suppose,' said Mara. 'Fritz Woestyn, too. They played soccer together, slept in a heap at the dump like stray dogs.'

'What did he talk about?'

'To me?' asked Mara, looking Clare straight in the eye. 'Not much. I know he loved his sister Sylvia and that he liked to draw.' She was quiet. Around them, the silence of the house was overwhelming.

'Tell me, Mara,' said Clare softly, 'what he dreamed.'

Mara slitted her eyes. 'How will his dreams get you to the truth of who did this to him, to the others?'

'Dreams take us to places we don't anticipate sometimes,' said Clare.

'He wanted to live. That can be quite an ambitious dream in a place like this.' The silence was taut, a tightrope between them.

'He wanted to go to school.' One tentative foot on the rope of her story. 'He wanted to draw.' Another. Mara looked at Clare as if she were searching for something. 'He wanted a mother. That's about it, as far as Kaiser's dreams went,' she said. 'Since I've been here so many kids I know have been sick, have died. It's Aids. That's why most of them are on the street in the first place. And if they didn't get the virus from their parents, then they soon catch it from their clients.' Mara's shoulders slumped.

'When did you see him last?'

'Friday afternoon,' Mara said with certainty. 'We always have practice and he never missed. I didn't see him at the Sunday practice. Weekends are different. The boys are less' – she pulled the cord of her sweatshirt – 'steady. Let me put it like that.'

'Did you ask where he was?'

'I was going to,' Mara replied, 'and then they found him, so I didn't need to.'

'The others?' asked Clare. 'Fritz Woestyn and Nicanor Jones?'

'I knew them,' said Mara. 'They played in my team.'

'What happened with Sergeant van Wyk and Kaiser?' asked Clare.

'I was stupid,' said Mara. 'Stupid and naïve. It was before Fritz Woestyn was found, so I wasn't worried. Just irritated that he didn't come to a weekend game. I asked and one of the boys told me he was in the cells, so I went to look for him.'

'Where was he?'

'By the time I found him he'd been dropped back at the dump,' said Mara. 'He'd been beaten. Badly. I tried to lay a child abuse charge.'

'What happened?'

'Sod all,' said Mara. 'Kaiser wouldn't say anything. I knew he'd been picked up near the harbour. Whoring maybe. I know that Van Wyk took him back to the cells and beat the shit out of him, but Kaiser wouldn't say nothing. I had to leave it …' Mara hesitated. 'You know Van Wyk used to be with the vice squad?'

Clare nodded.

'There've been rumours that he offers protection to the girls working the docks. You know, like … they have no choice but to accept it in return for a cut of their fee.'

'You think Van Wyk's running boys, too?' asked Clare.

'I don't know,' said Mara. 'I don't know if it's even true about the girls. I only know that Kaiser was with him and that afterwards he could barely walk. Van Wyk said he found Kaiser like that and picked him up to protect him.'

'That was the end of it?'

'Pretty much,' said Mara. 'Kaiser wouldn't say anything. Nothing more I could do.' Tears of frustration welled in her eyes. 'That's all I can tell you. Pathetic, right? To see someone every day and to know nothing about them.'

Clare stood up and opened the door. It was the end of the interview. They walked back to the kitchen where a woman in a blue dressing gown was stirring sugar into her coffee. A blonde plait snaked over one shoulder.

'Gretchen,' said Mara, disconcerted. 'You're up early. This is Dr Hart.'

'Hello,' said Clare.

Gretchen lit a cigarette. 'You're making progress, Doctor?' she asked. 'With these little boys?'

'I hope so,' said Clare.

'Good,' said Gretchen. 'So sad, what happened.' She sipped her coffee, her blue eyes fixed on Clare without a glimmer of recognition. She wouldn't have seen Clare at the bar of Der Blaue Engel the previous night. All she would have seen was a blur beyond the stage lights.

twenty-one

Captain Damases replaced the receiver when Clare walked into the office. 'You have a bad night?' asked Clare. There were dark circles under Tamar's eyes.

'Angela wasn't well. That was her nanny to say she was sleeping at last.' Tamar rubbed her temples. It was only eight in the morning, but she felt as if she'd been working for hours already. 'You look like you had a rough night too.'

'Just a late one,' said Clare. 'I'm not twenty-five any more so it shows if I don't get my beauty sleep.' She poured herself a cup of coffee. 'I hope Angela's on the mend.'

'Kids,' said Tamar, 'they bounce back so fast. I'm taking them into the desert this afternoon. Why don't you join us, see something other than Walvis Bay?'

'I'd like that,' said Clare, checking her schedule. 'I've got some admin to do before I see Darlene Ruyters, and I'm hoping that Helena Kotze's going to drop off her preliminary histology report.'

'Did you see Mara Thomson, by the way?'

'I did,' said Clare. 'She told me about that incident with Van Wyk and Kaiser Apollis, about why she tried to lay a charge against Van Wyk. I think we should talk to him again.'

Tamar stood up, acting on Clare's request. 'We'll try,' she said, opening her office door.

Van Wyk was sitting at his desk. He minimised the window on his computer screen when Tamar and Clare walked in.

Tamar did not greet him. 'Tell me again about what happened with Kaiser, that incident for which there don't seem to be any records.'

Van Wyk looked up and sat back in his chair. 'He was caught in the harbour,' he said wearily. 'Happens all the time.'

'What was he doing?' asked Tamar.

'Looking for shit,' said Van Wyk, his voice thick with insolence. 'And he got it, from whoever it was who'd paid him to take it. The harbour master called me. Apollis had been pimping himself. I picked him up and put him in the cells for the weekend for his own protection.'

'That's all?' Clare spoke for the first time.

'It was.' Van Wyk faced her, as contained and venomous as a cobra. 'Until Mara Thomson laid an abuse complaint. She claims I assaulted him in prison. Apollis denied that anything happened. He was glad to get out of jail without any charges.'

'It wasn't because he refused to pay you for working on your area?' asked Clare.

'You've got quite an imagination, Dr Hart,' spat Van Wyk. 'I'm sure that you can use it to picture what prison would be like for a pretty boy like Apollis. I did him a favour. Now, if you ladies will excuse me, I have things to do.' Van Wyk shut down his computer, pivoted on his heel and walked out of the office.

'I'm sorry,' said Clare, watching Van Wyk churn the gravel in the parking lot. 'That little piece of quiet diplomacy would've done Riedwaan Faizal proud.' Clare followed Tamar back to her office.

'Someone had to say it,' said Tamar, sitting down, 'and my life will be easier because you did it. I'm not sure that it'll make yours easier, though.' She pulled a folder on her desk towards her.

'What've you got there?' asked Clare.

'Ships' logs.' Tamar opened the file. 'Sailors' visits, harbour reports around the times these boys went missing.'

Clare skimmed through the papers. 'Still no pattern?'

'Not yet,' said Tamar. 'But I'm going to follow up on a few things that don't fit.'

twenty-two

Clare sat at her desk, trying to think of what to say to Riedwaan as she waited for her computer to boot up. She checked her mail: chit-chat from her sister Julia, one from Rita Mkhize saying Fritz was absolutely fine, two from Riedwaan. Clare opened the first e-mail. It was full of official attachments written in incomprehensible bureaucratese. She filed them to read later. The second e-mail had nothing in the subject line. Clare opened it, her mouth suddenly dry.

Clare, it read. *I fucked up. Talk to me. R.*

She smiled. She couldn't help it. The message was so like the man. Direct. For Riedwaan, emotion meant action. He had wanted her, needed her, when they first met. So he'd taken her, simple as that. And she had acquiesced, intrigued by the novelty of having her emotional defences so easily breached, and charmed by the simplicity of Riedwaan's desire for her.

That moment of curiosity had set her adrift in treacherous waters, and now here she was: snagged on the reef of her own vulnerability, with only herself to blame.

She took a deep breath and with one sure stroke deleted Riedwaan's message. Then she e-mailed a terse case update, copying in Phiri to neutralise any intimacy Riedwaan might have read into her 'best wishes' at the end.

By nine-thirty, she was walking fast down 2nd Avenue, ignoring the thin, chained dogs barking in each sandy yard. Number 53 had its back to the red dunes, and although the façade was ravaged, the paint blistered and the gutters sagged, the windows were clear. Clare rang the doorbell and waited.

'Darlene Ruyters?' The woman framed in the doorway was fortyish and too thin. The exposed ankles and neck too fragile. She pulled her fraying cardigan tight around her body. 'I'm Clare Hart.'

'How can I help you?' asked Darlene. She opened the door, feeling in her pocket for her cigarettes.

'I wanted to ask you about the murdered boy in the playground,' said Clare.

Darlene held the door open and Clare stepped into the dim hallway. A pot plant wilted over a pile of post on the small entrance table.

'Kaiser Apollis.' Darlene walked through to the kitchen, her gait uneven. 'Tea?'

'Please,' said Clare, looking around the tidy room. A pair of trainers stood at the back door, a box of brushes and shoe polish open next to them.

Darlene put on the kettle, and set out cups and sugar on a tray.

'Are you from Windhoek?' asked Darlene. She picked up the tray.

'Cape Town,' said Clare.

'My home town. I miss it. All that green.' Darlene led the way to a meticulously neat lounge and gestured for Clare to sit.

'What brought you to Walvis Bay?'

'The army,' said Darlene. 'My husband was posted here. He was a major in a special operations unit.'

'And now?' Clare looked at the floral-print sofas and porcelain ornaments.

'Oh, that was a long time ago,' Darlene said. 'He was handsome then. Forty. I was twenty-two and in love. What did I know? I followed him. Ten years later when Nelson Mandela gave Walvis Bay back to Namibia, he left me with nothing. I've been alone ever since.'

'You stayed?'

'I was used to it by then. My marriage was over. I'd started teaching. I liked it, liked the kids. So I took back my maiden name and started a new life.'

'That's how you knew Kaiser Apollis?'

'This is a small town.'

'You taught him?'

'A long time ago. Grade 1. He was such a sweet little boy. Desperate for affection.'

'Tell me about him,' asked Clare.

'Usual things. His father lost his job. Then he disappeared. Kaiser came to school dirty, then there were the bruises. His mother drank and worked the sailors' clubs.'

'What happened to her?'

'She died. Aids, I suppose. Although here it's just called a short illness.'

'When did you see him last, Darlene?'

Darlene swirled the tea leaves in her cup, as if hoping they would give her the right answer. 'He came to school. Last Wednesday.'

'What for?' asked Clare.

'I don't know. I hadn't seen him for months. He looked so' – she shook her head – 'alone. So I asked him if he wanted to come and help me.'

'Was he there to see you?'

'I didn't ask him. I assumed he was. He used to help me get ready for my art classes on Thursday. He loved doing that. He had talent too. Real talent. Maybe if he had been born into a different life, who knows?' She trailed off, as if exhausted by her speculation.

'What did he do for you?'

'He helped me with the desks, got the paint ready. I'm doing

136

a recycling project with my Grade 1s. Kaiser helped me cut things up. Prepare. He ate a sandwich I gave him.'

'Did he talk to you?'

'No, not really. He just liked to be busy.'

'How long was he with you?'

'An hour I suppose. Maybe more. He mixed the paints, then he said he was going to go. I gave him some money and he left.'

'He didn't say where he was going?'

'No. And I didn't ask.'

'How much money did you give him?'

'How much?' Darlene asked. 'I can't remember. Maybe ten Nam dollars in small change.'

'Is that why he came to see you?'

'Maybe.' Darlene shrugged. 'Like I said, we didn't talk much. He never begged. He hated it. He was a proud boy. I always gave him money for the odd jobs he did for me.'

'Were you surprised that it was him on the swing?'

'Herman Shipanga found him.'

'Shipanga doesn't wear high heels.' Clare's voice was uncompromising.

'No, he doesn't,' Darlene whispered. Her hands twisted around each other of their own volition. It was so hard to keep the sequence of things straight. She had been walking through the kindergarten playground when she heard the creak of the weighted swing, set in motion by a gust of wind that skittered papers across her path.

'Neither does Inspector Damases,' said Clare. 'There were holes in the sand leading up to the swings. I'm sure they would match the shoes you wore on Monday. The ones you cleaned.'

Darlene remembered walking towards the single occupied swing, transfixed, her ulcer stabbing. She had crouched down and thought about closing the lids of the accusing eyes staring

137

at her. Her fingernail had trailed over the shoulder and the twinned curve of his buttocks beneath the stained shroud.

'Not surprised. Shocked, yes. Horrified, yes. But not surprised.' Darlene returned to the original question.

She did not know how long she had crouched there, but her legs had cramped. When she stood up, the fog had lifted, and there along the fence trotted a dark, blue-clad figure, so she had picked up her basket and gone down the passage to her empty classroom.

'Why didn't you call someone?' Clare asked.

'Herman Shipanga found him. I knew he would. He called the police. I knew he would. What did it matter that I saw him first?' Darlene pulled a crumpled cigarette out of her pocket and fumbled about for a light.

'Is this what you're looking for?' asked Clare, picking up a battered Zippo from the floor. It had a topless mermaid engraved on it. Darlene lit her cigarette, and put the incongruous lighter on the tea tray.

'They don't care if he's dead or not, anyway. He was just street rubbish to them,' she said.

'Who doesn't care?' asked Clare.

'The police. The municipality. You ask them. They don't care about this dead boy or Nicanor Jones and Fritz Woestyn. They threw them into a grave to save themselves any trouble. There are so many orphans now that in their hearts people are glad when they're eliminated. They just hope it's the one who might've smashed their car window.'

'You care.' Clare's voice was gentle.

'That's why they came to me, those boys. I didn't judge them, or want anything from them. They were like my children. They wanted me when they needed something.'

'What did Kaiser need?'

138

'I don't know,' said Darlene. 'I just don't know. Maybe nothing. Maybe he just wanted some company. Maybe he wanted to tell me something but he was too shy. I don't know.'

'You said you were shocked to find him, but not surprised.' Clare's voice rose, questioning.

Darlene shrugged. 'There was something about him when I saw him last. Like he had crossed some line. His sister tried to look after him when their mother died. How does that work, a child-headed household? Bullshit. There is no household. Those kids just sit there, waiting to be picked off.' She took a deep, angry drag of her filterless cigarette. It made her cough. 'Sorry,' she said, waving the smoke away with her hand.

'After it happened,' Darlene continued. 'When I found him, it seemed as if he'd come to say goodbye. As if he knew what was going to happen. He looked so at peace, even with the wound.'

'That's because he'd been dead a while,' said Clare. 'All the muscles relax. That irons the expression from the face. Hence the peaceful look.'

Darlene recoiled and Clare regretted being so blunt. She stood up. 'You've been helpful.'

Darlene opened the front door and stepped onto the stoep. Clare was glad to escape the dank house. The fog had thinned, revealing the soft-swelling dunes.

'It's so beautiful, the desert,' said Clare, captivated.

Darlene's laugh was bitter. 'A jumble of women's tits. That's how my husband described it. He said it turned him on, the way it just lay there, waiting to be taken.'

Darlene's hands shook as she put another cigarette between her lips. The sleeve of her cardigan fell back. There was a bracelet of bruises around her wrist. Clare put out her hand and circled Darlene's thin arm.

'What happened?' she asked.

'I'm just clumsy.' Darlene snatched her hand back and pulled down her sleeve. She went back inside, closing the door behind her.

Clare expelled the stale, bitter air she had breathed in the house. She walked back, thinking about Darlene Ruyters and ignoring the cascade of twitching curtains that followed her progress. The learned cowering of a woman once battered runs deep and cold, habituating her to secrecy. It lasts long after bones knit and bruises fade. Those bruises, fingered around a resisting wrist, were fresh, a few days old.

On a woman who lived alone.

twenty-three

'It's so obvious to suspect a sailor,' said Tamar. She stood at the window, her hands wrapped around a steaming cup of coffee.

Clare had gone back to the station to meet with Tamar and Karamata, who had spent the morning interviewing the captains and crews of ships that had been docked when Kaiser disappeared. Most of the captains had given their crew a few hours off on Friday night, and the men had gone to town in groups. Alibis all around.

The window behind Tamar gave Clare a framed view of the harbour. A skeletal ship, long abandoned, rocked on the breakers. Black cormorants perched along the gunwales, silent as waiting widows.

'We've had enough murders because of drunk, lonely sailors fighting over women,' Tamar continued, 'but this case points the other way.'

'Inland?' asked Clare.

'On land at any rate,' said Karamata. He was pushing his muscular arms into a leather jacket. 'I'll catch you later. I've got a community policing forum meeting with the Christian Mission ladies.'

'Good luck,' said Tamar with feeling.

'They love me.' Karamata winked at her. 'It's single mothers like you that they pray for.'

Tamar rolled her eyes. 'Thanks for doing this, Elias.'

Clare poured herself some tea when he was gone. 'On land,' she repeated pensively.

'Whoever is doing this knows this desert, knows how to make things disappear in it,' said Tamar.

Clare's phone rang. She looked at the caller identity before answering. The little bubble of delight put a lilt in her voice. 'Riedwaan.'

'You picked up.' He sounded pleased with himself. 'You're missing me.'

Bastard, she thought. 'I'm putting this on loudspeaker,' she said.

'Hello, Captain Damases,' said Riedwaan. 'Dr Hart, tell me what you've got.' Clare couldn't decide if hearing his voice, disembodied by the speakerphone, clipped and neutral because of Tamar's presence, was disconcerting or sexy. She settled for disconcerting and sexy as she winnowed through the interviews, feeding him the scraps of information – evidence seemed too grandiose a word – she had gleaned.

'You're not exactly ready to do a line-up, are you?' Riedwaan said when she was finished.

'Not yet.'

'She's only been here three days,' said Tamar.

'I know, I know. I was joking.' Riedwaan paused. Clare could picture him rubbing his temples, searching for the right words. 'You'll look after her, Tamar?'

'I am.' Tamar smiled at Clare. 'But she seems quite capable of doing it herself. I'm going to leave you to finish this, Clare. I've got some things to see to. I'll see you at two? At the Venus.'

Clare nodded and switched the phone off conference as Tamar left.

'It looks like you've got a textbook series,' said Riedwaan.

'Looks like it.'

'You're not convinced?'

'Like you say,' said Clare. 'A textbook. The problem with textbooks is that the cases are exemplary rather than true.'

'Well, give me what you do have.'

'Three victims, same profile,' said Clare, summarising her notes for Riedwaan. 'The killer's used the same method for all of them. Ligatures. Head-shot wound. Missing joint on the ring finger. Two with their chests mutilated. Nicanor Jones as Number 2. Kaiser Apollis, Number 3. Fritz Woestyn, the first one with nothing on his chest, but the rest all the same.'

'What else links them?'

'All the boys are small for their age, feminine looking. They were shot at such close range. There's a kind of intimacy to that, I suppose, a complete absence of empathy and a need for total control. I kept thinking that this killer needs his victims to witness what is being done to them. They have to watch you as you kill them.'

'The crime scenes?' asked Riedwaan.

'Not much. Though it seems whoever did it wanted the bodies to be found.'

'Any other street kids missing?'

'None reported, which is hardly surprising. Nobody reported these boys missing,' said Clare.

'All homeless?'

'Most of the time, yes. Apollis stayed with his sister sometimes. The rest of the time, he lived with the others out at the dump. There's some kind of a shelter there.'

'Who's running it?'

'The guy in charge of waste management,' said Clare. 'George Meyer.'

'Wasn't he first at the school where Kaiser Apollis was found?'

'He was. Him and his son.'

'I'd question his altruism a bit,' said Riedwaan. 'How old is the son?'

'About seven,' said Clare. 'Grade 1.'

'That rules them out as a team, I suppose. Although stranger things have happened.'

'I talked to the homeless kids while I was out there. The second boy, Nicanor Jones, his body was found there.'

'Inside the dump?' asked Riedwaan.

'Propped up outside.'

'Have you got a perpetrator profile yet?'

'The basics,' said Clare. 'I'd say the killer must have a vehicle, something that doesn't stand out too much. He probably lives alone; otherwise his absences would be noticed. But everyone works shifts here, so that isn't a definite. One thing's for sure: these bodies are kept inside somewhere for a couple of days and then displayed.'

'Why inside?' probed Riedwaan.

'No predator marks. None of the boys was killed where he was found either. So they're shot somewhere, then kept, then moved and displayed where they'll be found.'

'Homosexual predator?'

'Hard to say. Could be. Homosexuality is illegal here, so I'd imagine that he's either deeply closeted or is some kind of mission killer. There's some evidence that Kaiser Apollis worked as a rent boy. I'd be surprised if the others didn't.'

'Sexual assault?'

'Nothing overt, but whoever he is he's organised. Arrogant, too, to risk displaying these kids.'

'Sounds charming,' said Riedwaan. 'You're going to have to bring your stuff down for the forensic tests. It can't be couriered.'

'Not before Friday,' said Clare. 'I'll catch an early flight.'

'I'll organise things for you, then,' said Riedwaan. 'And I'll pick you up from the airport.'

'I don't think that's the best idea.' Clare kept her tone businesslike.

144

'I wanted to talk to you about what happened before you left, about what I didn't say.'

'I got your e-mail,' said Clare.

Riedwaan must have got up to close his office door; the silence on the phone was absolute. He broke it. 'Are you not going to talk about us?'

'It's a bit late.'

'Okay, I should've told you. I'm sorry I didn't. How many times must I say this? It's my family, my daughter. How the fuck must I know how to handle this and them and you?'

'Just deal with them and leave me out of it,' Clare said. 'It's better that way.'

'Clare, I have to see you.' Riedwaan's voice was coaxing, as warm as a touch.

Clare inhaled and closed her eyes. 'We are going to see each other ... professionally.'

'Fine,' said Riedwaan. 'I'll see you professionally then.'

twenty-four

Riedwaan Faizal replaced the receiver, the click loud in the silence. He opened a window, letting in a rush of cool Cape Town air. He had meant to tell Clare. He had practised it in his car that morning: 'Their trip was cancelled. The trip was cancelled.'

'Their trip was cancelled.' He said it aloud again. Nonchalant. That was the trick, or, 'Shazia and Yasmin, they had to cancel, so …'

So what? Even he could see where that line of defence would go.

'I'm not coming,' his wife had said when she'd called the night before at home, when he was already two whiskies down. 'I want a divorce. You want a divorce. I can't afford to come back now, so I've changed the tickets. Yasmin will come to see you at the end of the year. If you can organise some leave. Oh, and I should tell you I've met someone.' Shazia had paused then, and in that suspended transatlantic moment, the memory of her pliancy, her eagerness as a young bride, was so immediate, he smelled for a moment the subtle, cinnamon scent of her skin.

'I'm getting married again,' she had told him.

'I'm pleased for you,' Riedwaan had said through gritted teeth, and she'd cut the conversation.

Riedwaan had tried to phone Clare after he got Shazia's call. It would have been easier if she had picked up then. It would have come out just as it was, unfiltered. But she hadn't, he thought, as he watched Superintendent Phiri park. The man reversed back and forth until his double cab was so precisely aligned that you could work out a geometry theorem with it. As his boss stepped over the scattered debris and disappeared around the building, Riedwaan's thoughts drifted back to his wife. His soon-to-be officially ex-wife. Some primitive part of his brain wanted to find the man who was sleeping with Shazia and brain him, even as he had felt the relief that came with resolution flood through him.

He poured himself a cup of coffee, his third, and put his hand into his pocket, looking for his cigarettes. His hand closed around the fax Yasmin had sent him: *Sorry Daddy, from my tears because we not comming to see u yet. Maybe in December. For my birthday.* The smudges of ink from her tears had been circled.

Riedwaan lit a cigarette and pressed his hands to his eyes, recalling the horror of his daughter's kidnapping. It was Yasmin's abduction that had brought him to Clare. She had profiled the men who had snatched his daughter and together they had found her.

He and Clare. They made a good team. Professionally.

'Why the long face?' Rita Mkhize sauntered in, saving Riedwaan from his tangled thoughts.

'Woman trouble.'

'No such thing,' said Rita. 'Man trouble, yes. Woman trouble, no.'

'Oh, really,' said Riedwaan. 'Then explain to me why Clare's not speaking to me.'

'Apart from the minor detail that you forgot to tell her that your wife was coming to stay?'

'She's cancelled her trip.'

'So she cancels and you phone Clare to say that all the problems are solved because Shazia's staying in Canada?'

'Well …' Riedwaan scrabbled about for a better light to cast himself in. There wasn't one. 'If you put it that way.'

'And Clare's still furious?'

'Yes.'

'You can't think why?'

'Because I didn't tell her,' he ventured.

'Oh my God.' Rita slapped her palm to her forehead. 'A doctorate in the female psyche coming your way.'

'So what do you suggest I do?'

'Grovel,' said Rita. 'That's always a good start. If you let me watch I'll put in a good word for you.'

'I know I'm not the brightest, but Clare clams up. She's like an oyster. Bang! You get near her and she closes up on you.'

'Well,' said Rita. 'Hang around. A piece of dirt like you, maybe she opens up again. My advice is to slip right in. With any luck she'll turn you into a pearl.'

'Why do women always side with each other?' asked Riedwaan. 'What did you come in here for anyway? Just to give me a hard time?'

'Phiri's looking for you. He asked me to tell you to join him for coffee.'

'That's all I need, his poison,' Riedwaan muttered as he walked down the passage.

'There you are, Faizal,' said Phiri as Riedwaan entered his office. 'There's an envelope for you on the table.'

Riedwaan opened it and flicked through the contents. Phiri was a stickler for paperwork and he had a reputation for turning it to his advantage. The file was full of the countless forms an officer needed before he could move. He checked: every single requisite signature was in place.

'Thank you, sir.'

'You're going next week?' Phiri straightened things on his desk.

'Sunday.'

'Close the door, Faizal.'

Riedwaan did so, praying that there would be no coffee.

'I signed that lot off yesterday.' Phiri pointed to the file. 'And it's been logged by Miss La Grange.'

'I'm surprised that Susannah processed me so fast.'

Susannah la Grange was Phiri's gimlet-eyed secretary. She shared Phiri's fanatical devotion to order; she was also devoted to the man himself. She was Riedwaan's nemesis, returning his sloppy leave forms and expense accounting with metronomic regularity.

'Your paperwork shows no sign of improvement, Faizal.' Phiri looked him in the eye for the first time. 'But I asked Miss La Grange to expedite it, not something I intend to make a habit.'

'Thank you, sir,' Riedwaan said again, wondering where this was headed.

'I had a call this morning,' said Phiri, 'asking me to let things … drift for a while.'

'You mean someone asked you to kill the investigation?' Riedwaan did not like the idea of Clare so far from home with her back-up pulled away from her. 'Why?'

'I'd be hard-pressed to say it was as definite as that. Perhaps drift was not quite the right word.'

'Who called and what did they want?'

'It was … indirect.' Phiri steepled his fingers in his ecclesiastical manner. 'A whisper in a diplomatic ear over cocktails, a private call to me.'

'Clare is up there, already working on it.'

'Faizal, Faizal. I know she is. Relax and stop thinking about hitting me. It's not God's answer to everything.'

Riedwaan uncurled his fists and put his hands behind his back. He tried the deep breathing that the last cop shrink had taught him. It worked. He stopped wanting to punch Phiri and tried listening to him instead. 'What was the concern?' he asked.

'My little bird told me that it'd be better if the Namibian police handled this on their own.'

'A serial killer?' Riedwaan laughed. 'Apart from Captain Damases, most of Nampol wouldn't know one if he came at them with a meat cleaver.'

'Faizal, that's most uncomradely. That's not what we need right now.'

'What does Captain Damases say?'

'I spoke to her this morning. She told me things were progressing as well as could be expected for such a complex case.'

'So who's complaining?'

'Hard to say. It's all been unofficial, circuitous,' said Phiri. 'There seems to be some military interest in the case.'

'Military?' said Riedwaan, surprised.

'Rooibank, where one of the bodies was found, is on the border of an old military site that has a sensitive land claim on it. Some desert nomads, I understand. The Namibians are concerned that all this attention will stir up dormant issues like what happened in Botswana with the San.'

'This sounds ridiculous,' said Riedwaan. 'Have you told Clare?'

'It's not ridiculous, Faizal. It's politics. But so far, I've told no one.' Phiri controlled his irritation but with visible effort. 'When are you going up?'

'Clare's coming to Cape Town this weekend with the physical evidence. I was thinking of leaving on Sunday and going up by bike.'

'Good. Better than flying, under the circumstances.' Phiri walked to the door, but he did not open it. 'You might want to keep out of the station for the next couple of days. Not that you'd break the record for regular attendance, Faizal.'

'Why might I want to do that, sir?' Riedwaan asked with exaggerated politeness.

'If you're not here, Faizal, I can't cancel your trip.' Phiri's eyes gave nothing away. 'If it comes to that, of course.'

'Clare?' Riedwaan started, not sure how to articulate the unease he was feeling.

'She'll be fine. She knows how to look after herself, I'm sure,' said Phiri.

Riedwaan stopped at the door. 'This military angle ... What is it? Something new?'

'No, no,' said Phiri. 'It's just that this is a volatile region, awash with new money and old grudges.'

twenty-five

Helena Kotze dropped off her preliminary report with Clare when she was back at the station. Clare scanned through it, most of Helena's findings confirming things she already knew. There was nothing revealing from the geologist boyfriend either, though some of the sand on the boy's shoes was from surprisingly far inland. There were still a couple of things that Clare could confirm once ballistics and forensics in Cape Town had had a look. She flipped through to the histology report, hoping that it would give her something new. The carpaccio-thin slices of lung lining that Helena had stared at through her microscope had shown a residue of deep-fried batter and cayenne pepper. Fast food, spicy chicken, so probably Portuguese. It wasn't much to go on, but it was a start. It made sense of the till slip Tamar had found in Kaiser's pocket. Clare turned the receipt over, wondering if the boy had known it was going to be his last meal. Twenty-four Namibian dollars was expensive for a destitute child.

Clare spread out a tourist map of Walvis Bay. The list of food outlets was unimpressive. She eliminated the restaurants, as she did the township's fish-and-chip shops and shebeens. They never gave receipts. That left five establishments, two of which were Portuguese takeaways.

The closest one was the Madeira, right at the entrance to the docks. It caught the trade from the harbour and from the factories that spewed out their workers at lunch times. A few men in blue overalls sat outside eating fish and vinegary chips with their fingers as Clare pulled up. Inside, a young woman with braided hair was texting with one hand, cigarette dangling from the other. Clare ordered a Coke from the pasty girl serving. The girl dragged herself off her stool and brought Clare her drink.

'Three-fifty.'

'Could I have a slip?' Clare asked.

The girl rolled her eyes. 'The people who eat here don't have expense accounts,' she said, pocketing the money Clare had given her for the drink.

In the centre of town, the streets had emptied of adults, filling instead with groups of raucous children heading home, white shirts grimy after a day of school. The Lisboa Inn was quiet. An old man was reading the takeaway menu. Clare approached the counter and asked for chicken peri-peri.

'Sorry, Miss. Just fish or Russians.' The pink sausages glistened in a greasy tray. Behind him, a score of splayed carcasses basted in the rotisserie oven. 'Electricity went this morning. Chicken's ready in half an hour.'

'No fried chicken?'

'No.' The cashier folded his hands across his belly, ending the conversation. His eyes moved to the man who had stepped up next to Clare. 'Yes?' he asked.

'Two Russians.' The Spanish cadences of the customer's accent lilted his English. He clicked his rosary beads as he recited the rest of his order. 'Onion rings, chips, two Cokes.' The man turned to face Clare. 'Try Lover's Hill.' His features were sculpted, his skin fine beneath the sunburn. 'They do the best chicken there. Spicy. Hot.'

'I'll try it then,' said Clare, trying to place the man's face.

'At the end of the Lagoon, you find it there. Sit and watch the flamingos while you eat.' He flashed her a smile and turned to collect his order.

'Thanks.' Clare left the gloom of the café, blinded by the sun that had fought off the sea mist outside.

'Hello, Dr Hart.' Mara's hand on Clare's arm was strong for such a skinny girl.

'Hello, Mara,' said Clare. 'What are you doing here?'

'Juan Carlos got some shore leave. We're just getting something to eat.'

'Your handsome boyfriend?' Clare asked. 'I think I just spoke to him inside.'

The young Spaniard strolled over to them. 'You two know each other?'

'Yes,' said Mara. 'This is Dr Hart. This is Juan Carlos. Dr Hart is here to investigate the murders. Kaiser and the other boys. You'll let me know when you find who it is?' Mara's eyes glistened at the mention of Kaiser's name.

'I'm sure it'll be all over the news when we do,' said Clare.

'You better be quick,' said Juan Carlos. He circled his fingers around Mara's slender throat and dropped a kiss onto her mouth. 'She's leaving me soon. If she wasn't so beautiful I might have to do something about it.' Mara blushed to the roots of her hair.

'When are you leaving?' Clare asked.

'Next week.' Mara looked down at her hands. 'My visa runs out. Come to my farewell if you're still around. On Saturday night.'

'It's better you don't talk about her leaving in front of me.' Juan Carlos wrapped his hand around Mara's waist and pulled her close to him. He slipped an intimate hand under her shirt as they walked off. Clare walked along the lagoon towards the café on Lover's Hill, aware of how acutely she missed Riedwaan. The takeaway was empty except for a woman at the till, and the cook leaning against the counter, reading the football results.

'Can I help you?' The woman did not take her eyes off the television screen.

'Chicken peri-peri,' said Clare.

'Antonio! Chicken 'n' chips,' the woman bellowed. 'Anything to drink?'

'Nothing, thanks.'

The woman took Clare's money and gave her a slip. 'Give that to Antonio.' The cashier turned back, riveted by her soap opera.

Clare handed her slip to the cook. He checked it and gave it back to her.

'Our best, the chicken peri-peri,' he said, picking up a piece of chicken and coating it with crumbs and spice. It sizzled when he threw it into the vat of bubbling oil. The thick potato wedges crisped golden. Clare could imagine a hungry boy's stomach contracting at the smell.

The sound of a car engine drew her attention, a Land Rover hurtling past.

'The desert road,' said Antonio. 'They drive so fast. So many accidents, especially if they drink.'

'It happens often?'

'These Namibians. They drink to drive; they kill each other every day like this.'

'You're not from here?'

'Not me, I'm from Angola,' said Antonio. 'I come here for work. In my country, there's nothing. Used to be war; now there is just nothing.' He wrapped Clare's order in paper and put it into a bag, tucking napkins and tomato sauce into the side. '*Bon apetito.*'

'Thanks.' Clare pulled a series of photographs out of her bag. 'I was wondering,' she asked, 'did any of these boys ever come here?'

Antonio looked at one of the photographs. 'Funny face, he's got,' he said. 'Like a frog.'

'You know him?'

'He was a soccer fan. What's his name?'

'Fritz Woestyn,' said Clare.

'He supported Brazil.' Antonio grinned, opening his white chef's jacket to reveal a yellow and green T-shirt. 'Like me.'

'How did you know him?' asked Clare.

'He slept there sometimes.' Antonio pointed to a padlocked glass door behind him. It was so covered with salt and grime that Clare hadn't noticed it. The kitchen vent was above the doorway. It would have been a warm refuge for a cold child at night. 'I gave him food sometimes.'

'When last did you see him?'

'One month ago, maybe. The owner put spikes there to keep them away. He didn't come to sleep here after that. Maybe you find him at the shelter at the dump.'

'And these boys?' Clare put the pictures of the other two boys on the counter.

'I never see them,' said Antonio. 'Who are they?'

'This was Nicanor Jones,' said Clare. 'This was Kaiser Apollis.'

'Why you ask me?' asked Antonio, anxiety in his eyes.

'Maybe one of them was here,' said Clare. 'With someone.'

Antonio shook his head. 'I don't remember.'

'Think about it.' Clare wrote down her name and cell number on a serviette. 'Call me if you do. This one loved Portuguese chicken.' She pointed to the picture of Kaiser. 'It was the last thing he ate,' she said as she walked towards the door.

Antonio picked up the napkin and folded it, watching Clare step out of the way of an accelerating 4x4 as she crossed the road. Antonio put down the forgotten serviette. Another car had flicked its lights, the roar of its engine disappearing into a quiet, star-spangled night with the child's familiar face in the window.

He wiped his hands on his apron and pushed open the swing doors. 'Wait!' he shouted to Clare. 'Let me look again. I think maybe I see one of them.'

Clare spun around and crossed the road again. 'Which one?' she asked when she reached the door. She took the photographs out of her bag again and held them out for him.

Antonio looked through the photographs again. 'This one,' he said.

'Kaiser Apollis?'

Antonio nodded.

'When? When did you see him?' Clare asked.

Antonio was weighing up whether he could trust her or not. 'I think it was Friday night. One week ago,' he said. 'He came in last. Was only me here, and I'm already closing up. He had money, new money, in his hand, a rich person's money. He asks me for chicken and chips. I make it for him, give him a Coke and then he went.'

'Where?' asked Clare.

'He walked back to town; I saw him. I see him walking, yes. Then I lock up and I also walk home.'

Clare let out her breath. She hadn't realised that she had been holding it. Back to town, that made no sense. The straw she had been grasping at was slipping away from her.

'Then I see the car. It's waiting for him.'

'What car? Where?'

'A car pull to one side of the road.'

'Did you know it? See any number plates?'

'It looks like all the cars here. White double cab.'

'Did you see the driver at all?'

Antonio shook his head. 'That is all I see. This boy.' He tapped the photograph of Kaiser. 'He talked to the driver, then he got in the back and they drive away, into the desert.'

'Thanks.' Clare was smiling at him. 'If you remember anything else, anything at all, you give me a call.'

He went back inside and watched Clare walk down towards

the lagoon. She sat down on a bench and took out a notepad, her parcel of food unopened beside her. The boy had ordered the same meal, but the sound of the café door opening interrupted Antonio's thoughts.

'Gretchen.' The cashier greeted the blonde stripper without moving her eyes from the television. 'What you want?'

'Give me what she had,' said Gretchen, pointing outside to Clare.

'Antonio!' the cashier boomed. 'Another chicken 'n' chips.'

twenty-six

It was three o'clock by the time Clare went to meet Tamar outside the bakery. From beneath the shade of a palm tree, a knot of boys untangled themselves, offering to guard Clare's car, wash her window, sell her an old newspaper.

'Where's Lazarus?' Clare asked one of them, exchanging fifty cents for yesterday's news.

'He went to the docks,' said the child.

'Tell him I want to talk to him,' said Clare. The boy looked around furtively. 'It's nothing bad,' she added. She slipped ten Namibian dollars into his hand. 'Tell him to find Dr Hart.' The boy nodded, sidling away before a bigger boy could twist the money out of his fingers. Clare went inside to buy the last cake, a sticky chocolate confection.

It was hot on the desert side of town, the morning's mist a ragged memory suspended above the ocean. Clare drank some water and watched the street children hustle. Tourists looked furtive, then handed over handfuls of coins. Locals walked on, oblivious. Clare pulled her notebook from her bag and read her notes. The desert revealed its secrets, everyone kept telling her, but when it was ready and in its own way. Someone has been very determined that the three bodies were found. That part was easy. Why they were so determined was less easy. The seduction, the trust quickly established, quickly broken. The bullet, the knife flashing across a chest. The severing of the fingertips. That small, nail-tipped joint from the ring finger lying, oozing, in the palm of a killer's hand. Everything about it said mission killer to her, cleansing the streets of rubbish, mending what had been broken by illegitimacy, poverty and delinquency, but the detail refused to crystallise into a coherent whole. The ghost, the killer, glided away from her when she reached for him.

'Come with us.' Tamar's voice at her window made Clare jump. 'It's half an hour, the drive. We don't need two cars.'

Clare got out and locked the car, balancing the cake box on the bonnet. 'Dessert,' she explained. 'I think your niece will like it.'

Tamar stopped the vehicle near a copse of acacias huddled against the cliffs. The children exploded from the car, dashing across the hot sand to the shadow of the trees, shrieking as if they had driven five hundred kilometres instead of fifty. Only a dark line marked the flow of underground water. Clare turned her back on the sprawled plain with its encrypted alphabet. Everything left a trace on this vast Rosetta stone of a desert.

She and Tamar set down their laden basket on the cement picnic table. It was cool, shaded, where they were. Water welled to the surface at the crook of this elbow of river. The children shouted, splashing in delight because there was enough water to swim in. Another day, perhaps two, and it would be gone, as the river retreated underground, leaving nothing but cracked earth and insect and rodent corpses trapped in the mud. Clare flicked some eggshells and a curl of orange peel off the table, shook out the tablecloth and settled it over the rough round surface.

'I'm glad we could come,' said Tamar. She settled herself onto a cement bench, cradling her belly between crossed knees. 'I've been promising to take them on a picnic for weeks, but this business has taken all my time.'

'It's nice to catch my breath before I catch my plane,' Clare commented. The children splashed, slick as otters in the water, and Clare sipped her lemonade. 'It doesn't feel real out here.'

The breeze came up off the desert, hot and short-lived. When it dropped, the mantle of air settled again. Clare leant back against the tree. She was tired and the heat made her sleepy. Tamar unpacked the picnic basket, setting out mounds of white bread.

'Here,' she said. 'Butter these.'

Clare took the knife. It sliced through the margarine, separating into an ooze of bilious yellow oil. Tamar sliced cheese, waving away the clumsy flies flustering towards the exposed food. Slices of anaemic tomato wilted under plastic wrap.

'How are you finding Walvis Bay the second time around?' Tamar asked as Clare buttered the bread.

'Quieter. Like half the town left in the middle of the night. Its soul seems to have gone.'

'But it grows on one, despite itself and against one's better judgement.'

Clare looked at the dunes, auburn tresses of sand rippling next to the black parting of the Kuiseb River. 'I suppose it does,' she said.

'Your profile? How do you feel about it?'

'I still feel like I'm missing something.' Clare put the last buttered slices of bread on the plate. 'Like a conversation I can hear through a door but that's just too low to distinguish the words. I get the emotion, the tone, a sense of a dialogue, but the words elude me. Maybe being outside of all this will clear my head.'

'Phiri called before we left. Captain Faizal should be here early next week. It's all sorted.'

Riedwaan's name lay between them. A challenge or an offering of sympathy, Clare wasn't sure. She wondered what Tamar knew, if anything. Not that there was much left to know.

'Aunty, Aunty, come and look!' The children burst from the undergrowth, a flutter of shrieks and pigtails and wide-eyed horror. Tamar's hand went straight for the pistol tucked inside her trousers, nestled next to the foetus, free-floating in its watery cave. A breeze curled off the dunes and around Clare's neck, lifting the downy hairs.

'What is it, Angela?' said Tamar.

'Come see, come see.' The child was hysterical, hopping from one pink-sandalled foot to the other. Further up the river bed, the children had discovered a tunnel in the scrub that had grown up over three seasons of good rain. Clare had to bend as Angela and Tupac wove through the bush. The pathway twisted and turned, as disorientating as a maze. Some of the branches had been cut back to clear a path. The cloying stench of death filled the air. Clare's blood ran cold as she thought of who might have been there before them.

The little girl stepped into a sun-dappled clearing. A semicircle of stones faced a small cave in the sheer, black cliff face. In front of it was a makeshift altar; the stumps of a few candles leant drunkenly, melted by the heat. A small body hung limp, a shrivelled fruit among the profusion of white blossoms at the entrance to the clearing. Clare stepped forward to touch the corpse's ginger fur. The skin was starting to slough off, leaving grotesque strips of exposed flesh. Flies clustered where its life had bubbled away.

'Tupac, take your sister back to the picnic place,' said Tamar.

Angela clung to her aunt, tears glistening on her plump cheeks. 'Who do it? Who do it to the kitty, Aunty Tamar?'

Tamar squatted down beside her distraught niece and drew her into the circle of her arms. The child buried her head in Tamar's shoulder.

Clare walked around the semi-circle. Faded Coke tins and discarded cigarette butts littered the place, the milder brands bearing telltale lipstick stains. She picked one up. A menthol ultra-thin. A teenager's nicotine starter pack.

'I'm going to take her back to the car,' said Tamar, gripping Angela firmly by the hand. 'Will you check here, Clare? Come on, Tupac, you too.'

The undergrowth closed on Tamar and the children, leaving Clare alone. On the other side of the makeshift altar lay a brandy bottle and a red G-string. Clare took a tissue out of her pocket and picked up the wisp of stained underwear. It was dim inside the cave. Once her eyes had adjusted, though, Clare could make out the graffiti: Chesney and Minki. The girl's name had been scored through when LaToyah had replaced Minki in Chesney's affections. There wasn't much else – a couple more empty bottles, a bottleneck with the remnants of a filter in it, a filthy old mattress. Unimaginative, small-town Satanism. A lizard bobbed on tensed elbows, liquid black on the sun-ravaged rocks, watching Clare duck into the tunnel of undergrowth.

'You get a lot of this Satanic stuff?' she asked Tamar when she got back to the picnic site.

Tamar had her niece on her lap. Tupac was sitting close to her too. He sidled away when Clare reappeared, an eleven-year-old sensitive about his image. Clare sat down opposite them.

'There've been a few incidents: bored teenagers wearing black nail polish and experimenting with group sex. Nothing too serious.'

'Crucifying cats is something else. The men I go for often start their careers torturing small animals.'

'I want to go home, Aunty.' Tamar stroked the hair out of Angela's eyes and popped a piece of bread into her mouth.

Clare packed up the picnic. 'Do you know anyone called Minki?' she asked.

Tamar shook her head.

'LaToyah?'

'Dime a dozen in Narraville, LaToyahs,' said Tamar. 'Three in my street.'

'And Chesney?'

'I know him,' said Tupac. It was the first time he had said a word. 'Chesney used to go to my school, but then he left to go to the school in town, the one where you found that dead boy in the swing.'

The two women looked at each other over the children's heads.

'I'll talk to him,' said Tamar quietly, strapping Angela into her seat. They were all silent as they drove back to town through the gathering dusk.

twenty-seven

Music blasted through the girl's iPod as the bike hurtled through the desert. She snaked her arms under the driver's leathers, and he accelerated, pluming dust behind the bike. It shimmered across the sinking sun as they passed the rusted no-entry sign. 'Danger/Gevaar' said the next one. The girl hopped off the bike and opened the gate. In among the trees were the remnants of three huts and a car wreck.

'Who lives here?' she asked, climbing back on the bike.

'Nobody now,' said her companion. 'Some Topnaars used to, but the South African army kicked them out twenty years ago.'

The man hadn't been this way in what … ten years, twelve? He hadn't even thought of the place since his unit had given up, rolling south in their Bedfords when Walvis Bay was handed back to the Namibians. For their sins, he thought. What anyone wanted in this godforsaken dump was beyond him.

'When're you going to stop?' the girl whined. It would be dark soon and she wanted a fire and a joint. The man was enjoying the feeling of a girl's tits pressing into his back. It made him feel young again, like the soldier he had once been and not the overweight husband he had become.

'Where's the fucking road gone? It should be here.' Instead of a track leading to a hut under a gum tree, there was a bank of sand, pocked with branches and other long-stranded flood debris.

'That flood, a few years ago, it shifted the course of the river. It must've blocked Memory Lane,' said the girl matter-of-factly. 'Let's stay here. The desert's all the same, anyway.'

The man parked the bike under a canopy of gnarled acacia, thinking of the girls he and some of the others in his unit used to pick up and bring out here. Army mattresses, they had called them. A couple of days in the desert made them docile, amenable. Not like this wild thing with the same name as his wife's fancy perfume.

The girl had logs and kindling assembled before he had the panniers unpacked. She put a match to the grass and blew, showering red sparks across the satin sky. She leant back and offered the man a drag of her deftly rolled joint – another thing girls seemed to have learnt to do in the last twenty years. He traded his hip flask for the joint.

The girl tilted her head back and he traced down her throat as she drank, stopping at the hollow between her collarbones where her breath fluttered below his thumb. She put his hand to her mouth, flicking her tongue along his fingers, clicking the piercing in the centre of her tongue against his wedding ring. Then his knee was between her thighs and he was spreading her legs and mounting her. He was finished before he'd really begun. The girl sighed, turning away to light a cigarette. He tried to kiss her, but she brushed him aside.

'I'm hungry,' she said, rummaging for food in the bag next to her, propped up on one elbow. She considered brushing her teeth, but the man had fallen asleep beside her, his arms around her stomach. She covered them both instead and lay, watching the stars wink, bright as lanterns in the branches of their tree canopy.

When the girl woke, it was dark. No moon. No wind either. She guessed it was two o'clock. Maybe three. The silence filled her ears, her lungs, making it difficult to breathe. She snuggled back into the man's arms, but the pressure of her bladder would not relent, so she wormed her way out from under the covers and felt around for the torch and her shoes. She picked her way towards a denser patch of darkness on the edge of their campsite.

When she flicked on her torch, nosing the light ahead of her into the trees, he was waiting for her. Grinning.

The girl's scream ricocheted into the night.

twenty-eight

Keening. High and wild. It feathered fear up Clare's spine. She sat up, putting her hands to her temples and trying to order her thoughts in the wake of the nightmare. She had been running, faster and faster. Her feet had been bare and bleeding, the flesh ribboned by the broken shells littering a beach. Spectral hands plucked at her legs, pulling her down towards the lagoon, wrapping around her throat. Clare looked around her room and orientated herself. She had been asleep. It was just a dream.

She was reaching for the water next to her bed when the terrible keening started again. Of course. Her cellphone.

'What?' Manners would be pushing it at three in the morning.

'Dr Hart? I woke you?' She tried to place the voice. 'It's Van Wyk.'

Of course it was. The receding dread of her dream circled back.

'What?' she said again.

'Another body. I'll pick you up.'

'Where? Who?'

'From your cottage,' said Van Wyk. 'I'll pick you up.'

'I meant where was the body found? Who is it?'

'Out in the Kuiseb, the old military site past the delta. Couple of bikers found him. I wouldn't be disturbing your beauty sleep if he didn't fit your bill.'

'How long have I got?' Clare needed coffee.

'Ten minutes.' Van Wyk hung up.

Clare made coffee and drank it while she dressed. Jeans,

anorak. It would be cold out. She was finishing a second cup when Van Wyk pulled up in the double cab. He handed her a packet of rusks and a flask. Clare bit off a piece of the rough, dried biscuit.

'Thanks.' She hadn't thought that she would be hungry.

'My mother makes them.'

Clare hadn't thought of Van Wyk with a family either. If her brain had been functioning better, she might have ventured a question about them. Instead, she kept quiet, watching the streets slip past.

Tamar was waiting for them, her house dark except for the light in the kitchen. 'Is Elias out there already?' she asked, getting into the back of the vehicle.

'He took the call, Captain,' Van Wyk said. 'So he went straight out.'

'Is an ambulance on its way?'

'Karamata said there's no need,' said Van Wyk, skirting the sleeping town. 'It would be impossible to get one out there, anyway.'

The road forked at the salt mine, which gleamed white under the floodlights. Van Wyk turned into the dark cleft of the delta. He drove fast along the twisting track, never hesitating about which tributary road to take, which to speed past. He veered left, heading for a dense thicket of trees. The track narrowed and the tamarisk trees cut out the starlight. Van Wyk braked. Ahead of them was a gate, the only breach in an endless garland of barbed wire. Clare could just make out the sign· 'Danger/ Gevaar'.

'What is this place?' she asked.

'It's part of an old military site,' said Tamar. 'The whole delta used to be the army's. This place has been off-limits so long that everyone forgot about it.'

'Not those little lovebirds,' said Van Wyk. He switched on the hunting lights, serried like evil eyes on the roof of the truck, flooding the clearing with white light.

A whippet-thin girl was hunched over her knees, a jacket wrapped tight across her back. Her eyes sparked with defiance. Fifteen, thought Clare. Sixteen, if you wanted to believe it. A man stood near his motorbike. His wedding ring glinted as he took a deep drag of his cigarette. Ponytail, pushing forty. The proverbial rabbit in the headlights. Wife and children blown for the brief thrill of a nubile body in his hands. The dead boy was slumped against a tree on the edge of the circle of light. A still from a horror movie until Karamata stepped out of the shadows, unfreezing the frame.

'Elias,' said Tamar, getting out of the vehicle, 'phone Helena Kotze and tell her I need her here this time. This one we'll autopsy tonight.'

'Has he been moved?' asked Clare, approaching the body cautiously.

Karamata shook his head.

Tamar handed Clare a pair of latex gloves, then pulled on her own pair before lowering herself next to the dead boy. A child drooped in jest against a tree at the end of a game. He had been secured with riempie, the same strips of cured leather that had kept the shroud around Kaiser Apollis's corpse.

'Same shroud for this one.' Tamar lifted away the gauzy fabric and shone her torch into the boy's ruined face, revealing a mouth wide open in amazement and a forehead that was nothing but shards of bone and burnt flesh.

'Lazarus,' gasped Clare, the shock of recognition a body blow.

'Lazarus Beukes,' said Tamar. 'He's got a record for petty thieving so long you could knit a jersey out of it.'

'What's his story?' Clare wished that she had heard it earlier.

'He had a mother who loved him when she was sober enough to remember he existed,' Tamar said, 'but she disappeared a few years ago. He's lived at the dump ever since.'

Tamar circled the body, resisting the urge to close the lids on the dulling eyes, to wipe away the fluid seeping from his forehead, eyes and slack mouth. The cold eye of her camera flashed on Lazarus's shattered face. The rope, a nylon washing line around the wrists, had been knotted, so that it would pull tighter as the victim struggled. It had been cut through in the middle, and the boy's hands lay between his knees, bloody tracks scored deep into both wrists. Clare envisaged the moment Lazarus had realised it wasn't a game, when he had fought for his life.

'Have a look at that rope,' she said. Tamar lifted the jaunty blue and white nylon. The ends around the wrists were cut clean through.

'This is frayed,' said Tamar, pointing to the longer piece that would have held his hands tight behind his back. 'Cut with a different knife. The same as Kaiser Apollis.'

'Two weapons,' said Clare. 'Two places. Two people? Or just one crime in two parts?'

'There's no blood here,' said Tamar. 'This isn't where he was shot, so there're your two places.' She put her hand against the boy's skin. It was cold, his body flaccid. She tried to move one of his fingers. He was starting to stiffen.

'It doesn't look like he's been dead long enough for rigor to reverse,' said Clare. 'There are no visible signs of decomposition. Looks like he was shot yesterday evening.'

A week since Kaiser Apollis had climbed into a vehicle and been driven into the desert to be displayed on a Monday. Now there was this one, Friday's Child. Loving and giving. Clare checked his left hand. The ring finger ended in a bloody stump. 'The signature,' she said. 'He's taken his trophy again.'

Tamar pointed to the pullover. 'This'll be the second signature,' she said, pushing back the bloody fabric, revealing ribs concaving into the stomach suspended between delicate hips. The flesh, as smooth as a girl's, had been ribboned by a series of sure, deep knife strokes. Tamar dropped the fabric.

'One with nothing, a 2, a 3 and now a 5,' said Clare.

'Please, God, there isn't a fourth victim waiting to be found,' said Tamar, supporting her lower back as she stood up. She turned to Karamata. 'You looked for a gun?' she asked.

'I did,' he said. 'I checked both their hands for residue. Nothing. It would last four hours on the hands of a live person after they'd fired.'

'Unless they washed their hands,' said Clare.

'I checked,' said Karamata. 'No sign that anyone washed their hands.'

'Knives?' asked Clare.

'Just this.' Karamata held up a small penknife. 'It had scraps of biltong on the blade, nothing else.'

'Who found him?' asked Tamar, walking over to the forlorn couple.

'Me.' It was the girl. 'I called the police too.'

'Your name?' Tamar pulled out a notepad.

'I'm Chanel,' the girl replied. 'That's Clinton.'

Tamar turned to the man. 'Why didn't you phone?'

'He was afraid to,' said Chanel, giving the man a look of withering post-coital clarity. 'He wanted to leave, but the bike's not working.'

Van Wyk walked over to the bike. 'This isn't going anywhere,' he said. 'Someone cut your fuel pipe. You're lucky you didn't end up with brain splattered across the desert like him.' He gestured to Lazarus's body.

The girl shuddered and Tamar put a blanket around her

shoulders. Still a child under the smudged make-up, her face was drawn, foxy with fear and cold.

'What were you doing out here?' asked Tamar. 'This is a restricted area.'

'He wanted to come out here.' Chanel pointed to the ashen man.

'Why here?' Tamar addressed Clinton.

'Old times' sake.'

'Why here and why now?' Clare persisted.

'No reason really.' Clinton looked besieged.

'So let me get this straight: you just decided on the spur of the moment to bring an under-aged girl to a restricted military site?' asked Clare conversationally.

Clinton shrugged, a failed attempt at cockiness. 'I saw an old army connection the other day and it made me think about this place. We used to come here in the old days. Then Chanel wanted to go somewhere, and I thought, why not here? Seeing as we can't go anywhere together in town.'

'Who's your connection?' asked Clare.

'I don't even remember his name any more. Something foreign. Polish. Russian maybe, I don't know. It was years ago. He was an officer in some unit that used to work out here. I was just a troepie. I saw him there in the strip club, sitting alone, as cool as ever in his cowboy boots, and it reminded me of this place,' said Clinton, his shoulders sagging in defeat. 'It seems fucking stupid now.'

'How do you know him?' Tamar asked Chanel

'I babysit for his wife,' the girl replied. 'Mrs Nel's going to kill me. So's my mother.'

'Tell me what happened,' said Tamar.

'Can I have a cigarette?' Chanel asked.

Clare tossed her a box of cigarettes. The girl lit one, hands shaking. Then she told them: they'd gone to sleep, she'd woken up, needed a pee, gone over to the trees, and there was the boy, staring at her like some sick joke.

'Did you look around before you went to sleep?' asked Clare.

'Not really,' said Chanel. 'It was getting dark when we arrived.'

'No other cars?' asked Tamar.

'We saw no one,' said Clinton. 'Heard nothing either.'

'And you?' Clare asked the girl.

'Just those geckos that call at night. Listen …' She held up her hand. 'You can hear them now.'

Clare listened: the chill, moaning laugh of a jackal, then there it was in the distance. Tjak. Tjak. Tjak. The knocking sound that solitary reptiles make to claim their territory, to attract a mate.

'Go and wait in the car,' Tamar said to Chanel. The girl was shaking now. Cold and shock. 'There should be some coffee there to warm you up.'

When Van Wyk cut the lights, the starlight washed over the scene, soft-focusing the horror. A bat swooped low along the ground, hunting. The wind rattled through the trees, then died away, leaving a silence so absolute Clare felt it as a pressure in her ears.

Like she was losing altitude too fast.

twenty-nine

Helena Kotze kicked her motorbike into life, the sound like a volley of machine-gun fire down the quiet street. Typical that the call had come once the pulse of the clubs and bars had ebbed, allowing her to plunge into the deep sleep she craved. She did not want to think of what was waiting for her on the indifferent desert sand. She did think, as she curved around the belly of the lagoon, that she was following the path the killer had taken. There was no other way into the delta. The trees closed in on her when she turned east.

She rolled the bike into the amphitheatre of dunes. Tamar and Dr Hart stood beside the body trussed against the tree. Van Wyk sat smoking inside the double cab. A blanket-swaddled girl leant against the window. Karamata and a middle-aged man stood near a motorbike.

'Helena, glad you're here,' said Tamar. 'Let's get started.'

Helena set down her sturdy bag on the sand.

'You've got your crime-scene kit there?' Efficiency smoothed out the edge in Tamar's voice.

Helena nodded. 'You got all the pictures you need?'

'I think so.'

'Close-ups of the gunshot wounds?'

'See if these are good enough.' Tamar scrolled through the pictures on her digital camera.

'Looks fine.' Helena palpated the boy's unresisting flesh.

'Time of death?' Clare asked.

Helena took out an instrument that looked like a sharpened bicycle spoke. 'I'm going to do a sub-hepatic probe. Taking a rectal temp can damage the tissue, making it hard to prove sexual assault later.'

Helena found the correct place just beneath the boy's chest. She pushed firmly downwards, puncturing the skin and driving the metal deep into the recesses of his body below the liver. She jotted down some notes about air movement and the number of clothing layers the boy was wearing. 'I need to get the weather report to check against body temp.'

'Would that shot have killed him instantly?' asked Clare.

'In a child, yes,' said Helena. 'Looks like whoever shot this boy was taller than him, or ...' Helena stood up and clasped her hands as if she were holding a gun. She softened her knees and angled her hands towards Lazarus. 'Or the victim was sitting or lying down.' She turned to face Clare and Tamar. 'Like it looks he was.'

'The gun?' asked Clare.

'Pistol shot again,' Helena said. 'Nice and clean and efficient. Punctured forehead. I'd say it's the same guy.' Helena took the boy's mutilated hand in hers. 'Your bridegroom has left his mark again.'

'I saw,' said Clare. 'Pre- or post-mortem?'

'Very little blood here,' said Helena. 'Between ten and thirty minutes post-mortem, it'll be bloodless unless a blunt instrument is used. Then you could get damage to the blood vessels. It'll cause a welling of blood and obscure the fact that it took place post-mortem. It's bloodless, just a little oozing. I'd say the two end joints of his finger were removed with a pair of pliers. And soon after he died.'

Helena pushed back the boy's shirt and shone her torch on the ravaged chest. The knife had cut through the skin. 'Looks like he used a non-serrated knife to cut the boy here. And quite a while after death. So a non-serrated knife for the chest and a pair of pliers or something else for the finger.'

'A strange calling card,' said Tamar.

'A warning, perhaps. To sinners,' said Clare.

The ebony night had thinned to pewter, giving form to the ghostly outlines of branches. Tamar moved off between the trees, following an invisible thread through a maze of bent grasses and shifted stones. The faint marks were familiar.

'He came this way,' she said. 'Carrying the boy. It's the same pattern as the school. Same print.' Clare followed Tamar over the stony ground along the river's edge. There was a thin track snaking through the sand, the ancient tracery of animals migrating in single file in search of water or food. Something you'd miss in the crushing light of day.

Tamar followed until she reached a pile of animal droppings. 'He would've gone back that way,' she said, 'but there's not much point in going on.' A flock of goats was moving down the riverbed. They had churned up the sand with their sharp little hooves. A couple of them stopped browsing and looked up at Clare and Tamar. They would obliterate any trail more efficiently than water.

'I'll send some men out later. See what they can find,' Tamar said, as they headed back to where Helena crouched by the boy. She had spread a tarpaulin sheet on the ground and lain down Lazarus to examine him. She was moving her competent, gentle hands across the boy's supine body, under his clothes. She had made swabs and was combing the body for a killer's DNA, which might have confettied onto the boy.

'Let's get him out of here,' said Tamar 'I want to autopsy him as soon as possible.' Karamata and Van Wyk stepped forward and lifted the body as one would lift a child who had fallen asleep. Tamar closed the lids, shutting Lazarus's dead eyes.

'The body?' asked Clare.

'Back seat,' said Tamar. 'With me.'

The police vehicles, Van Wyk and Tamar in the double cab and Karamata on his quad bike, disappeared over the dune. The hunting bats, flying low over the ground, returned to roost in the large Ana tree where Lazarus had been tied.

'I need to make a call,' Clare said to Helena. 'Can you hang on a minute?'

'Sure,' said Helena. 'Let them get ahead or we'll sit in their dust.'

Clare climbed halfway up a rise, hoping she would get cell-phone reception. Nothing. She stood in the scrub, like any other predator, and scanned the dunes. A thickening of the darkness on the opposite dune caught her eye, thudding her heart against her ribs again. The shadow moved, lengthening down the swell of the dune. Then it stopped and Clare heard the eerie chuckle of a brown hyena, a rare and persecuted animal. She exhaled, and watched the animal lope, swift and sure, into the scrub. Its presence meant that people rarely passed through here. It also meant that no body would last long. Half an hour alone, and the soft bits – stomach, buttocks, face – would be gone. The small bones would be ground away, the long bones cracked open for their sweet, nutritious marrow.

The killer must have kept the dead boy somewhere. He had been able to predict where a sleepy girl would go to relieve herself. He had displayed the body just there, so that her torchlight would find his face leering at her. Clare scanned the empty gulley, the motionless trees. He had to know this place. Like the back of his hand. The phrase echoed through Clare's mind as she moved out of the shelter of the trees, climbing to the lip of the dune. One bar. She crossed her fingers for the satellite to be around long enough for her to make her call.

'Faizal,' mumbled Riedwaan. Half asleep. Warm. Naked in bed. Clare pictured him, one sinewy arm over his eyes to keep the morning at bay. The unexpected ache of longing was a knife-twist.

'Riedwaan.' Despite herself, she listened for the muffled sounds of somebody else. 'It's Clare.'

'Baby.' Worry clear as a bell in his voice. 'What's wrong?'

'What did you just call me?' she asked.

'I called you baby. It's ... fuck, it's five o'clock in the morning, Clare. Get off your feminist high horse. What's happened?'

'Another boy, Riedwaan.' Clare put her hand to her mouth. 'I spoke to him two days ago. Now he's dead.'

'What is it now? Three? Four?'

'Four. Four bodies. But this one had a 5 carved on his chest. I'm scared it means there's another one out there that no one's found.'

'Where are you?'

'Out in the Kuiseb Delta. Some old military site.'

'Military?' Riedwaan was awake now, his ambiguous conversation with Phiri making his hair stand on end. 'What are you doing there?'

'A couple of bikers found the body,' said Clare. 'Well, a married man and an under-aged babysitter. It must've seemed like the ideal place. It's the middle of nowhere. Someone cut the bike's fuel pipe so they had no choice but to call for help.'

'Is there any connection between that place and the school? The other places where the bodies were dumped?'

'If there is, I'm not seeing it yet,' said Clare. 'Other than whoever is dumping these kids intends them to be found.'

Need and opportunity, she thought: malevolent twin moons that guided the ebb and flow of her killer's mind.

'You have to find some way of connecting these boys and the dump sites,' said Riedwaan. 'If the choice is purely opportunistic, then what does this guy do that allows him to be in the right place at the right time? Then you've got a chance of finding where he's shooting them.'

'Riedwaan, do you know how big this place is? It's like looking for a needle in a haystack.' The desert rolled away from Clare, ashen in the starlight.

'That's your job, Doc,' said Riedwaan. 'Unless this killer is a spook, someone's going to see him sometime.'

'It feels like I'm chasing a ghost sometimes,' said Clare, watching a moth alight on a cluster of creamy blossoms.

'What's the plan now?' asked Riedwaan.

'Captain Damases went back with the body. We'll do the autopsy immediately. I'm going back now with the pathologist.'

'Clare.' Riedwaan's tone softened. Not now, thought Clare. Not here. 'I wanted to tell you …'

Clare broke off a flower-laden branch from the tree she was standing under. She didn't recognise the species, but the plants that grew in deserts were unique, each evolving to fit some tiny niche. The fragile blossoms smelt of honey, a subtle fragrance as out of place in this harsh place as the delicate, pollen-laden moth that fluttered in the moonlight. She waited.

'It's not what you're thinking. I just—' he started, but the satellite moved, cutting him off.

Clare wiped her hands on her jeans. Her palms left a swirl of Van Gogh yellow against the blue. She looked at the pollen smudge. It clung to her jeans, her hands, her watch strap. It would travel with her no matter how much she tried to rub it off. She thought of the dead boys and the unchartered paths they had followed to their deaths. All the signs they might have left – footprints, hair, skin particles – had been erased by the desert wind and the tenacious insects that fought for survival. Clare looked again at the pollen clinging to her, determined to journey with her on the off-chance that it would brush against a receptive female plant. She felt her pulse quicken as her idea coalesced. If Lazarus had brushed against a tree or a flowering shrub in the Kuiseb Delta, surely the traces of these plants would have adhered to the tiny crevices in his skin or the folds in his clothes. Adrenaline surged through Clare as she thought of the invisible code encrypted on the dead boy. On the others, too: Kaiser, Nicanor, Fritz.

'Clare.' Helena's voice cut through her thoughts. 'Shall we head back? I'll need to get to work on that boy if you're going to have anything to take to Cape Town with you later.'

Clare went to join her, picking a branch of every flowering tree she passed. 'I need to find someone who knows about plants.'

'Tertius Myburgh's your man then,' said Helena, giving her a strange look. 'Plant nut, works at the desert research institute in Swakopmund. Tell him I sent you.'

Helena's bike roared back to life and Clare got on behind her, cradling her bouquet in front of her. They bumped down the track and turned onto the gravel road that would take them back to Walvis Bay. The bike's lights flashed over objects, pulling them towards Clare: an old car wreck, a gnarled tree and a donkey cart clip-clopping along, the driver hunched against the cold, a sleepy huddle of children on the back, lulled by the regular thwack of the leather on the donkey's withers.

Helena parked in the hospital parking lot. Clare needed a hot shower and coffee, but neither of those was going to happen any time soon.

Tamar was waiting for them. 'Lazarus's inside already,' she said, leading the way up the steps of the morgue. 'Elias has gone over to the dump to try to trace his movements.'

'And Van Wyk?' asked Clare.

'At the station with Clinton and Chanel getting statements.

His wife and her mother were waiting for them when we arrived,' said Tamar. 'They'd figured it out already.'

'Ouch!' said Clare.

In the antechamber, the three women pulled gowns over their dusty clothes before following Helena into her makeshift mortuary. The sheet draped across Lazarus peaked over his nose, his hands folded across his lacerated chest, over his too-large adolescent feet. In the dim light it looked like the marble tomb of a medieval crusader; then Helena flicked on the lights and he was a dead boy on a dented metal gurney again.

'Okay,' Helena said. 'Shall we start?' She drew back the sheet to reveal Lazarus Beukes, his gangly legs straightened, arms folded, eyes closed.

The scab on his knee was easier to look at than the neat cross bang in the middle of his forehead. Clare turned away, holding her hand up in front of her face. The gun here, ten centimetres from his forehead. Close enough to see each calibration of expression, but calm, contained, without the aggression of the barrel rammed against the flesh, twisting it. For the boy it was all the same, the end. The bullet tunnelling through the brain to lodge against the cradling skull at the back of his head.

Helena worked methodically, undressing and packaging the boy's clothes, recording her initial observations, her soothing tone in stark contrast to the unsettling details she was describing. The amputated tip of the Apollo finger, the 5 scored into the bony chest, the old scars, the new ones, the mapping of a rough and abbreviated life.

'Yes!' said Helena, turning Lazarus over. 'There's no exit wound here.' It took a second for the implication of what she was saying to sink in.

'Are you going to open his head up?' Clare asked, not sure

how much time she had to get to Tertius Myburgh before her plane left.

'I am,' said Helena. 'Hang on, Clare. Five minutes and you're free.'

Clare felt the bile rising in her throat as Helena picked up the instruments that would tease the last secrets from Lazarus Beukes's brain. She went over to the window and rubbed one pane clean. With intense concentration she watched the day-shift nurses arrive, ten large women spilling out of the minibus taxi. The doors of the hospital closed on them, silencing their ribald banter. Clare wished the night staff would start their exit procession so that they would distract her from the quiet sawing going on behind her.

There was a low whistle from Helena, followed by a tiny clink. A gasp from Tamar. Then another clink. Clare cursed herself for feeling faint. Helena picked up the bullet in the metal dish with tweezers, rinsing the blood and scraps of brain that clung to the lead. She dropped it into an evidence bag and handed it to Clare. Small, spent, malignant in her hand. Her skin tingled.

'A bullet.' Helena's tired face was triumphant. 'And here's another. Two bullets, one behind the other. Means that the first bullet lodged in the tip of the barrel and was forced out simultaneously with the next shot. So when your killer fired again, Lazarus got two for the price of one.'

thirty

Four pairs of shoes rested on the back seat next to the labelled bundles of clothes packaged in brown paper, as neat as gifts. Clare's desert bouquet was in the boot. She drove through Swakopmund, a quaint holiday town, thirty kilometres north of Walvis Bay. Its coffee shops displayed dripping slices of Black Forest cake, and its snow-roofed German colonial houses seemed outlandish in the desert. But the street children were the same: wheedling, coaxing or pickpocketing money from flustered, sunburnt tourists. Clare turned towards the copper-domed aquarium, tarnished a Florentine green by the sea air. It was sequestered at the end of the road parallel to the beach.

It was early still and no one was about. Clare had made her way around the back of the building to find the air-conditioned shipping container. She pushed her way into the gloomy interior. The dim, dusty windows and the narrowness of the space gave it the air of a mausoleum. A young man was hunched over a microscope. Long hair curtained his face.

'Dr Myburgh?'

The man turned. His face was narrow, ascetic. He held out a pale, eager hand. 'Dr Hart?' His voice was soft, the hand that enveloped hers warm and dry. 'Tertius Myburgh.'

'I hope I'm not disturbing your work.'

Myburgh smiled and gestured to the phials and jars on his shelves. 'My companions are very quiet, so I'm quite happy with the occasional interruption. Helena Kotze said you'd be coming. What can I do for you?'

Clare put the parcels of shoes and clothes and the posy of

desert plants on a trestle table. 'I'm helping with the investigation into the murder of four boys in Walvis Bay,' she said. 'The ones Helena autopsied.'

'Those Aids orphans?'

'A couple of them were, yes. Homeless children.'

'How can I help?' Myburgh looked puzzled.

'Their bodies have been dumped all over the place,' said Clare. 'At a school, on the Walvis Bay pipeline, at the dump. The latest in the Kuiseb Delta. None of them were killed where they were displayed.'

'Ah, you want me to tell you where they've been?' asked Myburgh, fingering the pale blossoms on the table.

'Can you?'

'I can try.' Myburgh's eyes gleamed at the challenge. 'Pollens are unique and they're tenacious. If they brushed a flowering plant, it's going to stick somewhere. Shoes, laces, hoodie ties. Pollen is the most conservative part of the plant. Mutations are rare. That's why we can pinpoint it so accurately. If there's a mutation it's like a red flag, pointing you in the direction of the correct species.'

'How long will it take?' Clare asked.

'This can wait.' Myburgh gestured at the leaves, seed pods and dissected buds arranged on his table. 'But it'll take a day or so. Plants are like people. It's the little differences that make them unique. What distinguishes one type of pollen from another will be just the tiniest mutation, the smallest difference. With a killer I suppose it's the same: you look for that one calibration of difference that distinguishes him from me ... or you.'

'Those tiny discrepancies,' said Clare, 'that's what I look for.'

'My mother always told me you could judge a man by his shoes,' said Myburgh. 'When you have a suspect, bring me his

185

shoes. They'll tell me where he's been. Take this in the mean-time. It's the plant list I've been working on, and here are the corresponding pollens.' He handed her a pile of paper.

'These are beautiful,' said Clare, looking at the magnified photographs of the desert pollens. 'How long have you worked on this?'

'About two years, but most of the groundwork was done by an American ethno-botanist,' said Myburgh.

'He's no longer involved?'

'She,' said Myburgh. 'Virginia Meyer. She was killed in a car accident last year.'

'Oh yes,' said Clare. 'I've heard of her, and I've met her son Oscar. One of the bodies was found at his school. Outside his classroom, in fact.'

'Strange little boy, he is,' said Myburgh. 'He used to do field-work with her. Him and an old Topnaar man called Spyt, who was Virginia's guide. Knows the desert like you and I know our own faces. If you want to know anything about anything in the Namib – plants, stones, animals – he's your man.'

'Where is he now?' asked Clare.

'Spyt?' said Myburgh. 'He could be anywhere. He's even more of a recluse since the accident. He was devoted to Virginia and he loved Oscar.' He paused. 'I suppose Oscar was too young to see how odd Spyt is. All he knew was the magic places Spyt could find in the middle of nowhere.'

Myburgh walked Clare back to her car. 'Give me your cell number. I'll call you as soon as I have something.'

Clare wrote down her number for him. 'There was one more thing I wanted to know,' she said. 'Maybe you can tell me.' She stretched over to open the cubbyhole. The insect husks that Herman Shipanga had found tumbled onto her hand. She was revolted again by the scratchiness of the little ball of carcasses.

'What's that?' asked Myburgh.

'Something else's dinner,' said Clare. 'I was hoping you could tell me more about it.' She handed it to him.

Myburgh peered at the orb. 'Moth wings,' he said. 'And long-horned grasshoppers. Some termites. Where did you find this?'

'The school caretaker found it in the swing where Kaiser Apollis was found.'

'Impossible,' said Myburgh, looking at the insects again. 'You won't find these at the coast. Inland, yes. I'd say this comes from where Egyptian bats have been feeding. They don't need full darkness, so they roost in large trees in the delta; otherwise caves or other shelters.'

'So you'd find them in the Kuiseb?' asked Clare. The importance of what Myburgh was telling her banished her exhaustion.

'Yes,' said Myburgh, 'but they're rare. There's not enough food to sustain more than a few colonies, and the curious thing about bats is that they keep returning to established feeding sites with their prey. Find that, then you know where these little mummies came from.'

thirty-one

The flight from Walvis Bay circled Table Mountain, which stood in isolated splendour above the squalor of the Cape Flats. Clare was first off the plane. She slid her passport across the counter, her mind shuttling between everything she had to do in Cape Town and the fragmented picture she had of events in Walvis Bay.

'This way please, Doctor.' The immigration officer pulled down the grille in front of his booth. He had Clare's passport clasped in his hand.

'What is it?' All she needed now was officiousness about smuggling body parts across international borders.

'Come with me.' He opened a door marked 'Customs', standing aside so that she could enter. Riedwaan was leaning against the wall, his shirt white against his throat.

'Thanks.' Riedwaan was speaking to the customs official, but his eyes were on Clare.

'Any time, Captain.'

'Can I have a look at those?' said Riedwaan. Clare put her assortment of packages on the scuffed table and folded her arms.

'You need anything else, Captain Faizal?' the official asked. Riedwaan shook his head, and the man left, closing the door behind him. Riedwaan picked up the box of samples Helena Kotze had packed for Piet Mouton.

'What are you doing?' Clare hissed.

'I'm here to see you. Like you said. Officially.' Riedwaan opened the door. 'Shall we go?'

'Where are we going?' asked Clare. 'Officially.'

'Security exit. It's much quicker.'

'Riedwaan,' said Clare with an incredulous laugh, 'you know I have appointments.'

'I know. I'm driving you, officially.' He turned to look at her. 'Don't look at me like that. Orders from Phiri.'

'Well,' she snapped, 'I don't really have a choice then, do I?'

'Doesn't look like it to me.' He was relieved that she didn't phone Phiri to check.

Getting her this far was easier than Riedwaan had thought. She got into his old Mazda and he inched through the chaos at domestic arrivals. He turned east along the N2, heading away from Cape Town. So far, so good. He suspected that getting her to talk – or to listen – might be harder.

'Where did your friend at customs spring from?' Clare asked.

'An old friend from my narc squad days. He owed me a favour.'

'I can just imagine.'

'Aren't you going to ask me about my family?' asked Riedwaan.

'After you've practically kidnapped me, does it matter what I do or don't ask?'

'It matters to me,' Riedwaan said. 'Yasmin is my daughter. I love her. And you … Look Clare, I'm sorry about that back there.' He gestured at the space between them. 'All this …' He gave up.

Clare stared at the shabby houses blurring past her window. Her autonomy had been so hard-won; loosening the bonds of her damaged identical twin Constance had left her determined to resist the lure of losing herself again in another person.

'Aren't you going to say anything?' asked Riedwaan, exasperated with her silence.

'You've missed the turning.'

'For fuck's sake.' Riedwaan did a U-turn, bumping over the traffic island. He accelerated across three lanes and took the turn-off to Bellville.

'It's red,' said Clare. Riedwaan braked at the traffic lights. 'There is the tiny issue of your wife, Riedwaan.'

'Why's it so difficult to tell you anything?' he asked, running his hands through his shock of hair.

'What you *didn't* tell me is what matters. You never gave me the chance to decide about things. You just ducked behind the luck that I was going to Namibia. A most convenient coincidence, seeing as you organised me to go there.'

Riedwaan parked in a visitor's bay at the large teaching hospital in Cape Town's northern suburbs. He turned towards Clare, but she spoke before he could say anything: 'We have to work together on this case, Riedwaan. It's just easier if you sort your family situation out yourself.' Clare needed air. She opened the door.

Riedwaan got out too. 'What're you so afraid of, Clare? With people, things are messy. That's how life is.'

'I'm not up to a philosophy lesson, especially if it's just a rehash of what some cheap cop shrink tells you when you drink too much.' Clare picked up her box, holding it like a shield across her chest. 'Let's just stick to the case, shall we?' Easier terrain that, the mechanics of death.

'Explain your case then. Tell me something I don't know.' Riedwaan took the box from her hands. His skin was warm where their hands touched.

Clare snatched her hand away. 'Leave it.' She sounded adolescent, even to herself. 'Let me get this to Mouton.' She marched over to the hospital's forensic pathology entrance.

The rotund security guard at the entrance beamed at her.

'You don't need to sign in if you're with Captain Faizal,' he said.

'He's responsible for you.'

'That'll be a first.' Clare could not help herself.

'The doc's waiting for you, Captain. In the morgue.' The guard waved Riedwaan and Clare towards the lift.

'All I need,' muttered Clare, standing aside as a group of chattering students rushed past. She followed Riedwaan down the corridor. He opened the last door, revealing Dr Piet Mouton bending over his large stomach, his hands careful as he worked on the yielding body laid out in front of him.

'Sorry about this.' Mouton spoke without looking up. 'I'm almost done. Move my tape recorder a bit closer, Faizal man.'

Riedwaan pushed the trolley with Mouton's notes and small black recorder closer to the gurney. Clare made herself look at the naked body on the slab – an elderly woman, ribs pulled open.

Mouton lifted the heart and laid it in a dish. 'Car crashes. I hate them,' he said. 'Make an Irish stew out of anybody, the way people drive. BMW jumped a barrier on the N1. Speedometer at 190 when it jammed.'

Whatever it was Mouton was doing made a horrible sound. Clare looked up at the vaulted windows, light-headed. 'She was driving?' she asked.

'You must be joking. She was just on her way to see her grandchildren. The fucker in the BM is fine, just worrying about his insurance and trying to stall a blood alcohol test. You know what it stands for, Faizal? BMW?'

Riedwaan shook his head.

'*Bankrot Maar Windgat*,' said Mouton in disgust. 'So, Dr Hart.' He had always refused to call her Clare. 'Post-mortems are not a spectator sport yet. I presume you want something?'

'Riedwaan told you?' Clare had moved to the window. The sun streaming in did nothing to counter the air conditioning, but she was glad of it; the cold stifled the smell of chemicals and bodily wastes.

'He did.' Mouton went to rinse his hands. He pulled off his gown, releasing his belly from his tight scrubs. 'I don't know who they make these things for. Midgets, I suppose,' he muttered. 'So this Namibian serial killer. You had another victim?'

'Same thing,' said Clare. 'Single gunshot to the forehead, body displayed where it would be found. Outside again, and some time after death. No scavenger marks, so someone was keeping him somewhere.'

Mouton ushered them out of the mortuary and into his adjoining office. He opened a cake tin and offered them each a slice of succulent apple cake. Riedwaan accepted but Clare refused.

She took a sip of the tea that Mouton passed her. It was lukewarm and tasted as if it had been brewing since lunch. She put her cup down.

'We wanted you to look at these.' Clare handed him the four autopsy reports. 'In all the cases there's been a delay between the death and finding the body. I want to find out where they were kept before being displayed.'

'You got a keeper?' Mouton looked up from the reports.

'Seems like it,' said Clare. 'It would help me if I could work out where he was keeping these boys and why. What he was doing with them before he shoots them. And why he waits afterwards.'

'Gunshot wounds. Desert corpse. Mutilation. It's like Namibia when it was still South West Africa, South Africa's Wild West,' said Mouton. 'I'll take a look.'

Riedwaan drove fast, rejoining the cars speeding towards Cape Town. The vivid red sky set off the mass of Table Mountain and Devil's Peak to perfection. Clare felt a pang for the simplicity of the Namibian landscape, composed of horizontals: sea, sand, sky. The Sea Point Boulevard seemed too crowded, the rough swell too boisterous. She wouldn't really feel at home until she had finished her business in Walvis Bay. With Riedwaan, a mountain of unspoken unfinished business lay between them in addition to the silence that had filled the car on the drive back to her apartment.

'Rita asked me to give you these,' said Riedwaan. Clare took the keys he held out. She got out of the car and picked up her scattered belongings from the back seat.

'Give me that,' said Riedwaan, pointing to Clare's evidence box for ballistics. 'I'll drop it with Shorty de Lange. He said he'd look at it for you.' Riedwaan took it from her, his hand brushing against hers. 'You look exhausted.'

'I'm finished,' Clare confessed, before disappearing up the stairs. She picked up an ecstatic Fritz at the door and stopped herself from turning around to watch Riedwaan drive away.

Inside, she ran herself a bath and lay in it, letting the hot water soothe her. She listened to the waves beating against the boulevard, drowning the sound of the evening traffic and the noise in her own head. Her thoughts drifted to Mouton and his plump hands conjuring the secrets from the dead. 'A keeper' he had called this killer.

'Finders were keepers. And losers were weepers,' she said to herself as she towelled her body. She didn't aim to be one of those.

Clare took her supper onto her balcony and watched the filling moon rise up over Devil's Peak, but she didn't see it. Instead, she saw red sand bleeding to ash in the moonlight. The lights of a plane flying over the city transformed, in her mind's eye, into a vehicle, headlights dipping as it summitted her imaginary dunes. The lights vanished, and Clare imagined distant doors opening, slamming shut. A hand on a boy's skinny nape. Comforting in the emptiness. The fingers tightening. The food in his belly a nauseating lump. No struggle in the end.

She put her half-eaten meal aside and went through to her study. From the top of the bookshelf, she pulled down a couple of files with articles on profiling. She flicked through them, reading again about the progression of sadistic complexity that was, in Clare's mind, the hallmark of organised serial killers: the repeated attempts to recreate a fantasy, the perfect blueprint of which existed only in the mind of the killer. The fantasy behind these desert killings, so organised, so similar in outward appearance, had something cursory, something improvised about it which irked. The symmetry of the killings, the trophy-taking, the mutilation of the chest were textbook signs of a copycat killer. But her thoughts chased their own tails, so when the phone rang at nine she pounced on it. It was Mouton.

'What you got, Piet?' she asked.

Mouton got straight to the point. 'Helena Kotze did a good job on Lazarus Beukes and Apollis. The other two are a first-class bugger-up. Looks like they were done by some idiot who wouldn't be able to dissect a frog.'

'I'm not going to contradict that,' Clare said with feeling. 'Can you tell me anything about where they were kept?'

'If they were shot out in the desert?' asked Mouton.

'That's what I'm assuming,' Clare said.

'Then I'd say these boys were kept inside, somewhere where the temperature was even. I checked on the weather,' said Mouton. 'There were some pretty hot inland temperatures around when these boys were missing. Some isolated showers too.'

'That'd explain the termites,' interrupted Clare. 'Sorry, Piet, go on, I was just thinking aloud.'

'You think away, Dr Hart,' continued Mouton. 'Now, if they'd been outside, and someone had been there to keep the predators off them, they would've burnt in that sun.'

'So where should I look?' said Clare.

'A well-insulated house – definitely not one of those tin pondoks. Possibly a deep cave. Somewhere where the temperature would've been constant.'

'That's it?'

'That's it,' he said. 'I hope it helps.'

Clare put down the receiver and walked to the kitchen in a daze. She made tea and took it into the lounge. She put on a CD. She had missed Moby while she was away. 'Where were they?' Clare asked Fritz.

But the cat just purred and curled up like a comma against her back. Clare spread out the photographs of the four bodies and shattered skulls on the coffee table. She stood up, spilling the cat to the floor, and fetched her phone. 'I need to discuss the case with Riedwaan,' she told her baleful cat as she dialled, believing herself.

'Faizal.'

Her heart gave a leap when she heard his voice. 'It's Clare.'

'I know it's you.' Riedwaan was guarded.

'I needed to talk to you … about the case,' said Clare, watching the sea tumble against the rocks beyond the boulevard.

Riedwaan waited. In the distance, the foghorn wailed into the night. 'Are those the terms? For us to have a conversation?' he asked.

'Mouton called,' said Clare. 'There's a lot to discuss.'

'You're telling me? I'll be there when I can,' he said. 'On your terms.'

thirty-two

Clare loosened her hair and leant back on the sofa, drifting with the haunting music that filled the room. The sea, moving with repetitive restlessness beyond the grey rocks, lulled her and she gave up trying to archive the fragmented information she had gleaned. Instead, she gave herself over to the pleasure of being at home, cocooned in the textures and views she had chosen. She picked up a celebrity gossip magazine that Rita must have left behind. Five pages of the antics of footballers' wives and she was asleep, her hair tumbling over one outstretched arm.

The hand under Clare's shirt caressed her bare skin. She arched towards it instinctively, fitting her breast into the familiar palm, a tiny involuntary gasp parting her lips as forefinger and thumb teased her sleepy nipple to a rosy peak. She breathed in the familiar smell: the tang of cigarette smoke, cold night air, biker's leather. The low laugh pulled her awake and she brought her knee up hard, the groan telling her she was satisfyingly on target. Clare opened her eyes to see Riedwaan leaning over her. She pushed herself upright, straightening her clothes and pinning up her hair. Riedwaan sat down beside her, keeping a wary eye on Fritz, who had leapt to a belated but impressive defence of her mistress.

'That was a nice welcome,' he grinned. 'The first bit.'

'How did you get in?' Clare was wide awake now. She sat on the edge of the couch and decided to ignore the self-satisfied smile playing in the corners of Riedwaan's eyes.

'Spare key.' Riedwaan dropped it on the table.

'You copied one?' Clare's skin was fiery where Riedwaan's hand had been. 'You broke in.'

'You could look at it like that, I suppose.'

'What do you mean, you could look at it like that?' she snapped. But she was pleased to see him and he knew it.

'I've brought you a peace offering.'

'What?'

'Coffee and a message from Shorty de Lange,' said Riedwaan. 'He says he's got some news for you.'

'I accept,' she said, holding out her hand for the steaming espresso.

'On one condition.' Riedwaan held the coffee just out of her reach.

'This is like the Gaza Strip,' said Clare. 'First an invasion, then unilateral conditions.'

'It's felt a bit like Gaza to me recently.' Riedwaan ran his fingers along the inside of her arm. 'But the strip sounds good.'

'What's the condition?' asked Clare, folding her arms.

'You stop being so angry with me,' said Riedwaan.

Clare considered, her head on one side. 'Okay,' she capitulated. 'It's late and I'm tired. Give me the coffee and I'll consider an armed truce.'

Riedwaan put the coffee down and pulled her towards him. 'No haggling?'

'I thought you said ballistics had something for me,' said Clare, disentangling herself. 'That was part of the deal.'

'Shorty wants to meet,' said Riedwaan, letting go reluctantly.

'What? Now?' Clare looked at her watch. It was close to eleven.

'Yup. He's waiting.'

The flag above the khaki-green shipping container that served as Cape Town's Ballistic Unit testing range was at half-mast, indicating that the unit was in use. From inside came the muffled thud of bullets. It had to be De Lange. At eleven o'clock, his was the only car left in the parking lot. Riedwaan lit a cigarette and waited. When there was an interval, he banged on the door.

'You still trying to kill yourself, Faizal?' At six foot six, Shorty de Lange looked like a Viking. He pushed open the door, releasing the smell of cordite into the cold night air.

'Sounded like Baghdad in there,' said Riedwaan, grinding his cigarette under his heel.

'Taxis,' said De Lange, 'are worse when they get going. I tell you, they're cooking now. Three shootouts today. Two commuters dead, a little kid shot walking to school. Two drivers. It's a fucking war.' He tucked the AK-47 he had been testing under his arm so that he could lock up.

Clare got out of the car as Riedwaan and De Lange walked over to the low buildings that housed De Lange's office.

'Hi, Shorty,' she said, joining them.

'Clare,' he said, a delighted smile on his face. 'A sight for sore eyes, as always. What a pleasure to see you. You need an Irish coffee?'

'I'd love one.'

De Lange ducked into his office, then took them through to the bar. One wall was covered with pictures of his rugby-playing days. He looked around. 'No kettle,' he said. 'You'll have to settle for whisky.'

'Suits me,' said Riedwaan.

'You pour then, Faizal. One for me too. Here you go, Clare.' De Lange tossed a folder onto the bar counter. He looked pleased with himself.

Clare flicked open the report, excitement flooding through her. She smoothed out the crisp pages. Nobody would accuse De Lange of being talkative, but his pictures were. There were two images of the striations on a bullet. They would match if you overlaid the one with the other in the same way as a fingerprint would. The concentric patterns were the unique print of the gun from which they had been fired.

'Where did you get this?' she asked.

'There's more.' De Lange unrolled a long sheet of white paper. The image spread out on the table was an explosion of colourful lines, branching off from clusters of dates and place names.

'What is this?' asked Clare. 'A family tree?'

'It is, in a way,' said De Lange. 'Although a tree of death would be a better way of describing it. I told you I've been working on the gang wars. I started mapping them to see if I could link specific firearms to different crime scenes. This one was done during an upsurge of fighting about drug turf and taxi routes. I fed your bullets from Walvis Bay into our computer system, and, bang, this is what came up.' He pointed to a small gold star on a branch that ended in a cul-de-sac.

'All on its own?' Clare leaned in to decipher De Lange's writing. 'In McGregor? Who was it?'

'I don't usually ask,' said De Lange. 'If I start with a name, then next thing I've got a wife and kids crying and then objectivity is in its moer.' He pushed the docket towards Clare. 'I pulled this for you, though. Ex-army. A Major Hofmeyr found in a vineyard off the main road into McGregor a few years ago. His car was left at the farm entrance, and two little girls found him at midday. He'd been dead for a few hours already. According to the pathologist he was shot at about seven in the morning.'

Clare paged through the thin report. There wasn't much to go on. Major Hofmeyr was survived by his wife and daughter, but there were very few details for such a gruesome killing. 'No evidence?' Clare looked up at De Lange.

'No tracks, no witnesses. Nothing.'

199

'Nothing except a bullet embedded in the tree where Hofmeyr's body was found,' Riedwaan pointed out.

'The police speculated a gang killing, maybe an initiation,' said De Lange. 'He was tortured. His skin was carved up, all over. It hung in ribbons, looked like broekie lace.'

Clare turned to the crime-scene photographs. A man's body was slumped against the tree, blood and flies crusting the shattered forehead and lacerated chest. 'Hofmeyr must've welcomed the final shot when it came,' she said, looking at the skin hanging from his fit soldier's body.

'Could've been a hired gun,' Riedwaan said to De Lange. 'What does it cost now, a weekend special on the Flats? Fifty bucks to hire, ammo thrown in?'

'Pretty much,' said De Lange. 'But how did it get to Walvis Bay?'

'A gun like that could easily make its way up the West Coast,' said Riedwaan. 'The border is as porous as a sieve, so it could be in Walvis Bay in a couple of days.'

'I've thought of it,' said De Lange. 'But I've never seen this before or since. It bothered me, this one. That's why I kept a copy of the docket.'

'What bothered you?' asked Clare.

'Same thing that bothered Februarie, the officer who investigated the case. The ammunition,' said De Lange. 'Full metal jacket. That's professional. It's what the security industry uses, the military. Not drug lowlife.'

'We'll check it out tomorrow,' said Clare. 'Talk to his wife. Is she still in McGregor?'

De Lange nodded. It seemed he knew more about surviving relatives than he cared to admit. 'Keep those then,' he said, pouring himself another whisky. 'You go ahead. I've got some things to finish.'

It was nearly one o'clock before Clare and Riedwaan were back on the empty highway. 'Does he ever go home?' Clare asked.

'No,' Riedwaan replied. 'He's looking for the gun that killed her.'

The whole force knew that the murder of De Lange's wife had nearly killed him too. She'd been shot in a botched hijacking over a year ago. 'He's convinced that once he gets *that* gun,' said Riedwaan, 'then he's got the tik-head who killed her, and his life will be what it was before. In the meantime, he's trying to keep track of every stray bullet in the Cape.'

'Which works for us,' said Clare, looking out at the cityscape. Compared to the desert sky the few visible stars were faint, eclipsed by the carpet of streetlights and the flashing neon signs.

'We'll see.' Riedwaan parked in front of Clare's apartment.

His hand on the back of her neck stopped her from opening the car door. He turned to look at her, his face faceted by the orange glow of the street lamp. He brushed his thumb across her full bottom lip, silencing her protest.

'I missed you,' he said, moving his hand down her neck, seeking out the hollow at the base of her throat, down further, his hands on her breasts, knowing, peaking her nipples beneath his palms. Clare closed her eyes. Riedwaan's skin was warm against hers as he kissed eyes, ears, mouth, tunnelling desire through her. She put her hands on his chest, felt his breath coming sharper, faster. Gathering what was left of her will, she pushed him away.

'I can't do this.' Clare yanked the door open and got out. She stood on the pavement, her arms folded across her chest.

Riedwaan looked straight ahead at the Atlantic hurling itself at the rocks.

'You're coming to McGregor tomorrow?' she asked. She was starting to shiver.

'I'll pick you up at six.' Riedwaan started the car. Still Clare stood on the pavement. 'Go in,' he said. 'I can't leave till you're inside.'

'I ...' Clare started.

'You what?'

'I ... I'll see you later.' She disappeared up the staircase.

When her bedroom light came on, Riedwaan drove home. He let himself in to his empty house and sat down in his only chair. He couldn't decide which maudlin cliché suited him better: Leonard Cohen or Tom Waits. So he sat and smoked until the dawn call to prayer crackled from the mosque down the road.

thirty-three

Clare was ready and waiting when Riedwaan fetched her at five-thirty. Dressed in a black poloneck, black trousers, her hair tamed, lipstick in place, she had the carapace of her professional self firmly back in place.

Riedwaan took the N1 through the dilapidated fringes of Cape Town towards the forbidding mountains that were the gateway to the interior. McGregor was eighty kilometres beyond them. The sun was up, stirring the hamlet awake, when they reached it. Smoke wisped from the crowded houses on the eastern edge of town. Higher up the hill, larger houses were spread out around a sturdy white church. A few children in sports uniforms were chattering their way to school along the main road.

'Voortrekker Road.' Riedwaan read the sign in disbelief. 'This is like a movie set. No burglar bars. No armed response. How do they sleep?'

'I'm with you. You'll survive,' said Clare. 'Lie your urban hackles down.'

'I don't like it.' Riedwaan tapped his fingers as he waited for an old lady to coax her moth-eaten terrier across the road. 'It's like the whole place is waiting for something to happen.'

'Something did happen. Why else would we be here?'

'Connecting things will be tricky,' said Riedwaan. 'If there is a connection.'

'It's worth a shot, so to speak,' said Clare. 'Mill Street. Turn here.'

Goedgevonden was the last house. A low, dry-packed wall kept the flinty Karoo scrub out of the lush garden. They hadn't called. Clare and Riedwaan preferred to see people without warning, before the battlements of the self could be checked for a breach.

'That's a welcome mat, not a dog,' said Riedwaan, ringing the bicycle bell on the gate as a German Shepherd ambled over to the gate and whined. A woman straightened up from her rose bed behind the wall.

'Mrs Hofmeyr?' asked Riedwaan.

The woman who approached, secateurs glinting in her hand, was maybe fifty-five, her iron-grey bun severe. She looked at Clare, took Riedwaan in.

'Can I help you?'

The dog was at its mistress's side with a single click of her fingers, its eyes wary. Not such a doormat after all.

'I'm Riedwaan Faizal, SAPS special investigations. This is Dr Clare Hart. It's about your husband Captain Hofmeyr.'

Mrs Hofmeyr squinted into the sun. 'Have you got new evidence?' she asked.

'Not exactly,' Riedwaan replied. 'But we need to speak to you to find out.'

'If you've driven from Cape Town, I'm sure you'll need some coffee. Come into the kitchen. We can talk more privately there.'

They followed her inside and sat down at a scrubbed yellow-wood table. The coffee pot hissed on the stove. *Moerkoffie*. Mrs Hofmeyr slipped a doily off the milk jug. Its little fringe of glass beads clicked in the silence, disturbing the cat coiled asleep on a blue cushion. The animal took one look at Riedwaan and arched its back and hissed.

'What is it with me and cats?' Riedwaan muttered.

'Rasputin isn't used to visitors,' said Mrs Hofmeyr, stroking the cat's gun-metal coat.

'We need to ask you some questions about Captain Hofmeyr's

death,' said Clare. Murder was too brutal a word for the ordered domesticity of the room.

'Major Hofmeyr,' corrected his widow. 'Why do you want to stir it up again?'

'I'm very sorry,' said Clare, 'but we suspect that the weapon used to shoot your husband has been used in another crime.'

'How awful,' whispered Mrs Hofmeyr, bringing her hand to her mouth. 'Near here?'

'In Namibia,' said Riedwaan. 'Walvis Bay.'

Mrs Hofmeyr frowned. 'What happened?'

'Four shootings,' said Riedwaan. 'It'd be a great help if you could tell us what happened to your husband.'

'I've already told everything to the police, but all right. He was shot in the head. Close range, single pistol shot. I identified him.' Mrs Hofmeyr trembled, but there were no tears. She had used up her quota long ago. 'He looked so young again when I saw him. All those years gone. A life erased.'

'What time did he leave the house?' asked Clare.

'Early. Before seven, I'd say. I was asleep when he left. When I woke at seven-thirty the tea he had left for me was ice cold.' She twisted her cup in its saucer. 'Who would want to torture him?'

Riedwaan could think of quite a few people who might want to leave a trellis of knife wounds on a man who had commanded a special operations unit during the dirtiest years of South Africa's war in Namibia. Hearts and minds. You could say that Hofmeyr's killer got both. He didn't say that.

'One of the officers here said it was gangsters,' said Mrs Hofmeyr. 'People in the village said some 28s had been here.'

The number gangs. South Africa's apocryphal grim reapers, trailing fear and destruction in their wake. Sliding like a knife through the soft underbelly of a country where all felt their houses to be chalked with crosses, where the vultures of fear circled above the living. The perfect slipstream for another kind of killer, well dressed, without tinted windows, to follow. He would have been smoke against a heat-whitened sky, invisible until the roar of the flames was too close. If he existed.

'They never traced them?' asked Riedwaan.

'No,' said Mrs Hofmeyr, acidly. 'How often do the police find anyone?'

Riedwaan shifted in his chair. He had no answer for that.

'What did he do, Major Hofmeyr, with his time?' Clare changed tack. 'After the army?'

'Rugby-coaching at the school. He'd started teaching science too. He was a physicist. The army was good to ambitious Afrikaners born on the wrong side of the tracks. Teaching science was his way of saying sorry for what happened' – she hesitated – 'for what happened before.'

'He see anyone from his army days?'

'Not really. He was a loner. After Bishop Tutu's thing, the dust settled and we didn't see anyone much. I suppose they didn't need each other any more, didn't need to check up on who was going to say what. Sometimes his old army friends would come through, drink a bit, hunt a bit in season, but other than that the past just went away. We were quiet here. I liked it like that.' She twisted the obsolete wedding ring on her left hand.

'I'm sorry to bring up the past,' said Clare.

Mrs Hofmeyr shook her head. 'Where does it start? That's what I never know about the past. Kobus was a soldier. The army was his life and 1994 was the end of it. Is that the beginning or the end of the past?'

'That's why you came to McGregor?' Clare asked.

'I don't think my husband cared where he went. He just came here to wait until his heart stopped beating.'

'Depression?'

Mrs Hofmeyr batted the word away with a dismissive hand. 'Psychological labels. Human beings aren't bottles of jam. Depressed, obsessive compulsive, paranoid. Giving it a name doesn't make it feel any different.'

'He came out of it?' Clare guessed.

Mrs Hofmeyr looked up at her, surprised. 'He did. Slowly. Despite himself. It helped that our daughter came to visit with her baby from Australia. The first time they had spoken in fifteen years, but not even he could fight with a baby. It was as if some knot inside him loosened, released the man I had married. I don't know. He kept on worrying about the world, about terrorists and bombs, and about what could happen to his *skattebol*.'

'What was he like, your husband?' asked Clare.

Mrs Hofmeyr sighed as she cleared away the coffee cups. 'If you want a sense of my husband, go and look at his den.' She opened the kitchen door and gestured down the passageway. 'I suppose you could say that is what his world shrunk to.'

Apart from the kitchen, the house was dim. The shutters were closed, the curtains drawn. It had the stillness of a museum. Clare opened a door off the passage. A masculine seclusion, free of ornaments. It was irresistible. She stepped inside. The desk was clean, the letter opener and pen standing in quartz holders. A perfect desert rose on an ugly little plinth held down a pile of till slips. Clare checked the dates. All from a few days before Hofmeyr was killed: bottle store, DIY, cigarettes and a paper from the café. Next to the desk was a hollowed-out elephant's foot. A trophy hunt. Caprivi, Kaokoland, Angola. Clare wondered where the helicopters had hovered, machine-gun bullets studding into the fleeing animals below. She pictured the elephant cows herding their panic-stricken young towards the tree line. One sinking to her knees as her calf nudged her with his forehead, then retreated and watched as the men, laughing, hopped down to hack off the cow's foot as the last light in her wise eyes was extinguished. Then again, the murdered man could just as easily have bought it in a junk shop and brought it home for a laugh.

One wall was covered with photographs. Clare went to look at them. A 1960s wedding picture. Later, Mrs Hofmeyr in a halter-neck top, a baby in her arms. Then another baby, the first child now a thoughtful little boy bracketed around his mother's slim legs. Another photo showed a sturdy young woman on a speedboat, a greying Major Hofmeyr grinned next to her.

'My daughter,' said Mrs Hofmeyr, coming to stand next to Clare. 'She moved to Australia.'

'They seem happy here,' said Clare.

'They were,' Mrs Hofmeyr replied. 'Eventually.'

Clare guessed that politics would have come between them. A father with a decorated career in the defence force of the apartheid years did not go down well in the new South Africa.

Mrs Hofmeyr trailed a finger across a picture of her husband saluting troops on a dusty parade ground. The undulating sweep of sand was unmistakable. Strange, though, to see the vast plain covered with tents. They seemed to stretch from horizon to horizon, a regatta of triangular khaki sails on a sea of sand.

'Walvis Bay?' asked Clare.

'Where else? It looks so different now,' said Mrs Hofmeyr.

'How long were you there for?'

'You want me to give you the hours and seconds? The heart-beats?' Her bitterness flared, a naked flame. 'We were there from 1989 to 1994. Five years, three months and eleven days. Before that at the weapons testing site in Vastrap in the Northern Cape. God knows what we were supposed to do there in the middle of the Kalahari Desert. No people. No trees. Nothing but heat and dust and secrets. Not a place to go if you had a family.'

The large photograph hanging behind the door caught Clare's attention. She stopped, arrested by the photograph of Major Hofmeyr. Lithe and brown, his eyes the blue of the sky above the dune rising in a majestic sweep behind him. Three soldiers, equally confident, were draped over a dusty Bedford. The man next to Hofmeyr, his swagger evident in his muscular, khaki-clad legs, had a hard face. The third one was as thin as a whip, his expression shadowed by his cap.

'That was Kobus's unit.' Mrs Hofmeyr pointed to the date on the bottom. 'It was taken when they were disbanding. This was the last picture of all of them before they returned.'

'They came back then?'

'Kobus and a couple of officers wrapped up the last things, then came back. The troops returned by truck and on the train.'

'You know them? The others?' Riedwaan asked.

Mrs Hofmeyr shook her head. 'Kobus kept us separate, me and his life.' She stood closer to the photograph. 'I can't remember their names.' She pointed to the shadowed figure. 'He came to the house sometimes near the end. He and Kobus would talk. He never said anything to me. This one' – she pointed at the man next to Hofmeyr – 'had such a young wife. She was a dancer before she married.' She frowned at the tug of memory. 'Maylene or Marlene was her name. Something unusual.'

Clare pictured a house on the edge of the dunes. A bracelet of bruises. 'Not Darlene?' she asked.

'That was it: Darlene. Her husband stamped on her ankle at a party. He said she'd been flirting. She never danced again.'

Darlene walking down a dim, polished passage. The awkward gait. A surname jettisoned to mark the end of a marriage. 'She's still there,' said Clare.

'In Walvis Bay?' Mrs Hofmeyr was appalled. 'I suppose it was the only way she could escape her husband.'

'You never went back?' asked Riedwaan.

'Never. Neither did my husband. There was nothing left for him there. Or the others. They all got sent home to garden and become security guards in the new South Africa.' She stood transfixed by the picture as if it were a cobra weaving in front of her. 'He said it was better to leave things in the past, where they belonged. Walvis Bay was the place where all his dreams died. Fool's gold is what he called the past.' Mrs Hofmeyr tapped the photograph of her husband standing in a typical soldier's pose, unfiltered cigarette in his hand. 'A fool,' she said. 'They were all fools.'

'Did your husband keep any kind of record of his time there?' asked Riedwaan.

'Never. He kept everything in his head. Habit from working with classified stuff. He was proud of the fact that he remembered everything even though he wrote nothing down.'

They stood looking at the fading photographs. Deep within the house, a clock chimed ten.

'There's nothing else,' said Mrs Hofmeyr, 'is there?'

'He never fought back.' Clare broke the silence of the journey. They had travelled from McGregor to the outskirts of Cape Town without saying a word.

'Hofmeyr?' Riedwaan's thoughts had been elsewhere.

'There were no injuries. No defensive injuries. You think he wanted to die? Just gave up?'

'It's possible he felt certain he was going to die and decided just to go with it, without the ritual of begging and pleading and trying to run away,' Riedwaan suggested. 'Or he knew his killer and he'd reached the end of a road that only the two of them knew about. The war in Namibia was a dirty one, and most of the dirt was brushed under the carpet.'

'That's not much help, is it?' Clare played with the new puzzle pieces Mrs Hofmeyr had given her. 'I guess we should talk to Darlene Ruyters again. Find out about her ex-husband.' There were links, but no perfect fits. 'She's not very forthcoming, though. If she knows something, I doubt she'll talk.'

'Let's go and talk to the investigating officer, if he's sober enough.'

'You know him?'

'Eberard Februarie. Old connection,' said Riedwaan, taking the Stellenbosch turn-off. 'I probably owe him a drink anyway.'

thirty-four

The Stellenbosch police station was quiet when Clare and Riedwaan arrived. Clare waited in the car while Riedwaan went inside to extricate the officer who had worked on the Hofmeyr case.

'Where's Captain Februarie?' he asked a bored-looking constable in the tea room. Talking to Eberard Februarie always cheered him up. No one had hit rock bottom at quite the same speed as the former narcotics unit captain.

'Out.' The woman ate another biscuit.

'Out where, Constable?' said Riedwaan, patiently.

'Are you a cop?' She looked him up and down.

'I suppose you think I dress this badly for fun?' said Riedwaan. The constable looked at him blankly. 'Of course I'm a cop. Captain Faizal.'

'Captain Februarie's investigating a case.'

'Which case?'

'He didn't write it on the board.' It was true. Everybody else had a neatly printed note next to their names on the whiteboard. Everybody except Februarie, that is.

'Can I have his cell number?'

'Sure.' The constable flipped through a grimy file. It was the wrong file. She found the right file. Found the right page. Found the number. Found a pencil. Found a piece of paper. Wrote it down. When she looked up to give it to Riedwaan, he was gone. She shrugged and went back to her tea.

Riedwaan and Clare were already three blocks away. The chances of Februarie not being at the Royal Hotel on a Saturday morning were minimal. Riedwaan pushed open the saloon doors, letting Clare precede him. It was dim inside the bar. The smell of last night's drinking hung on the air. There was only one cigarette going: Februarie's. He was sitting in the corner, a Castle lager in front of him.

Riedwaan sat down on the stool next to him. 'Breakfast?' he asked.

'Faizal, you fucker. What are you doing here?'

'Come to see you. You're looking good.' It was not quite true. But Riedwaan had seen him look much worse at this time of day.

'I'm cutting back, man. This is my first.'

'Why don't you just stop?' asked Riedwaan.

'Not good to rush things,' said Februarie. 'You can shock your system. That's not healthy.'

'This is Clare Hart,' said Riedwaan, his hand on Clare's elbow.

'Hello,' said Clare.

Februarie looked her over, taking in her slim figure, the determined set to her jaw. 'The head-case doctor. I've heard about you,' he grunted. 'I didn't know they only let you out under guard these days, Faizal.'

'As charming as ever,' Riedwaan retorted. He ordered a Coke for himself and a soda for Clare and waited for the barman to leave. 'The constable said you were working on a case.'

'Of course I'm working on a case. I'm always working on a case. Someone's bicycle will be stolen any minute, then I'll have another case. You?'

'No, I'm working too.'

'You're lucky they left you in town, man. This exile story is terrible. It'll kill you quicker than cigarettes.'

Riedwaan took the hint and offered him one. Februarie took two.

'You want something, Faizal? Or is this just a social call?'

'We wanted to ask you about a case.'

'So, ask.' Februarie inhaled deeply, then coughed.

'You sound like you're going to die, Februarie.'

'I told you, it's being out here in the countryside. It's unhealthy.'

'Tell us about that shooting in McGregor,' said Clare.

'The army major? Hofmeyr?' Februarie asked. He shifted his eyes from Riedwaan to Clare. Sharp. Calculating. In spite of the drink. 'Why you asking?'

'I'm on a case in Namibia. Looks like a serial killer,' said Clare. 'But the bullet found in the head of one of the boys threw up a match with Hofmeyr.'

'Shorty de Lange tell you that?' Februarie guessed.

'He did,' said Riedwaan.

'All I know is they pulled that case from me quicker than a virgin crosses her legs.' Februarie drained his glass.

'You think it was a gang hit?' Clare asked.

'Nah,' said Februarie. 'Andrew,' he called the barman over. 'Pour me another beer; you're not pretty enough to be useful just standing around.' He turned to Riedwaan again. 'I thought it was something else. They tortured him first. It looked professional to me, not the usual mess a tik-head leaves. Whoever did it wanted something specific.'

'Have you got any idea what?' asked Riedwaan.

Februarie shrugged. 'He was in the army. Old regime. Special ops. He probably knew stuff. They all did, those fuckers. The list of people who want them dead is longer than the list that wants them alive.'

'What did he know?'

'I'm speculating. The case was pulled, I told you. Some desk jockey said they were shifting it higher. Giving it priority.'

'What happened?'

'Don't fuck with me, Faizal. You know what happens when that happens. The case dies.'

Februarie drank his beer. Riedwaan drank his Coke. Clare watched them.

'There was one thing,' Februarie said at last.

'I thought there might be,' said Riedwaan. 'You follow it up?'

'Of course I did.' Februarie was affronted. 'That's when the case was kicked upstairs and I got stolen-bicycle duty.'

'Sorry.' Riedwaan put down enough money to cover the drinks. 'What was it?'

'They were army,' Februarie continued. 'The killers.'

'How do you know?' asked Clare.

'The way he was tortured. They used to do that in Namibia. To insurgents, if they caught them. To civilians, if they were bored.'

Riedwaan was quiet.

'So watch your back in Walvis Bay,' muttered Februarie.

'That's touching,' said Riedwaan. 'You find out anything else?'

'After I got taken off the case?'

'Ja.'

'Sommer for the cause of justice?' said Februarie.

'Something like that.'

'Do I look like I have a death wish? My life might look like a fuck-up, but it's the only one I've got.'

Riedwaan waited. He and Februarie went back a long way and he had learnt to read the man's silences. The barman went to the other end of the counter to serve a new customer.

'I've got an old friend,' said Februarie. 'She did a search for me. Nothing on Hofmeyr. Fuck-all in any army record, old or new.' He looked up at Riedwaan. 'Funny that, for a decorated major, wouldn't you say?'

'Hilarious,' said Riedwaan.

215

'His unit's there on the record,' said Februarie. 'But no Major Hofmeyr. No fellow officers either, those ones you'll find in the picture in his study. Erased, all of them.'

'So you gave up?'

'Nearly,' said Februarie, finishing his beer.

'Then I found a footnote in one of those truth and reconciliation cases that went nowhere. Some secret weapons-testing site up north.'

'Yes?' said Riedwaan.

'There was a reference to this covert unit in Walvis Bay. There was a Hofmeyr there. A major. He and a couple of friends were implicated. The whole thing folded, so nothing more was heard about Major Hofmeyr.'

'Until he was shot.'

'Exactly,' said Februarie. 'Until he was shot.'

'I owe you,' said Riedwaan.

'You want me to check out his friends?' asked Februarie.

'Depends how many bicycles get stolen.'

'Fuck you too, Faizal.' Februarie counted the money Riedwaan had left on the bar and ordered another beer.

The gathering clouds had thickened when Clare and Riedwaan got outside. It was starting to drizzle.

'I'll be in Walvis Bay in a day or two,' Riedwaan said. 'I'll see what I can find out by then.'

Clare checked her watch. 'I hope I'm going to make it to the airport,' she said.

'You *are* going to make it,' said Riedwaan. There had been an accident on the highway. Rubbernecking drivers had slowed the traffic to a crawl. He pulled in to the emergency lane and speeded past, siren blaring.

'I always wondered why you kept that thing,' said Clare,

with a smile.

'You're going to make it,' said Riedwaan, taking the plunge, 'without asking me a single question.'

'I need to think,' said Clare. 'It's not making sense. It could be that the gun used to kill Hofmeyr was sold or stolen. Male victims, there's a match, I suppose, but Hofmeyr was cut up before he was shot.'

'I wasn't thinking about Hofmeyr.'

'I know,' said Clare, 'it's those boys that get me.'

The rain started to come down in earnest, making it difficult to see through the windscreen.

'I was thinking about us,' said Riedwaan.

'Don't start again,' said Clare, holding her hands up. 'This is your thing, your wife here, all that. Why must I take the responsibility for talking about it?'

Riedwaan took the airport turn-off, parking outside the international departure drop-in. He turned to face Clare. 'She never came.'

Clare glanced at her watch again. She had five minutes before check-in closed. 'Why didn't you say anything?'

'I tried to talk to you,' said Riedwaan. 'I've e-mailed you, but you disappear behind work and theories and business.' He stopped, startled at this uncharacteristic burst of articulateness. It was a mistake. Clare opened the car door, slipping her bag over shoulder and the thin Hofmeyr file underarm.

'You know this whole debacle could've been avoided if you'd just said something in the beginning?'

'I know.' Riedwaan's dark eyes flashed with the temper he had been keeping in check. 'And you wouldn't give me an inch. I'm trying to fix things, with Shazia, with my daughter.' Riedwaan got out of the car too. He leant on the roof, his eyes on Clare until she looked away. 'With you too,' he said softly.

'Riedwaan, it's not going to fix, especially not in the five minutes I have before the flight is closed. Just forget it. Let's just get this case done.' Clare was through the automatic doors before Riedwaan could say another word. They closed behind her, leaving him with nothing but his own reflection and a couple of porters shaking their heads in sympathy.

'Women,' said one of them mournfully.

'Women,' agreed Riedwaan.

Five o'clock the next morning and Riedwaan was throwing a couple of pairs of jeans, four clean shirts and underwear into the bike's pannier. He wheeled his bike into the cobbled street. The foghorn wailed as the sea mist stole through the sleeping suburbs fringing the Atlantic. In the distance, the whine of a car or two. Clubbers heading home, Riedwaan's favourite time of day. He fired the bike's engine. Two minutes and he was on the elevated freeway above the harbour, where construction cranes, still as herons at the water's edge, waited for the day's activity to return.

Riedwaan accelerated north where the road ribboned into the clear morning. He had hairpinned up the first mountain pass by the time the sun was up, the roar of the bike lifting his mood.

It was getting hot when he refuelled. Riedwaan checked his map. A hundred or so kilometres to the Namibian border.

An hour later, he was through the border and driving through the emptiness of southern Namibia. Marooned in the desert, a thousand kilometres northwest, was Walvis Bay.

thirty-five

In the cool sanctuary of his laboratory, thirty kilometres north of Walvis Bay, Tertius Myburgh picked up a cloth and wiped down his microscope, though his equipment was immaculate. His prepared solutions waited for him, labelled, ordered. His heart beat faster. It always did before he plunged into the secret world of plants. He set to work on the pathetic bundles Clare Hart had brought. The dead boys' shoes were covered in pollen. Invisible hieroglyphs that mapped the journeys they had made.

He prepared his first slide and placed it on the stage, leaning in to the eyepiece and adjusting the lens to bring the grains of pollen into focus. He exhaled. They floated before him, the cellulose grains that carried the fragile male plants to a waiting female, if there was one. More often, they were stranded on un-receptive surfaces. Like a murdered boy's shoes. Myburgh prepared another slide, then another, and another. He matched the pollen grains against what he already had, checking off the species that flowered in response to the desert's waterless spring.

No *Sarcocornia*. The humble, stubby-fingered plant grew in profusion in the shallow, saline water around the lagoon and in the river mouths along the coast. It occurred for about two kilometres inland. If there was none on the boys' shoes, then it meant that their Calvary was further inland.

Plenty of *Tamarix* pollen. Not surprising, as tamarisks grew in profusion in the Kuiseb. They also grew from Cape Town to Jerusalem. He would need more.

There were traces of *Acanthosicyos horridus*, the seasonal Nara plant that crept from the Orange River in the south over the dunes to the Kuiseb. The spiny melons provided food for the Topnaars, the desert people, and their animals, and the inherited stands were as valuable as the secret sources of water in the desert. Myburgh paused to admire their distinctive pollen walls covered with exquisite striations, which, under his microscope, looked as if someone had drawn meditative fingers through sand.

He found *Trianthema hereroensis* pollen, a tough plant that occurred from the Kuiseb River for about a hundred and fifty kilometres to the north. The overlap of the plant distribution was bang on the Kuiseb Delta.

Myburgh was beginning to see the outline of a map for Clare Hart, but he needed more coordinates. One distinctive, triangular pollen pattern eluded him. There were traces of it on all four pairs of shoes. He checked back through Clare's samples.

Nothing.

He picked up Mannheimer and Dreyer's classic **Plants and Pollens of the World** and flicked through, finding the matching pattern that would help him place the pollen. Fear dry-tonguing his neck, Myburgh propped a ladder against the bookcase so that he could reach the top shelf, which held the stained, cloth-bound book that he had hidden months earlier and tried to forget. He opened Virginia Meyer's blue journal. It was still filled with her detailed drawings, her cramped notes on ethnobotany, gleaned from Spyt, the wary old Topnaar man who had shared what he knew about the plants of the Namib, the desert's secret treasure trove. Myburgh paged through it until he came to the last page of entries. Times, abbreviations, Latin names. He ignored those. Instead, he cracked the book open and swabbed the margin. He wiped what he had collected onto a glass slide. A thin yellow smear appeared down the centre of the pane. He placed this on the microscope's stage, the eyepiece cold against his skin once more. His hands shook as he adjusted the lens. They appeared with magical precision, the distinctive triangular pollen grains, perfect equilateral triangles.

Myrtaceae: Eucalyptus. The ghost gum.

The scientist lifted his head and stared at the surf. He heard again Virginia Meyer's soft voice, telling him of secrets too dirty, conspiracies too complex, which she had unearthed in the heat-raddled desert. He closed his eyes and pressed his palms against his lids, but he failed to block the memory of a car upturned, its wheels spinning against the blue sky.

In the back, the boy Oscar sits in wordless terror. In the front, his mother's life trickles down her face, into her hair, the same colour as the boy's halo of curls. It runs into her unblinking eyes, over her hands and pools on the floor. Eventually, it seeps into the orange sand at the base of a tall alien tree.

Myburgh shook off the memory with an effort and returned to his desk to type up his findings, the routine of recording method, results and conclusions soothing him. He printed the document and put it into a large envelope with the journal. He thought for a long time about what his discovery might mean for pretty Dr Hart; then he locked his laboratory and slipped away, taking care not to be seen.

thirty-six

Clare parked next to Tamar's car when she got to the Walvis Bay police station on Monday morning. She was impatient to be busy after the town's Sunday torpor. The constable at reception greeted her as though she had been gone for weeks. Clare could see a strip of light coming from Tamar Damases's office. She knocked and went inside.

'How was your Cape Town trip?' Tamar asked, after offering Clare a cup of tea.

'Interesting,' said Clare.

'Chinese interesting?' Tamar gave her a sidelong glance.

'Pretty much,' said Clare, with a rueful smile. 'Ballistics tracked that bullet we found in Lazarus Beukes.'

'To the murder in McGregor. Peculiar,' said Tamar. 'I spoke to Captain Faizal.'

'Same gun,' said Clare, 'doesn't make it the same killer. Guns change hands so fast and for so little. How were the interviews about Lazarus?'

'No family, so no one to break the news to,' said Tamar. 'Should have been a relief that, but it made me feel worse. The other kids told me he was in town on Wednesday, doing his usual trick, selling out-of-date newspapers. The little kids who were with him went back to the dump. They don't get a meal if they're late. Lazarus said he'd be along later. He wasn't, but nobody thought much of that. He's older, did his own thing anyway.'

'Did they notice he was missing on Thursday?' asked Clare.

'They did. They were afraid.'

'But nobody said anything?'

'Habits don't change that quickly,' Tamar said. 'They're boys for one, so no telling tales. And second, the police give them a hard time. Particularly some of my own colleagues.' She rose and picked up her jacket. 'I'm going to the school. Mr Erasmus has asked me to talk to the Grade 1s. They all want to know what we did with the body, if we're going to catch the murderer. If they're safe. Would you like to come with me?'

'I'll come,' said Clare, finishing her tea. 'I want to see Darlene Ruyters anyway.'

Tamar picked up her keys and they walked out together. 'You missed Mara Thomson's farewell party, by the way,' she told Clare. 'The school hosted a little ceremony for her.'

'How did it go?'

'Sad, considering the circumstances. I think she felt that everything she'd worked for came to nothing.'

They arrived at the school at the end of first break. Tamar parked under the palm tree as the bell rang. Erasmus came out to welcome them while the older children drifted back to class. He directed them to the section of the school that overlooked the playground where Kaiser Apollis's body had been found. The corridor that housed the youngest children was crowded with satchels and pungent lunchboxes. Solemn-faced six-year-olds dropping glass, paper and tins into recycling bins stared at them as they walked to Darlene Ruyters's classroom. It had a clear view of the playground, the emptied yellow swings slow-moving in the breeze.

Darlene Ruyters sat at her desk, her right arm around a plump, pig-tailed girl. The child spun around when she saw Clare and Tamar at the door. Darlene patted the little girl on her bottom, despatching her back to her seat.

'Good morning, Captain, Doctor.' Darlene extended her slender right hand. The children shuffled to their feet and greeted the two interlopers in a singsong chorus. A wave from Darlene seated them again.

'Finish your seascapes,' she told the class. Small heads bowed over sheets of colourful paper. After a few furtive glances, they were absorbed once more in scissors and glue and bits of glitter. As Tamar discussed what she'd tell the children with Darlene, Clare drifted to the back of the classroom. A series of poster-sized self-portraits were pinned to the wall. Cheery collages with a smiling child, a few blonde, most dark, at the centre of each one. Pictures of parents, siblings, houses ranging from modest to mansion, ice creams, braaied fish – the small, familiar pleasures that made sense of life for a child.

The lone redhead caught Clare's eye. Oscar. He had given himself wild hair out of orange twine. When she turned to look for the original, his green eyes were riveted to her. She smiled at him. He looked down at once, a startling blush creeping up from under his collar.

Clare looked at his portrait again. The images were skeletal, arresting, executed in the colours and form of the rock paintings found in the desert. Oscar's drawings told a story that the other children, who could speak and shout and laugh, did not need to. Clare looked at his picture of a woman with a mass of hair twisted out of fraying yellow wool. The next picture had the same feeling of bell-jarred silence. A man and boy sat side by side; in a second chair, a woman, taut as a wire, watching television. Another drawing with the woman absent, and Oscar plastered to the man's side, his limbs uncurled as if they had been released from invisible ropes. Ordinary scenes made extraordinary because of the sense of menace that pervaded them.

Clare felt Oscar's presence next to her, as she had on the

couple of occasions when he had fallen in step beside her on the boulevard. She looked down, startled to see the contusion on the cheekbone, just below his left eye, and a small, livid tear in the tender skin. Clare put her hand on Oscar's thin shoulder; feeling across his back where there would be more bruises. The child winced.

'What happened?' asked Clare, concerned. Oscar avoided her gaze as he tumbled his hands over each other.

'You fell?' she asked. 'Off your bike?'

He nodded and pointed to the single photograph on the wall. It was fuzzy, printed on cheap paper.

'Mara?' asked Clare, bending closer. The boy nodded.

'You'll miss her now she's gone.' In the photograph Mara Thomson stood exultant on top of a dune, arms and face lifted towards the sun, eyes closed in delight. The shadow of the photographer had splashed against her feet, giving the picture an odd perspective.

Oscar was seated next to her shadowed feet, swathed in a hat and long sleeves.

'You know the desert though, don't you? That's the place you went with your mother, isn't it?'

Oscar nodded, shoulders bowed like an old man.

'Clare?' Tamar and Darlene Ruyters were looking at her. So were the children.

'Sorry,' said Clare. 'I was lost there for a minute.'

Oscar looked down, the thick fringe of auburn eyelashes hiding any expression.

'Mrs Ruyters says the children will want to ask you some questions too,' said Tamar. 'They're always curious about foreigners.'

'Being South African is hardly foreign,' said Clare.

Darlene raised an eyebrow. 'They think Swakopmund is a foreign country and it's only thirty kilometres away.'

'Let them ask, then,' said Clare, smiling.

'Thank you, it'll help them be less …'

'Afraid?' offered Clare.

'I was going to say fascinated.'

Tamar explained that the dead boy had been taken to the morgue. And that they were safe. The half-moon of children sitting at her feet stared at her with wide, solemn eyes. Only the bravest had questions: where would he be buried? Could they go to his funeral? Tamar fielded them with practised empathy. Soon the children had sidled closer and she got them talking about other things.

'This has been a big help,' Darlene said when she had winkled Tamar away from the children and ushered them out of the classroom. 'Thank you.'

'That little redhead,' Clare said.

'Oscar?' said Darlene.

'Yes,' said Clare. 'His face is bruised.'

'Oh, Tamar can tell you, we have such bad cases …' Darlene's voice trailed off. She looked at Tamar for support.

'What do you think?' Clare was thinking that somebody's ring held a trace of the child's blood in its setting.

'I don't know what to think,' said Darlene. 'The children come to school with bruises, but you want to see some of the mothers on a Monday. They bear the brunt of it.' She closed the classroom door behind them. The corridor was cold and quiet after the buzz of the children.

'I met an old friend of yours,' said Clare. 'In McGregor.' Her voice was loud in the empty corridor.

'Oh?' Wary.

'Mrs Hofmeyr,' said Clare, watching Darlene closely. 'She told me why you stopped dancing.'

'I've got to get back to my class.' Darlene cut her short.

226

'It was an army boot on your ankle.'

'So what if it was?' hissed Darlene. 'Since when is it a crime to be beaten?' She put out her hand to open the door. The amethyst bracelet of bruises Clare had seen a few days earlier gleamed citron.

'You've got my number.' Clare placed her index finger on Darlene's wrist.

'I don't need it.' Darlene had her mask-like smile back in place when she stepped back into the classroom. Her voice calling her giggling charges back to order followed Tamar and Clare down the passage.

thirty-seven

It took forever for the lights of Walvis Bay to roll up towards Riedwaan. He had slept over in Solitaire, a half-abandoned hamlet in the southern Namib Desert. The miles are longer on roads where there is nothing to measure distance. The last stretch through the Namib had been bone-shattering. No other vehicles except a donkey cart. Not even telephone poles. He tried phoning Clare, but all he got was an automated voice telling him she was out of range and that he should try later.

'This whole country is out of range.' He said it aloud, just to hear a human voice. Then he dialled Tamar Damases's number.

'Yes?'

'Sorry to call so late,' he said. 'I thought I'd be in before sunset.'

Tamar laughed. 'Did you believe the map? They make things look much closer than they are. You must be finished.'

'I am,' said Riedwaan. 'I need a shower and some sleep before I do anything.'

'You're booked into a guesthouse on the lagoon. It's called Burning Shore Lodge. Don't be deceived by the fancy name, but it's close to the station and to where Clare's staying.'

Riedwaan jotted down the address. The town was quiet, only the pizza place open. He was hungry but too tired to stop. He hoped there would be something for him to eat where he was headed.

The guesthouse was a facebrick nightmare on the lagoon. It seemed to have been designed to avoid the view. Riedwaan rang three times before someone buzzed him in. He pushed his bike into the courtyard.

The only light on was at the bar. Inside, the walls were covered with signed snaps of Hollywood celebrities who had washed up on this barren stretch of coast to make B-grade movies, a couple to give birth to A-list children.

An overweight man took down Riedwaan's details and gave him a key.

'Show him to his room, Rusty,' he said to a morose youth hunched over a beer at the counter.

The boy heaved himself off his stool. He was a replica of his father, down to the tatty white vest and the plain cigarette curling smoke between his fingers.

'This way.' The boy eyed Riedwaan and thought better of offering to take his bags.

The room was clean and, if one ignored the red and black colour scheme, comfortable.

'Thanks.' Riedwaan dumped his bags on the floor. 'Can I get something to eat?'

'Nah,' said the boy. 'We only do breakfast.'

'Jesus, man. I've ridden from Solitaire with nothing to eat. Can't you do me a toasted sandwich or something?'

'Ham?' said Rusty.

'With a name like Faizal? You must be joking,' said Riedwaan.

The boy looked blank.

'Get me cheese or something.'

'Come through to the bar. I'll get it for you. But you explain to my dad.'

'I'll be there in ten minutes.'

Riedwaan opened the curtains. The fog had closed in. He couldn't make out if he was looking at a parking lot or the lagoon. He closed them again and went to shower. The hot water dissolved two days of grime and stiff muscles. He pulled on his jeans and a clean shirt and went through to the bar.

His supper was waiting: toasted white bread and cheese, swimming in butter, no sign of salad. Lots of tomato sauce. Just how he liked it.

'You want a drink to go with that?' said the old man.

'Whisky. No ice,' said Riedwaan.

The man poured him a double. 'Name's Boss,' he said. 'What you doing up here? A holiday?'

'Kind of,' said Riedwaan, his mouth full. 'This is a good sandwich.' He washed it down with the whisky. 'Boss. Is that a nickname?'

'Short for Basson. My surname.' He poured himself a shot and shook a cigarette out of the pack lying on the bar. 'You want one?'

Riedwaan took one and leant forward so his host could light it for him.

'So where you headed?' asked Boss.

'I'm going to be here for a bit. Not sure how long.'

'Where you from?'

'Cape Town.' Food, whisky and a cigarette. Riedwaan felt human again.

'Oh,' said Boss. 'The States.'

It was Riedwaan's turn to look blank. 'The States?'

Rusty rolled his eyes back. 'It's what they used to call South Africa pre-94, when there were all those little fake countries. Transkei, Ciskei. All those independent states. You remember, the whole apartheid thing.'

'Oh that,' Riedwaan said dryly. 'I remember.'

'What line of work are you in?' asked Boss.

'Investigations,' said Riedwaan.

'Insurance?'

'No.' Riedwaan pushed his glass forward for another shot.

'You must be in the police,' said Rusty, a rare flash of

understanding in his eyes. 'Remember, Pop, Captain Damases made the booking?'

They both eyed Riedwaan. Riedwaan stubbed out his cigarette.

'You working up here then?' asked Boss.

'A bit.' Riedwaan did not care to elaborate.

'Those fishing scams?'

'Not really,' said Riedwaan. 'Thanks for supper. I need to sleep.'

'It's those kids they keep finding in the desert, I bet,' said Rusty. Another light-bulb flash. He was going to wear himself out at this rate. 'I think it's a sailor. One of those Russians. They're all faggots. Drinking vodka, living on those ships for so long. What do you say, Pop?'

Boss ignored his son, turning to rinse the glasses in the sink.

'You must know that lady policeman staying at the cottages down the road,' Rusty said excitedly.

'I think I do,' said Riedwaan, getting up.

'She's hot,' said Rusty. 'I've seen her run past here in the mornings. Nice little tits. I bet I could get her to work up a sweat for me.'

Rusty's fingers were in Riedwaan's muscular hand, bent further back than their original specifications should have allowed. Riedwaan's voice was low, intimate in Rusty's ear. 'You go near her and you'll be combing the desert for your balls.'

The boy rubbed his hand. He decided it was best to say nothing.

Riedwaan finished his whisky. 'What time is breakfast?'

'Six-thirty on. You want bacon and eggs?'

'No bacon. Just the eggs. Thanks.'

Riedwaan went back to his room and checked his cellphone. A missed call. Yasmin, his daughter. Damn, he'd forgotten his bi-weekly call. He pulled off his boots and lay on the bed, meaning to phone Clare. Instead, he fell at once into that deep, untroubled sleep that is the gift of innocence or physical exhaustion.

thirty-eight

Four o'clock and Clare was wide awake, her duvet on the floor, a sheet tangled around her bare legs. Her dreams had been horrible: the dead boys winking at her with their bloody third eyes. The laugh of the hyena echoed through her subconscious, mocking her in a language she could not understand. She got up, opened her stoep doors and stepped onto the balcony. The silence pressed in with the fog. Not a sound, not a car. Roosting seabirds rustled their wings, calling softly, occasionally, as if to reassure themselves that they weren't alone in the vast salt marshes. The cold, and the pulse of an idea, drove Clare back inside; if she couldn't sleep, she might as well work.

She dressed quickly, flattening two cups of coffee in quick succession. The sound of her car starting was so loud she was convinced that she had woken the whole town, but nothing stirred. No lights came on.

A sleepy night sergeant waved her through the police station gates. In the special ops room, dim light filtered in from the street, making Clare's pinned-up victims look like a macabre boy band. She flooded the room with neon and sat down at her desk. Opening her notebook, she drew up columns, one for each boy. The first victim with nothing on his chest. Then 2, 3. The missing number 4, and 5, the last one. Five columns, four bodies. Clare wrote down what she knew about them, what she knew about their deaths. Then she wrote down what she didn't know.

She made another column for the killer. Nothing to put there, but a bullet matched to a shooting two thousand kilometres away, and a white vehicle glimpsed in the dark. A predator that slipped through the night, unheard. Utmost secrecy and yet the bodies displayed where it would be impossible to miss them. She looked again at the map of the place where Lazarus had been found. One road in. One road out. Beyond it, tracks of sand unmarked by vehicles; the only tracks left were those of animals. Kaiser Apollis, too. Moved unseen and in silence. How? When she reached for the answer glimmering on the horizon of thought, it slipped away like a mirage on a desert road.

Debit and credit. No matter which way she juggled it, she could not get the books to balance. The truth was hidden below the surface, like the rivers that coursed deep underground. Clare put her head on her arms and closed her eyes to think and promptly fell asleep. Fully clothed, under a flickering neon light, Clare did not dream at all.

It was the smell of fresh coffee that woke her. 'Not like you to sleep on the job.' A voice that should have been in her dreams but wasn't, a gentle hand smoothing the hair from her forehead.

'Riedwaan.' Delight in her voice. She looked a mess; she could feel it. Hair all over the place, her cheek red from where it had rested on her sleeve. 'What are you doing here?'

'I made you coffee. Here.' Riedwaan pushed a steaming cup across the desk. 'And I got you a Florentine from the Venus Bakery. Your favourite.'

The honeyed almonds glistened in their nest of chocolate and dried fruit. Clare picked it up. It was too early in the morning to resist. She bit into the tiny biscuit. It was delicious. Useful too, because she couldn't eat and grin. Which was what she felt like doing, seeing Riedwaan sitting on the edge of her desk.

'Thanks for letting me know you were here,' she said, with her mouth full.

'I did try. Check your phone.'

Clare pulled it out of her pocket. 'Damn. So you did. It's been on silent.'

'What are you doing here?' asked Riedwaan.

'I couldn't sleep,' said Clare.

'You could've fooled me.'

'In bed I couldn't,' she said.

'So you came in here?' asked Riedwaan. 'Odd choice for soothing company.'

'I'm going crazy with them.' Clare gestured to the boys on the wall. 'Just as I feel I have something, it vanishes like water on hot sand. Have you seen Captain Damases?' she asked.

'Not yet. Only Van Wyk, I think it is. He's about as warm as a KGB agent.'

'That's Van Wyk for you,' said Clare. 'I don't think South Africans are at the top of his hit parade. Did you meet Elias Karamata?'

'Looks like a prizefighter? He said I'd find you in here.'

'Oh God, I suppose everyone knows I've been sleeping here.'

'Pretty much.' Riedwaan walked over to the displays, concentrating in turn on each of the four clusters, absorbing what Clare and Tamar had set out.

'I'm impressed,' he said. 'Fritz Woestyn, the one without a number carved on his chest, he was the first one?'

'Yes. We've been thinking of him as Number 1. Head shot, but not as close as the others. No tattooing that the pathologist could see. So definitely more than two, three metres. The others are all close-up.'

'Show me where he was found.'

Clare pointed to a red pin on the aerial map. 'His body was dumped here, but it wasn't where he was shot.' Riedwaan was standing close to her, raising the tiny hairs on her arms.

'Some guys checking a fifty-kilometre stretch just happened to find him?' asked Riedwaan.

Clare nodded. Riedwaan thought of the vast desert he had just passed through.

'You could go missing in this desert and not be found for weeks,' Clare said, reading his mind. 'The chances of the boys' discovery were so slim that whoever shot him probably calculated that he wouldn't be found until he'd been reduced to just another heap of bones. Or they dumped him where they knew he'd be found.'

'The others?' asked Riedwaan. 'Jones, Apollis, Beukes. Run me through them.'

'The killings get more elaborate after that first one. Nicanor Jones with the 2; Kaiser Apollis had a 3 on his chest. Then a skip to Lazarus Beukes with a 5.'

'Where's your Number 4?'

'Alive and well, I hope. No one's been reported missing.' Clare fanned out a series of close-ups: the faces, their mutilated chests, the missing finger joints on the left hands. 'It's the same person killing them,' she said. 'We don't have a bullet from each scene, but it looks like the same calibre gun and the same rope – nylon washing line – on the wrists. Same victim profile, too. Marginal boy, fifteen or so, fey, small, nobody to look for him. Also, there's a time thing. It looks like the murders were done on or around a Friday night, except for Lazarus. At least close to the weekend.'

'And your man?' asked Riedwaan. 'Where does he hang out?'

'This is the only place I can fix him,' said Clare, pointing to the first red pin on the map.

'The takeaway place at the lagoon?' said Riedwaan.

'Lover's Hill. They went there. Well, I know for sure that Kaiser Apollis was there. The cook saw him on the Friday evening he was killed. He ordered some food and then got into a car a few metres down the road.'

'Okay,' said Riedwaan. 'I'm with you. What happens?'

'This guy picks them up somewhere, probably in town where it wouldn't be noticed. Then he drives out, dropping them off to get something to eat. The cook noticed Kaiser because it was quiet, but otherwise the boys would be in and out. Invisible. Then they go outside, walk down the road a bit and get back into the car and they drive out into the desert.'

'There's no sign of recent sexual assault, is there?' said Riedwaan, checking the post-mortem results.

'No. Maybe he's impotent. Maybe he's a romantic. Maybe they laugh at him, threaten him. Maybe he gets his kicks in his own special way.'

'By shooting them?' asked Riedwaan.

'Maybe.'

'So who moves them?'

'Maybe I'm looking at this all wrong ...' Clare's voice trailed off as she stared at the accumulating bank of information. 'Maybe he meets someone out there. They both do something together ...'

'What's he like, this romantic of yours?'

'He'd have to be a loner, maybe a shift worker, so no one notices late comings and goings.' Clare finished her coffee. 'A textbook killer for a textbook case.'

Riedwaan walked over to the window and looked out over the flat, featureless town. 'How do people get around this place?' he asked.

'On foot or bike, if you're poor,' said Clare. 'A 4x4 if you're somebody.' She cocked her head and looked at her display. 'He'd have a car, or access to a car. Enough money to lure these kids and then buy them food. Something to drink. I'd put his age at around thirty-five, forty. Maybe a bit more. He might be someone the kids think they could take advantage of, but they'd go with just about anyone with a bit of cash.'

'Even after a couple of them have been killed?' asked Riedwaan. 'It must seem like someone they can trust, someone they don't expect to be a danger.'

'I agree,' said Clare. 'Someone they wouldn't see as a threat. The car will also look like everyone else's here.'

'White double cab, if what I've seen is anything to go by,' said Riedwaan. 'What would've triggered this spree?'

'Something unravels, the guy ropes of self-control snap,' said Clare. 'Stress does it usually. And there you go: a killer on the loose.' She looked at the pictures of Lazarus's bloodied face. 'Whoever it is knows how to seduce. There's no sign of a struggle and such an intimate death. Blood would splatter on your hands and face as you fire. Quite a sophisticated rush in a way, the symbolism of it: the union, the consummation. Weird.'

'With you involved it's going to be weird, Clare,' said Riedwaan, looking at the pictures of a dismembered hand. 'You're sure it's someone local?'

'Whoever's doing this knows this place very well. He wouldn't be able to be invisible otherwise.' She paced up and down in front of the pinboard, stopping in front of the photograph of Kaiser Apollis's shrouded figure. 'My profile's still off-kilter,' she said.

'Why do you say that?'

'The display aspect of the murders. Herman Shipanga went on about bodies being exhibited as a kind of warning. It's not just the rush that comes with pulling the trigger. Our killer's trying to communicate something too, through the bodies. Out in the Kuiseb, where Lazarus's body was found, you had to ask how he got to be there exactly, where Chanel would find him. I keep thinking: someone knows this place, knows where people will stop in this vast desert, knows its secrets and can work with them. I wonder—' The door swung open, interrupting Clare. It was Tamar. 'Did you sleep well, Riedwaan?' she asked. 'Comfortable where we put you?'

'Good bar, good bed, good food. Thanks.'

Clare had hardly noticed Tamar come in. 'What is this?' she said, almost to herself. She was rifling through the photographs, pulling out the one Tamar had taken of the alleyway behind the schoolyard where Kaiser Apollis had been found. She spun around. 'Riedwaan?'

'Morning to you too, Clare,' said Tamar.

Riedwaan peered at the photograph. 'Looks like dirt to me,' he said, puzzled, passing it to Tamar.

'It's shit,' said Clare.

'What did you say?' Riedwaan looked at Clare, startled. She saved swearing for emergencies. A grainy crime-scene photo was not an emergency.

Clare strode over to the desk, opened the interview file and flipped through the transcripts. 'Remember, what you asked me, Riedwaan?'

'Which question?' he said. 'There were twenty or more.'

'About how people get around?'

'Yes, by bike, foot, car ... it was just a check.'

'Okay then,' said Clare. 'Look at this.' She brandished a carefully typed page. 'Tamar, remember, you said the recyclers use the alley behind the school.'

'They do,' said Tamar.

'And that woman we talked to, the one hanging up her washing, said she heard nothing?'

'I remember.'

Clare walked back to the pinboard. 'When I came back with Helena Kotze after we found Lazarus, I saw a family going home on their donkey cart. I didn't hear them until I was practically upon them. You wouldn't really hear a cart if you were inside and the television was on.' She pointed to a small heap of dung in the photograph. 'Look here,' she said. 'A pile of donkey shit, right by the opening of the fence. They must've passed right here and we never thought to question them.'

Riedwaan was still confused. 'Who uses donkey carts?'

'The Topnaars,' said Clare. 'The desert people. Their settlements are marked on the aerial survey photos. Here.' She gestured to a series of little black crosses. 'If you look closely, you'll see their shanties. Hot as hell they are. I just didn't put recyclers and the Topnaars together. But of course it would be them, scavenging bits of scrap for the cash even they need to survive.'

'It's so risky,' said Riedwaan.

Clare turned to look at him. 'Not if you've got nothing left to lose.'

'Your invisible man?' Tamar said to Clare. 'A Topnaar?'

'Who else moves with such ease through the Namib?'

'A desert nomad doesn't fit with your profile,' Riedwaan noted. 'They're as poor as the dead kids.'

'No,' said Clare, 'but surely they'd know who's moving in and out of the Kuiseb. They'd see.'

'Wouldn't they tell?' asked Riedwaan.

'Not necessarily,' said Tamar thoughtfully. 'They're a marginal people, pushed further and further out. Persecuted by the army, silenced by this administration that wants them all settled and schooled and controllable. The Topnaars have a couple of hundred years' worth of knowing that the underdog gets the blame. If they found a body, they'd want it as far away from their land as possible.'

'So they wouldn't want to attract attention.' Riedwaan was looking at the map.

'Tertius Myburgh mentioned an old man called Spyt to me. Virginia Meyer used to work with him, because he knew the desert like the back of his hand. Do you know him?' Clare asked Tamar.

'I know of him,' said Tamar. 'He's very secretive, avoids people like the plague. He doesn't speak.'

'Give me a straight-down-the-line gangster any day,' muttered Riedwaan.

'I think we should try to talk to him,' said Clare. 'Stupid of me, not to have gone out there before.'

'We can give it a shot,' said Tamar sceptically. 'We've got to show Riedwaan around anyway, so we'll kill two birds this way. I'll get Van Wyk and Elias. Meet you outside in five minutes?'

Clare nodded.

'Your profile doesn't fit,' Riedwaan said again as Tamar left the room.

'What if there are two people involved?' asked Clare. Her voice was very quiet.

Riedwaan pulled on his jacket, suddenly chilled. 'Two?' he prompted.

'One who kills.' Clare tapped her pen on the window as she stared towards the desert. 'For whatever reason. And another who displays.'

thirty-nine

'Spyt's going to hear us long before we're even close,' said Elias Karamata. 'We won't find him unless he wants to be found.'

Clare, Riedwaan, Tamar and Karamata had left Van Wyk at the station. Claiming that he wanted to see what else the South African experts had missed was his tactful way of putting it. After showing Riedwaan where the bodies had been found, they had gone from one Topnaar settlement in the Kuiseb to the next, each one drier and dustier than the last. An old woman, her weathered skin the same texture as her cloak, had said she knew where Spyt lived. She had led them through a lattice of desiccated tributaries to a desolate refuge.

'It looks as if he lives here alone,' said Clare. Unlike the other settlements, there were no dogs, no goats and no bug-eyed children staring at them from the inside of tin huts.

The camp was well hidden, backed up against a protrusion of black rock. Rusting lumps of metal and old tyres lay around between the little pyramids of bottles and old tins.

'Bully beef,' Tamar said, picking up an old tin. 'Old army issue. This must be twenty years old.'

Nothing moved on the black rocks. High above them a lone vulture drifted in the wash of blue sky. The Namib's eyes and ears, its silent witness. Like Spyt, Clare thought, hidden in a place that even his practised eyes would struggle to find.

'*Eitsma miere*, Spyt,' Tamar Damases called in Nama, the ancient mother tongue that she and Spyt shared. Her voice echoed off the rocks, the only reply.

The old woman led them around the side of the rocky protrusion to a small cave. A ring of stones circled the shelter, demarcating the point at which the desert ended and Spyt's dwelling began. A fireplace marked the epicentre of the domestic circle, the coals half-covered with sand.

'Still hot,' said Riedwaan, putting his hand close. The back of Clare's neck prickled as if she were being watched. She looked about; there was nothing but a lizard sunning itself on a rock.

A shallow oval of bark had been abandoned alongside the cave. Karamata picked it up and moved it back and forth between his hands, winnowing the wild grass seed Spyt must have harvested from a termite heap. He blew away the husks, and the breeze caught them, dust-devilling them across the sand. The chaff landed in the fireplace, the coals flaring briefly. 'You make pap with these,' he explained to Clare and Riedwaan. 'Spyt has to eat food that's as soft as a baby's because of his mouth.'

'His name means regret in Afrikaans,' said Riedwaan. 'What happened to him?'

Tamar asked their wizened guide, who burst into an animated tale in Nama. Clare could not understand a word, but the lilt of the tonal language, punctuated by a complex series of clicks, carried her with the emotional flow of the tale.

Tamar translated: 'She says that when he was a toddler his mother went to work on a farm on the edge of the Namib. Spyt ate caustic soda and it dissolved the inside of his mouth. That's why his mother took him back into the Namib. They lived together, just the two of them until she died. Then he lived alone. It was his mother who taught him how to hunt, how to hide.'

'Must've been why the military were always after him,' said Karamata.

'Were they?' Riedwaan asked.

'Oh yes.' Karamata gestured at the sand sprawling into the horizon. 'They made him work as a tracker for a while. They

243

wanted to know everything about the desert, claim it, then own it and keep everything secret.'

'Let's look around,' said Tamar, 'but I don't think he's going to pitch.'

Clare went into the small cave shelter. It was narrow, dark beyond the splash of light at the entrance. There were few things inside, a sleeping roll, a leather bag, a pair of handmade shoes with pieces of tyre serving as the soles. Strips of cloth hung off a hook. Clare touched the fabric. It had perished from the heat, but the green stripe was still visible. The faint lettering too.

'Looks like old army sheeting,' said Riedwaan, following Clare into the cave. 'SWATF. The letters make the green stripe.'

The smell of years of wood smoke, of stale human sleep was overwhelming. Clare stepped outside, her heart pounding. It was a relief to be in the open air, but it did nothing to clarify her dervishing thoughts.

'A scavenger,' said Riedwaan, ducking out of the cave. 'Looks like he collected all sorts of rubbish lying about the desert, but not your boys. They were kept for a couple of days at the most and then displayed where you couldn't miss them. And they couldn't have been kept in there. It's too hot. Mouton said that the bodies must've been kept somewhere cool.'

'Give me your binoculars,' said Clare. 'I'm climbing up there to have a look.' She scrambled to the top of the cliff face and scanned the desert. The sand roiled in the east, where it had been agitated by the wind. Apart from the slender sentinel of a distant gum tree, there was nothing to see that way. To the south and west was a sea of dunes, some covered with spiny Nara plants, which flowed towards the ocean. Nothing moved. No tracks. No trail of dust to indicate a retreating cart.

'What've you got?' asked Riedwaan.

'Nothing,' said Clare, climbing down again. 'No donkeys, no cart, no Spyt, no tracks. Just sand.'

'You have to learn to see,' said Tamar. 'Not just to look.' She tugged Clare's arm, getting her to crouch alongside her. The light, angled low, transformed the blank slate of the desert sand, revealing the crisscrossings of jackal, oryx, lizards, the circular twist of seed pods eddied by the wind. And wheel tracks, barely visible. Neat crescents, close together, paired.

'Your donkeys.' Tamar stood up.

'That way?' asked Clare, pointing down the gulley that twisted away from them.

Tamar nodded. 'Elias, stay here on the off-chance he comes back.'

Clare and Riedwaan followed Tamar past a midden. Bones and shells, and other waste that had no further human use, were scattered about. They went on further; the ground became increasingly flinty.

Tamar stopped. 'I've lost them,' she said, frustration clear in her voice. Clare looked ahead. The shallow canyon they had entered broke into a labyrinth of tributaries. The sunlight shimmered on the mica, distorting the distances.

'Where to begin?' asked Clare.

'We'll need a helicopter if you want to pursue this,' said Riedwaan, turning back.

Tamar followed him, drinking from her water bottle. Clare waited. The silence the other two left in their wake was profound. She could hear the rush of her own blood, pulsing with frustration.

The sound came when she was halfway back to Spyt's cave. The sharp clink of a stone dislodged. Clare stopped, every sense alert. She looked about. Nothing but sand and rock and the sheer wall of the canyon. An agama eyed her, its reptilian body vibrating with anticipated movement. Clare let out her breath. The lizard bolted, vanishing straight into the rock. Curious, Clare went over to see where he had gone. To her surprise, she found a fissure in the rock, eroded by some prehistoric river that had long since changed its course. She stepped through the entrance into an amphitheatre of rock.

In the shade of an acacia thicket stood two creamy white donkeys. The animals shifted, pulling their tethers tight, as Clare approached them. She made a series of quiet, soothing clicks deep in her throat, and the donkeys were still again, motionless except for the occasional twitch of a velvet ear.

The entrance to the second cave was a dark opening in the cliff, a cool vestibule to the large cavern that opened to the right.

Clare ran back to the entrance. 'Riedwaan,' she yelled, her voice echoing behind her. 'Tamar, come back.'

The other two returned, Riedwaan's look of anxiety disappearing as soon as he saw Clare was unharmed.

'I think this is it,' said Clare, leading them back.

It was cool inside the cave, as dark as a crypt. A bat, disturbed by their presence, swooped low as they entered. Clare shivered at the little rush of air it left in its wake.

Riedwaan flicked on his torch and passed it to Clare. She shone it around the cave, bringing the beam to rest on the cart standing right at the back of the cave. It glinted in the light. The cart had been made from the back of an old bakkie. It had a bench in the front for the driver. Clare went closer and shone her torch over the back. Several empty jerry cans were secured on one side of it. On the other was a narrow space fitted with an old mattress, blotted with dark stains.

Riedwaan let out a long, low whistle. 'You are so lucky, Clare. What were the chances?'

'This'll teach you to be a nature lover,' she teased.

'We're going to need luminal to see if that's blood,' said Tamar, businesslike.

'You've got some here?' Riedwaan asked, impressed.

'I have. And a UV light.'

'Sharp,' said Riedwaan. 'Field forensics.'

'If you've got six months, then send the cart to Windhoek and file an official request to move and test a vehicle,' said Tamar. 'This works. If we need more we take it all in and fill in the forms.'

'Where is the stuff?' asked Riedwaan.

'On the truck. There's a trunk on the back.'

Riedwaan slipped out of the cave entrance. Clare switched off the torch while she and Tamar waited, sheltered from the heat of the desert. Safe and cool and restful. It was not a bad place to be alone.

'You'll need a slow exposure to get the patterning … if there is any.'

Clare jumped. She hadn't heard Riedwaan come back. He handed Clare the camera and sprayed the luminal over the back of the cart. Tamar held up her handmade ultraviolet light. For a second, there was nothing, then it glowed purple, a small patch on one end of the mattress.

'We'll send that through to the lab,' said Riedwaan. 'But I know what they'll take five pages to tell us: something or somebody was on this, something not that long dead. But they didn't die here.' He pointed to the contained patterning. 'It would've pooled a little when it was moved for transport. Post-mortem.' Riedwaan looked around the cool, clean cave. 'Doesn't look like they were killed here either.'

'No,' said Clare. She shone the torch into the recesses of the cave. On the floor were gossamer heaps. Wings, discarded exoskeletons. She arced the beam up towards the roof, the light exposing the huddled, roosting bats.

Riedwaan ducked instinctively as a dozen or so of the tiny, disturbed creatures took off.

'These must be the bats whose droppings got caught in Kaiser Apollis's hair.'

'So what was Spyt doing, bringing dead bodies here and then dropping them off in public again?' Tamar asked the question they were all thinking as they walked back towards Karamata and the vehicle. 'And how are we going to find him if he doesn't want to talk to us?'

'Why would Spyt have done this?' wondered Clare. 'Knowing that eventually someone would come out here and look for him? What was he trying to say to—?'

The roar of a vehicle cresting the dune cut Clare off.

'We've got company,' said Karamata as they joined him.

The doors opened and Van Wyk emerged, followed by Calvin Goagab, incongruous in his city suit.

Goagab reached them first. 'Mayor D'Almeida will be pleased to have a suspect after so much investment in this case,' he said. 'We should get back to the press conference.'

'What are you talking about, Calvin?' Tamar's voice rose with fury.

'Captain Damases,' Van Wyk interrupted. 'I tried to call you, but got no reply. So, I called Mr Goagab.'

'You know there's no cellphone reception out here, Van Wyk.' Tamar's voice vibrated with anger. 'And you were supposed to be checking interviews, not making public announcements.' She watched him as one would watch an unpredictable dog. 'What did Van Wyk tell you, Calvin?'

'That our experts have led us to a suspect,' Goagab replied. 'We're very pleased. It'll allow me to justify the expense.' He nodded towards Clare and Riedwaan. 'And it vindicates my policy to get the desert nomads properly settled.'

'He's not a suspect yet,' Clare observed.

'Oh, we'll have him soon enough and then he will be.' Van Wyk put his hand on Tamar's shoulder. 'The mayor is waiting for you to address the press conference, Captain Damases. We'd better head back if we're to make the news tonight.'

'We'll discuss this, Van Wyk,' said Tamar. 'This insubordination.'

'I did a little check,' he replied, 'and I don't think we'll be discussing anything in the near future. I see our very progressive leave policy stipulates that pregnant officers go on leave from the seventh month. I looked at your medical records and noticed that your due date is next week.'

'How dare you go through my private records?' asked Tamar.

'We care, Captain Damases,' said Goagab, with an oily smile. 'Our administration's concern for gender issues means that we can't allow you to jeopardise your unborn child. We must ask you to return to town immediately.'

Speechless with rage, Tamar looked from Van Wyk to Goagab.

'Let's go, Captain,' Karamata said, his hand on Tamar's elbow. He walked her back to the vehicle.

Van Wyk turned to Riedwaan. 'It's going to look good, Captain Faizal. An almost-arrest the day you arrive,' he said. 'I'm sure you're looking forward to addressing the media. It's all been set up.'

'I wouldn't like to see what Spyt looks like after a night in the cells with him in charge,' Clare said under her breath, watching Van Wyk and Goagab swagger back to their vehicle.

'I'm not sure I want to see what we are going to look like after this press conference,' said Riedwaan.

They joined Tamar and Karamata at the car and were forced

to follow Van Wyk and Goagab out of the Kuiseb, tagging behind in the vehicle's dusty wake. Van Wyk angled his rear-view
mirror so that he could catch Clare's eye. He grinned. He had
won his battle. She'd helped him win. Clare wished she could
figure out what the war was.

forty

The yacht club bar was still crowded at eight-thirty when Clare arrived. The after-work crowd had gone home, but the professional drinkers had settled in for the night. A fug of smoke had settled over the bar.

'Give the lady a drink,' ordered a belligerent drunk. 'She looks like she could do with it.'

'No, thank you.' Clare raised a deflecting hand at the whisky sloshed into a shot glass. She ordered wine and went to sit in one of the booths. Calvin Goagab's press conference had been worse than she imagined, with Goagab and Van Wyk posturing before the cameras, and Clare expressing doubt in spite of all the evidence.

'I said: give the lady a fucking drink.' The drunk's voice rose a threatening notch.

'Tell him, thank you, but no.' Clare fixed her blue eyes on the barman.

'Frigid bitch,' muttered the heavy-set man on the other side of the bar. 'Just a bit of hospitality.'

'She's not interested.' A woman's voice. 'She's not going to get interested either, so why don't you leave her alone?' Clare was surprised to see that her defender was Gretchen von Trotha, seated a few seats away from the drunken men.

'Thanks,' she mouthed, raising her glass in salute.

'You stay out of this, Gretchen,' said the man.

Gretchen did not bother to reply, turning her attention instead to the lean man beside her. Clare recognised him from Der Blaue Engel: the man who had pulled Gretchen from the icy

Atlantic. It looked as though he was still cashing in on her debt to him. Gretchen certainly looked adoring.

'Sorry I'm late.' Riedwaan slid into the opposite side of the booth, distracting Clare.

'It's fine,' she said. 'You look cleaner and calmer.'

'You need a drink?' he asked. 'I need a double after that. More like a lynching than a press conference.'

'I'm fine.' She tapped her full wine glass and scanned the bar. Gretchen had vanished, so had the man she'd been with.

Riedwaan came back with his whisky and a new pack of cigarettes. 'I have to eat,' he said, taking the menus from a plump waitress. 'I'm starved. Steak and chips for me,' he said.

'Steak? At the sea? Order the fish.' There was no arguing with that.

'What do you think about Spyt?' Clare asked when the waitress had left with their orders.

Riedwaan buttered some bread and took a bite. 'I don't think it was him. But the local politicians want the Topnaars out of the way. This is all a convenient way of getting this land claim business to disappear. But Nampol have to work that out themselves. Let's just hope they do it before someone else dies.'

'I feel it'll be my fault if anything happens to Spyt. I don't like the thought of Van Wyk and his cronies hunting him like a dog.'

'I don't think they'll catch him that easily.' Riedwaan said. 'What's happened with Tertius Myburgh, by the way?' he asked, shaking a cigarette from his pack.

'I'm still waiting for his pollen analysis,' said Clare. 'I'd love one of those. I need it after this afternoon.'

'Have one.' Riedwaan lit one for her and placed it between her lips.

'Smoking's like sex,' said Clare, inhaling deeply. 'It seems

252

such a good idea at night. Not so brilliant when you wake up in the morning.'

'You can give that back to me then,' said Riedwaan.

'No, let me smoke it,' she said. 'Just so that I can remember what a stupid idea it is.'

'The smoking or the sex?' said Riedwaan.

'I haven't decided yet,' said Clare, tension coiled in her belly. 'I feel so stupid, that I set myself up. Van Wyk and Goagab had me checkmated at that press conference. All that bullshit about Cain and Abel, nomads being vagrants. Just an excuse to persecute people whose land you want.' Clare took a deep drag of the cigarette. 'Yes, it was my idea. Yes, I went out there. Yes, there was evidence that the bodies were in Spyt's cave at some stage. And me like an idiot, saying he didn't kill them.' Clare put out her half-smoked cigarette when the waitress brought their food. 'While Goagab and his goons are flattening the desert in their 4x4s, there's a killer sitting eating dinner and planning Number 6.'

'There's nothing more we can do tonight,' Riedwaan pointed out.

'What're we going to be able to do tomorrow?' snapped Clare. 'Van Wyk has pushed Tamar into a bureaucratic corner and me and you are supposed to be off the case.'

'Not quite,' said Riedwaan. 'But let's leave that for tomorrow.' He put his hand on hers. 'Right now the moon is nearly full. I'm here, you're here, so why don't we talk about something else?'

'Okay,' said Clare. She took her hand away and fussed with her table mat. 'Suggest something.'

'Smoking maybe,' said Riedwaan.

Clare didn't laugh.

'Me? You?'

'Me and you?' Clare toyed with the idea of asking him about

253

Yasmin, or of telling him she was sorry that she hadn't listened to him earlier, but she couldn't find a way to start. She gave up and pushed her food around her plate. She looked at Riedwaan, looked away.

'Talking about something other than work take away your appetite?'

'No,' she said. 'It's just that my stomach's in a knot.'

'Does your having dinner with me mean I'm forgiven?'

'Don't rush me.' Clare picked up her wine glass. 'I'm deciding.'

'I'm useless on parole,' Riedwaan warned. 'It brings out the worst in me.'

'You're not—'

Clare's phone rang. She looked at the screen. 'I've got to take this,' she said. 'It's Constance.'

Riedwaan shook his head at her, irritated, but Clare had already taken the call. He waited for a second, but all her attention was focused on the identical twin murmuring into her ear, drawing her away from him and into a place he could never follow.

He picked up his cigarettes and went to the bar.

The barman poured him a sympathetic double whisky.

forty-one

The dark was thinning when Clare awoke, smiling, expecting to find herself circled in Riedwaan's arm. Then she remembered that she had gone to bed alone. She got up and opened the curtains. A sodden west wind was blowing. She pulled on her tracksuit and a waterproof jacket, zipping her phone into her pocket as she left her room. She headed north towards the harbour. Once she was past the Burning Shore Lodge, she found her stride, finally eliminating all thoughts of Riedwaan.

Sweat bloomed under Clare's shirt. She slowed as the path narrowed, snaking between the lagoon shore and a new hotel. Discarded building materials and other debris littered the track. She waved at the little red-haired boy sitting huddled on a bench.

'Hello, Oscar,' she called as she went past. 'You're up early.'

He raised one hand in reply, his face solemn.

She whipped her phone out of her pocket when it rang.

'Riedwaan?' He had said he'd call first thing.

There was nothing but a hollow echo.

'Hello?'

No answer. The chill played over Clare's skin. She ducked behind a wall when her phone rang again.

'Hello?'

'Is that Dr Hart?' An unfamiliar voice. Faraway. Foreign.

'It is.'

'I'm sorry to disturb you. I know it's early.'

'Who is this?' asked Clare.

'She didn't arrive,' a woman said.

'Who didn't arrive?'

'Mara.' There was a break in the woman's voice. 'This is Lily Thomson. Mara's mother.'

'How did you get my number?' Clare asked.

'I phoned the police station. The man I spoke to, Van Wyk' – she struggled with the unfamiliar name – 'said it was too soon to do anything. He gave me your number when I asked for you.'

'Where are you?'

'I'm at home again, aren't I?' Lily Thomson replied. Clare envisaged the bleak courtyard of the housing estate that Mara had escaped. 'I went to Heathrow.'

'Yes?' prompted Clare, unease prickling the nape of her neck.

'She didn't come. She was meant to be on that flight. That's all I know and all I can find out, because she's not answering her phone.'

'Might she have changed her mind?'

Lily Thomson clutched at Clare's straw. 'That's what I said to myself: she's changed her mind. I tried her mobile.' Her voice broke. 'But she's not picking up.'

Clare pictured Lily Thomson in her spring-cleaned flat. The supermarket flowers on the kitchen table. Mara's single bed made up in crisp white sheets, a chocolate under the pillow, teddies perked.

'Mara told me about you coming there from South Africa,' Lily Thomson continued. 'About the investigation. She was so upset about those boys. That's just how she is, our Mara: always responsible, trying to make the world right, especially after that trip that went all wrong.'

'What trip?' asked Clare. Anxiety tightened her spine. Mara and her soccer team. She had known the murdered boys better than anyone else had.

'She took them camping or something,' said Mrs Thomson.

'She felt so guilty about leaving them out there in the desert like that. But I told her it was fine, if it was the only time she could see her boyfriend, that Juan Carlos, then why not? She was so head-over-heels and she knew she didn't have long with him.'

Clare thought of the last time she had seen Mara, entwined with Juan Carlos, sharing fish and chips, glowing with whatever he had been doing to her to make her so hungry.

'Did you report her missing?'

'I tried. They said they have this all the time with travellers, with volunteers. They meet a new person, go somewhere else. To Botswana. Maybe Cape Town. That the mothers panic because it's Africa. Van Wyk said to wait twenty-four hours.' She stifled a sob. 'But when do I start counting, Dr Hart? When she didn't come I thought the worst. I thought ...'

Panic hit Lily Thomson, doubling her over. It was impossible for her to say what she had thought, as if saying the words would conjure up what she feared most.

'Please find her for me, Dr Hart. I'm so far from there. You speak English. You can understand me. You knew her.'

Lily Thomson caught it. Clare did too, that slip into the past tense.

Clare set off at a run for George Meyer's gloomy house where Mara had rented a room. She clung to the hope that she would find her and Juan Carlos asleep in a tangle of sheets and salty limbs. When she got there, the only signs of life were in the kitchen. Clare knocked over Oscar's fishing rod standing at the back door. She righted it, disentangling it from the roll of washing line as Gretchen, wrapped in her sky-blue robe, opened the door.

'Yes?' Gretchen jabbed her cigarette into her mouth, still stained with last night's lipstick. Smoke curled up to the ceiling.

George Meyer and Oscar were sitting opposite each other at the kitchen table, Oscar staring down at the rheumy eye of a fried egg. He looked up at Clare, his face lighting up. George Meyer paled.

'Dr Hart, please come in,' he said. 'How can we help?'

'I'm looking for Mara,' Clare said as she walked inside.

'She left.' Gretchen tossed her cigarette into the remains of her coffee.

'When?'

'Yesterday, must've been,' said Meyer. 'The Lufthansa flight.'

'You didn't see her?'

'No.' He shook his head. 'I saw her on Sunday evening. She had supper with me and Oscar and then she went out with her Spanish friend.'

'How was she going to go to the airport?'

'I offered her a lift, but she said she was sorted,' said Gretchen. 'Go and look; her room's empty. She took all her stuff.'

'What time did she leave?' Clare asked.

'I don't know.' Gretchen's mouth twisted, thin as wire, around a fresh cigarette. 'I work late. I must've been asleep.'

Oscar coughed, his delicate ribcage heaving under his shirt. 'Do you want to show me Mara's room?' Clare asked. 'Do you mind?' She turned to George Meyer.

He shook his head.

Oscar slipped his hand into hers and led her down the passage to Mara's room.

Stripped bare of Mara's belongings, the room was smaller than Clare remembered. The overhead light had been left burning, the bulb feeble in the daylight. A pile of soiled bed linen was bundled on the floor. On the bedside table were a couple of abandoned paperbacks and an old *People* magazine. Clare sat down on the bed. The little boy sat next to her. The mattress sagged, leaning the child's warm body against her.

'Where is she, Oscar?'

Oscar's hand in hers was clammy, as he tugged her off the bed and led her to the other side of the room. There he lifted up a loose square of carpet to reveal a shallow depression in the concrete.

'What is this?'

Oscar lifted out a cheerful yellow and red Kodak envelope, taking out some folded drawings, childish representations of Walvis Bay, the desert, and trees against orange sand.

'Did you do these?'

Oscar nodded again, pointing to where he had written his name. An O bisected with an M inside a heart.

'They're good.'

Clare took out the photographs. They were mostly of Mara. With her mother in London, looking triumphant and nervous at Heathrow. Standing against a Tropic of Capricorn road sign, her arms spread, bisecting the featureless plain behind her. Surrounded by grinning children at a school. Camping in the Namib. Her soccer team holding a cup, looking like the cats that had the cream.

Oscar was growing agitated, tugging at Clare's arm. 'What is it?' she asked.

He pointed at the pictures again.

'Are you upset that she left the drawing you gave her?'

Oscar inclined his head. His expression was unreadable.

'Was she in a hurry to——?'

Oscar was shaking his head before she was halfway through her sentence.

'You don't think she would've left a present behind?'

Oscar nodded, this time certain. He turned to face the window that overlooked the concrete yard of the house and lifted his index finger, seeming to point to the sky. Clare frowned, struggling to see through the grime and dew misting up the glass. Oscar touched the pane. He wasn't pointing; he was drawing, tracing a familiar shape in the condensation on the window: the scored-through heart on Clare's bedroom window which had so startled her.

'That was you,' she said, 'watching me.'

Oscar's nod was almost imperceptible.

'You were checking on me. Did you watch Mara, too?'

The child nodded, tears welling in his eyes. Clare's heart went out to the fragile boy. The little Clare knew of Mara convinced her that she would not have rejected the child's shy gesture of love.

'And Mara wouldn't leave a present behind, because she loved you,' she guessed.

Oscar nodded again.

'What happened to her, Oscar?'

He shook his head violently and then stopped, his eyes fixed behind Clare's shoulder. She turned to see Gretchen leaning against the door frame. Clare wondered how long she'd been there.

'Silly boy,' Gretchen laughed, low in her throat. 'Why would she keep your stupid pictures?'

'When did you see her last?' Clare asked Gretchen.

'Sunday night,' said Gretchen, giving it some thought. 'She was at the bar of Der Blaue Engel. I was working.'

'Who was she with?'

'Juan Carlos.' Gretchen was quick to answer. 'Her boyfriend. She loved him, Oscar, not you.'

'Do you know what time she left?' asked Clare. She felt Oscar shake.

'I did my show,' said Gretchen. 'I left straight after. Maybe two?

260

When I got home, everything was dark. I watched TV for a while, then I went to bed. She would've left while I was still asleep. Her flight was nine-thirty. So check-in time seven-thirty for international.'

'You didn't hear a taxi come? A car?' Clare put her hand on Oscar's shoulder.

'No,' Gretchen said blandly. 'I sleep deeply. Is there anything else we can help you with, Dr Hart?'

'No,' said Clare. 'Not now.'

Gretchen lingered in the doorway until Clare stood up to leave, then she turned and ascended the stairs, her blue gown sweeping over the steps. Oscar tucked the envelope into Clare's jacket pocket as they walked back to the kitchen. He fiddled with his fishing bag, humming to himself to fill the space around him, and then he took his rod from behind the kitchen door, averting his eyes from Mara's empty room. The sound of running water came from the bathroom upstairs.

'You'll excuse us, Dr Hart?' said Meyer. 'I have to get to work.'

George Meyer picked up his keys and walked Clare to the front gate. 'Be a good boy, Oscar,' he said, as the boy wheeled his bike around to the front.

'Call me if you hear anything about Mara.' Clare said it to George, but her hand was resting on Oscar's cheek. She felt him nod.

forty-two

Clare cut back alongside the rubbish-snagged razor wire that sequestered the harbour from the town. She called Tamar, but her phone went straight to voicemail, so she left a message with the news about Mara. She turned in at the police station. At seven in the morning, the parking lot was empty except for Van Wyk's white 4x4.

She pushed open the office door, her running shoe protesting against the linoleum floor. Van Wyk was engrossed in whatever was on his computer screen, his hand on the mouse. One click and the image shut down. So did his expression.

'I'm surprised to see you here, Dr Hart.' The hurried crackle told Clare that he had hit sleep mode. 'After yesterday. But if you're looking for Captain Damases, you're a bit early.'

'I'm always early,' said Clare, wondering what had piqued Van Wyk's interest in office work. 'But this morning I also had a call. So I thought I'd come and see you about it.'

'The media?' Van Wyk said 'For another interview with our … expert from South Africa? I'd say your case is dead in the water. It's just a matter of time before we find that old desert beggar.' He leant back in his chair, arms behind his head, legs splayed, the denim tight across his thighs. The door clicked shut behind Clare, making her jump.

'It was Mara's mother,' she said. 'Mrs Thomson.'

A pause, a heartbeat long. 'What must I say to the mother? That her daughter got an itch for a sailor?'

'Has it crossed your mind that something might have happened to her?' said Clare.

262

Van Wyk spread out his hands and examined his fingernails. 'If she's dead, her body'll pitch up sometime, and we'll send her home in a box. If she's alive, she'll run out of money and go home anyway. All the same in the end.'

'To you maybe. Not to the desperate woman I had on the phone.'

Van Wyk uncoiled himself from his chair, his pupils pinpricks. 'Mara was nothing but trouble. She lodged a complaint against me after we picked up one of those street kids of hers stealing in the harbour. She got me shunted into this pointless fucking unit. And now it's my job to look after a stupid little foreign slut who can't keep her knees together?'

'She's missing, Sergeant,' said Clare.

Van Wyk was close to her now. Clare kept her eyes on his.

'You don't belong here, Dr Hart.' His fingers closed around her wrists. The bones shifted when he twisted. 'Just like Mara didn't, so you stay away from things that don't belong to you.'

'Don't you ever threaten me,' said Clare, bringing her right knee up, fast and accurate.

Van Wyk let her go, his eyes glazing with pain as the office door flung open.

'Morning, Clare.' It was Karamata, cheerful and crisply dressed for the new day. 'Morning, Van Wyk. You're here—' He looked from Clare to Van Wyk. 'Is something wrong?'

'Everything's fine,' Van Wyk managed to say. 'I was working most of the night. Dr Hart and I were just talking about solving cases, weren't we?' He didn't give Clare a chance to reply and walked down the passage, his tall, thin body cutting through a sudden flood of early-morning arrivals.

Clare flexed her wrists. She made herself breathe deeply, slowing her heart rate and ordering her jumbled thoughts. 'He's like a hand grenade without a pin,' she said.

'Oh, you mustn't worry about him too much,' said Karamata. 'He's always touchy first thing in the morning.'

'I won't,' said Clare, with feeling. 'I was worrying about Mara Thomson. Her mother called to say she never arrived home.'

Karamata stirred sugar into his tea and shook his head. 'If we followed up every report like this, we'd never do anything else. She'll call her mother when her money runs out.' His cellphone rang. He nodded at Clare and went into the corridor, firing a rapid volley of Herero into the receiver.

Clare sat down at Van Wyk's desk to get Mara's number from the case dockets on the shared server. She found it quickly and dialled. Mara wasn't answering. Unease, long since upgraded to anxiety, turned into fear.

Clare massaged her wrists, working out what to do, watching the screensaver on Van Wyk's computer. Her curiosity was piqued at his unprecedented diligence. She didn't imagine he'd been working on an expense report on the hunt for Spyt. She reached for the mouse. There were a couple of cases in the documents folder, but when Clare opened them, they were empty. She called up the mail programme minimised on the bar at the bottom of the screen. Viagra spam, a couple of e-mail memos from police headquarters in Windhoek. Routine stuff from Tamar. The sent box was sparse too. Nothing in the delete box either. She checked the file history. Nothing there. Clare sat back in the chair for a second. There was one last thing for her to try. She went to the recent items in the menu. Google. She clicked on the search history. One website only. Van Wyk had spent some time on it.

The site was dark, almost black. Explicit content warnings competed with the pop-ups of beckoning girls inviting viewers to 'cum see my first time'. So this is what he does in his spare time, Clare thought. Her mouth dry, she clicked on the entrance portal. The names and images of twenty half-naked women appeared. Amateur shots in suburban homes, classrooms, offices. Clare scrolled down the web page. The photos had been posted from all over the world, but they had two things in common: the youthfulness of the girls and the subtle brutality of their submission. In offices, classrooms and toy shops, around family dinner tables and in everyday places, were images of girls doing everyday things. One click transformed the image, and the girl was stripped, splayed and penetrated.

Clare scrolled through the images, but there was nothing to identify the anonymous postings. She was about to log out when the name of a video link caught her eye: Namib Nature Girls. Clare opened the first video. It was grainy, downloaded from a handheld camera, but it made her stomach turn. It was Van Wyk all right. He was standing in his uniform, his cap jaunty, his belt unbuckled, poised behind a naked, spread-eagled body. It was impossible to identify the recipient of Van Wyk's attentions. Then the film cut to a wide shot.

Clare froze. The ghost-smell of a putrefying cat caught at her throat. The altar, the ring of stones, the amphitheatre, the encircling trees. She looked closer at the body on the altar. It was a girl, her eyes glazed, limbs limp, a blank smile on her face. Her clothes in a pile on the floor. She looked drugged. LaToyah or Minki. The names scrawled on the cave. And Chesney, the other name. It must have been him holding the camera. There were other videos too. She flicked through the site, looking for Mara, but there was no sign of her. There were no boys either. The videos were strictly heterosexual. There were a couple of Angolan girls who Clare had noticed hanging around the entrance of the docks, so young that the breasts had barely budded on their skinny chests. She wondered how much these girls, paying in kind in the revolting little films, paid him in cash as well. Fury surged through her as she e-mailed the link to Tamar and hurried out of the office.

Riedwaan was pacing in front of the cottage when Clare got back. 'Where were you?' He flicked his cigarette away and followed her in. 'What took you so long?'

'What's the matter with you?' Clare asked.

'Unfamiliar territory.' Riedwaan's desire for an argument had ebbed as soon as he had Clare safe in front of him again. 'It puts me on edge.'

'I went past the station,' said Clare, making coffee.

'So early?'

'I got a call from Mara Thomson's mother,' Clare said. 'From London. Mara was meant to arrive there yesterday, but she never got off the plane.' Riedwaan looked blank. 'Mara volunteered at the school, teaching the homeless kids soccer,' she explained.

'So what's bothering you?' he asked.

'She knew those boys better than most people in this town,' said Clare, the kernel of anxiety unfurling from the pit of her stomach. She pushed the coffee away. The caffeine would only make her feel worse. 'She looked like them, too.'

'Did you go past her place?'

'Yes, and all her stuff's gone.'

'Boyfriend?' Riedwaan knew more about missing girls than he cared to.

'Yes,' said Clare. 'A sailor. Nice looking. I've met him.'

'If she's young and she has a boyfriend, that can mean two things,' said Riedwaan. 'She's safe and fucking him silly and her mother will be furious. Or she's dead. Either way, the boyfriend's your first port of call.'

'I'm going to see if she missed her flight first,' said Clare.

'Fine. I'll catch you later.' Riedwaan stopped in the doorway, silhouetted by the sun. 'Clare,' he said.

'What?' She turned from the sink where she had been rinsing her cup.

'You'll call me if you need me?'

'Of course, I'll call you.'

Clare locked the door behind Riedwaan, walked to the bath-room and turned on the shower tap. Her wrists hurt. They would look like Darlene's by tomorrow. It was only when she was in the shower, hot water needling down her back, that she realised that she hadn't told Riedwaan about Van Wyk. She pulled on her clothes, wishing that she had.

forty-three

Riedwaan's cellphone beeped as he parked his bike outside the police station. *Call me,* read the text. He dialled, smiling.

'Februarie, you cheap bastard.' Riedwaan could hear maudlin country music playing in the background.

'You still interested in that murder in McGregor?' Februarie grunted.

'You had an outbreak of altruism or what?' Riedwaan closed the door to the office. Neither Karamata nor Van Wyk was in. Tamar's door was closed.

'You wouldn't know altruism if it gave you a blow job,' said Februarie.

'What then?' said Riedwaan. 'You think I'm phoning you back because I like the sound of your voice? Just like I came to see you because of your pretty face.'

'As charming as ever, Faizal. No wonder you're such a one-hit wonder with women.'

'What have you got?'

'Some more background on your Major Hofmeyr. Seems he started in Pretoria with some obscure unit doing research. He was from the wrong side of the tracks with no links in the Afrikaner establishment. But he was a bright boy and he did well. Soon he had a beautiful wife from one of the oldest Cape families, nice house, fancy car, and trips overseas. Then he was transferred to another unit and sent to some hellhole in the Kalahari where—'

'Vastrap,' Riedwaan interrupted. 'His wife's already told us. She was less clear about what he did there.'

'That's the odd thing,' said Februarie. 'It looks like it was a promotion. More trips overseas. More money. He didn't do the party circuit like some of the others, but he had what he wanted in terms of research and travel. I can't find much, but it looks like it was weapons development and testing.'

'What kind of weapons?'

'Possibly nuclear. It looks like it was part of Operation Total Onslaught, PW Botha's baby. Born in 1972, baptised with the Soweto riots in 1976. The best minds; the best facilities; unlimited funding. It makes sense that it would be nuclear.'

'And then?'

'He was sent to Namibia in the eighties, where you could do what you liked, pretty much. Play God, and no one would ever know. And if they found out, what would they do about it?'

'Why was he shunted sideways?'

'Can't say if he was really. It was all classified. And shredded in the early nineties before Mandela could say *amandla*. De Klerk sold them down the river by decommissioning unilaterally in 1990.'

'What else have you got?'

'Well, I had another look at that TRC stuff. Like I said, Hofmeyr's name came up in a few of the hearings. The usual things: torture, a few extra-judicial killings, assaults. Him and two others, all from the same unit in Namibia, but it didn't look like he was going to apply for amnesty. And because nobody said anything, it just went away.' Februarie paused. 'Never happened for me,' he added.

'You fucked up in the wrong direction, Februarie. You went after the guys with money to buy enough politicians to make their own parliament.'

'That's my problem with altruism,' said Februarie.

'It's terminal,' said Riedwaan. 'You're born with it. This

therapy session is costing me five bucks a minute. I'm sure you can get it cheaper down there. Tell me what happened.'

'Extra-judicial killings,' Februarie mused. 'A good concept that – always makes me wonder what a judicial killing is.'

'No philosophy either, Februarie. What else? How is this connected to Hofmeyr's murder?' Riedwaan tried not to sound impatient; withholding information was Februarie's favourite game.

'Ja, well, Hofmeyr had a change of heart. He approached someone to make a full disclosure about what they'd been doing up there in Walvis Bay. Him and his friends.'

'He must've stood out like a parade ground corporal in a ballet tutu,' said Riedwaan.

'Funny, you mention Tutu. The only person who looked like he might be happy about it was the Arch. Hofmeyr wanted forgiveness, I suppose. The major was dying of cancer, so I guess he was afraid of that final court date. His offer was shoved from one desk to another, and then he was murdered. So it all went away overnight.'

'Until you started looking,' said Riedwaan.

'I was shafted,' said Februarie. 'Apparently my paperwork was bad.'

'Was it?'

'Of course it was. My paperwork's fucking terrible. But it always was before I got into any of this.'

'Why then?' asked Riedwaan.

'I found out that he had visitors before he died,' said Februarie, after a pause.

'Who told you?'

'The maid. Who else?'

'She see them?'

'No. Hofmeyr told her not to come for a couple of days. But

270

the woman who worked next door told her anyway. Two men. They argued on the second night. Then they left, and two days later, he was dead. Too many coincidences. The visitors while the wife was away. The convenient gangsters.'

'You think it was the wife?'

'You know what I think of wives,' said Februarie. Riedwaan knew. The whole force knew. Februarie's wife left him for her boss. Februarie had refused to take the fact that the boss was solvent, always sober and never violent as mitigating circumstances.

'But no. Not her. It's the visitors. I've been looking for them since I last saw you.'

'And did you find them?' Riedwaan felt his fingertips tingle in anticipation.

'No. But I did get the names of the two friends Hofmeyr was going to implicate in his disclosure.'

'Where did you get this from?'

'It might be hard for you to swallow, Faizal, but I still have a few chips to call in.'

'Who are they?' Riedwaan asked. 'Hofmeyr's friends?'

'Malan.'

'Malan?'

'Malan.' Februarie was enjoying Riedwaan's discomfort.

'Now there's a helpful name. There must be thousands of them.'

'This one runs a security consulting business out of Goodwood in Cape Town.'

Riedwaan knew the area well, poor and working class, clinging to respectability despite the backyards filled with cars on bricks. 'You got a number for him?'

'Jesus, Faizal. You ever heard of a phone book? Phoenix Engineering. Look it up.'

'Give it to me, Februarie. I know you've got it.'

'Okay, I'm standing in front of the place right now,' Februarie laughed.

'I thought you were at the Royal,' said Riedwaan. 'That shit music I heard in the background.'

'Don't insult the Man in Black,' said Februarie. 'That was Johnny Cash on my new tape deck.'

'Sorry, sorry,' said Riedwaan. 'Tell me what you see.'

Februarie was parked at the end of a littered cul-de-sac. 'Spanish burglar bars on the front,' he said. 'A pile of mail at the front door. Nothing inside. Empty. Everyone gone.'

'When would you say?' asked Riedwaan.

'The neighbours round here aren't that chatty, but one old lady told me no one's been here for a month.'

'She know the people?'

'No. Keeps her curtains shut. This isn't the type of neighbourhood where you pay too much attention to what your neighbours do. All she would say was that a man came here, used it for storage. Then he left and … nothing. I've done a company search. Not much, except some import/export permits to Pakistan.'

'And the other one?' asked Riedwaan.

'The other who?'

'Hofmeyr's other friend?'

'Oh him … Janus Renko.'

'Russian. That must've caused him trouble in the army.'

'From what I heard, he didn't take any shit. Parents were immigrants.'

'Do you know where he is?'

'No sign of him for ten years. No parents, no siblings. No ex-wives like Malan. No children like Hofmeyr. Could be he changed his name. Maybe he bought another passport, moved

272

elsewhere,' said Februarie. 'Could be dead, in which case you'll be hunting a ghost.'

'Where did your witness in McGregor see them?' asked Riedwaan, lighting a cigarette and going over to look at Clare's display.

'She didn't. All she saw was two extra sets of dirty sheets a couple of days before the major was shot. Made me wonder who Hofmeyr had had to stay.'

'Thanks, Februarie. I'll buy you a case of beer when I'm back.'

Riedwaan put down the phone and looked again at the places the boys had been found. A triangulation between Rooibank, the Kuiseb Delta and the ugly cinder-brick town. Pretty much the area where South Africa had camped thousands of miserable, sand-blasted conscripts in their decades-long war in Namibia. Why would any of these men come back? Walvis Bay had been about the worst army posting anyone could get.

Riedwaan looked closely at the pictures of Kaiser Apollis, Fritz Woestyn, Nicanor Jones and Lazarus Beukes. Why would anyone bother to shoot them? Scrawny little rejects, unlikely to live past their teens anyway.

He sat down at Clare's desk and opened her neat folders, looking for her interview transcripts. Details. The devil gave himself away in the detail. Riedwaan opened the first interview and started to read again.

forty-four

The plump blonde put down her coffee when Clare pushed open the door of the only travel agency in Walvis Bay.

'Can I help you?' she asked, almost cracking her heavy make-up with the first smile of the day.

'Morning, Sabina,' Clare said as she sat down opposite her.

'Have you been here before?' The girl looked disconcerted.

Clare pointed to the girl's name tag.

'Of course,' said Sabina. 'How can I help you?' She pecked at her keyboard with crimson-tipped nails, bringing the computer to life.

'I was wondering if you knew Mara Thomson.'

'Yes.' The girl's pretty mouth closed on the single syllable. 'I booked her ticket home for her. So if you're looking for her, she's gone. She would've left yesterday.'

'Will you check her booking for me?' Clare asked.

'Sure,' said Sabina. The printer muttered and whirred. 'Here you go. Yesterday. Lufthansa. Nine-thirty a.m.'

'Did you issue the ticket?'

'Oh yes. A week ago.'

'How did she pay?'

'Credit card,' said Sabina. 'But it wasn't hers. Someone from England paid. Look here. Mrs Lily Thomson, it says. Battersea. Where's that?'

'It's in London,' said Clare. 'Can I keep this?'

'Sure. Is there something wrong?'

'She never arrived. Her mother phoned this morning, frantic.'

'Shame!' Sabina's hand went straight to her mouth, though

her eyes glittered at the prospect of gossip. 'Poor lady. I told Mara she was leaving it late.'

'Leaving what late?'

'Telling Juan Carlos she was going home. It's hard for them when they stay long, these foreigners. I warned her that Juan Carlos would be angry if she didn't give him enough warning. Her boyfriend. He's Spanish and a sailor. You know how they like to be the ones who leave, not the other way round.'

Clare did not know that, but she let it slide.

'You ask my boyfriend.' Sabina wrote down an address on a slip of paper and handed it to Clare. 'They had a terrible fight, Mara and Juan Carlos, outside the club where Nicolai works.'

'Which club is that?' Clare asked.

'Der Blaue Engel. You must've been there. Everyone goes.' Sabina paused. 'Check at the airport first, but if she didn't leave, go around and wake Nicolai up. He'll know what's what.'

As Clare left, she heard the girl sharing the news with a friend over the telephone. Mara's disappearance and Clare's interest would not stay secret for long.

The morning plane to Walvis Bay had landed, loaded and taken off again by the time Clare had parked her car and entered the bleak airport terminal.

'Flight's left,' the check-in clerk told Clare as she approached the counter. He settled his shades on his nose and zipped up his bag.

'I'm not flying,' said Clare. 'I wanted to see if somebody flew yesterday.'

'Can't help you. The flight lists are confidential.'

'It's important. I'm investigating a missing person.' Official idiocy provoked in Clare an overwhelming desire to inflict grievous bodily harm. 'A girl who was meant to arrive in London and didn't.'

'Then you must get a warrant and come back.'

The man stood up, slipped on his jacket and went through the door behind his chair, closing it in Clare's face.

Clare suppressed an urge to swear. A customs official drinking tea at the café table gestured to her.

'Dr Hart,' the official said. 'Did you miss your flight?' It was the large woman who had stamped Clare's passport when she arrived.

'I'm not leaving,' Clare explained. 'I was trying to find out if somebody left on the Lufthansa flight yesterday.'

'That plane,' said the customs official, 'it was two hours late. It left at eleven-thirty eventually. Everyone was crazy here. Who were you looking for?'

'An English girl. I can't find her here, and she never arrived in London. The check-in clerk refused to help.'

'I can help you.' The official looked around. There was nobody in the terminal. 'Follow me.'

The woman led Clare through the restricted area to a heavy metal door. She twisted the combination lock, and the safe swung open, revealing an untidy Aladdin's cave of boxes, full of small square emigration forms.

'There must be thousands of them here,' said Clare.

'Ja, there are,' beamed the customs official. 'If your lady's here, we'll find her.' She picked up a box and cut open the seal. Lying on top was a muddle of forms from the previous day. She gave half of them to Clare. 'What's her name?' she asked.

'Mara Thomson,' said Clare. 'Thin, brown skin, lots of wild hair.'

'I didn't see her,' said the woman, ferreting through the forms. 'But she could've been processed by one of my colleagues.'

They sat down on the floor and rifled through the forms, deciphering the cramped handwriting of yesterday's passengers. Most of them had ticked 'holiday' under 'reason for visit', a few 'business'.

Clare read through the last form for the second time, fear returning, as cold as ice, in the pit of her stomach. 'It's not here,' she said. 'Could she have got on without handing in a form?'

'Not at all,' the woman bristled. 'We're very professional. Maybe she just changed her plans, didn't tell anyone. Young people are like that.'

Clare thanked the woman and went back to her car. She stood without getting in for some time, looking at the horizon. A fiery haze was erasing the thin line separating the sand and sky. A gust of east wind blew sand into her eyes. For the first time since she had arrived in Walvis Bay, she felt the implacable heat of the desert.

forty-five

'What?' A man's bleary eye appeared through a crack in the door. The heavy chain did not let the door three inches from the steel frame.

'Police,' chanced Clare. 'I have a question for you.'

A sharp-featured man unchained the lock. Nicolai, with a dirty sarong wrapped around him, was as unattractive a sight as his dingy flat above Der Blaue Engel.

'Come into the kitchen. I need some coffee.' Clare followed him into a gloomy room. A week's worth of dishes stood in the sink.

'I know you,' he said, sitting down at the table. 'You came in the bar the other night. Gretchen was dancing.' He smiled, revealing uneven and slightly yellow teeth.

'That's me,' said Clare, sitting down.

'So, Miss …'

'Dr Hart,' said Clare.

'So, Doctor,' Nicolai drawled, 'to what do I owe the honour of your presence?'

'I'm looking for Mara Thomson.'

'Why are you asking me?' The man's voice rose defensively.

'I wanted to speak to her. I heard she was at Der Blaue Engel the night before last.'

The sound of running water came from the direction where Clare guessed the bathroom was. It stopped, thickening the silence in the rancid kitchen. 'Where is she?' she asked.

'How the fuck would I know?'

'Did you see her last night?' Clare persisted.

'No.'

'The night before?'

'Yes. What's the deal? She's a big girl.'

'Who was she there with?'

'Juan Carlos, her boyfriend. Works on the *Alhantra*. Spanish. Pretty boy. I thought he went the other way, but then he arrived there with Mara. Not my type, English virgins,' said Nicolai, 'so you won't find her anywhere here.'

Nicolai leant back, his eyes sliding away from Clare to the doorway. 'This is more my type,' he added.

A Rubenesque woman strolled into the kitchen. She looked Clare over dismissively, poured herself a cup of coffee and strolled out again. Clare wondered if the woman had met Sabina.

'The maid,' said Nicolai, with a smirk. 'We were doing the bed.'

'When did Mara leave Der Blaue Engel?'

'Sometime after Gretchen's show.' Nicolai sipped his coffee. 'Must've been about two. She and Juan Carlos had a fight. Why don't you ask *him* where she is?'

Clare ignored his question. 'What did they argue about?'

'How should I know?' Nicolai said glibly. 'I went outside and saw them in the parking lot. They'd both been drinking. She was crying. He looked angry. Same old, same old.'

'Did they come back inside?'

'Juan Carlos came back later. I didn't see her again. He was upset and said that she'd walked home. Later he left with Ragnar Johansson. You know him, I think?' Clare nodded. 'Ask him. But the last time I checked there wasn't a law that the barman has to know what his customers do in their spare time.'

'There isn't,' said Clare, standing up. 'But there'll be consequences if you're withholding information.'

Nicolai stood too. 'If what I've heard is correct, Dr Hart, you've been paid by me and my fellow taxpayers to catch the motherfucker who's been cleaning up Walvis Bay.' Again, the suggestive smirk. It made his ratty features even less attractive. 'She looked very like those boys of hers, Mara did. Let's hope for her sake there hasn't been a mix-up.' Nicolai moved even closer to Clare. The implication of what he said, his breath rank in her face, made her shiver. 'Now, if you'll excuse me, I have some housework to finish.'

Clare needed no further encouragement. She breathed a sigh of relief as she went down the stairs from Nicolai's apartment. When she got to her car, she pulled out her phone and dialled Tamar's number; she was going to need help getting to Juan Carlos.

'Tamar.' Clare was very happy to hear her voice. 'Mara never arrived home.'

'I got your message,' said Tamar, concerned.

'I've checked at the airport. She didn't take her flight, but all her stuff's gone from George Meyer's house.'

'You need to go out to the *Alhantra* to talk to Juan Carlos?' Tamar guessed.

'As soon as possible,' said Clare.

'I'll organise you a motorboat. Give me a few minutes.'

'Thanks. Any news about Spyt?'

'I'm not holding my breath,' said Tamar. 'Spyt knows this desert too well. If he is found it'll be because he wants to be caught. Van Wyk disappeared out that way early. The evidence that the boys could've been there is all Goagab needs to get his lynch mob going. At least it gives me a bit of breathing space.'

'Did you look at that website I sent you?' Clare had almost forgotten to ask.

'I did. I'm working out what to do. I'm not sure if he's done anything illegal. The site claims all the girls are over eighteen. If they are, my hands are tied.' There was a beat of silence. 'I'm also putting out fires here,' Tamar added.

'What?' asked Clare. 'Riedwaan?'

'He and Goagab haven't exactly hit it off,' said Tamar. 'I had Goagab in my office, raging that the reason we invited you here was to look for a killer, not for young Englishwomen who stir up trouble.'

'I need to know if she was more than just their soccer coach,' said Clare. 'We need to find her.'

The skipper and speedboat were ready, the engine idling, when Clare got to the harbour. Five minutes later, the nose of the boat was chopping through the swell, to where the *Alhantra* and other ships were anchored, beyond the bay, where they could avoid harbour fees.

Clare plunged her hands into the front pocket of her jacket, her fingers wrapping around the envelope of Mara's photographs. More precious than a passport, which could be replaced by enduring the supercilious smile of a British embassy official. She opened the envelope, sheltering it from the wind with her body, to look at Mara's well-thumbed photos, the dainty drawings Oscar had done for her. The surreal whimsy of the drawing of a tree, ghostly against the endless dunes, hinted at the child's strange inner world. It was a haunting image. Why had Mara left them?

There was the picture of Mara and Oscar together. Mara searching for a place to belong; the mute boy, yearning for affection. The image caught their fragility and isolation. Mara and Oscar. They had understood each other. The little boy knew that Mara would never leave her pictures, her memories.

That is what he had been trying to make Clare understand.

Clare put herself in the place of the silent, unnoticed boy.

She pictured him opening the door off the kitchen. She saw him glide down the passage, a silent red-haired ghost, into Mara's room. Oscar would have found her room emptied but for the photographs hidden in their secret place. He had given them to Clare, so that she would do something.

Clare looked at them again. The last picture, the date in the corner six weeks earlier, was the photograph of Mara and her team. She had the triumphant smile of someone who has beaten the self-timer. She stood in the middle of the group, wiry-haired, boyish, wearing skinny jeans, with her arms around two boys who had turned up dead. The thought that the predator she was hunting had seen the same androgynous likeness in Mara goose-fleshed Clare's arms. She put the envelope back in her pocket.

The water unfurled a fringe behind the boat until it came to a bobby halt next to the *Alhantra*. The ship was high in the water, its hold emptied of fish. A ladder lolled like a tongue down the side. At the top of it stood Ragnar Johansson. Clare swallowed the fear that had balled tight and cold in her stomach. She put her hands on the ladder and began to climb, thinking of Mara at the rubbish dump, playing soccer in the dust and broken glass. So needy of love, of acceptance. She thought of her twined around Juan Carlos and wondered if Mara had given everything of herself over to him, if he had made her pay the ultimate price to assuage his loneliness.

Ragnar helped Clare aboard, his delight in seeing her obvious; his disappointment, when Clare told him the real purpose of her visit, equally apparent. He had half-hoped she had come to find him.

'Wait here,' said Ragnar, escorting Clare to the bridge. 'I'll fetch him for you.'

Ragnar took the steps into the dim interior of the vessel. The metal door screeched when he pushed it open. 'Juan Carlos,' he called into the gloomy cabin. The Spaniard lay on the top bunk. He grunted, without looking down to see who it was. 'You have a visitor.'

Juan Carlos turned onto his back and punched the metal ceiling above him. He licked the blood welling red on his knuckles, then he swung his legs off the side of his bunk and dropped, agile as a cat, to the floor and followed Ragnar to the bridge. He stopped when he saw Clare Hart, pulling his rosary beads from his pocket and passing them through his fingers until the crucifix halted them. Mara had given them to him. If he held the wood to his nose, it whispered of the hot interior.

'You know Dr Hart?' asked Ragnar.

Juan Carlos nodded.

'Where is Mara Thomson?' Clare dispensed with the formalities.

'In London,' said Juan Carlos, the vein at the base of his throat pulsing. He looked from Clare to Ragnar and back again. 'She left yesterday.'

'She never arrived,' said Clare. The creak of the ship was loud in the silence that Clare let stretch between them.

'Maybe she didn't go to her mother's house,' Juan Carlos tried. 'Her mother drive her crazy. So lonely.'

'She didn't check in at the airport.' Clare stepped closer to him. 'Where is she?'

'I don't know.'

'You were with her the night before she left.' Clare kept her voice low, intimately aggressive. 'You went home with her, made love to her, I imagine.'

Juan Carlos shook his head. 'No, no, I said goodbye and then I come back on board.' He looked at Ragnar. 'I had a pass. Twenty-four hours.'

Clare took Juan Carlos's hand in hers, tracing his bloodied

knuckles, the scratch along his sinewy wrist, his signet ring, a silver skull and crossbones.

'You didn't take her to the airport?'

'She didn't want me to go with her,' he said. 'What's happened to her? Why are you here?' He snatched his hand back.

'Why did you hit her?' asked Clare.

'I love her.' Juan Carlos said the words with no trace of irony.

Clare pictured the darkened parking lot. The hand raised. Mara's smooth cheek. The ring tearing open her taut skin. The contusion that would be developing.

'I was angry because she was leaving,' Juan Carlos went on. 'I was … I don't know the word.'

'Upset?' said Clare.

'Yes, yes, upset. I was very upset. She was too. She was sad to go from Namibia; she loved it here, her work. She was sad for saying goodbye to me too. So we fight. And then she go away.' He looked Clare in the eye, shifting the balance of power away from her. 'You never fight with someone before you go away?'

'That is the last you saw of her?' Clare shifted the control back. 'In the parking lot? Where you hit her?'

'Yes,' he said, leaning against the metal railing. 'No.'

'You were away from the bar a while.' Clare listened to Juan Carlos's beads clicking persistently in the quiet. 'Nicolai says an hour. That's a long time to spend in a parking lot.'

'Okay, okay,' said Juan Carlos, lighting a cigarette. 'She left. I was very angry to start with, but then I think, is she home? I want to tell her I am sorry, so I follow her. Nothing. She was walking fast when she left, so I go to her house. Her light is on and I knock on her window. She doesn't answer. I call her phone. She doesn't answer. I think she's in the bath maybe. But she doesn't want to speak to me. I leave her a message to call me, that I'm sorry. It's cold and I don't want to wake up the other people in the house. She's angry. She's still a woman, even if she looks like a boy. And I think, what more can I do? So I come back to the bar.' He looked at Ragnar, who nodded.

'What time was that?' Clare asked.

'About three, three-thirty, I suppose,' Ragnar answered. 'Just before I left.'

'Then I get her text message to say sorry the next morning from the airport. Here, look.' Juan Carlos pulled his phone out of his pocket, found the text message and shoved the screen in front of Clare. 'I was already on board ship,' he said. 'I couldn't see her again. I sent her a text, but nothing. It's too late. She was on the plane already.'

'You hit her because you were upset, and she forgave you that easily?' asked Clare. 'You're lying, Juan Carlos.'

'You see that?' Juan Carlos flung his arm towards the desert. The wind whipped tongues of flame-coloured sand into the sky. The sandstorm was preparing to strike the bunkered town. 'That is what we fought about,' he spat.

'I'm not following you,' said Clare. 'Explain.'

'The east wind … it is on its way,' Juan Carlos continued. His tone was resigned. 'It was the same weather the weekend that we fight.'

'What happened that weekend?'

'She went out to the desert, and the east wind, it was blowing. She take her soccer boys – Kaiser Apollis, Lazarus Beukes, I can't remember the other names – to camp in the Kuiseb River. It was a reward because they did well in some five-a-side tournament. We came in to port for the weekend and I phone her. She didn't want to come back, because she always put them first. She say that's what they needed to see: someone putting them first. But I tell her to leave them and come and see me. I say she should fetch them in the morning. I told her they were

285

used to looking after themselves. That they would be fine. It was true.'

Juan Carlos watched a gull turn on a column of air, mesmerised by its flight. 'They *were* fine that weekend, except the one who got sick. That is what we fight about. She felt bad that she left them out there. She blames herself. We went back to fetch them the next day and they were not there. She found them later at the dump. They say they had walked back; that is why the young one, he got sick.'

'And that's why you hit her?' asked Clare.

'I didn't want her to tell you.' Juan Carlos looked down at his feet. 'She wanted to come to you or the other lady cop and tell you that she had been with them all and that now they were all dead. She was crazy about it. I tell her it was just coincidence. I was saying, no, if she tells, then the police will want to question her and me. And the ship is sailing tomorrow. If the police want to ask questions, then I can't go too and I won't get my fishing bonus.'

'How many boys did you say there were there?' asked Clare.

'Five. It was the five-a-side tournament.'

Two. Three. Five. One with no marking. One unaccounted for. Clare calculated how long it would take to get to the dump when she was finished. Half an hour, she reckoned.

'You'll have to stay on board,' said Clare. 'Captain Johansson will keep you under guard.'

'Why?' Juan Carlos pleaded. 'What have I done?'

'You were the last person seen with her,' said Clare. 'If you'd prefer you can come ashore and go to the cells.'

Juan Carlos paled.

'I'll need your cellphone.' Clare held out her hand.

'For what?' asked Juan Carlos. 'I tell you already, she text me.'

'I want to track all the calls on your phone,' said Clare. 'Calls in and out. You can choose: I take your phone and check, or you can come in with me and I put you in the cells for refusing to cooperate.'

Clare was bluffing, but he was a foreigner, wanting to get home. It worked. Juan Carlos handed her the phone, the fight gone out of him.

'Ragnar,' she said, 'can you keep him under guard?'

'No problem,' said Ragnar. 'We're out of here soon. If you want him longer, and you've got grounds, I'll have to hand him over to the Namibian police.'

Ragnar walked with Clare to the top of the ladder. 'You think he did something to that girl?' he asked.

'The odds are against him.'

'You're not a gambler, Clare.'

'No, I'm not. But I won't take any more chances either. If Mara knew something about what happened to those boys, then Juan Carlos might too. I'd watch him. It might be for his own sake.' Clare stepped onto the ladder to climb down to the speedboat waiting for her. 'Where are you headed?' she asked.

'Luanda tomorrow, after the shareholders' inspection,' said Ragnar. 'Then Spain. You can imagine that I need this like a hole in the head.'

forty-six

It was quiet at the rubbish dump. The first flurry of trucks had come and gone and the incinerator was pluming smoke into the sky. The boys who had been so eager to greet Clare the first time she had visited slunk away. She went to the lean-to where Kaiser Apollis and Fritz Woestyn had shared a mattress. The bed was untouched, as was their meagre assortment of garments. One of the braver boys hovered in the doorway, a younger child sheltering behind him.

Clare called him over and showed him Mara's team photograph. 'Where is this boy?' she asked.

The boy's expression closed down like a mask. 'Ronaldo's gone,' he said, his voice low.

'Where?'

The boy shrugged. 'Miss Mara took him.'

'Mara took him? Where? Where did she take him?' Clare's voice wavered.

'To the desert.' Emotion flickered in the boy's eyes, but Clare could not read it. 'He never came back again.'

'Okay, where did she take him?' Clare softened her tone.

'Ask Mr Meyer,' the boy said. 'He knows where they go.'

The younger boy cupped his hands and looked at Clare, eyes wide, pleading. 'You got some change for bread, madam?' Clare fished in her bag for money.

George Meyer was alone in his office, his hands folded on the empty desk. His tie, knotted too tight below the Adam's apple, bulged a fold of skin onto his collar.

'What do you want this time, Dr Hart?' he asked when Clare

appeared in the doorway.

'These boys. Four are dead. Now Mara's missing.' Clare propped the photograph against his hands. 'Where is this one?'

Meyer picked up the photograph and looked at the frail boy. The child's bony ribs tented the skin on his chest. 'Ronaldo. I haven't seen him for a while. He was sick.' He handed the photograph back to Clare.

'Where will I find him?' said Clare. 'If he isn't dead yet.' Clare leant close to Meyer. She kept the impatience from her voice.

'The only place that would take him would be the Sisters of Mercy.'

Clare remembered Lazarus's fear of the nuns. 'Where are they, these Sisters of Mercy?'

'Out in the Kuiseb, past the delta. The road to Rooibank. You'll see the turn-off there.'

'A convent?' asked Clare.

'It's a hospice now. The sisters take people who no one else wants.'

'And it was Mara who took him there?'

'Yes. Those boys on the dump are like a pack; they look after their own. But this child was the runt of the litter. Mara was attached to him. She has a thing for underdogs. Why do you think she liked Oscar?' Meyer's voice snagged in his throat. 'Or me for that matter?'

Clare turned off the tar road, leaving the row of pylons and phone lines that trudged on to the airport. There was nothing to see but the mesmerising expanse of gravel rolling up to meet the car, then fanning dust behind her. The outcrop of black rock reared above the red sand like the exposed skeleton of some ancient animal. Clare bumped down the track towards it, surprised by the alluring green cleft in the heat-cracked surface.

The convent had been built into the cool overhangs and caves that formed the oasis.

Clare parked and walked down the swept path that led into a perfect amphitheatre. A woman came towards her, her welcoming smile a startling splash of white against her dark skin. A loose wimple covered her head, her gnarled feet secured in sturdy sandals. A Sister of Mercy.

'Welcome.' The woman took Clare's hand between her cool palms. 'Come out of the sun.' She led Clare to a shaded veranda. 'Wait here. I'll fetch the Mother Superior.'

Clare sat on a bench and closed her eyes, the cloistered tranquillity of the oasis working its seductive magic on her.

'My child.' A gentle voice broke the spell.

Clare opened her eyes. A tall woman stood before her. Her habit fell from broad shoulders that looked as if they carried the weight of the Lord with ease. The hand she offered Clare was muscular, calloused. Her face had been weathered down to its essence: a beaked nose, arched iron-grey eyebrows, a tapestry of lines and crevices on the tanned skin.

'I'm Sister Rosa. You're welcome here.' Her accented English gave an old-fashioned lilt to her words.

'Good morning, Sister. I'm Clare Hart.'

'You have no bags with you. I presume that you want something specific from us?'

'I wanted to ask you some questions about a child who was brought here,' Clare explained.

'Follow me.' Sister Rosa's habit swished wide, drawing Clare into its wake. Clare followed her into a cool study. On a low table was a pile of dog-eared pamphlets about prayer and meditation, healing and love, HIV/Aids and dying with dignity.

'What is it that you are looking for?' Sister Rosa asked, sitting down.

'A boy,' said Clare. 'I'm hoping he is here with you, alive.'

'His name?' asked Sister Rosa.

'Ronaldo. That's all I know. He doesn't seem to have a surname.'

Sister Rosa opened a leather-bound ledger. She flicked through it until she found the page dedicated to him. 'Here you are.' She pushed it over to Clare. 'All I have about him.'

The notes were brief: the boy's name. His age: barely fourteen. Parents: unknown. Previous address: none. Date of arrival: four weeks earlier, just before Fritz Woestyn was found dead by the pipeline.

'A young English girl, Mara Thomson, brought him here,' said Clare.

'Poor child,' said Sister Rosa. 'She lost her heart to this place.'

'You knew her well?'

Sister Rosa nodded. 'She came out here a few times.'

'Four of the boy's friends are dead. And now Mara has disappeared,' said Clare.

'Where is she?' Sister Rosa's voice was full of concern.

'I'm trying to find that out,' said Clare. 'When last did you see her?'

'About a week ago. She came to see this boy you seek.'

'I'd like to see him. Maybe he can help.'

'Come this way then,' said the nun after a moment's hesitation. 'He has some lucid moments.'

Clare followed Sister Rosa down a path shaded by tamarisks. At the end of it was a sparse row of old stone-crossed graves. Alongside these was an abundance of new mounds, lozenge-shaped heaps with wooden crosses. The newest graves had posies of veld flowers on them. The rest were bare. Sister Rosa passed the graveyard and walked towards a stone building shaded by vivid green trees.

The interior of the building was dim and cool. An old nun, her face wrinkled as a walnut, rose as they entered. 'The sick boy?' Sister Rosa asked the nun. The woman pointed to an open door and they went inside.

'There he is, your Ronaldo.'

A child, impossibly thin, lay on a narrow bed with a drip attached to his arm. His breathing was laboured; the lips were cracked and dry; his skin was a dull grey. There was a photograph on the bedside table. The same boy propped against plumped pillows, a toothy grin on his gaunt face.

'Mara took that the last time she was here,' said Sister Rosa. 'He was so pleased with it.' She moistened a cloth under the tap and wiped the boy's face. Ronaldo's eyes flickered open, then closed again.

'Mara knew how ill he is?' Clare asked.

'She phoned a couple of days ago and I had to tell her he was much worse,' said Sister Rosa. 'It happens like that, with his condition, but she was distraught. Kept on saying it was her fault.'

'Has Mara brought other boys to you?'

'No,' said Sister Rosa. 'Only him, although she used to raise money for us. Ronaldo played in her soccer team and she said something about him being pushed too hard. It must've broken his immune system, because he collapsed after a camping trip that Mara had organised for the team. She brought him here afterwards, asking us to keep quiet. Ronaldo was afraid other people would find out. There's a terrible stigma about this illness.'

'What's killing him?' asked Clare.

'Technically, a single-digit CD4 count. He has no immune system and a host of secondary infections. That's what will stop his heart from beating in the end.' Sister Rosa stroked the boy's forehead. 'But his heart was broken a long time before.'

'Abuse?' asked Clare.

'Abuse, poverty, Aids. It's not hard for a child to support himself in a place like Walvis Bay, but the way he had to make a living is a death sentence. It was too late for treatment when we got him, so I suppose you could say he came here to die.' Sister Rosa turned to Clare. 'What was it that you wanted to ask him?'

'I wanted to ask him about that camping trip in the desert.' Clare looked down at the boy, the sheets barely raised over his emaciated body. 'About where they went and what happened. Seems to me it was the start of something that played out to a very bloody finish.'

'At least these have healed,' said Sister Rosa, picking up the child's right hand and smoothing open the palm.

'What was there?'

'Blisters, deep ones. It's only the scars now. They were infected and then healed so slowly. Poor child, he was in agony.' She drew Ronaldo's thin sheet up to his chin and smoothed his pillows.

'Do you know what they were from?' asked Clare, her pulse quickening.

'I asked him; he said it was from the digging they did, but I couldn't work out where. Somewhere in the desert. Maybe they had casual work on the water pipeline. He had some money when Mara brought him.' The nun opened the Bible lying next to the boy's bed. There was forty Namibian dollars in notes tucked into Revelations. Clare thought about Kaiser Apollis and the diary with one hundred dollars in it. She tried to remember the boy's hands, but all she could picture was the tipless Apollo finger.

'He was terrified of the desert,' Sister Rosa continued. 'It must've been torture for him to camp there with Mara. I sat up with him one night. The moon was full, and he couldn't sleep with the curtains open. He kept saying they would see him.'

'Who?'

'Who knows?' said Sister Rosa. 'Whoever it is that you see when your temperature hits forty.'

There was no point in asking the boy any questions. Each shallow breath marked a loosening of Ronaldo's tenuous hold on life. Clare stood up and followed Sister Rosa to the entrance lobby. The old nun they had passed on the way in nodded politely to her.

'Did anybody come to see the boy apart from Mara?' Clare asked on impulse.

'Nobody,' said Sister Rosa. 'Except you.'

'You,' the old nun interrupted, 'and one of the missionaries.'

'Who are they?' Clare swung around to face the woman.

'The Christian Ladies' Mission. A group of worthy wives. Protestants,' Sister Rosa said with a wry smile. 'They work with prostitutes. They rarely come out here. I suppose they've given up on us Catholics.'

'When was that, Sister?' Clare asked the old nun.

'Three days ago,' she replied. 'Just before Ronaldo started slipping away from us.'

'What was she doing here?' Sister Rosa asked. 'Why was I not informed?'

'I'm sorry, Sister,' said the older nun. 'I forgot my sewing in the convent and when I came back the woman was here. The child was very upset, but I got her to leave and he settled down again.'

'Did you know her?' Clare asked.

'She was young. Fair. I don't know her name. She said she wanted to save him, but I think that even she could see that it was too late.' The nun hesitated. 'They can be … agitating, re-formed sinners. Zealous.'

'You'll find them easily, Dr Hart,' Sister Rosa said. 'They have their haven, as they call it, down near the docks.' The woman's hand on Clare's elbow propelled Clare back into the heat.

Clare's car was a furnace when she got back to it. She opened the window, letting the hot air escape before she got in. The heat swam on the surface of rocks, the road and the car as she drove back to Walvis Bay, mirroring her thoughts. What did Mara know? Why had she hidden the boy Ronaldo out here? And why had she not said anything? Why had Lazarus said nothing? This circuit of questions was interrupted only when Clare found the Christian Ladies' Mission. It was situated opposite Der Blaue Engel, where the ladies could keep an eye on their husbands while saving the town from moral turpitude. Housed on the ground floor of an ugly facebrick building, the entrance to the Mission was decorated with watercolour landscapes and crocheted doilies, no doubt donated by its members.

The woman who got up to greet Clare was slender, her hair set in even, rigid waves. 'Dr Hart?'

Clare was getting used to strangers knowing her name. She nodded.

'How can I help you?'

'I need to know about one of your members who visited a boy out at the Catholic hospice in the desert.'

'Why, may I ask, should I give you this information?' The woman's mouth was a red-lipsticked slot in her face.

'I'm working on the investigation into the recent murders of—'

'The boys?' the woman interrupted.

'Them,' said Clare.

'Well,' said the woman, pursing her lips, 'we've tried to reach out to street children before, especially the Aids orphans. But it's difficult to get children who have strayed from the authority of adults to conform.'

'Which of your members would've visited him there?' asked Clare.

'I'll check in the record book. But I can't imagine anybody did. When was it?'

Clare gave her the date, and the woman opened the book and paged through to the relevant entry. 'Nothing then.' She shook her head. 'Not to the convent at any rate.'

'The woman who visited him was blonde apparently. Young,' Clare said.

The woman frowned. 'I can't think of anybody who fits that particular description.' She pushed the ledger over to Clare. 'And see for yourself. Nobody went out that day. Everything's logged, because our volunteers can claim for petrol.'

'Would one of your members have gone without filling in the forms?' asked Clare.

The woman drew herself up, offended. 'All our volunteers are working here towards salvation and rehabilitation. Part of that process means that they must follow procedures in all situations. The leadership, and I include myself in that, are unwavering about such details.'

'Who could it have been, then?'

'Dr Hart, I'm a lay preacher, not a detective.'

forty-seven

Riedwaan was in the special ops room, a takeaway coffee in hand and Clare's notes and several official-looking printouts spread out in front of him. The sheets spiralled on a gust of wind when she opened the door.

'Where've you been?' Riedwaan got up to retrieve the pages.

'Out in the desert,' said Clare. 'At sea.'

'That's how I feel, going through all of this.' He gestured to Clare's notes.

'Did I miss anything?'

'Nothing that I can see.' Riedwaan sat down again and picked up a heap of papers. 'I was just checking through these car rentals. See who's been passing through.'

'Any patterns?' Clare asked.

'Not yet. German tourists mainly. A few businessmen coming up for meetings. I'm working through them. You haven't come across the name Phoenix Engineering while you've been here?'

'Doesn't ring a bell,' said Clare. 'Why? Are they on your list?'

'Februarie mentioned the name to me,' he said. 'He phoned earlier about Hofmeyr's murder. It's the name of a company that one of Hofmeyr's connections set up after he left the army. A guy called Malan.'

'Haven't heard of him either,' said Clare. She picked up the car hire lists, scanning the names. 'No Phoenixes here,' she said. 'Although there're a couple of other Greek names sprinkled in. Here's one: Siren Swimwear. That sounds promising. How about this one: Centaur Consulting?'

'The advantages of a classical education revealed,' said Ried-waan.

'Funny ha-ha,' said Clare. She scanned the list again. 'There's also Arizona Iced Tea and New York Trading and Washington Pan-African Ministries. What're you looking for?'

'I'm just casting about for an easy answer, I guess. A psycho ex-soldier running amok would be easy to explain. It'd certainly make the Namibians happy.'

'You've had Goagab on your back then?' Clare sat down on the edge of the desk.

'I had the pleasure. He was in here demanding a resolution before his tourism press junket or whatever it is that makes him sweat in his Hugo Boss shirts.' Riedwaan crumpled his coffee cup and pitched it into the bin on the other side of the room. 'Tell me about Mara's sailor boy. You think he did something to her?'

'I don't know what he's hiding, but he implied that she was.'

'You could hide an army out here and no one would find it,' said Riedwaan, pointing to the waves of sand on the map.

A movement at the door caught their eye, and they both looked up to find Tamar standing in the doorway. 'You see nothing,' she said, her voice soft. 'Everything's hidden by the heat and the distance, then these dunes pick up their skirts and move and everything's exposed. What did you find out about Mara?' she asked Clare.

Clare gave her the rundown: that Mara and Juan Carlos had fought about a camping trip; that Mara had wanted to tell the police that she'd left the boys alone in the desert while she was servicing Juan Carlos's needs for the night; that the boys were being targeted now; and that Juan Carlos had shut her up.

'They fought about it again the night before Mara was supposed to leave,' Clare said. 'Mara went home and he says he went back to the club. Says he never saw her again, though she apparently sent him a text message from the airport.'

'What do you think?' Tamar asked Clare.

'About him?'

'About her, her and the boys?'

'Hard to say. If someone is targeting homeless pretty boys, then it could be a coincidence, I suppose. She was working with them, spending more time with them than anyone else does, so a "wrong place, wrong time" is possible.'

'Funny things, coincidences,' said Riedwaan.

'Never happens in movies, because no one will ever believe them,' said Tamar. 'In real life they happen all the time. Wrong place, wrong time. There's you: dead.'

'She left all her photographs behind.' Clare put the envelope of snapshots on the table.

'Memories go sour sometimes.' Riedwaan flicked through them. 'You move on, leave the past behind. Could be that.'

Clare was sceptical, but said nothing. 'Tamar, do you know the Sisters of Mercy?' she asked. 'Out in the desert, in an old castle?'

'Yes, towards Rooibank. There's an oasis there. Some German count built a castle for the love of his life and she never came. So he donated it to the Catholic Church, specifying that it be run as a convent. Now it's a hospice.'

'There's a lesson in that,' said Riedwaan. 'I'm not quite sure what.'

'Why do you ask?' said Tamar.

Clare picked up the photograph of Mara and the five-a-side team and pointed to Ronaldo. 'A boy who played in Mara's team was out there. George Meyer told me about him. I went to talk to him.'

'What did he say?' asked Tamar.

'Nothing. He's on his way out,' said Clare. 'Full-blown Aids. Too far gone for treatment.'

'He's the last boy alive,' Riedwaan said. 'Her whole team, red-carded.'

'There's something else,' said Clare. 'The Mother Superior told me a woman had visited him. She thought it was one of the Christian Mission ladies, but I went past there and they have no record of anyone visiting.'

A sudden gust of the east wind sprayed sand against the office window. Clare jumped, then continued: 'His hands were infected when he came in, blisters all over the palms. His illness was triggered by exhausting himself doing some kind of digging.'

'Digging where?' asked Tamar. 'None of those kids would be picked up to work. First, nobody would trust them, and, second, if anyone did hire them, they'd be bust under the child labour law – one of the many unintended consequences of a progressive constitution.'

'Catch-22,' said Clare.

'I wonder what they were digging for,' Riedwaan said. He opened the files of autopsy photographs and sorted out the close-ups. 'Look at this.' Kaiser Apollis and Lazarus Beukes both had thin, livid marks across their palms.

'Could be blisters,' said Clare, looking at the photographs. 'Easy to pass over in a homeless child whose hands and feet would be rough and cracked.'

'You get anything else from your interview with Juan Carlos?' asked Tamar.

'His phone.' Clare held it up. 'I want to check out his story about the night Mara went missing. I've asked Ragnar Johansson to keep him on board until you've decided if you want to keep him here. In the meantime, I want to check some phone records.'

'There's a place out in the industrial area that'll figure it out for you in no time.' Tamar wrote down the address. 'Cell City. They'll help you out.'

'Did you talk to Van Wyk?' Clare asked Tamar, folding the piece of paper.

Tamar shook her head. 'He's still out of cellphone range. He's scouring the desert with Goagab, but I did find Chesney, the name we saw painted on the cave. Turns out he's Van Wyk's nephew.'

The mention of Chesney's name made Clare shiver: Chesney, Minki, LaToyah, the heat and the stench of the dead cat. 'What did he say?' she asked.

'Not much at first,' said Tamar. 'But Elias can be persuasive when he needs to be. He convinced Chesney that it'd be simpler if he just showed him a couple of files, his web cam, and some other incriminating evidence. The girl you saw, LaToyah, is fifteen, so as far as Van Wyk goes, it'll be a fairly straightforward case of statutory rape.'

'All we need to do is find him then,' said Clare.

'What's this?' Riedwaan asked. 'Van Wyk been cradle-snatching?'

'A cop getting freebies off the girls he protects. Oldest trick in the policeman's book,' said Tamar. 'How about you find this killer now.' She was standing in the doorway, keys in hand. 'My water broke half an hour ago and I'm off to have this baby in peace.'

Riedwaan went pale. 'We'll take the bike.' He tossed Clare the spare helmet.

Outside, the sun sparkled off the razor wire, the snagged plastic flapping, its colour bleaching in the heat. Even the black slagheap across the road managed to give off an ebony gleam.

Clare slipped her arms around Riedwaan and her hands under his jacket.

'It is better with you here,' she said as they drove through town.

'I was waiting for you to say that,' said Riedwaan.

'Only because I like having a driver,' she teased him. 'There it is. Cell City.'

The two chinless wonders who ran the cellphone shop looked as if they could hack into the Pentagon. Darren was blond, his hair hanging in greasy rats' tails over the faded picture on his T-shirt – some heavy metal group doomed to permanent obscurity, Clare hoped. She explained that they wanted to know where Mara's last SMS had come from.

'No problem,' he said.

'You want a list of all the numbers called? Texts?' asked Carl. He had dark hair, and was as soft and blubbery as his friend was bony. 'I can download the pictures too.'

'That'd be great,' said Clare, writing down Mara's number. 'How long will it take?'

'I can do that for you straight away,' he said. 'Darren'll take a bit of time, but this is a small town, so there's just a couple of thousand cell users. Do you want to come back?'

'We'll wait.'

Darren beamed up at them from behind his laptop. 'Go get some coffee there.' He pointed to a Portuguese café across the road. 'A watched hacker never cracks.'

Carl found this hilarious. He emitted a series of stricken hoots that passed for a laugh.

'Come on,' Riedwaan said to Clare. 'We'll get some coffee.'

The café served unexpectedly good coffee. They took their cups and some rolls to the only table outside.

'So, tell me about Van Wyk,' said Riedwaan.

Clare smiled grimly as she told him of Van Wyk's sidelines

in extortion and amateur porn. Nothing pleased her more than ridding the world of another corrupt bully.

They had just finished eating when Carl undulated across the road. He grabbed a Coke and a Peppermint Crisp on his way to their table.

'Darren,' he said admiringly. 'He's a fucking wizard.' He placed a single sheet of paper on the greasy tablecloth. A list of numbers in one column, coordinates in the other. Carl bit off half of his chocolate bar before pointing to the last number. 'There you go. The SMS you were looking for. That's it.'

'Where was it sent from?' asked Riedwaan.

'The airport tower is where it's first logged.'

'So she was there?'

'Who was there?' Carl shovelled the second half of the bar into his mouth and washed it down with Coke.

'Mara Thomson. The girl who sent the message.'

'This one?' Carl scrolled through the photos in Juan Carlos's cellphone, stopping when he got to one of Mara, naked on a sand dune, smiling at the phone camera.

'That's the one.'

'So pretty,' said Carl wistfully. 'What's she done that you're looking for her?'

'It's what she hasn't done that's worrying me,' said Clare. 'She left Walvis Bay, but never arrived in London. Her boyfriend claims that the last he heard from her was this SMS from the airport.'

'Well, from the tower closest to the airport. But that covers quite a range out there. It could be anywhere from the Kuiseb Delta to Rooibank.'

'These other numbers?' Clare asked.

'Recent calls. A couple to Spain. The others are all local numbers. Looks like whoever's phone this is had this girl's number on speed dial.'

'I tried to call her earlier,' said Clare. 'It just says the number is unavailable and to try again later.'

'That means she's out of range or her phone is off,' Carl explained. 'Or her battery's dead.'

'If Mara was in the vicinity of the airport,' said Clare, 'then why did she never go in?'

'Oh no,' said Carl, excited at the prospect of playing detective, 'she got on the plane all right. Check this out.' He pointed to a column on the next page, listing all the SMS messages. 'This is what she said.'

Riedwaan looked at the screen: *On the plane. Sorry. I love U. X Mara.*

'I saw that,' said Clare. 'But it seemed pretty standard to me. Anybody could have sent that text.'

'Amateurish as a cover,' said Riedwaan. 'Someone was going to phone when she didn't get to London.'

'But if you go missing in the desert, it can be a long time before anyone finds you,' said Clare, deciphering the columns of digital information that Darren had teased from the phone.

'Unless you're a homeless boy. Then after two days you're stuck up like a billboard advertising the fact that someone really didn't like you.'

'Have a look at this.' Clare pointed to the time the message was received: nine-twenty.

Riedwaan and Carl looked at her blankly.

'Her plane was two hours late. Nobody was even on the plane until eleven.'

Riedwaan parked his bike outside the station. Clare was heading for the door before he even had a chance to switch off the engine.

'That schoolteacher you mentioned in McGregor,' Riedwaan called after her. 'Did she marry again?'

'Darlene?' Clare turned around, remembering that she had meant to talk to her again.

Riedwaan nodded.

'No, she'd had enough of men after her first husband. She just shed her married name. Why do you—?'

The shrill sound of Clare's phone interjected. She took it out of her pocket and looked at the flashing screen. 'Tertius Myburgh,' she said to Riedwaan. 'My pollen expert. I thought he'd vanished. Let me take this.' She held the receiver to her ear and nodded a greeting at the receptionist as she entered the station.

Riedwaan followed her down the passage in a daze, his manner unusually calm.

Clare sat down at her desk and disconnected. 'He's got my results,' she said, reaching for a mapbook. 'I'm going to meet him at Dolphin Beach. It's halfway between Walvis Bay and Swakopmund.'

'Can you handle this on your own?' asked Riedwaan. 'There's something I must do.'

'I'll call you when I'm back,' said Clare, grabbing her keys. 'Where are you going?'

'To see your ballet-dancing divorcée,' Riedwaan smiled. 'Darlene Ruyters. To find out what she can tell me about centaurs and phoenixes.'

forty-eight

One kick would have ripped the newly installed chain out of the door, but Riedwaan rang the doorbell.

'Yes?' Darlene Ruyters opened the door a crack.

'Captain Faizal. Police.' Riedwaan always felt stupid holding up his badge like an American movie cop, but he did it anyway. People watched so much television these days they expected it. Darlene put out a hand for the badge before sliding back the chain and letting him in. Riedwaan stepped into the gloomy hallway. The smell of a thousand houses he had visited: the combination of yesterday's cooking and fear.

'Where is he, Darlene?'

Darlene's eyes widened. 'There's nobody here.' She crossed her arms. She wasn't wearing a bra.

Pushing past her, Riedwaan went down the passage. He opened the first door, Darlene's bedroom. Peach nylon lace and pale-green walls. A worn, shaggy carpet and a pile of teddy bears on the bed. He opened the next door: a bed, a table, a chair, a lamp. Not a thing out of place, but the windows closed, and the smell of a man in the stale air.

'Where's he gone?' Riedwaan demanded.

Darlene was right behind him, her dark hair framing her pale, once-beautiful face. 'You can see. There's no one,' she said, turning away, but Riedwaan caught her arm and swung her around again, light as a bird against his arm. The bruises on her wrists had faded to shadows. Riedwaan nudged her collar away from her neck. There was a livid contusion on her clavicle. He felt the back of her head. She winced. The skin there was broken.

'Tell me where he is,' said Riedwaan. 'Your house guest, who left such a charming thank-you gift.'

'I don't know what you're talking about,' Darlene whispered. Riedwaan let her go. She swayed on her bare feet.

'The guy who hired the car. Centaur Consulting,' said Riedwaan. He pulled the car-hire forms out of his pocket and showed them to her. 'Fifty-three 2nd Avenue. Your address. He hasn't returned the car yet. Your ex-husband.'

'Malan.' The name twisted Darlene's mouth as if it were poison. She slid down the wall until she was folded, small as a child, on the floor.

Riedwaan was unmoved. 'When did he leave?'

Darlene stopped resisting, a drowning woman too tired to fight any more. 'The day before yesterday,' she whispered.

'Where did he go?' Riedwaan knelt down in front of her. He lifted her chin so that she had to look at him.

'To cash in his pension.' Darlene laughed, her bitterness corrosive.

'What're you talking about?' said Riedwaan. 'I'm out of time.'

'What are you going to do? Hit me too?' She looked him up and down. 'I'm an expert in that area and *you*,' she spat, 'haven't got it in you.'

'Why did Malan come here to you?' asked Riedwaan.

'I don't know. He didn't explain. He wanted somewhere to stay. Somewhere where he wouldn't be seen. I don't know.' Darlene got up slowly, the pain of movement making her wince.

'You didn't refuse?'

'This is what I got without arguing.' Darlene unbuttoned her blouse. Her delicate body was black and blue to the waist. 'I thought, it can't last forever. And it didn't. He left.'

Riedwaan put out his hands and gently buttoned up her blouse again. 'Where will I find him?' he asked.

'If he's not out in the desert then I hope to God he's gone.'

'The desert?'

'The sand on his boots. He made me clean them for old times' sake. They were full of the golden dust you find further in. Fool's gold.'

'Why would he be back? Think, Darlene.'

She shook her head. 'I don't know. But if I know them at all, I can guess.'

'Them?' Riedwaan took her by the shoulders. She winced again.

'Malan. Hofmeyr.' She waved her hand dismissively. 'Except he's dead now.'

'Janus Renko?' Riedwaan tested.

A shadow passed over Darlene's face. 'I haven't heard that name in a long time.'

'You haven't seen him?' asked Riedwaan.

'Not since the South African army left, and please, God, I won't see him again. He made my husband and Hofmeyr look like Sunday school teachers.'

Darlene took a packet out of her back pocket and fingered out a cigarette. Riedwaan held out his lighter for her.

'What was this pension?' he asked.

Darlene shook her head again.

'Guess then, Darlene. Guess.' Riedwaan kept the urgency out of his voice. It was like coaxing a wild bird to take food from his hand.

'I'd say it's something to do with the weapons they worked on during the war.'

'What?'

'You saw all that stuff, guerrilla fighters drugged and dropped from planes. People bleeding to death after being detained. Drugs that made your heart stop. Where do you think they practised?'

'Where did they do this?' asked Riedwaan.

'First at Vastrap, then they had a place out in the Namib, in the Kuiseb Delta somewhere. I never went there.'

'Would they have taken anyone else out there?' asked Riedwaan. 'Boys, maybe?'

She considered the possibility. 'Not likely,' she said, holding out her bruised hands. 'It's women he likes to see grovel and beg. He's very old South Africa, so if he had boys out there it's because there was hard labour to be done.'

'Where would they go,' said Riedwaan, 'if they've come back? Tell me, Darlene. If they've come back for some of their old toys and you say nothing, you'll have way more than a couple of homeless kids on your conscience.'

Darlene's resistance crumbled. 'There's one place. I'll show you.' Riedwaan followed her as she walked down the passage. 'Here.' She pointed to an old survey map taped to the wall. 'It's a map of the Kuiseb before the big flood a few years ago. This was an old army site, before the river changed course after the flood.' She pointed to a marking next to the old Kuiseb River. 'It's this area around the old railway line that caused all the trouble between the Topnaars and the army; it was full of Nara plants. Now it's giving Goagab headaches. Maybe that's where they tried to go. Some kind of sick reunion.'

'Can I take this?' Riedwaan asked.

Darlene nodded and Riedwaan rolled up the map.

He closed the front door behind him and heard the chain rattle as Darlene locked herself in. She must have slid down the wall and crouched there, because he did not hear her footsteps recede.

Riedwaan's bike surged to life. He made the short trip back to the station in record time. He closed the special ops room door and called Phiri, pleading with his acid-sounding secretary that she get him out of his weekly planning meeting. While he waited for Phiri to call back, he looked at Clare's map of where the dead boys had been found. Two, three, five, the first one with nothing. He plotted possible trajectories, trying to figure out where they had been killed from where they had been dumped. Two of them in the east; two in the west. No-man's-land in the middle.

'Faizal?' Phiri called back in five minutes.

'Sir, I'm glad you—'

'I had a call from someone called Van Wyk,' Phiri cut him short. 'He tells me that Captain Damases is off the case and that he's in command and, thanks, but no thanks for the assistance. I then had a call from Town Councillor Goagab saying that, apart from apprehending the suspected serial killer, who seems to be some kind of desert bogeyman, the show's over. What've you done this time?'

'I've done my job,' said Riedwaan.

'That's what I was afraid of,' said Phiri.

'Goagab and Van Wyk would like to see it as solved,' said Riedwaan.

'You and Clare don't?'

'No,' said Riedwaan.

'Despite the fact that the luminal showed positive for blood on the cart?' Phiri asked.

'The Topnaar could've moved the bodies when the boys were already dead,' Riedwaan explained. 'But I don't think he killed them. You dump a body out here, and no one will find it. Vultures, predators, heat. All you'll have is bleached bones in a couple of weeks. I'd put money on that Topnaar moving these boys to draw attention to their murders.'

'What for?' asked Phiri, puzzled.

'There's a weapons test site that a special ops unit used to use,' said Riedwaan. 'Bang in the middle of the Topnaar land. I want to check it out.'

'That's it?' said Phiri.

'That, and the fact that a couple of old soldiers who used to be involved in covert stuff seem to have been around.'

'That lot are finished, Faizal. They are all practising their golf swings in Wilderness.'

'If your intelligence is correct, this little game is not about ideology,' said Riedwaan. 'This is about money.'

There was a long pause. Riedwaan waited it out. 'What sort of weapons?' asked Phiri. 'What sort of money?'

'The records are all gone,' said Riedwaan, 'but I'd say bio-chemical.'

'I have one card left to keep you there,' Phiri said reluctantly. 'And that's a bluff. You've got twenty-four hours.'

'Thank you, sir,' said Riedwaan, breathing a silent sigh.

'This had better be good,' warned Phiri. 'If it's not, there's a post in Pofadder that needs filling.'

'I'm sorry, sir,' Riedwaan cut in, 'but I have a call waiting.' He saw with relief that it was Clare.

'What've you got?' he asked as he switched calls.

'Nothing yet,' said Clare. 'Myburgh hasn't pitched.'

'Wait for him,' said Riedwaan. 'I'm going to check out an old military site. If Karamata's around, I'll get him to take me.'

'Good plan,' said Clare. 'Elias knows the area well. What did Darlene tell you?'

'That her ex-husband's been back.'

'Surprise, surprise,' said Clare. 'With those bruises, who else? You think he's been killing these boys?'

'Why come all the way to Walvis Bay to kill street children?' said Riedwaan. 'There are enough in Cape Town.'

'Another coincidence?' Clare asked.

'That's what's bugging me. We'll discuss it over dinner.'

forty-nine

Clare was watching the fishermen, their rods sticking up like insects' feelers above the shoreline, when the battered red bakkie drew up next to her. She got out, the sand blowing off the desert stinging her calves. Tertius Myburgh unlocked the door and she slid in next to him, holding the door against the wind.

'Here,' said Myburgh, pushing an envelope across the cracked seat. He was tense; his hands were shaking.

Dr Clare Harriet Hart. Her full name in black ink: like an accusation. Clare opened it. Five pages of Myburgh's dense, looped cursive. Clare spread out the pollen report on her lap.

'There's the list,' said Myburgh. '*Tamarix. Trianthema hereroensis, Acanthosicyos horridus.*'

'What does that tell me?' asked Clare.

'The *Tamarix* and the *Hereroensis* grow in the Kuiseb River. This is where you'll find them.' He pulled out a map and sketched out two intersecting arcs. 'This section is where they overlap.'

'That's a huge area,' said Clare. The flicker of hope disappeared into the empty wastes that Myburgh's long, tapering fingers indicated.

'Well,' said Myburgh, 'you can cut out this bit. If they'd been near the mouth, you'd have found *Sarcocornia*, a stubby little succulent. You'll have seen fields of it beyond the lagoon. Nothing on them. They didn't even walk through it.'

'So they could've been anywhere in this area, except for this two-kilometre sliver near the shore?'

'No.' Myburgh looked around the parking lot before continuing: 'There's the *Acanthosicyos horridus*, the Nara plants that the Topnaar harvest. These grow in restricted areas along the vegetative dunes. It looks like a melon. Sweet, nutritious, full of fluid. Just what you need in a desert, but they only grow a few kilometres inland.'

'So that restricts us to this area, more or less?' asked Clare, pointing to the area of the Kuiseb Delta and just beyond.

Myburgh nodded.

'That's still a huge area.' Clare turned to look at the ocean of sand, rolling far beyond the horizon.

'Your needle in a haystack,' said Myburgh. 'I've got it for you.'

'What do you mean?'

'*Myrtaceae: Eucalyptus*.' Myburgh's dark eyes gleamed as he held out the branch to her: dark, pungent foliage, pale bark. 'The ghost gum,' he said. 'An Australian, alien. It would've had to have been planted near a water source.'

'How sure are you that you're right?' asked Clare.

'There'll only be a couple of spots in the Namib with this combination of plants.'

'So where do I start?' said Clare.

'With the gum, anywhere where there was human habitation,' said Myburgh, unfolding an aerial photograph. 'I looked and the only places I could find gum trees were these: two tourist camps and this old military area.'

Clare thought of Riedwaan's proposed destination. 'That's in the middle of nowhere,' she said, the puzzle pieces in her hand; the composite they made as shifting as the mirage dancing on the desert.

'It's the best I can do, I'm afraid,' Myburgh said, 'but there's more.' He handed Clare a slim journal, dark blue with embossed initials on it: VM.

Clare opened it. 'Whose is this?'

313

'Virginia Meyer's,' said Myburgh. 'It's all that was left of her work.'

Clare flipped through the book, glancing at the pages filled with spidery notes, the whimsical drawings of plants, birds and dunescapes so like her mute son's. Outside, the rising wind moaned around the car.

'I don't understand.' Clare looked up at Myburgh.

'I tested her diary for pollen,' he said, 'and it was a match. They were in the same place, Virginia and those boys.'

Clare's face remained expressionless.

'She was on her way to see me when the accident happened,' Myburgh explained. 'She'd been dead twelve hours when Spyt found them. Oscar couldn't loosen his seatbelt, so he was trapped, covered in her blood and flies. Spyt managed to resuscitate the child and get him help. And he brought me this.' Myburgh gestured to the journal. 'It had been hidden under Oscar's seat.'

'Why?' said Clare.

'Virginia wasn't where she should have been.' Myburgh must have crossed his Rubicon of doubt. When he spoke, his voice was quiet. 'It was the only bit of her work recovered after the accident. Everything else was gone. No one would've found them if Spyt hadn't come across them. She was on a side road out of the Kuiseb.'

'What was she doing there?'

'Virginia loved the Namib,' said Myburgh, 'and was enraged with the South African army and what they'd done to it. I always thought she was paranoid, seeing conspiracies everywhere. She was obsessed, Dr Hart, convinced that her beloved desert had been contaminated by the army. She kept on trying to expose what had happened, what she was convinced was happening again. She would've done anything to stop it.'

'Contaminated with what?' asked Clare. 'The South Africans left more than ten years ago.'

'They took their hardware,' said Myburgh, 'but they left some damaged people behind, as scarred and littered as the desert.'

'What had they been testing?' asked Clare.

'Overtly, the usual heavy weapons,' said Myburgh. 'Virginia was convinced there had been covert bio-chemical testing. Diseases, viruses, poisons that had leached into the underground water, and driven the Topnaars from their own land. Just before the accident, she phoned me to say there was something else, something much worse. She was afraid to tell me over the phone.' Myburgh looked away before continuing: 'She said the water table would be contaminated because of what they'd done.' He rubbed his eyes. 'Virginia was so paranoid, Dr Hart. It seemed easier at the time just to leave it.'

Clare thought of Fritz Woestyn, his lifeless body propped on the water pipeline, the artery pumping water into Walvis Bay, the lifeblood of the marooned town. 'Contaminated with what?' she asked.

'It didn't make sense to me then, still doesn't, because she said it in Afrikaans, but it stuck because she never spoke Afrikaans. She said it was the language of oppression.' Myburgh paused. 'She told me she was *vasgetrap*. Trapped fast. At least that is what I thought she said.'

'*Vasgetrap*, *vasgetrap*,' Clare repeated the syllables to herself. The word conjured up the quiet house in McGregor, the den with the elephant's foot. Mrs Hofmeyr with her iron-grey hair talking about her dead husband, her years as an army wife. 'She didn't say Vastrap, did she?' Clare asked.

'Vastrap, yes, that was it.' Myburgh looked at her. 'What is it?'

'It was a military base in South Africa, a secret weapons-testing site in the middle of the Kalahari Desert.'

A horrible image was forming in Clare's mind. She turned back to the last page of Virginia Meyer's diary. The digits 2, 3 and 5 were ringed in red. Clare looked at Myburgh's beaked profile.

'Tertius,' she asked, 'what do the numbers 2, 3 and 5 mean?'

'Nothing,' he said.

'Stop lying to me,' said Clare.

'Well, 235 is nothing on its own,' said Myburgh, his voice a monotone, his eyes trained on the heaving sea. 'Except with uranium. U-235 is an isotope. Highly enriched uranium. It's what you use for a nuclear weapon.'

Myburgh looked Clare in the eye for the first time, his knuckles were white on the steering wheel.

'That's what she meant about the desert being contaminated, Dr Hart. Those boys and Virginia Meyer, they were in the same place and now they're all dead.'

fifty

The sound of the off-road bike was a flinty staccato across the plain. Riedwaan stopped to get his bearings. He had gone to find Karamata, but there had been no sign of him at his desk, and Riedwaan hadn't looked for him for long. He preferred being alone. The sun bellied orange over the sea as he passed the place where Lazarus Beukes had been found, but the shallow valley was a dead end, blocked by a wall of sand. So he left the relative sanctuary of the dry Kuiseb River behind him, trusting that his cheap Chinese GPS would see him through the expanse of desert.

The disused railway track, a spine from which the desert fell away, soft as a woman's flesh, came from the north, running aground in an ocean of red sand. Riedwaan checked the coordinates against the GPS. They told him the same thing as his old survey map: he needed to be on the other side of this waterless strait. Out here, the temperature would strip a body of its cloak of skin, hair and flesh. In weeks, he'd be nothing but white bones and a skull staring up at the blue vault of the sky. Riedwaan calculated the descent of the first dune and the elevation of the second and pitched over the edge, opening the throttle to the full, praying that the momentum would carry him to the top. It did, but all he had in front of him was another dune, then another.

Again Riedwaan took his bearings, trying not to picture his own demise. He made himself go on, following, more or less, the tracks of a vehicle that had preceded him. Three more dunes, and the railway reappeared, its ironwood sleepers scattered like matchsticks in the sand. A kilometre ahead was his destination. He could just make it out: some scrubby bushes and a gnarled eucalyptus tree next to two weathered huts. Riedwaan rode alongside the railway line, stopping under the tree, a ghostly sentinel in the dunes. Apart from the rattle of seeds feathered across the sand by the east wind, the place was silent.

The ground fell away from the huts towards two concrete-capped mounds. They could have been a century old, or a single decade. The tracks he had followed were neither, thought Riedwaan, bending down to get a closer look at the compacted earth. A heavy vehicle, a Land Rover perhaps, had passed through recently. An empty bottle of brandy lay discarded against the pale tree trunk. Scattered near it were a few cigarette butts. Riedwaan bent down to look. Two different brands.

It was cooler in the shade, but that did not account for the chill that played over Riedwaan's skin. A grimy white T-shirt was snagged against the bole of the tree, sweat stains indelible under the arms. The Pesca-Marina logo was only half-hidden by the shovel lying on top of it. Riedwaan stood where the men must have stood, the image forming as crisp as a nightmare in his mind. The back door of a vehicle would have opened, releasing the men's hurriedly collected human cargo – five boys, hired to harvest a deadly crop planted in another lifetime. Riedwaan lit a cigarette, imagining how their presence would have absorbed the vestiges of warmth from the night air.

The brandy, neat, burning down the throat of one man, then the other. Impossible to say how many, but Riedwaan would put his money on two. The men watching the activity below them would have been accustomed to the backs of others bending rhythmically to their wills.

For the boys, coming out here must have seemed safer than standing against a wall, legs astride, for a paunchy truck driver or a sailor with a knife. They wouldn't question a hundred for the night. Sickness or fear might have tightened the chest of one boy, hot from digging. The youngest boy slipping off his shirt, the moon sculpting his slender torso, as he stopped to rest. But when he caught the man's eye on him, as cold as a switchblade, he would have bent down again. And dug.

Riedwaan's mouth was dry from the heat. He fetched his water from the bike and tried to phone Clare. No reception under the tree, so he walked towards the shelters. One bar, he noted. The door to the first hut was ajar. Two bars. He dialled, ducking inside to avoid the sun.

The blow came without warning. For a brief moment before silence blossomed from agony, Riedwaan heard it: the quiet crack of his own skull.

fifty-one

There was no one at the station when Clare got back from her meeting with Tertius Myburgh. She closed the door to the special ops room and sat down at her desk. She dialled Riedwaan's number. Nothing. A flash on her screen told her she had a call waiting.

'Dr Hart?' It was Karamata.

'Yes?'

'George Meyer's son is missing.'

'Where from?' Clare felt faint at the inevitability of it, her own failure to protect the child.

'Kuisebmond beach.' Clare knew the beach. It was a crescent of grey, littered sand near the harbour.

'I'll come over.' Clare cut the connection, but not the image of cold water creeping over the face of a lonely, wide-eyed boy.

She drove fast along the beach road, which glistened like a strip of kelp stranded by a receding tide on the high-water mark. Karamata was there with a couple of uniformed officers. George Meyer stood with his hands thrust into his pockets, his shoulders hunched. The vehicles blocked off the area of beach where the boy had been. The wind was too strong for tape.

'He must've been here,' said Karamata, beckoning Clare over.

The yellow rod was wedged into the ground. Next to it was Oscar's khaki bag. The bottle of water was still full. A half-eaten sandwich was wedged in next to his bait. Peanut butter and Marmite.

'You didn't see him again, did you?' Meyer asked Clare. The question was framed around the hopes to which the parents of missing children cling. But with George Meyer, it was a formality. Hope was absent.

'I didn't see him,' said Clare, her chest tight with sadness.

'He was upset this morning after you were there. He was upset that Mara had left. I thought maybe he'd tried to find you.' Meyer moved out of the way of a wave that reached up the beach. It retreated, leaving a fringe of foam. 'He liked you, Dr Hart. He thought you'd be able to find Mara and bring her back.'

Clare saw Oscar's face before her, eyes accusing at her inability to understand his mute explanations. 'When did he disappear?'

'When I got home at lunch time, he was gone. His rod was gone too, so I came looking for him at the beach. I found the bike and the rod. No Oscar.'

'He wouldn't have gone off somewhere?'

'Not without his bike,' Meyer said.

'That taxi driver saw him here earlier.' Karamata gestured towards a man leaning against a battered red Toyota, talking to a couple of uniformed officers.

'The sea's been rough today,' said Meyer. 'He couldn't swim.'

Rough and cold, Clare thought. The Atlantic was not a place for a little boy alone.

'They're going to put a radio alert out,' Meyer said.

'And we'll search the harbour,' Karamata added. 'Why don't you go home, Mr Meyer? Maybe he's been somewhere and he'll turn up.'

'Maybe.' Meyer looked at the keys in his hand as if he had never seen them before.

'I'll take you back.' Karamata pointed to the police car. Meyer walked towards it, obedient as a child.

'Where was he?' Clare asked Karamata.

'At work all the time. I checked. They were doing an audit,

so he was with the accountant. There will be a search, so there won't be anyone at the station for a while.'

'Did you speak to Captain Faizal?' Clare asked. 'I thought he'd arranged with you to take him to the Kuiseb Delta.'

'He's said nothing to me.'

'I can't get hold of him,' said Clare.

'I hope he doesn't go out there alone,' said Karamata. 'It looks so easy on the map, but once you're in the desert a map's useless, especially with this east wind.'

'Don't count on it, Elias,' said Clare. She knew Riedwaan too well to assume he'd do the sensible thing. She tried his number again. 'Caller out of range,' said the electronic voice. 'Try again later.'

'I have a sea search,' said Karamata. 'All I need is a desert search during a sandstorm.'

With an effort of will, Clare put her anxiety about Riedwaan on hold. 'You've spoken to Gretchen, I presume?' she asked.

'I did,' said Karamata. 'On the phone. She said she was in the bath when Oscar left the house.'

'That polite?' Clare raised an eyebrow.

'Not actually,' said Karamata, with a rueful smile. 'She told me to fuck off, that he wasn't anything to do with her and that she was busy.'

'Charming.' Clare looked out at the choppy sea. 'He was a little boy to be out fishing alone.'

'Nobody's child,' said Karamata. 'There are so many of them here, not all of them poor.'

'Who uses this beach, Elias?'

'The Chinese come and fish here. Couples with nowhere else to go. Kids come to fish. No one else really.' Karamata's phone was ringing. 'I must go and speak to the divers. They're here.'

Clare picked her way to the last rocks on the small headland that protected the harbour and looked back at the beach where Oscar had left his rod and his frugal picnic. Litter circled the small bay, nudging against the man-made promontory where she stood. The first diver splashed off the bobbing rescue vessel. If the boy had drowned, then his body would have been sucked down and flung up here, against these rocks. She worked her way back, her heart beating fast when she spotted a red smudge, but it was an old piece of T-shirt.

A wave ran high up the beach, obliterating all trace of Oscar and those who had been looking for him. Half an hour later and nobody would have known where he had stood and cast his line. Clare looked up the beach towards the road. The sand behind where Oscar's things had been had not yet been smoothed by the water. She walked towards his last-known location. Several mussel shells lay crushed in the disturbed sand. It looked as though a vehicle had stopped right behind where Oscar had been standing. It had stopped and then reversed and gone back onto the road.

Clare picked up a fragment of shell.

Oscar wouldn't have gone swimming and he hadn't fallen in. They weren't going to find Oscar's body here. She felt it with chilling certainty. Someone had picked him up and taken him elsewhere. Someone he had had to obey. Clare thought of the portraits hanging in her gallery. Each had slipped from life without a ripple.

Fritz Woestyn.

Nicanor Jones.

Kaiser Apollis.

Lazarus Beukes.

Mara Thomson. A girl, but so similar. The slenderness of the limbs, the brown skin, the faces planed and angled.

Now Oscar.

The coda to this symphony of pain. Small, russet-haired, pale … he struck the wrong note.

Clare dropped her head into her hands and imagined herself sliding under the translucent skin of the child, the silhouette of evil taking shape in her mind. She pictured him watching Mara pack, holding the break in his heart in, locking away this new loss with the loss of his mother. And then before the allotted, dreaded time of the taxi, before the final flurry of packing and goodbye, a gun in her back. The middle of the night. The shadow-man removing his last witness. Mara's room brutally emptied of everything except the secret pictures that she and Oscar shared.

Mara hurtling towards the desert, her life receding with the grey fishing village sinking behind the horizon. Oscar shrinking back, unheard, unseen, except for the crack in the upstairs curtain. And now he was gone, the witness. Like the others. Killed not for the way they looked, but for what they knew.

Clare looked out to sea. A fishing ship, laden and low in the water, made her way between the buoys towards the quay where the *Alhantra* had docked to be loaded. One last shot, thought Clare, at finding where they had all connected.

She parked outside the Pesca-Marina factory as the shift-change siren went, the silver fish in the logo catching the light. She slipped in unnoticed through the stream of workers on their way out. On the wharf, front-end loaders scurried back and forth, heavy with stacked boxes. She went past the men concentrating on offloading the catch and slipped on board. There was no sign of Ragnar Johansson on the bridge, so she went below in search of Juan Carlos.

The second-last cabin door was closed. There was no answer when she knocked, but, to her surprise, when she tried the handle it opened. She went in and sat down to wait. It didn't take long for the door handle to turn again. Juan Carlos closed the door behind him, the expression on his handsome face unreadable.

'Dr Hart,' he said. 'Again.' The hum of the engines preparing to sail seemed to have restored his confidence.

'You're free to move about?' Clare asked.

'Change of command.'

'I need to know where Mara went camping,' said Clare.

'You didn't get a warrant?' Clare's beat of hesitation was enough for him. 'What do you have to trade?'

'You're free to go,' Clare bluffed. 'No word to the police in Spain, so no trouble when you dock.'

'I'm innocent?'

'Not the word I'd have chosen,' said Clare. She took out her map. The coordinates Myburgh had given her needed to be narrowed, and fast.

She spread it out in front of Juan Carlos. 'Show me.' The tone of her voice brooked no argument.

'Here. This is where Mara went.' Juan Carlos took the pen from her hand and marked a place with a sure, black X alongside a railway line. An arc of dunes had moved across it, severing the dry tributary from the rest of the delta.

Clare thought of Lazarus Beukes, the no-entry signs shining in the dark. She had been there, or near there, before. The hairs on her arms stood on end. 'What happened there with Mara?' she asked.

'Nothing. I've told you. She went with those street boys of hers. She loved them.' He smiled a slow, smug smile. 'But she loved me more. Once I show her how.'

'What do you mean?' Clare did not like him so close to her. He made her skin crawl.

'I told you, I got a pass, so I call her and tell her to meet me.

325

She left them out there. Her boys. It was late. We met. We made love. She go back to fetch them, but they were gone. She found them at the dump again. They say they walked.'

'All of them? Were they all there?'

Juan Carlos looked down and said nothing. Clare waited.

'Okay, okay, all except for one,' he said at last. 'He only turn up later … dead.'

'Why didn't you tell me earlier? Why didn't Mara say anything?'

'She was too ashamed. She was afraid. She say she should have stayed with them. Take your pick.'

'Which one's your choice?' asked Clare.

'It was me or them.' His eyes glinted with the subtle charge of sexual power.

'What did you do, Juan Carlos?' asked Clare. 'Four boys are dead and a girl who loved you is missing.'

'The ship is full. I've made my money. I don't want delays,' Juan Carlos shrugged. 'Why would I do something?'

'Where is Captain Johansson?' asked Clare.

'Go and check on the bridge.' Juan Carlos turned his back on her. 'I say nothing more.'

The passage was a relief after the closeness of the cabin. Clare went up to the bridge before the boxes were stowed. A half-smoked pack of Marlboros was wedged on the barometer. It was Ragnar Johansson's brand, but there was no other sign of him. Clare looked below. The centre of the ship was open as the winch lowered packed fish into the refrigerated hold. She guessed that Ragnar would be directing things from below.

There was a metal staircase near the bridge. Clare closed the door behind her and swung down. The metal banister was slick and cold and her feet tingled as she spiralled down into the dark hold.

Ragnar wasn't on the first level. She asked one of the packers if he had seen him, but he shook his head. Clare went lower into the ship's belly. It was eerie, just the roar of the engines and the thud of the winch as it lowered its precious load. Something gleamed on the floor next to the packed and padlocked cold room. A Zippo. Clare picked the lighter up and rubbed away the dark fluid staining the engraving of a mermaid. Not Ragnar's, but familiar. She slipped it into her pocket.

'Are you looking for something?' Clare swung around. She didn't recognise the voice. Light and chill, as dry as ice.

The man was blocking the light in the narrow corridor. He had his cellphone up, directed at Clare, and he snapped her as she turned.

'Hey, what are you doing?' she asked, furious. 'Who the hell are you?' But she remembered the leanness. She had seen him at Der Blaue Engel. It was the man who had pulled Gretchen out of the sea.

'I like a record of the people who come onto my ship without permission.' The man was blade-thin, his face sculpted, handsome. He pressed a button on his phone, a smile creasing his tanned cheeks. Then he slipped his phone into his pocket and looked directly at Clare for the first time. 'Janus Renko. The new owner.'

'I've seen you,' said Clare. 'With Gretchen von Trotha.'

He raised an eyebrow.

'I'm looking for the captain,' said Clare. 'Where is he?'

Renko lit a cigarette. 'Ragnar Johansson?' He flicked the name away with the match. When he took off his dark glasses, he exposed pale, blank eyes. 'Ragnar went kite-boarding.'

'When will he be back?' Clare asked. Renko had not moved from the doorway. Clare glanced towards the light behind him, the smell of diesel oil, cold and fish heavy in the air. Renko smiled at her discomfort.

'He was made an offer he couldn't refuse,' he said.

The churn of the engines crescendoed. The ship was ready to sail.

'We're on our way, Dr Hart.' He rolled her name in his mouth, the intimacy of it was chilling. 'If I speak to him, I'll tell him you were here.'

Then Renko's hand was on her elbow, his grip a vice, propelling her back down the icy corridor, walking her faster than was comfortable. Clare's heart hammered against her ribs when she saw the refrigerated room ahead of her, the door into its icy maw now ajar.

She tried to pull free, but Renko had her arm twisted up her back. He was very close, his arm, sinewy and hard, was round her throat, cutting her breath. He laughed when she kicked backwards at him.

'This can be slow, Clare.' His voice sibilant, his breath intimate on her neck. 'Or it can be qui—'

'Janus!' A voice from above. 'Goagab's here with your authorisation. He wants us out of here.'

Renko's grip loosened an involuntary fraction, enough for Clare to twist herself free of him. In three strides, she was clear of him and past the startled harbour master holding out a sheaf of papers. Back on the deck, she dashed towards the gangplank; the shouts of the men she pushed out of her way were snatched away by the wind. Clare sprinted past the packers, through the ice shed and out of the factory gates.

fifty-two

Clare yanked her car into gear and cut in front of a hooting taxi, her heart thudding against her chest. She drove towards the lagoon, the tears coming without her noticing.

There was no truck and no dog at Ragnar's flat. She looked across at the harbour to see that the *Alhantra* was halfway down the narrow shipping channel, heading for the open sea. She drove back along the lagoon, but there was no sign of Ragnar there either. One place left to look. In five minutes, Clare was bumping along the track that led into the salt marshes where the Kuiseb Delta blurred into the sea. A dangerous place to kiteboard, but one that Ragnar loved.

The first thing she saw as she approached the beach was the Labrador circling the vehicle, yelping in distress. The kiteboard was still tied to the roof racks, ready. Clare did not like the feeling in her chest. It felt like something hard and cold was expanding, squashing the air from her lungs. She drove towards Ragnar's truck.

'Come boy,' Clare called to the dog.

The dog whined, but refused to move away from the vehicle. Clare approached slowly, expecting the worst, but Ragnar was sitting inside, staring straight ahead at the sea. Clare opened the door and to her horror he toppled towards her. She caught him in her arms. He beamed up at her, his eyes ice blue, the wound in his forehead blooming. He was warm against her breast, his blood on her shirt a cheerful red. Clare bit back a scream. She manoeuvred him back into the seat and placed a finger against his neck. A pulse.

'I'm getting you help,' she said.

Ragnar started to slide towards her again. She propped her hip against his weight and pulled out her phone. Her hands were shaking, but she managed to key in Tamar's number. It was ten rings before anyone answered. Clare counted every one of them. It felt like a lifetime.

'Hello.'

'Tamar?' asked Clare. The voice didn't sound right.

'She's asleep right now.'

'Helena?' said Clare.

'Yes,' said Dr Kotze. 'I'm sorry—'

'It's Clare Hart. Send an ambulance.' Clare could not get the words out fast enough. 'The road past the saltworks, towards Pelican Point. Ragnar Johansson. Head shot. He's still alive but only just.' She disconnected without waiting for an answer.

Ragnar slipped further. Clare dropped her phone and turned to the stricken man. She pulled his seatbelt across his chest to hold him upright.

'Keep still,' said Clare, her heart thudding. 'The ambulance is coming.'

'Angel.' Ragnar's breath was feather-soft against her ear. The blue eyes flared. The wound in his forehead oozed, and his eye-lids started to flutter.

'Don't pass out, Ragnar. Look at me. Talk to me.'

Ragnar obeyed and looked up at Clare, struggling to focus, his breathing coming in sharp jerks. There was nothing to do but wait. Clare looked out at the deserted beach; it was hard to believe that on other days, it would be dotted with kites and dogs, and families enjoying a weekend outing.

Ragnar groaned and his eyes rolled.

'Come on, Ragnar.' Clare touched his face. 'Stay with me.' She settled him against the door and went around to the back of the truck in search of water. When she came back, the blood from his forehead had trickled over his lips. She sprinkled the water over his mouth.

'Talk to me, Ragnar. Tell me who did this to you.'

'Angel,' he slurred.

'Not yet,' said Clare. 'No angels for you.' She cradled his bloodied head, counting the minutes.

A chopper at last, she could hear it. Ragnar inched his hand across the seat, as if he were looking for something. There was nothing there.

'Here's help for you now. Hang on.'

The helicopter hovered, buffeted by the rising wind blowing off the desert. An enormous flock of flamingos took off, turning the sky deep pink as they circled before heading for safety. Two paramedics jumped out, neat as paratroopers.

'What happened?' the first one asked as soon as he was within earshot.

The sound of the chopper drowned out Clare's attempts to explain. She stepped aside so the paramedic could see Ragnar.

The colour drained from the man's ruddy face.

'Shit,' he said as he bent over him. 'Pulse is here. Just.' He signalled the other paramedic over. 'Let's get him out of here.' There was an efficient flurry of drips and needles.

'Where are you taking him?' Clare asked.

'To Windhoek,' the man said. 'There's no ICU at the coast.'

'Will he make it?' She was starting to shake.

'If he made it this long, he has a chance. Sometimes the bullet lodges between the brain lobes. If nothing's damaged, he might make it,' said the paramedic.

Clare stood back, watching as the paramedics worked to stabilise Ragnar before lifting him into the chopper. They pulled the door closed and were gone, lifting up and over the dunes.

331

Clare closed her eyes, but it did not drive away the image of Ragnar's punctured forehead.

She walked around to the other side of Ragnar's truck and opened it. A file of official-looking papers fell out. She picked them up, wondering if it was what Ragnar had been looking for. The Walvis Bay Port Authority letterhead. Records of load, of taxes paid, of inspections done, of a route filed. Spain via Luanda.

Clare thought of the *Alhantra* rocking next to the stone quay. Its sudden turn of fortune. Two. Three. Five. It was adding up. Ragnar was a sore loser and she knew he'd bent the law before: illegal crayfish, some dope, a bit of recreational coke. But transporting the ingredients for a dirty bomb was not his thing. He must have found out about his ship's secret cargo and threatened to talk. The helicopter had vanished, leaving only the wind and the calls of seabirds in its wake.

Clare snapped the file closed as a car door slammed behind her. It was Van Wyk and a sergeant she did not recognise.

'Captain Damases is off this case,' said Van Wyk. 'And I'm on it.' He held out a hand and Clare reluctantly handed over Ragnar's file. 'It's an offence to remove evidence from a crime scene,' he added, tossing the file into his vehicle. 'I'm running this case now, Dr Hart. So I suggest you run along.'

Clare let a violent fantasy that involved her, Van Wyk and a machine gun run its course before getting back into her car, his smile a knife in her back. She calmed herself with the knowledge that Tamar's inquiry would put him behind bars and wipe that arrogant smile off his face for a long time.

The maternity ward was surprisingly quiet. It was not visiting time, but Clare had slipped in without anyone noticing. Tamar's room was at the end of the passage. A single bunch of flowers – hand-picked by Tupac and Angela, Clare guessed – stood by her bedside. The aftermath of labour had smoothed the guarded toughness from her face. She looked fifteen, lying on her heap of starched white pillows. The baby curled in her arms was slack with sleep, a drop of milk pearled in the corner of its small, pink mouth.

'Tamar,' Clare whispered. 'Tamar.' It felt like sacrilege to wake her.

Tamar opened her eyes, and the illusion of the Madonna vanished. 'Hi.' She drew her child closer to her before she smiled. 'What is it?'

'I'm sorry, I know you're off the case, but I really need your help.'

'Any time,' said Tamar. 'What is it?'

Clare closed the door and told Tamar. The horror of it seeped through Tamar's exhausted postpartum tranquillity like a poison. The baby's face crumpled in distress, feeling its mother slipping away from it.

'Pass me my phone. It's in my bag.' Tamar rocked the child and it settled again, lulled. Clare handed her the phone.

'We'll do a swap,' said Tamar. 'You take her.'

'Who is she?' asked Clare, taking the infant. 'This new little person.'

The child was unbelievably light in her arms.

'Rachel.' Tamar ran a gentle finger over her baby's plump cheek. 'Rachel Damases.'

Clare looked at the child. 'She's beautiful.'

Clare watched Tamar's features sharpen and her eyes focus as she made the calls Clare needed.

'It's done,' Tamar said, snapping the phone closed. 'Now you do what you have to.'

She held out her arms for her baby and Clare handed Rachel over.

'Look in that drawer,' said Tamar.

Clare walked to the bedside table and pulled open the drawer. It contained a tube of cream and a pistol.

'You can leave me the hand cream,' said Tamar.

fifty-three

Out in the desert, Riedwaan's stomach had hollowed beneath his jeans, but the belt buckle stood clear of his skin. He could feel the place where the sun had bored heat through the metal to brand the tender skin. He tried to calculate how long he had been out, measuring the air in even packages of breath. In. Then out. Pacing himself.

He remembered the road, winding through the tamarisk trees. He had passed the no-entry sign where Lazarus Beukes had been found. He had gone on, his bike churning the virgin sand in the riverbed. He had found the place Darlene had told him about, the tree a dark-green sentinel, a couple of kilometres east of Spyt's makeshift hideout. He could see the old railway tracks sinking into the heaped sand. The ruined roof of the huts, the rafters protruding like the ribs of a carcass picked clean by scavengers. The stationmaster's house, the red sand curved through the windows, heaped like treasure in the front rooms. The track. The end of the track, the riverbed again, the ghost gum tree towering above him, the entrance to the hut. Then nothing. Except this blinding pain.

Riedwaan opened his eyes. The sun was dipping west. He closed his eyes against the searing light, the sand whirling in the wind. He made his mind work. Remember.

There had been tracks everywhere. He had gone into the building. A pick, shovels too, standing against the wall. New ones. A boy's peaked cap, tossed in a corner. The pit, recently dug. A single drum standing against the wall, the hazard sign visible beneath the crusted sand. The others had been dug up

335

and were no doubt now on the *Alhantra*, moving towards their targets like deadly wraiths. The pain. That's when it had come, from behind him when he stood inside the room.

'You're awake.' A woman's voice. Riedwaan could just make out her figure stacking a pile of wood into an ashy hearth. Her fire would be going in minutes. His eyes fluttered closed.

He opened them again and looked at the woman standing above him now, her hair gleaming in the angled light. Riedwaan tried to move his arms. They were tied tight around the trunk of a tree, the slender nylon rope cutting into his wrists. The ground was hard. Riedwaan's cellphone was in his back pocket. It bit into his back. He shifted his weight and hoped it was on silent. His gun was gone.

'Who are you?' Riedwaan's own voice sounded unfamiliar. It hurt his cracked lips when he spoke. The woman dropped to her knees beside him, fanning her cool fingertips over his hot skin. He concentrated on her face, trying to get his vision to stabilise.

'Your guardian angel.' Her voice was husky. 'You're going to need one. The Namib Desert's not safe.' She held out her hand. 'Oh, you can't shake. Sorry.' She returned to the fire and turned the metal fence dropper she had placed in it. The tip glowed an ominous red.

'Water,' Riedwaan begged.

The woman turned to look at him, not a glimmer of compassion in her pale-blue eyes. 'You must learn to ask nicely.' A shadow passed over her face. Pure menace.

She pressed the dropper into the smooth skin on Riedwaan's chest. The acrid smell of charred skin hit him before the pain convulsed his body. He bit down on his bottom lip, the taste of his own blood sharp on his tongue.

'A perfect circle,' the woman said, admiring the mark she had made. She lifted the rod to do it again.

'Give me some water,' croaked Riedwaan, watching her face, trying to judge how far she would go, how much he could take. 'Please.'

'You can do better than that,' she laughed, the soft red dunes echoing the curves of her body, but she put the rod down.

Riedwaan felt like he was walking a tightrope in the dark. If he was sure-footed, he might rekindle some empathy in her. If he got it wrong, he would fall, triggering a release of cruelty.

He thought of Clare, the gentleness in her face when she thought no one was watching her. Yasmin, his daughter. She would be calling tomorrow at their usual time.

Riedwaan knew if he drifted, he was going to pass out. And if the woman drifted any further, the slender thread of empathy would snap and he would die. He fought off the siren call of unconsciousness.

Shift things.

That's what he had learnt when he had trained as a hostage negotiator. Shift things and get them to talk, to trust you. Then the hostages have a chance of survival. It seemed like a rather fragile straw to cling to now that he was the hostage. Unlike Clare, he was a betting man, but he didn't like to think of his odds.

'Talk to me,' said Riedwaan, watching the woman, ignoring the stabbing pain in his bound arms, his seared chest. She was so at home, preparing things. The fire, the rope, the gun. Riedwaan had not picked a winner in this charnel-house hostess. He had to bring her back to him.

'Give me some water.' He said the words with an authority he did not feel. His tongue was swelling in his throat.

The woman glided towards him and held the flask to his mouth, the liquid pouring in, hot and choking at the back of his throat. She was so close Riedwaan could feel the warmth of her body, smell the unsettling, feral mix of perfume and adrenaline. Her hair swung over her shoulder and brushed his skin. It was bleached and porous, the colour and texture of dried grass left from last year's rain. The desert wind made it crackle with static.

'Just swallow,' she said, holding his chin expertly. Riedwaan choked, his lungs burned, but the alcohol gave him a kickstart. 'It's only the first time that's really bad,' she added.

Riedwaan looked at her face. Her cheekbones, the sweep of her eyebrows were sculpted, beautiful, but the eyes were blank. All he could see in them was his own reflection, twice in miniature.

'Who taught you that?' he asked. He could imagine. She had such a perfect mouth, full and red. Made for a certain kind of love.

The woman sat down opposite him, intrigued by his question.

'A boyfriend?' guessed Riedwaan. 'A teacher?'

She clasped her slim arms around her knees, as if folding her forgotten vulnerability away from his prying gaze.

'Your mother's boyfriend?'

The woman said nothing, but she shivered. Riedwaan was on target. He had to keep her talking.

'Your mother?' The wind had dropped and Riedwaan's words reverberated in the sudden lull. The pain in his arms was unbearable. He was glad of it. It distracted him from the charred skin on his chest. He inched himself higher up the tree.

'Not my real mother,' the woman spoke at last, though she did not look at Riedwaan. 'The woman who took me after my mother died.'

'Tell me what she made you do,' Riedwaan coaxed.

The woman got up and walked away as if she had not heard Riedwaan. She walked into the hut, leaving him alone. Riedwaan moved his body a little higher up the tree. The trunk narrowed a little, a dry cycle must have stunted its growth.

When the woman returned, she was holding a box of menthol cigarettes and a lighter. Riedwaan, though desperate for nicotine, feared what she might do. 'Can you—?'

'He was old,' the woman interrupted. 'In the army, but he always smelt dirty. He used to come to see her.'

Riedwaan nodded. 'And he decided he liked the look of you?'

Again, she seemed not to hear him. 'I choked and he hit me, but she made me finish.' The memory of it danced like a blue flame as she raised her expressionless eyes to stare at Riedwaan. 'Once you get used to it,' she said, 'it's such an easy way to pay the rent.'

Riedwaan kept moving his body upwards. He could flex his wrists a little now. 'How old were you?' he asked.

The woman picked up a stick and jabbed it into the sand. 'I was eleven.'

Riedwaan pictured the hand, nails lacquered red, holding the child's small, round chin to wipe her face clean.

'Tell me about those boys you shot,' said Riedwaan.

'What about them?' she asked.

'So close,' he said. 'You did it so close. I'm impressed.'

Her eyes glittered. An arc of light again. He had to keep her facing him.

'Tell me about it, what it felt like.'

She hesitated.

'Come,' he said. 'You don't want to rush this, do you? When I'm gone, then your fun is over.' It was true; he could see it in her face. Clare would be impressed with him, he thought. His new conversational ways with women. 'How did you feel?' he pressed.

'How do you think?'

'Like no one could argue with you. Powerful.'

'More than that.' She came closer.

'Tell me,' he said. 'Tell me where it all began.'

'I can tell you where it's going to end.'

'With me?'

The woman smiled at him and lit a cigarette. 'Why not? Any requests?'

'A cigarette,' he said.

She held the cigarette to his lips.

'But we aren't at the ending yet, are we? So why don't you start with the first one, Fritz Woestyn?'

'Oh, was that his name?' she asked. 'I didn't do him.'

'Who killed him, then?'

The woman hesitated. 'Don't be clever with me. You think I'd betray him, my guardian angel. I told you, you need one.'

'Nicanor Jones?'

'He was sweet,' said the woman. 'My dry run.'

'The others?'

'Those were all mine. You'll see later,' she said. 'I've learnt to be a good shot.'

'I can't wait,' muttered Riedwaan.

The woman stirred the fire with the fence dropper. He didn't think he could endure another session. 'Why?' he asked. It was a weak question, he knew, but he had to do something.

'Why what?' the woman shrugged.

'Why did you do it? Love?'

'I suppose you could call it that.' She considered the notion.

'Who are we waiting for, out here in the middle of nowhere?' Riedwaan asked.

'This time' – she leant close to him – 'it'll be just the two of us. Tête-à-tête.'

'So why did you do it?'

'It made me feel. He made me feel, standing close to me. Here.' She put her hands on her hips. 'Close.'

Riedwaan could feel it with her. The man behind her, close, his hands under her elbows, adjusting them, helping her aim, sliding back the smooth upper arms, under the breasts. Stepping back as she fired to watch the dénouement. There didn't seem any reason why it shouldn't be pleasurable.

'Why did the Topnaar move them?' Riedwaan asked.

'I don't know,' she said, agitated. 'I don't know who moved them. Nobody's business, but ours.'

'And why didn't you stop?'

'We had to finish what we started.' She looked at him, surprised that this logic had eluded him. 'That is what he taught me; to finish what you start.' She stirred the fire, mesmerised by its flames. 'And I always pay what I owe.'

'So now you get the clean-up?'

Rage flared in the woman's eyes. 'He's not like that.'

Her phone purred on cue. She fished it out of her jeans and looked at the screen. Riedwaan watched the pulse at the base of her slender throat. He inched his arms up the tree, closer to where it narrowed. Blood oozed where his skin tore on the rough bark.

'Who?' he managed to say. 'Who's not like that?'

The woman laughed, the sound low, malignant. 'You think you're so clever, making me talk to you, distracting me. You think I haven't seen it before?' she sneered. 'You'll stop being so full of yourself when you meet him. He'll fix you as soon as he's finished.'

'Finished with what?'

'Your little doctor friend.'

Riedwaan was quiet. The stakes had just notched higher, and the woman knew it.

341

'You want to see?' She held up her cellphone, so Riedwaan could see the screen: Clare, half-turned, startled, in a narrow passageway.

Horror made him lucid. Riedwaan played his last card. 'You believe he's coming back for you?' he asked.

'He's coming,' said the woman, petulantly.

'He's finished with you. He didn't even bother to kill you, did he?' The air pulsed. The wind was rising again, fast, and visibility was dropping.

For a moment, the ghost of the broken child the woman had been softened the carapace of her adult face. But only for a moment. It was gone when she started to strip. She unbuttoned her shirt. Off it came and her bra, her jeans, the shoes, the watch, even her rings.

Riedwaan watched her, riveted. A quick shower and any traces of his blood on her skin would be gone. This perfect woman, naked except for the wings tattooed on her back and the pistol in her right hand. She flicked off the safety catch. She was so close, he could feel the warmth of her. It chilled him. She touched the gun against his forehead – cold, like a dog's snout, and stepped back.

Knees soft, elbows locked.

She breathed in slowly.

Then out.

She knew what she was doing.

fifty-four

Visibility was getting worse. Clare could see a few metres ahead. That was it. The wind was a keening banshee. It hurled the sand in stinging waves off the tops of the dune, driving them down like vengeful furies that flayed the skin and tore at the eyes and ears. Her mouth was soon filled with choking red dust. Clare stopped to orientate herself. The stand of trees was thick, the black bark coated with mica. She fought her way towards the outflung arm of dune in the lee of the wind. Here, the wind was less constricting and she could make out the outlines of trees. She was close. She had to get to the top of the dune. She looked for the signs of human habitation that would be there. Eucalyptus. Here in the desert it would have been planted and nurtured for some time so that its delving roots could tap into the subterranean lake where the Namib hoarded its water. She closed her eyes and pictured the aerial map. If she pulled it out here, it would be whipped out of her hands.

She had seen the eucalyptus earlier, exactly as Oscar had drawn it, with its dark spire squared against the undulating horizontality of the desert. She had seen it and then it had disappeared, so it must be behind the ruff of dunes that had formed in the last flood. She would have to go up and over the dune she was sheltering against. Due east. At least the wind would help her orientate herself: she had to face down the Valkyries of sand that screamed past her towards the sea. It was horrible going forward: two steps forward was one backwards.

Her throat was dry and cracked, and her muscles screamed at her to stop. There was a momentary lull. An absolute and deafening silence fell. The dust hung in abeyance, waiting for the next onslaught.

Janus Renko. The unfamiliar name. The hard face familiar. And not just from Der Blaue Engel. The chord it had struck echoed through the chaos of sandy wind. The quiet kitchen. Clare saw it with startling clarity: the woman with her gun-metal hair, pointing out her husband in the desert. In the photo, one arm draped over a friend, the unknown man standing aloof, shadowed. The same face, distilled down to its cruel essence. The half-empty ship. The numbers: 2, 3 and 5. Coded for her, inscribed upon the dead boys' chests by Spyt, the desert's silent witness. The drums loaded, not with the obscuring load of fish, but with the deadly treasure dug up by five boys, watched, found and delivered by Spyt.

Two, three, five. Unleashed in air or water, a stealthy death no one could fight. Enriched uranium: more than a pension that. A fortune for anyone willing to sell mass murder to the jostling numbers eager and able to make a dirty bomb. She couldn't think of that now. Not here. She was concentrating on one life. One death.

She was on the summit. Below, a vortex of red dust writhed beneath the yoke of the wind. Her heart thudded at the thought that she had lost her way, but the storm was so wild, the only thing to do was to struggle towards the tree she had glimpsed earlier. It offered the only sanctuary. She plunged over the edge of a dune, into the comparative silence in the well of sand. She rested, recovering from the assault of the wind.

Ahead of her was a mound where the desert had heaped against something. Shelter. She made her way to it. The shape, the outline, a flash of colour. The familiarity of it caught like a cry in the throat. She crawled forward and collapsed against the mound.

Mara.

Clare repressed the hot flare of panic. Face to face with her, the girl's expression rigid, the eye sockets already emptied. The final bullet a rose on her forehead. Beautiful, for a split second. Mara had been dead a good twenty-four hours, by the looks of her. The wind howled over the top of her discarded body, her outstretched hands covered in sand. Clare brushed the insects away from the girl's face, curling her hand into hers. Mara's paisley jacket was open, hanging loose from her body, revealing her white shirt. A few strands of hair stuck in the bloodstain drying on her sleeve.

Clare touched the stain. It was still moist. She picked up one of the blood-sticky hairs. It was a deep auburn where it wasn't stained. The colour of the dunes where Mara lay.

It could only be Oscar's hair. There was a faint impression on the sand where the boy had curled, nestling into the stiffening curve of the dead girl's body. He had crawled here, inching his way across the dune, as she had, to find shelter. Clare shivered, looking out into the wind-blurred sand. There was no sign of the boy.

She wound her scarf tighter around her face. The series of regular impressions leading away from Mara's body was nearly obscured. The lure of them, the possibility that they were footprints, that Oscar was alive, was overwhelming. Clare stood up and looked north, the direction into which the tracks vanished. There was a gulley on the other side of the dunes, and then nothing but an ocean of dancing sand. If she followed these ephemeral marks she would be lost in minutes. Oscar had survived the desert before. She had to hope that he could do it again.

She struggled up the incline, leaving Mara's lifeless body to be buried in the desert. Below, she could make out the broken spine of the railway line and the eucalyptus standing in solitary splendour, marking where someone had tried to make a home, or coax a crop out of the sand. Clare made her way down, zigzagging along the contour, dreading what she was going to find. The wind had sculpted the sand over the low scrubby bushes, rocks and any detritus that lay on this dry tributary. It moulded sand over everything, making the shifting landscape surreal, blurred by the whirl of fool's gold.

Clare crouched as her eye registered a movement at the tree. A woman with her knees parted and bent just a fraction. The arms locked, clasped in front of her body. The man bound and watching the woman's face as one would watch a weaving mamba.

Riedwaan.

Clare slipped the dust-sticky safety off Tamar's gun. Before her mind had a chance to even register, she fired.

Riedwaan felt the blood spurt from his right wrist as he wrenched it free. He grabbed the metal rod beside him and brought it across the woman's knees as she fired, felling her like a ham-strung animal. She lay across his lap, completely motionless. He worked his left arm free and slipped his arms around her. They were both slick with her blood. There had to have been two shots; Riedwaan was sure of it. That was the only thing that explained the sound. He turned Gretchen around to reveal a gunshot wound on her shoulder.

'Well caught.' The catch in Clare's voice undid her attempt at a joke.

Riedwaan looked up. 'About time,' he said. The blood was rushing back into his arms. It was excruciating, but the sight of Clare was like a shot of morphine. 'Who is this?' he asked. 'If you don't mind me asking.'

Clare knelt beside the bleeding woman and turned her head towards her. The woman moaned.

'The Blue Angel,' said Clare. 'I thought it might be.'

'A friend of yours?' said Riedwaan. He pulled off his shirt and wrapped it around Gretchen's naked form.

'In a manner of speaking. You could say we have a couple of mutual acquaintances.'

'She's not going to last long,' said Riedwaan. He pulled out his phone and gave it to Clare. 'You dial. My hands aren't working that well at the moment.'

Clare took the phone and dialled Tamar's number, ducking into the hut to get reception.

Riedwaan found his cigarettes. He put one between his lips and felt around for his lighter. It was gone.

'You don't have a light, I suppose?' he said to Clare as she came out of the hut.

'I do actually,' she said, offering him the Zippo with the mermaid on it. 'I picked it up outside the freezer just before Gretchen's friend tried to push me inside.'

Riedwaan turned the lighter over in his hand so that he could read the inscription: Magnus Malan. He lit his cigarette. 'On the *Alhantra*?' he asked.

Clare nodded.

'No sign of its owner?'

'Just a trace of blood.'

Riedwaan took a deep drag. 'How much will you bet that Darlene's husband is freezing in the hold with his uranium cakes?'

Clare sat down next to him and watched him smoke. 'I'm not much for betting,' she said. 'But if I were, the odds would be so low it wouldn't be worthwhile.'

She thought about kissing him, but the sound of the helicopter approaching drowned out the wind and by then it was too late.

347

fifty-five

The bundle of dollars Janus Renko handed over to the port captain in Luanda meant that the *Alhantra* had no trouble docking at the Angolan port. He leant against the rail, waiting for his man. He had not met him before, but they all looked the same: shirt pressed and crisp despite the humidity, linen suit, shades mirrored, black hair precisely cut. He scanned the girls displaying their wares on the other side of the razor wire. There. Newly budded breasts. The girl held his eye, deliberately hooked a nipple on a barb. One crimson bead of blood spread across her tight white shirt.

'Delivery complete?'

Renko turned towards the soft voice.

'Of course.' He took the case the man had placed at his feet and opened it. The diamonds, nestled on green velvet, winked at him, complicit, true.

'You want to look below?' Renko asked, putting his eyepiece away.

The man shrugged, his expression hidden behind his dark glasses. 'It's there. We checked.'

Renko handed over the ship's papers. The keys. Docking papers. Orange roughy, such a delicacy. Especially the way this lot was going to be prepared. Renko disembarked, avoiding the filth on the wharf. The girl peeled away from the others. She fell into step beside Renko once he was clear of the docks.

'You lonely?'

Renko checked his watch. He had a couple of hours.

'A little,' he smiled.

*   *   *

When his plane flew low over the Luanda Hilton, the sun was dropping westward, the roofs of the town shining in its light. In the east, darkness.

Hours later, the stars hung low. On the horizon, Scorpio setting as the plane touched down. Janus Renko's shirt was white against the smooth, dark skin of his neck, despite the long flight to Johannesburg. He was tired. It took a second before he noticed the man in the black suit peel away from the shelter of the wall.

That fraction of time was all Phiri needed. The Browning was hard in Renko's kidneys; his arms high up his back, the sharp intake of breath indicating just how far.

'Funny,' said Phiri, his mouth close to the man's ear. 'A perfect fit.'

Renko knew better than to fight. 'Goagab?' he asked.

'Singing like a bird,' said Phiri.

In the time it had taken Renko to get to Johannesburg, Goagab's fear of prison had him confessing to every crime he'd ever even considered committing. The *Alhantra*, he told Karamata, had been ferrying six cakes of uranium 235. The highly enriched uranium had been siphoned off from Vastrap and buried in the Namib by Hofmeyr and Malan when they were in charge of destroying the nuclear programme in 1990. The cakes had been buried there for over ten years, waiting for Janus Renko to broker a deal with some Pakistani businessmen. When he did, Goagab had signed off the safe passage to Spain for a cut.

'One city, one cake,' Phiri said. 'Enough highly enriched uranium to make dirty bombs for six European cities. Which were they? Paris? Berlin? Antwerp?'

349

'You'll be sorry for this,' said Renko calmly, 'when my lawyer gets hold of you.'

'I hear the Americans are clearing a cell for you in Guantanamo,' Phiri continued, unperturbed. 'But I think that might have to wait a bit. That little mermaid you pulled out of the water in Walvis Bay, the one you got to shoot those boys who did your dirty work, she's decided that her debt to you was cashed up when you left without her.'

'A whore,' said Renko. 'Any lawyer would shred her in court.'

'Hell hath no fury ...' Phiri let the phrase linger. 'After Clare Hart put a bullet through her shoulder, and then kept her alive long enough to get her to ICU, it seems she switched allegiance,' he went on. 'Never underestimate a woman scorned. Dr Hart got the lot. You. Gretchen. The boys. Johansson, who incidentally looks like he'll be testifying, too. Malan.'

'Malan.' The name erupted from Renko. 'Too fucking lazy to do his own labour.'

'We found him,' said Phiri. 'Not a pleasant sight. What did you use? A filleting knife?'

Renko was silent again, contained fury vibrating through his body.

'Now, if you'll excuse me ...' Phiri pulled out his cellphone and dialled the number. 'Faizal,' he said when Riedwaan picked up. 'Tell Dr Hart we've got her man.'

Riedwaan put his finger on Clare's lips, stopping her question. She waited impatiently, recognising Phiri's voice on the other end of the line but unable to make out what he was saying amidst the noise of the restaurant.

'They got him,' Riedwaan said, snapping his phone shut. 'And his cargo.'

'I've had enough to eat,' said Clare, relief washing over her.

'Shall we go?'

Riedwaan signalled for the bill. He winced. The skin on his chest was healing and his shoulder had been expertly bandaged by Helena Kotze, but even after three days in hospital, movement was not easy.

Outside the restaurant, it was clear, the sky heavy with stars. A curlew on the lagoon called, the sound piercing the cold night. Riedwaan put his arm around Clare's waist.

'Sexy dress this. I was wondering who you were going to wear it for.'

Clare unlocked her cottage door. Somehow, they had walked past Burning Shore Lodge.

'You want some coffee?' she asked, running a tentative finger down his neck.

'Maybe a whisky.'

Clare poured two and took them through to the sitting room.

'You didn't miss these?' Riedwaan put his hand into his jacket pocket and pulled out a scrap of silk.

'Whose are those?' Clare grabbed the black knickers.

'Yours, I hope,' he laughed. 'I took them before you left Cape Town. A memento.'

Clare reached under her skirt and pulled off the pair she was wearing. 'You want me to check?'

'Not really.' He caught both her hands in one of his. The other one he slid up her bare thigh. 'I'd just have to take them off again.'

'True,' said Clare, pulling him with her onto the couch. 'And that would be a waste of time.'

scorpio setting ...

Oscar.

You hear it, your name formed as a series of soft clicks in the back of a throat. A drop, then two, of water on your lips, your eyelids. You open your eyes. The familiar weathered face: Spyt.

You try to say his name. Nothing comes but a croak. The man sweeps the flies sipping from your forehead, split by a rock. He disentangles you from the dead woman, Mara, lifting you into his arms, cradling you against his chest. He carries you to the cool shelter of his cave, out of the wind. The silence in the wake of the storm is overwhelming. Spyt lays you down, gentling his donkeys, restless at the intrusion, before he sets to work on you ...

Three days later, the moon is full, obliterating all but the brightest stars. Spyt puts out a hand for you. Together you listen, ears catching the distant purr of an engine, which is nothing but a texture in the silence. You retreat deeper into the shadows when the lights break over the dune, sweeping across the moonlit sand. When the engine cuts, the restored silence is deafening.

Their voices are low murmurs as the couple unpacks, lights a fire. The pungent smoke purls into the sky. It is getting colder. The man twists the long rope of the woman's hair in his hands. She sinks into him. The soft undulation of their bodies mimics the desert, radiating away from them. When they subside into sleep, the old man walks with you down to the dying fire. In sleep, the woman has turned her back on the man, but his hand rests on her hip. She is familiar, this woman, the woman who reads your mind. It is Clare. You have watched her sleep before, standing by her window, tracing a heart in the mist your breath made.

Spyt crouches, holding your hand close to her mouth. Her breath is warm on your palm.

When the moon arcs up and over, sinking into the ocean to the west, the cold desert wind knifes down the gully, rattling dry grasses. She turns towards the sleeping man; you imagine her breasts soft on his chest. Spyt takes your hand, and the two of you leave. The man and woman will head south to Cape Town, and you, here, will melt into the sheltering desert.

A jackal cries, unfurling the rosy dawn. Scorpio defers to the new light and sinks below the horizon.

a short history of walvis bay

Walvis Bay is Namibia's only deep-water port. It is situated on the mouth of the ephemeral Kuiseb River. This underground river, in effect a long linear oasis that supports an infinite variety of plants, animals and people, halts the restless, constantly moving Namib sand sea that flows up from the south.

The town is isolated: to the south lies the Sperrgebied, the Forbidden Territory, where diamonds have been mined for over a century. To the north is the Skeleton Coast. Here, shipwrecks slowly disintegrate along the elementally beautiful stretch of sea, sky and sand.

People have lived in and around Walvis Bay for about five thousand years. Hunter-gatherers, ancestors of the Topnaar people who live in the Kuiseb fished and harvested the Nara plants, as the Topnaars still do to this day.

The Portuguese named it Bahia das Baleas, the Bay of Whales. Diego Cao erected a stone cross to the north, at Cape Cross, but he sailed on, leaving the bleak and waterless tracts of land unoccupied. During the eighteenth-century whaling boom, American whaling ships filled the bay, decimating the animals that gave this remote place its name.

In 1793, Walvis Bay was occupied in the name of Holland, but in 1795, the British occupied the Cape and claimed the port at the same time. But it was only in 1878 that Walvis Bay and the surrounding land, now a busy trading port, was formally annexed by the British. In 1884, the scramble for Africa reached a feverish pitch and the territory that is today Namibia was claimed by Germany. The British proclaimed Walvis Bay to be part of the Cape Colony, however, and it remained a tiny British enclave until 1915, when South African troops seized German South West Africa and imposed military rule. In 1920, after the defeat of Germany in the First World War, South Africa, then a British colony, was granted a mandate over German South West Africa by the League of Nations. Walvis Bay was integrated into the rest of the territory and it was known as the South West African Protectorate. South Africa's segregationist laws, including the migrant labour system, were extended to the whole territory, including Walvis Bay.

Walvis Bay was of strategic importance to South Africa, and in 1962 a large army base was established – part of it in the town, most of it in the desert – as internal and international resistance to apartheid in South Africa and South West Africa grew. In 1977, it became clear that South Africa would have to give up control of the territory. The South Africans appointed an Administrator General for South West Africa/Namibia (as the territory came to be called). On the same day, however, they annexed Walvis Bay, justifying this on the British annexation on behalf of the Cape Colony a century earlier. As apartheid laws eased in the rest of the country, they were applied ever more strictly in Walvis Bay.

Namibia became independent in March of 1990, but from 1990 to 1994, the South African army consolidated its presence and continued to control the harbour, leaving the town in a strange economic and political limbo until South Africa's transition to democracy in 1994, when Walvis Bay and its population of about forty thousand were reintegrated into Namibia.

Taken from Melinda Silverman's *Between the Atlantic and the Namib: An Environmental History of Walvis Bay*, published by the Namibia Scientific Society (Windhoek, 2004).

Thanks to Willie Visser and Sharon Roberts, for patiently explaining ballistics to me and for teaching me to shoot straight; to Johan Kok, for detailed information on blood splatter patterns and forensics in out-of-the-way places; to Leanne Dreyer, for introducing me to the microscopic wonderland of pollens and forensic palynology; to Colleen Mannheimer, who told me which plants grow where in the Namib Desert; to Bruno Nebe, for rescuing me at the last minute with information about the bats that live in the Kuiseb River; to Johann Dempers, for giving me so many rivetingly gory pathology lessons; and to Andrew Brown, for letting me borrow his wonderful *Coldsleep Lullaby* cop, Eberard Februarie. Special thanks to Martha Evans for being such a creative and patient editor, and to my literary agent, Isobel Dixon, my heartfelt thanks. Also, to Michelle Matthews, for having faith again.

Any mistakes and all fabrications are mine.

Margie Orford

THE CLARE HART SERIES

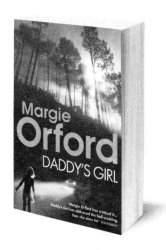

The street was empty; only one car near the park. Dog walkers. Yasmin could hear barking. She told herself that an hour was not so long, not while it was still light. *She looked up when she heard the car...*

TO PREVIEW DADDY'S GIRL TURN THE PAGE

The afternoon sun broke though the cloud, splashing small hands on the barre and pooling on the floor; the girls' serious faces looked straight ahead. From the piano, a simple minuet. One, two, three. One, two, three. Slow enough for everyone in the class to keep up, their tummies tight drums in new pink leotards.

'First position. Heels together. Feet out. Hands held correctly, chins up, plié. And smile and turn. And smile. And turn. And hold. Hands in front and second. Curtsey.'

The ballet teacher marched down the line of little girls, adjusting a hand, a foot, tapping at protruding bottoms, bellies. She paused next to the dark-haired girl at the front of the line, touching her long nails to the girl's cheek.

'Smile, Yasmin. This isn't a funeral.'

The child smiled obediently. Her slender limbs were correctly positioned; she knew this from her ballet teacher's approving frown. Madame Merle moved on.

'Hands graceful, girls. First position and music, Mister Henry. And smile. And smile. And curtsey.'

Clapping her hands, she dismissed the class and accepted a cigarette from the pianist. Mister Henry lit it for her.

'What, Yasmin?' Madame Merle became aware of the lingering child.

'Isn't it too early, Madame?' Madame Merle blew a smoke ring, round and perfect, over the child's head.

'Darling, it's the gala tonight.'

Persephone. The ballet about the girl who disappears,' Mister Henry explained. 'At Artscape.'

'Oh.' Still, Yasmin lingered.

'Run along.' Madame Merle turned away. The class was over.

The beam of her attention switched off.

Yasmin felt Mister Henry's eyes on her as she negotiated the stream of six-year-olds rushing to the cars idling outside. Ever since her older friend Calvaleen had stopped dancing, hers was the only dark bun among the blondes.

The change-room door burst open and the older girls billowed out, all tulle and chatter. Yasmin pressed herself against the wall, and then went to her locker. She had a proper ballet dancer's crossover cardigan, which Amma had knitted for her as an early birthday present. She tied the bow. Thinking about her birthday gave her a knot in her stomach. It was her birthday that had started all the trouble. Last year, when she turned six. In three sleeps she would be seven. She hoped it would be better this year.

Yasmin reached into her bag for her takkies. Her mother always threw a fit if she went outside in her satin pumps. She pulled out her old shoes, dislodging a piece of green paper as she did so. She unfolded it, her heart beating faster. Zero-to-panic. That was Amma's nickname for Daddy. That's how she felt now. Zero-to-panic. She realised that it was another thing she'd forgotten. Madame Merle had handed out the notices with strict instructions that they get them signed and return them to her.

'So I can be absolutely sure that your mummies and daddies know to fetch you early, darlings,' is what Madame Merle had said in her posh voice.

Another thing that would make her mother strip her moer. Two things! She'd forgotten to give her mom the paper. And the picking-up time had changed. Yasmin felt shame wash over her. She tried so hard to do everything right, to make her mother happy, to make her smile like she used to. But everything she did just seemed to make her mother angrier. Ever since her daddy had kept her for the weekend and that Aunty Ndlovu had come with the police papers that said her father was bad like the gangsters he was meant to catch, things had been even worse.

Yasmin smoothed open the notice that Madame Merle had handed out. The notices were only mailed if you missed a class. 'Saving money, darlings!' said Madame Merle. 'Do you think a person can eat from teaching ballet?'

Her mother wouldn't know that the school was closing early today because of the performance of Persephone. Calvaleen was meant to be the star, Persephone. But she'd have got the notice in the post because she had stopped going to the older girls' class a long time ago. Yasmin missed her. She crumpled the paper. She didn't like to think about girls who disappeared. She didn't like to think that her mother was on shift and that she would shout at Yasmin if she phoned her. No one would come to fetch her for a long time.

She was going to be in trouble again. She knew it.

She could hear Madame Merle's voice.

'One, two, three.' Madame Merle's voice cut across the music. It was the end of dance: swan-like in their white skirts, the girls would be skimming across the room, their necks elongated, trailing their arms behind them.

'Like air, girls. You're ballerinas, not bricklayers. Jeté, jeté, jeté.'

The tight burn in Yasmin's throat told her tears were coming. She took a deep breath and made herself think. She was a big girl. She could make a plan. She unzipped her emergency money pouch and looked at the coins in her palm. Two fifty cent pieces. She repeated the cellphone number she needed to

360

dial and stood on tiptoe in front of the call box in the passage. She slotted in the first coin, then the second.

'Oh Eight Two,' she whispered. 'Five Four Two Two Oh Oh Seven.'

The coins clicked down the gullet of the call box. Yasmin's tummy unclenched when the phone began to purr.

'Faizal.'

'Daddy.' A lilt in her voice.

'Leave a message.'

Her father's voice for other people.

The call box swallowed the last coin, cutting the connection before she could leave a message. She replaced the receiver. The piano had stopped. Mister Henry would be closing the lid, gathering his score. His eyes were always watery behind his glasses. He smelt funny. Calvaleen had told her. Yasmin didn't want to have to wait with him. She hoisted her pink rucksack, then slipped past the security guard and through the gate to wait until her mom came.

The afternoon sunlight slanted between the Roman pines lining the steep street. Yasmin did not like to look at them. They were like the trees in the dark Russian fairytale forests in her book. Forests where cannibal crones like Baby Yaga Bony Legs lurked, waiting for young girls. The street was empty; only one car near the park. Dog walkers. Yasmin could hear barking. She told herself that an hour was not so long, not while it was still light.

She listened to Madame Merle herding the older girls into the parking lot. When the security gate opened, unleashing the minibus with its cargo of sylphs, Yasmin pressed herself deep into the bougainvillea hedge. She put her hand to her mouth, sucking the bright bead of blood where a thorn had pierced her skin.

The saltiness reminded her how hungry she was. She had nothing in her bag but a peanut butter sandwich from yesterday. The bread was dry and the peanut butter stuck to the roof of her mouth, but she took another bite as she watched two bergies make their way up the steep hill. The woman stopped to rummage in a dustbin over the road, giving Yasmin a toothless smile. Yasmin did not smile back, but she did wave. The hand with the sandwich she hid behind her back, ashamed to eat in front of people looking for food in a bin. The homeless couple drifted up the road towards the mountain and she ate again.

She looked up when she heard the car, swallowed, a smile starting as she stepped towards the opening door.

The arm snaked around her body, squeezing the narrow cage of her ribs until she felt the bones would snap. She bit down hard when the hand clamped over her mouth, pushing her scream back down her throat. The hand fisted into her upturned face. Another slammed into her belly, winding her. Yasmin crumpled forwards into the pizza boxes and Coke bottles littering the floor of the car. The driver slid down the hill, and Yasmin rolled sideways as he turned. He cut the engine, but neither he nor his passengers moved as the afternoon faded into night.

The beginning of forever.

She lay still, her mouth full of blood. The tooth that had wobbled for days on its last thread lay on the cradle of her tongue.